THE SALACIA PROJECT

A BEN DAWSON NOVEL

BILL DUNCAN

Best Wishes,

BRYSTOL
FOUNDATION

Published in the United States by Brystol Foundation, LLC
St. Louis, MO

More information, photographs, and background about the author's experiences that inspired The Salacia Project can be viewed at www.bill-duncan.com. Additional copies can be purchased there as well.

Cover design by Andrew Wredberg - AWArtworks, LLC
Salacia patch design by Brian Dupont - Cerebral Design Studio

Library of Congress Control Number: 2013956692
ISBN: 978-0-9911213-0-4

I have been privileged to work with some tremendous members of the United States Armed Forces over the last several years, including: General Vincent Brooks, United States Army, General Ed Cardon, United States Army, Colonel Christopher Hamilton, United States Marine Corps, and Colonel Michael Kelly, United States Marine Corps.

I have also been privileged to observe many others who provided the United States of America with intelligent leadership and unflinching resolve in some of the darkest hours of modern American history. They demonstrated profound courage in the theatre of war, and I am still humbled at the memory of watching them at work in the field. These men include General David Petraeus, General Stan McChrystal, and General John Allen.

But far beyond the leaders who make headlines, the men and women who wear the uniform of the United States of America with honor and courage are the heroes of our modern age. From the teeming streets of Baghdad and Kabul to the parched and deadly hinterlands of Basrah and Marjeh, I worked with these soldiers and Marines and watched in awe at their self sacrifice. I thank Almighty God for them every day.

Bill Duncan
St. Louis, MO

THE SALACIA PROJECT

In ancient Roman mythology, Salacia was the female divinity of the sea, worshipped as the goddess of salt water who presided over the depths of the ocean. She was the wife and queen of Neptune, god of the sea and water.

But to the US intelligence community, the Salacia Project represented the difference between maintaining military superiority for at least another decade, or losing the country's edge almost overnight.

CHAPTER 1

A single Blackhawk helicopter skirted the mountaintops, bobbing and weaving like a prizefighter as it traced the lowest passes available, homing in on the designated landing zone. No one spoke—either on board or via radio—since leaving the long-deserted airfield just north of the Pakistan border. The old airfield was just a couple of buildings and a level patch of broken concrete that had once been enough runway for the occasional missionary visit. Now it was just one more among the thousands of relics from historic acts of kindness fallen into decay, nearly swept away by the endless wars of the Middle East. But it had made a perfect refueling area for the Blackhawk whose flight originated in Kandahar and was now bound for a classified destination.

The night sky over southern Afghanistan was inky black, blanketed with stars so bright they shone like brilliant diamonds over the craggy mountains below. But the pilot didn't care about the dome of stars in the heavens above; he was focused on the potential hell waiting below. Accustomed to piloting general officers and State Department VIPs, he hated these classified night flights. No chase bird covering his "6" (his back), no radio contact, and if there was trouble, it was very unlikely the QRF—Quick Reaction Force—would find them at all and certainly not in time for a rescue.

The only light was the green instrumentation glow from the cockpit, so all six passengers either stared straight ahead or just closed their eyes inside their goggles. Three of the six wore a night vision apparatus, but it wouldn't be engaged until they were on the deck, which, if Dawson's calculations were correct, should be very soon. By now, he figured, they were somewhere around the marble quarries and less than ten minutes out from their target. The man he knew best in this team, his old colleague Billy Winger, was chewing a big wad of gum with his eyes closed and a meditative non-expression on his face.

Ben Dawson and his security detail wore black from head to toe and were decked out in body armor and helmets, ear plugs, clear goggles, and lightweight fire-resistant gloves. Only the pilot and copilot were in camouflage. The windows had been removed from the chopper, and the wind roared as it whipped frantically at their shirtsleeves. But no one minded. A little breeze, Dawson thought, made the cabin almost comfortable at this altitude and at this time of night, even inside a Kevlar vest. As they began to slow, the copilot signaled to the passengers via a small amber light; they were over the landing zone, and about to descend. The five men in the security detail charged their weapons.

Those wearing night vision equipment jumped out first, before the prop wash had even cleared, and began scanning the area. The rest of the team followed until Dawson was on the ground. The Blackhawk's engines came to a stop, and once again the pilot whispered aloud: "I don't like this. I don't like it at all." He knew full well how long it would take to cycle the engines back up again. If they had to leave in a hurry, well, it wasn't going to be pretty. But his orders were clear. They couldn't afford the sound of running even at a low idle while the team was operating on the ground. The risk was just too high. The copilot quietly agreed: "We're sitting ducks." But all they could do was wait while Dawson did his work. Wait and hope the security detail could keep them all alive.

The sand beneath his boots as Dawson hit the deck was as fine as baby powder, poofing away from his feet as he walked. The 120-degree heat was stifling, and beneath forty pounds of body armor, helmets, and gloves the sweat began to form in slick pools around his back and arms. His equipment added another eighteen pounds. The security team was even more encumbered with their weapons, additional magazines of ammo, equipment, and Camelback canteens of water or Gatorade. Winger stayed behind Dawson, visually sweeping the surrounding terrain and watching his friend's 6.

As arranged, two of the night vision-equipped operators took up positions along the edges of the clearing, one on each side of the helicopter. The other took point, leading Dawson and the remainder of the security detail in a wedge formation toward the spot Dawson had designated back at their refueling point. Getting the exact target position information so late in the game didn't set well with the team, but money talked, and this mission was paying handsomely. So they gritted their teeth and took it in stride. About fifty meters along their journey, the cry of jackals erupted from just over the rise to their east. It was hideous, and Dawson always imagined it sounded like the cry of a Comanche war party as they crested a butte and road down in waves so many years ago in his native Texas. No matter how many times he'd heard the blood-curdling cry before—which unfailingly splintered the night when all was quiet and the wind was absolutely still—it always startled him. Young inexperienced Marines with hair triggers from the grueling duty in Helmand Province often found themselves shooting at shadows before they realized it, and sheepishly had to confess to their commanding officers that they'd fired needlessly into the darkness.

Their objective was on the other side of the ridge and down the mountainside about 150 meters. The combination of altitude and uphill trek had Dawson breathing hard by the time they cleared the ridgeline and started down the other side. The loose rocks and sand, coupled with the fact that he was moving by starlight with just a sliver of moon, didn't help. More than once he reached for his flashlight but then caught himself. The flashlight would have to wait until they were inside the cave. As he crossed the ridge, only one security man flanked him, and the only other team member he could see was one of the men wearing night vision goggles. The others had spread out to each side and were slowly converging on a dark spot below—an empty black crescent-shaped opening in the rock surface that made the outcropping seem like an unlit jack-o-lantern with the cave entrance forming the misshapen mouth.

When they reached entrance, one of the security team pulled two cylinders from his vest, triggered the mechanisms for each, and tossed them inside. Then they stood aside and waited. About ten seconds later two muffled pops could be heard from inside and soon gray smoke began to waft into the night air from the opening. No one knew what creatures might inhabit the cave—snakes, bats, jackals—it was impossible to say. But anything in there would find the combination of smoke and gas sufficiently noxious to exit quickly, and that's all the team needed.

The cave roof was too low for walking upright for the first twenty meters, and by the time they reached their destination, they were all getting a bit claustrophobic. The cavern was only about the size of a large SUV, but at least they were able to stand. As soon as it was clear that there was no human or animal threat inside the cave, the rest of the team was ordered back out, leaving only Dawson and the team leader, a man named Romero whose team just called him "Chief." Winger guarded the entrance to the cave.

Dawson stretched his back, looked around, and spotted what he was searching for almost immediately. Moving quickly and efficiently, he got to work. First he unpacked an instrument that looked like a tricorder from the old Star Trek TV series, and snapped on a flashlight-looking device on one side. The instrument was a sort of combination video camera, Geiger counter, mass spectrometer, and light spectrum analyzer. It also contained a chamber about one inch in diameter for on-site destructive sample analysis and a satellite uplink device which would almost certainly be useless while inside the cave.

The vein, darker than the stone surrounding it, was deep green and smooth to the touch. It stood out against the relatively soft sandstone, but was not as crystalline as the local granite. Dawson wished again he could use his laser to remove the section he needed—he had a portable unit in his pack that was more than capable—but with the limited amount of breathable air in the confined space, a mechanical method was the only reasonable solution. He hacked out a tiny sample, deposited it in the small analytical test chamber of his instrument, and confirmed he had what he was looking for. Then he went to work with a titanium-edged cordless power tool. Romero had laughed, saying that the tool looked like a large Dremel, but it got the job done and that was all that mattered.

It took him about fifteen minutes to get a sample about the size of his forearm, and once he had it extracted, he deposited a metal cylinder in its place. Then he packed away the sample and his equipment, nodded to Romero, and ducked back down to begin his crawl back out toward fresh air.

* * * *

Romero waited until Dawson was about fifteen seconds out ahead of him before turning back to the cylinder. He carefully pried free the outer casing and discarded it on the cavern floor. Then he lost no time getting back into the small shaft himself, and as quickly as he could, belly-crawled toward the surface. He had almost caught up with Dawson by the time they emerged, both of them sweaty and dirty and grateful for the fresh air. Only Dawson took a moment to breathe once he was out, though. Romero instantly signaled one of the remaining security team, and the man set to work installing two explosive devices, one basic C4 block at the entrance itself and a shaped charge just a few meters inside the shaft. Both were set up with remote triggers, and the triggers blinked tiny red lights in unison as the team moved away, returning toward the ridgeline.

Just as Dawson and Winger cleared the top of the ridge, they could see Romero stiffen perceptibly, working even harder than usual on his SA, his situational awareness. His head never stopped pivoting, and he was now clearly tense. Something was wrong. The remainder of the team picked their way down the side of the mountain, but they were more vigilant as well. About twenty meters from the landing zone, Dawson heard the engines of the Blackhawk coming to life and saw the big rotor blades beginning to move. Anticipating the prop wash, he pulled a balaclava up over his nose and his goggles down over his eyes, as he continued to pick his way through the rocks toward the helicopter. Winger stayed close behind him, his M4 constantly pivoting to sweep the terrain in tandem with his head.

Things began to go south just as Dawson reached the clearing. There was a double click on the radio earbud in Romero's right ear, a pre-arranged signal that one of the security team had detected unexplained movement or sound. Had the helicopter not yet restarted its engines, the team would have frozen in their positions until the signal originator conveyed an "all clear" or the situation escalated. In this case, because the engine restart had blown any opportunity for remaining undetected anyway, Romero signaled double-time. The team continued to shepherd Dawson, their VIP, toward the helicopter as rapidly as possible. Suddenly, although muted by the sound of the spinning-up rotor blades, Romero heard the distinctive report of a flare being fired into the air from the south, and within seconds, just as he and Dawson reached the bird, the sky lit up in an eerie orange glow. The landing zone, helicopter, and personnel lay exposed and easy to target. And then all hell broke loose.

The unmistakable bark of AK-47s coughed from two sides as dark shapes poured over southern and western ridgelines. There were about a dozen of them, and from the way they moved and the orchestrated way they deployed, Romero knew they were no ragtag local Taliban group. These were well-trained professionals, and they had been waiting. It was an ambush. Someone had leaked information about their arrival if not their purpose, and that leak had come from somewhere very near the mission planning source. After all, even Romero hadn't seen the actual coordinates until the very last moment, while staging for refueling at the abandoned airfield. The enemy, whoever they were, had waited for Dawson to extract the mineral, and now they were determined to take it from him.

That meant there was likely to be much worse news than a dozen men with AKs. The flare, which was quickly followed by a second, erased any advantage from the night vision equipment. Romero's primary objective now was to get Dawson and his cargo aboard the chopper and get him airborne. While he'd like very much to get all his team out alive, and himself for that matter, he knew they were all expendable. If the enemy got Dawson, and especially if they got his cargo and his instruments, the result would be disastrous. Romero wasn't going to let that happen and, he noted, neither was Winger.

As they moved, Winger ran in reverse—a nearly impossible maneuver in the rocks, in combat boots, and by moonlight—and stayed glued to Dawson's back, responding with sweeping volleys toward every location from which he perceived incoming fire. As Romero provided cover for Dawson and Winger, he noted enemy fire was still coming from only two directions, and they didn't seem to be trying very hard to hit the chopper itself. Because it was facing north, the enemy didn't have a good firing line, but why, he wondered, weren't they moving into a better firing position? After all, if they took out the pilot in the cockpit, the rest of them would be easy pickings.

By the time Romero, Dawson, and Winger made it to the edge of the clearing and were ready to make a run for the chopper, one team member was hit and unable to move, one was pinned down about fifteen meters out, and the last was hidden somewhere amidst the boulders. Once Dawson was safely aboard, Romero clambered in behind and basically on top of him, and Winger threw himself back out of the chopper, running toward the uninjured, pinned-down team member. Romero concentrated on keeping Dawson out of the line of fire and did his best to provide effective cover for the other two men while Winger pivoted and fired toward every enemy position until his man was on board. Soon the only men out were the one who'd already been hit and one keeping to the shadows on the perimeter. The man who'd been hit dragged himself toward the bird as prop wash from the rotor threw a cloud of sand and debris into the air, obscuring both his figure and the chopper. He had just a few feet to go when he took another hit—a head shot this time. Romero could see he was clearly dead before he hit the ground. Then the last man out took a round in his right leg as he sprang from his position to reach the bird. Between Romero and Winger giving cover, he was able to pull himself on board as Romero signaled the pilot to get airborne.

That's when Romero saw the real threat. Now he understood why the enemy hadn't tried to hit the cockpit with their AKs. Getting into position behind a substantial group of boulders along the eastern ridge, two men were preparing to blow the bird out of the sky. One was shouldering an RPG, a rocket propelled grenade launcher, while the other looked to be readying a TOW missile on a tripod masked in camouflage netting. The ground fire had just been a show. It looked as though they planned to simply shoot down the helicopter, killing its passengers and crew in one fell swoop, and then simply recover the valuable mineral from its charred remains. These guys might be trained professionals, Romero thought, but they had no idea how valuable Dawson and his equipment really were.

* * * *

Dawson felt useless and that just didn't suit his nature. He wasn't carrying an M4, an M16, or even an M9 sidearm. The rifles of the security team, being fired from a moving helicopter as it twisted and rocked with incoming AK fire pinging off the sides and whistling through the doorways and windows, were not effectively targeting the RPG-wielding enemy. And although the men on the ground were being painstakingly deliberate about getting into position and getting the helicopter into their sights, he knew it wouldn't be long before they'd be ready to fire. That moment was coming at them with the inevitability of death itself. He could hear Romero bellowing at the pilot to "Get us outta here!" but no one else could. Romero had his hands full firing off bursts at the enemy below and couldn't trigger his mike to communicate with the pilots, and of course the pilots were doing their best to gain altitude without verbal encouragement in any case. The situation was loud and it was lethal. Bullets ricocheted in every direction, and all of them were far too close for comfort. Dawson had to do something.

He yanked an instrument from his pack and rolled onto his stomach. As it powered up, he popped up into an open corner of the Blackhawk window frame and aimed at the silhouetted figures of the RPG-wielding soldiers just coming into clear view. He hit the on-switch, and, like a stream of tracer fire, his portable industrial laser burned a smoldering path from the boulder it initially struck across the images of the men below. Like the finger of God, the blinding, pencil-thin beam shone brightly against the eerie, flickering orange light of the flares descending through the night sky. As the beam encountered the enemy soldier, it sliced through him until it struck the weapon in his hands. When it hit the first RPG round, the projectile detonated with an earth-shattering roar, spraying rock and debris across the ridgeline and cascading down the opposing mountainside. "Not exactly a textbook application," Dawson said to himself as he grunted and fell back to the floor, "but I guess it worked."

As soon as they cleared the ridgeline, the pilot leaned into the throttle and the chopper began to climb safely away. Dawson watched as Romero pulled the remote detonator from his pocket, removed the cover, and pressed the blinking green button. Below and behind them, the charges Romero had placed into the shaft of the cave did their job.

The chopper skipped across several mountaintops, wending its way back toward the abandoned airfield for refueling. Only then did Dawson start to come out of operational mode and downshift mentally to consider what had happened. The idea had been to sneak in, grab the specimen, and sneak out with no trace left behind. They had lost one man, and another was wounded. Worse, the enemy—whoever the enemy was in this case—now knew the general location of their source. And worst of all, that enemy also had at least one mole somewhere deep in the intelligence community. Deep enough to know about one of the most heavily guarded and least known secrets of the most important US military research program in existence.

Someone somewhere was going to pay.

CHAPTER 2

Dawson scanned the small auditorium. The room was sparsely occupied, with the first two rows filled by assistants to the Joint Chiefs, high-ranking intelligence officers, and a couple of representatives from the scientific community with extremely high clearances. The only two others in the room were members of Brystol's staff, and they stood against the back wall.

Doctor Kenneth Brystol was speaking. A world-class physicist and educator, Brystol still seemed as vital and energetic in his seventies as Dawson remembered him twenty years earlier. He had lightness in his step and brightness in his eyes that conveyed energy and enthusiasm, and his attitude was infectious. He reminded Dawson of the professor played by Christopher Lloyd in the movie *Back to the Future*. Brystol wasn't some wild-eyed eccentric, but he had that energy level; it was just more structured, more constrained, and thereby more palatable to government research funding agencies.

"Today, the United States finds itself competing for global influence in an era in which it is neither fully at war nor fully at peace. While defending our shores and defeating our enemies in war remain the indisputable ends of sea power, the United States Navy must apply sea power in a manner that protects our vital interests while promoting greater national security, stability, and trust."

Dawson could see a few heads nod in agreement down front. Brystol was just creating the foundation for the case he intended to make. He continued,

"Guided by the objectives articulated in the National Security Strategy, National Defense Strategy, National Military Strategy, and the National Strategy for Maritime Security, the United States Navy will continue to act across the full range of military operations to protect the United States from direct attack, assure strategic access and retain global freedom of action, strengthen existing and emerging alliances, and establish favorable security conditions." Again, heads nodded, as they should. Brystol had basically paraphrased their own words from a US Department of Defense paper titled, "A Cooperative Strategy for 21st Century Sea Power."

Although Brystol was no stranger to the men in uniform, he needed to convince them he understood their challenge as well as they did, and that they were all of common purpose. He continued to speak directly to the first two rows, only occasionally lifting his eyes to check the clock and make sure he wasn't missing some other dynamic in the room. Seeing no reason to divert from his objective, he plowed ahead.

"Technology continues to expand marine activities such as energy development, resource extraction, and other commercial activity in and under the oceans. Climate change is gradually opening up the waters of the Arctic, not only to new resource development, but also to new shipping routes that may reshape global transportation. All of these are potential sources of competition and conflict, as they provide opportunities for new access to natural resources. Globalization also contributes to changes in human migration patterns, health, education, culture, and the way we engage in conflict. Conflicts are increasingly characterized by a shifting blend of traditional and untraditional tactics, decentralized planning and execution, and non-state actors. The parties engaged are now using both simple and sophisticated technologies in innovative ways. In fact, you will be hearing a great deal about one of those technologies today."

Brystol paused and took a sip of water; Dawson was never sure whether Brystol's throat was actually dry, or if this was some stage effect. "Weak or corrupt governments," he continued, "growing dissatisfaction among the disenfranchised, religious extremism, and many other factors exacerbate tensions and contribute fuel for the fires of conflict."

He paused for dramatic effect, and then said: "As our security and prosperity are inextricably linked with those of others, US maritime forces must be deployed with unprecedented speed to protect and sustain the peaceful global system comprised of interdependent networks of trade, finance, information, law, people, and governance. Please consider that. We have the most capable weapons systems in the world, but in this increasingly complex and volatile environment, we must be able to move our assets through the oceans of the world more quickly than ever before." At this point, he had them eating out of his hand. The room was his. They all understood that he understood what they were facing. He grasped the magnitude of the challenges and the critical nature of naval vessels in the management of future security and national strength. Now he needed to move from education to sales.

"Ladies and Gentlemen," Brystol intoned, "I have a question for you: What would it be worth to double the speed of our strategic naval vessels?" He paused for a moment, and then turned to a man in uniform in the front row. "Admiral Green, imagine if we could cut in half the time it takes for our navy to deploy anywhere around the world. How would that capability affect our naval superiority?" Green, one of the most experienced, storied, and respected naval officers in recent history, had of course been briefed and prepared to respond ahead of the session. He was ready to take the floor.

Standing and turning to face the audience, Dawson could see the admiral's silver head framing a tanned and rugged face. His bright blue eyes seemed to burn holes through bushy eyebrows, and the array of brightly polished medals across his chest gleamed as his gravelly voice captured the attention of the room. "It would not only greatly enhance our current capabilities, it would ensure our naval superiority for at least a decade. The ability to reach our theatres of operations more quickly would mean our ground-based forces would be safer, because we could be more responsive. We could deliver warfighters, reinforcement personnel, armament, weapons, ammunition, and sustainment materials faster, and we wouldn't need to maintain as many materials in storage locations in theatre awaiting potential use. Our projected casualty rates in theatres of armed conflict are estimated to decline by as much as eighteen percent due to improved responsiveness."

Protecting boots on the ground, Dawson thought. *This guy should run for office.* Green continued, glancing meaningfully at the representative from the Office of the Comptroller, a thin and mousy looking man, who he could see was already scribbling notes furiously. Dawson saw the corners of Brystol's mouth turn up ever-so-slightly in satisfaction.

"As to what such a capability might be worth, our logistics experts estimate the savings resulting from a doubling of speed could be as much as $3.4 billion a year." Passing his gaze over the audience one last time to make certain that he had communicated effectively, the admiral returned to his seat, and Brystol retook the platform.

"Thank you, Admiral," Brystol smiled. "And so that brings us, I think, to the point of our meeting today." Brystol nodded toward his assistant, Margaret, a spinsterish-looking woman standing beside the main doorway. She thumbed a button on the remote control in her left hand, and a projection screen lowered behind Brystol as the room lights dimmed.

"The Salacia Project" flanked by the Brystol Foundation logo appeared. Brystol left the cover slide up long enough for everyone in the room to know exactly who was in the driver's seat on this project. Then it faded, and the side view of a destroyer class naval vessel came into focus. Brystol cleared his throat. "I'm going to employ a communication principle I learned from a Marine Corps general officer some years back. It's called BLUF, or Bottom Line Up Front. Here is the bottom line: if you want to move quickly through the water, move the water out of the way."

Arrows appeared on the screen, and the outline of the destroyer glowed. "We all know water applies equal pressure against the submerged surfaces of a seagoing vessel. And in the case of submarines, of course, that means all external surfaces. But for the moment, let's talk about surface vessels, and let's focus on two specific areas. Area number one is the stern of the ship, the surface containing the engine's thrusters, typically mechanical propellers, and commonly the ship's rudder. Area number two is the bow, the two vertical planes comprising the sides of the ship, which join at the forward edge and cut through the water as the ship is propelled forward. Now, assume pressure from the water on the submerged surfaces remains constant, providing adequate buoyancy to support the vessel and keep it from sinking. Also assume normal pressure exists at the stern, pressing the ship forward. What would happen if the water pressing against the forward edge did not exist, if it was simply not there? Of course when your vessel is out in the middle of the ocean, this would seem to be impossible. But consider that under those impossible conditions, the existing pressure at the stern of the ship would provide a natural propulsion forward into the empty space, and the effect of the ship's mechanical propulsion would be multiplied dramatically. Relative acceleration and cruising speed would be much more akin to the performance of land vehicles."

It wasn't a gasp, precisely, but there was a significant intake of breath and general surprise among the audience. It was mixed, of course, among some frowns of skepticism and sporadic murmurs. Brystol raised his hands gently and smiled. "I know," he said, "the concept seems counterintuitive, and it appears to defy the laws of physics. But be patient with me a moment longer.

As many of you know, I have a little experience in the field of physics." Another friendlier murmur passed between some of the audience members. Dawson knew Brystol's reputation in the field afforded him quite a bit of leeway.

"You know," Brystol continued, now adopting a kindly uncle tone, "we weren't really looking for this here at the Foundation. The team that developed the critical enabling process was working on alternative energy sources for automobiles; specifically, they were doing research into hydrogen production and propulsion." Many of the scientific members of the audience were leaning forward at this point, hanging on Brystol's every word. "What we came across, and are now developing, is a process that splits the molecules of water just in front of the vessel, converting the bulk of the water into hydrogen gas just before it comes into contact with the ship's bow surfaces. Essentially, nothing remains in front of the ship but an evaporating gas, with the pressures of natural and mechanical thrust now free to provide that propulsion against minimal resistance. For the most part, the only static inertia remaining is a function of gravity, and the fact that the vessel remains afloat in water reduces even the effect of gravity substantially. One member of our research team commented that the effect was a bit like the suspension of an air hockey puck moving across the surface of the air hockey table. That's probably not a bad analogy." As Brystol spoke, the image on the screen zoomed in. The glow depicted along the front edge of the naval destroyer image moved outward from the vessel's surface, creating a small gap between the water and the ship's forward edge.

"This may sound like science fiction, but I can assure you it is not. By passing an electric current through H_2O, you can split the aqueous molecule neatly into its constituent elements. Hydrogen gas rises from the negative cathode, and oxygen gas collects at the positive anode. The process is called electrolysis, and it's been around since Jules Verne's time. Electrolysis produces a very pure form of hydrogen and it's simple enough to be widely adapted. Some futurists envision an electrolysis box in every garage, producing hydrogen from tap water. But in our case, of course, we have envisioned a somewhat different application." He smiled broadly, pleased that his audience was, for the most part, thunderstruck by the concept.

"Dr. Brystol?" A question came from Bill Tayaka, a physicist of some renown himself, and chairman of the National Science Board.

"Yes, Bill?" Brystol replied.

"As the water molecules are split into gases, what prevents the water surrounding it from immediately rushing in to fill the void, displacing the gases and replacing the surface resistance?"

"Ah, yes," Brystol smiled even more broadly. "That is precisely the question, and the toughest nut, shall we say, to be cracked. The answer to your question, Bill, is this: bubbles. One member of our research team was blowing bubbles with her young son a few months ago. You know what I'm referring to, Bill, the ordinary soap bubbles sold in toy stores. Well, they ran out of bubbles after a time, and rather than make another trip to the toy store, Carolyn Menlo—that is our researcher who had been working on the engineered performance of spherical objects at MIT—decided to concoct some of her own at her kitchen sink, using ordinary dishwashing liquid and a couple of other household ingredients. Carolyn, it seems, was thinking about the physics of bubbles as she was whipping up her replacement batch."

A few of the audience members were clearly wondering where this story was headed, but Brystol continued to smile and pull them along. "Now, as we all know, a bubble is a thin film of soapy water. Most of the bubbles that you see are filled with air, but bubbles can also be formed using other gases such as carbon dioxide. The film that makes the bubble has three layers. A thin layer of water is sandwiched between two layers of soap molecules. Each soap molecule is oriented so that its polar or hydrophilic head faces the water, while its hydrophobic hydrocarbon tail extends away from the water layer. No matter what shape a bubble has initially, it will try to become a sphere. The sphere is the shape that minimizes the surface area of the structure, which makes it the shape that requires the least energy to achieve. So Carolyn began to think about ways that the chemical composition of these remarkable products of nature might be altered to allow the hydrophobic hydrocarbon tail to fold inward under minor pressure without permitting the structure of the bubble to implode for a short period of time—mere seconds in some cases, and fractions of seconds in most cases—while the hydrophilic head remains much more resistant to the pressure of the water it faces. Essentially, the 'pop' one perceives when a typical soap bubble bursts is replaced with a more gradual dispersion of inner gases, owing to a very complex chemical reaction that alters the molecular decomposition rate and retards the sequence of decay. A good way to envision this is to think of the bubble bending in a concave fashion and then disappearing as though it is melting away from side to side, rather than merely popping all at once."

Brystol paused a moment for that to sink in. Dawson noticed that both Tayaka and another scientist just two seats away had removed their eyeglasses and were obviously thinking hard about this. Tayaka was holding his hand across his mouth, leaning on one elbow and frowning. It was almost comical that the other scientist was mimicking the gesture exactly but with his opposite hand.

"If you'll take a look at this next slide," Brystol continued, "you can see the principle elements of our system and the concept of operations." A nod to his assistant, and the slide advanced. "As you'll recall from my earlier remarks, electrolysis causes hydrogen gas to rise from the negative cathode and causes oxygen gas to form at the positive anode. So electrolysis on this scale must be performed by turning the forward quarter of the ship's hull from sea level downward, in the case of surface vessels, into positive and negative cathodes, with the arcing environment extending just a short distance into the surrounding water, as depicted here. This is achieved mechanically, of course, and the primary element of the system is a rather unique surface coating, applied to the hull of the vessel in the areas shown, that was developed here at the Foundation specifically for that purpose.

"The second element is a specially modified and enhanced set of planar lasers that emanate from each side of the bow in a fan-like configuration, dispersing its light at a naturally declining power level as it passes along both the port and starboard sides of the bow and toward the stern of the ship. Incidentally, there is a supplemental laser array, in case the water becomes densely comprised of particulates that diminish the strength of light as it passes along the surfaces of the ship."

"The third key element in our system is a chemical catalyst that is actually generated from the seawater itself in a rather unique—no, strike that—in a *completely* unique process. The catalyst issues continuously from tiny nozzles along the bow, as illustrated here. As it flows backward along the sides of the vessel, traversing along the same general paths as the laser generated light, it enables 'Menlo Bubbles' to form across the surfaces. It is the composition of the gases and the membranes of the bubbles that represent the great breakthrough here."

At that point, Brystol stopped and nodded toward his assistant again, and she in turn brought the house lights up with her remote. Dawson was so busy watching the faces of the audience, mesmerized at the presentation, he hadn't noticed another figure slip into the back of the room. Carolyn Menlo stood on the opposite side of Margaret. About five feet seven inches tall, with shoulder-length auburn hair and brown eyes, Menlo wore a simple gray blouse and navy slacks.

"Ladies and Gentlemen," Brystol beamed, "I want to take a moment here to introduce you to the researcher I spoke of a few minutes ago, and after whom these unique new structures are named. This is Carolyn Menlo." A polite smattering of applause began, and Menlo blushed. "In just a moment, Dr. Menlo will lead you into a lab down the hall and demonstrate our system. At that time, she will also answer, well, *some* of your questions." Gentle chuckles ensued. Everyone in the room knew the critical elements and formulae weren't going to be part of the information divulged today, or any time soon for that matter.

This is sheer Brystol. Deliver world-changing technologies, but at a price, and always with a splash, Dawson thought, *even when that splash had to be limited to a room full of high-clearance government weenies like these.* From the stage, Brystol shot him a sly glance. Less than half a dozen people knew it, but Dawson was almost as responsible for the now-revered Menlo Bubbles (a moniker Dawson suspected the femininely shaped researcher would likely come to regret) as Menlo was herself.

The catalyst that enabled the bubbles to form without soap and deteriorate in such a controlled fashion required a mechanism that was built on the splitting and disbursing of light in a very unnatural way. Only one crystalline substance had ever been discovered that produced this effect, and it was extremely rare. In fact, it was classified as a strategically critical material for national defense, beyond even the rare earths so prized for the high-tech electronics used in satellite and telecommunication technologies. At first it was only available in theory among the pages of textbooks. Then the first deposit of the substance, known only as "unobtanium" among the research staff, was unearthed in an African lithium mine in the 1950s. When it was discovered, no one knew what to do with it, and the only known specimen was finally located in a museum of natural history in South Africa decades later.

Now the Brystol Foundation possessed by far the largest known quantity in the world. How much existed elsewhere, no one knew. What Dawson did know, however, was that the best security measure was keeping the use of the material in the Brystol Foundation's new device a secret. Because the substance was sliced into a lens only a millimeter thick and attached to the end of an optic fiber for each application—in this case each ship—the Foundation had enough material in secured storage to power at least two fleets the size of the United States Navy with just a little left over.

Dawson knew all this because he and a small band of mercenaries, piloted by Special Ops personnel, had wrested the critical mineral from the wall of a hot, tiny cavern deep in the mountains of southern Afghanistan some eleven months earlier. Dawson sighed. The price they paid was a high one, and they had come within seconds of complete disaster. And they still didn't know who had tipped off the team of soldiers who had tried to take them out and steal the material. Dawson had his suspicions about who was behind the whole operation, but as far as who the mole was and in which operational organization he—or she—was posted, he still had no clue.

CHAPTER 3

The demonstration took place in a large laboratory with a long, narrow tank filled with seawater and replete with a sand-and-debris strewn floor as well as some live fish. The fish were small, as were the pieces of debris, in an obvious effort to keep things as close to scale as possible.

At one end of the tank were two scale model Nimitz class carriers. Each model was about four meters long. It was obvious that the vessel on the far side of the pool was fitted with some additional equipment, looking very much like what the audience expected from their images in the slideshow they had just witnessed. The other vessel looked as though it was unmodified from whatever its original designer had intended. The audience was positioned for the demonstration along one side of the pool near the center, but they were free to walk along the edge as they desired to gain whatever vantage point they needed.

"Ladies and Gentlemen," Menlo spoke through a portable microphone from the starting end of the pool, "as you can see we have two identical scale models of a modern aircraft carrier. Both of the models are electrically powered with identical horsepower ratings and identical propulsion systems all the way through the propellers. I am about to start them from this end with no enhanced performance, just to point out a couple of things."

At that, she nodded to a technician along the other side of the pool who pressed forward on a set of dual levers. Both of the ships sprang to life and began their journey down the length of the pool. "First of all," Menlo continued, "you'll see that they are not perfectly uniform in their speed through the water. A lot of things come into play, including the dynamic movement within the water at any given position and time. However, I think you'll agree that for the most part they are running along at the same pace.

"You will likely notice that by the time they reach the end of the pool the vessel fitted with the special equipment is actually a bit slower. This is owing to a minor amount of drag going through the water from the additional equipment along the bow, and—more importantly—because of the additional weight of the special equipment. Our estimates are that the equipment will produce a roughly nine-percent penalty in weight and diminished payload. Hence it sits just a little lower in the water, though it's not readily discernible even when you're looking for it." Dawson could see the mental wheels turning as each member of the audience attempted to weigh the cost and benefit of a more rapid transit time against a nine-percent reduction in payload. Again he noticed the small, bespectacled comptroller's office representative, Ralph Simons, making copious notations in his leather-bound notebook.

Menlo continued. "Our trial tank here is one hundred meters in length, twice as long as an Olympic pool, and the model ships we use are about four meters long. As you can see, the difference in elapsed time between the two vessels traveling from one end to the other is just a few seconds without our equipment engaged."

While she was speaking, two more technicians who had been quietly waiting at the far end of the pool retrieved the model ships and turned them end-for-end to begin their journey back to the point of origin. After they were set in place, Menlo said: "Now, Rebecca, please engage the Salacia System." The technician who had operated the throttles earlier now moved to a different bank of controls and flipped a series of three switches.

At once, the audience members could see a very faint light along the front edge of the ship, and just barely see a very tiny wall of bubbles, almost a micro foam, along the bow of the Salacia-equipped model. The bow seemed to lift slightly in the water. "I will pause for a minute," Menlo said, "in case any of you would like to walk down and examine the ship more closely."

As expected, everyone moved to the end of the pool where they could get a better look. There wasn't a lot to see—the wall of Menlo Bubbles was a very thin one. One of the observers said, "Looks like cherry club soda to me," which elicited a few smiles. One of the other military members of the audience, a rear admiral from the Coast Guard, called out: "How bright is the laser at night?"

"Good point!" said Admiral Green. "We don't want all of our ships to turn into visual targets when they're under way."

"You're right, and that's a great observation," Menlo responded. "The fact is that finding a color spectrum which remains transparent is one of the things we are still working on. The planar laser arrays currently used produce a red light, and the techniques we have experimented with to alter it thus far have disabled the catalytic reaction we need for the bubbles. We will continue to work on it, and even in darkness I think you'll agree that it's not exactly a lighthouse beacon. Rebecca, would you kill the lights in here for a moment, please?"

The technician left her station and walked to a bank of switches on the wall. A moment later the room went dark, and it became obvious that, as Menlo had said, there was a very faint light along the front of the ship but it certainly wasn't something that the unaided human eye would pick out from any distance. After about thirty seconds, the technician restored the lights and returned to her station at the control panel.

"Now, watch carefully," Menlo continued. "I am going to ask Rebecca to simply engage the catalyst production process. The system pulls seawater in from along the edges of the vessel near the stern of the ship, with a tiny resulting bonus in drag reduction, and chemically alters the seawater slightly—and temporarily—to form a chemical catalyst, as Dr. Brystol mentioned earlier. The catalyst is then disbursed from tiny nozzles along the frontal edges of the bow on both sides of the ship. Rebecca, please engage."

The technician flipped the last of the bank of four switches along one side of her console and immediately the ship began a slow advance. The speed of the advance appeared to Dawson to be about a quarter of the rate of speed at which the ships had traveled before. "This," Menlo smiled, "is merely the result of removing most of the pressure of the water in front of the ship. At this point, we are just 'moving water out of the way,' as Dr. Brystol often says. No mechanical propulsion is engaged. The ship is being propelled forward by the differential between the pressure of the water at the stern of the ship and the water at the bow."

As Dawson returned his gaze to the faces in the crowd, it was clear that they were impressed. Even the comptroller representative had stopped writing and was watching in awe. "All right, Rebecca," Menlo spoke again, "let's return the ship to its starting position, and we'll engage the two in their side-by-side run." She then turned back to the audience. "You'll want to return to about mid-point along the edge of the tank. It's the best perspective for comparing the relative speeds of the ships."

The group shuffled back to their mid-point position as suggested, exchanging brief observations along the way, and when they were back in place Menlo began the real demonstration. "Now," she said, "Rebecca will start both vessels out just as before at full speed with standard propulsion." The ships began to move, essentially in parallel.

When they reached a few meters into their run, Menlo said: "All right, Rebecca, engage Salacia." At that point, the technician flipped all four switches and the Salacia-equipped vessel moved ahead at what appeared to be twice the speed of the other ship, perhaps even faster. The observers were, as nearly as Dawson could tell, absolutely stunned.

The Salacia-equipped vessel basically "walked away" from its sister ship as though it was standing still. Although they had heard Brystol's description, seeing it before them was another matter entirely. It appeared to Dawson that it was significantly exceeding the prescribed improvement in speed, and he heard others in the room privately making similar observations.

Questions immediately ensued: What is that mist I see rising around the front of the ship? How is it affected by turbulence in the water? What is the energy consumption rate of the Salacia System? and so on. Menlo directed the technicians to keep running the demonstration continuously for about thirty minutes, so that everyone could see what interested them.

In answer to the question about water turbulence, Menlo instructed the technician at the control panel to engage a bank of oscillators at various locations around the tank. "We can simulate swells up to twenty meters here," she said. The performance of the ship through increasingly turbulent water seemed to be affected little, and Menlo reported that the simulations they had run indicated a degradation of about ten percent in the improved speed. Although they had several theories, the team was still trying to understand exactly what produced that loss. Even so, the difference in speed between the model fitted with the new equipment and the model under standard propulsion was almost unbelievable. Brystol had mentioned the seeming impossibility of removing water from in front of a ship in the middle of the ocean. Now, it seemed clear to Dawson that many members of the group simply couldn't believe what they were witnessing.

Finally, after all of the appropriate questions were answered, Brystol used the microphone to bring the demonstration to a close. He directed the group to follow him down the hallway outside the lab, up a beautiful winding marble-and-chrome staircase, and into a large conference room outfitted for the occasion with classical music emanating from hidden speakers, a bountiful spread of hors d'oeuvres, and an open bar. To say that the demonstration was a hit would be an understatement. Brystol was holding court, and everyone appeared to be enjoying themselves. Dawson noticed that even Brystol's assistant, Margaret, appeared to lose her usual dour expression and replace it with a sweet, matronly persona.

As he stood near the door, Dawson watched the crowd mingle. It included Brystol, his immediate circle of direct reports, a few of the Foundation's marketing people, Carolyn Menlo, several of her technical staff, and of course the dignitaries who had witnessed the demonstration. On a couple of occasions, Dawson thought he had caught Menlo watching him. She appeared to be watching in a distant, indirect way so that it would appear uncontrived, and never allowed herself to make eye contact. Dawson felt as though he was under surveillance of a sort; he had some experience with that, but Menlo had no particular reason that he knew of to be watching him.

Eventually, as the conversations in the room were beginning to wind down and the first few dignitaries began to say their good-byes to Brystol, Menlo broke away and walked directly toward him. She clearly had something to say. But as she drew close, Margaret appeared out of nowhere and swept her off to one side. Dawson could hear most of their conversation, though in muted tones, over the ambient strains of a distant concerto.

"My dear," Margaret said, "you must be very pleased about the way things have gone today." She spoke with animation and a sparkle in her eyes that Dawson thought endearing, and yet somehow a little out of place. It reminded him of a meeting he had been involved in with the tribal elders in Marjeh, in the Helmand Province of Afghanistan back in 2010. They were all seated around the perimeter of the room on cushions on the floor, cross-legged and facing inward from the walls. The elders looked as though they had come straight from the desert set of Ali Baba. Haggard, dressed in flowing tunics and turbans, and shod with sandals or no shoes at all, the tribesmen seemed sullen and lethargic, almost despondent most of the time. Dawson had been thinking that he would probably look the same way if he spent his entire life in 120-degree-plus temperatures and had the lack of access to medical care and nutrition these people experienced.

About midway through their talks, hot tea was served around the room in badly worn cups. As young boys were distributing the tea, a sudden burst of tinny techno-music burst into the air. It was as foreign to the environment as anything Dawson could have imagined, and everyone's heads pivoted toward the source of the sound. Slowly, one of the elders reached deep into the folds of his garment and retracted a cell phone. He stared blankly at it for just a moment, deliberately hit a button on its keypad with the index finger of his free hand—silencing the loud ring-tone—and replaced it again into the hidden pocket of his robe. It still stuck in Dawson's mind as one of the oddest events in all of his time in the Middle East. Now, watching the sixty-plus-year-old Margaret taking up the conversation with Menlo, he realized her manner seemed unrealistically energetic. Margaret had come to the Foundation after many years of service in the DOD Comptroller's office, with strong recommendations from Ralph Simons. Brystol, always alert to another means to ingratiate the Foundation with the funding agencies of the United States government, was pleased to bring a former "insider" into his inner circle. Usually a no-nonsense manager who ruled over the Foundation like a drill sergeant with an ax to grind, today she was all smiles, and her gestures revealed a fluidity Dawson would never have expected. Her movements were almost lithe.

As Dawson observed these two women, it seemed Margaret was trying to lead Menlo away, as a sheepdog would guide a wayward lamb from possible danger. Menlo was unmoving, however, and eventually broke off her conversation with the spindly assistant, reestablishing her vector toward Dawson. As she approached, Dawson stuck out his hand and smiled. "Dr. Menlo, congratulations. Great demonstration. I think you have a real game changer here." Dawson wasn't blowing smoke. Both in the lab and in the field he had seen big ideas come and go, but from his perspective this one looked like solid gold.

"Thank you," she replied soberly. "Of course, we have some work still in front of us to make the system scale up. Models are one thing; actual naval vessels can be quite another matter. Mr. Dawson, if you have a few minutes there are a couple of things I'd like to speak with you about."

"Of course," Dawson replied, "I'm at your disposal."

Menlo cast a wary glance about the room, arms crossed in front of her, and said, "Could you meet me in my office in fifteen minutes? I'd prefer to speak with you privately."

This was an unexpected turn, and the smile evaporated from Dawson's face as he said, "I'll be there."

* * * *

Fifteen minutes later, Dawson was waiting outside Menlo's door. He had a three-minute wait before she arrived, and she had clearly taken the stairs rather than the elevator. The exertion left her chest heaving a bit and had brought more color to her cheeks, making her freckles a bit less pronounced. She is an attractive woman, Dawson thought, and noticed for the first time the substantial wedding ring on her left hand.

"Sorry I'm late," she puffed. "It was harder to tear away from our guests than I anticipated." She slid her badge through the reader, entered her five-digit PIN, and pressed her right thumb against the glass of the fingerprint reader. The door of her office clicked open, and the lights illuminated automatically. There was also an old-style combination lock on all of the doors at the Foundation, but it was a mechanical backup in case the electronic devices all failed or in case Security needed to enter the rooms without their normal occupants.

"I'm not at all surprised," Dawson replied. "You have to be very much in demand right now." The office was large and tastefully appointed. A wall of windows overlooked the heavily wooded Virginia countryside with ancient oaks beautifully ensconced among contrasting birches stretched for at least a half mile in every direction. Along with her desk and wall cabinets, there was an impressive wall of awards, commendations, photographs with a few well-known military leaders, and a couple of US patent declarations. On her desk were several framed photographs of the Menlo family. Dawson could see that she had one son, and that her husband was a United States Army officer. The colonel had a bright smile, direct gaze, and chiseled features. They made a nice couple. Nodding to the photo, Dawson asked: "Is the lieutenant colonel still on active duty?"

Menlo closed the door behind him, waved him to a seat at the small round conference table in the corner, and took up a seat across from him. "Yes," she responded, "and as a matter of fact that is one of the things I wanted to speak with you about." She seemed to organize her thoughts for a moment, and then plunged ahead. "But before that, I wanted to say thank you."

"Thank you?" Ben repeated it as a question.

"Yes," she said. "By the way, I hope you will call me Carolyn. May I call you Ben?"

"Of course," he said, the smile returning to his face. "But I'm still not sure—"

"You see, Ben," she interrupted, "Dr. Brystol shared with me the fact that you are responsible for retrieving the material for our optic filters. He wouldn't tell me the details, of course, but I understand that a heavy price was paid, and that you were heroic in your efforts. Truly heroic, and of course you know Kenneth is very proud of you."

"Well," Dawson said, "first of all, Dr. Brystol shouldn't have been so glowing. We got very lucky that night, and most of us literally dodged a bullet. Many bullets, actually. But my actions were no more heroic than any of the other members of the team, and, in fact, I did very little."

"Yes," Menlo replied, "Kenneth said you would eschew any credit for your actions. He was right about that, as he is about almost everything. In any case, none of this would have been possible without what you did, and I just wanted you to understand that I realize that, and I am very grateful."

"Oh," Dawson replied, shifting a bit in his seat. He met her steady gaze and said, "Well, there was no need to thank me, really, Carolyn. I was just—"

"Doing your job." She finished the sentence for him with a soft smile. "Yes, I knew you would say something like that. So I won't embarrass you any further about it; I just wanted you to know that I know, and I'm grateful."

She paused for a minute and then said, "It's funny; I can't imagine you in that kind of situation. You seem like, well, if you'll forgive me saying so, a pretty normal guy. Certainly not like most of the security people I know, especially the military types."

"Ah, yes. I see what you mean." Dawson smiled. "Not exactly Arnold Schwarzenegger." At this point, Menlo began to look as though she was sorry for ever having made the offhand remark. "Oh, don't be embarrassed," Dawson continued, "you're absolutely right. Most people describe me as 'average height, average build.' I'm an intelligence guy, not a security detail type. Blending into a crowd is a good thing in my line of work. I'm always reminded of an old movie called *Road House* with Patrick Swayze. You know it?"

Menlo shook her head.

"Anyway, Swayze plays a bouncer in the movie, and again and again other characters who meet him for the first time keep telling him, 'I thought you'd be bigger.'"

Menlo laughed, and a faint blush colored her cheeks.

"You're right. I'm no Rambo, but I'm often called to work on difficult problems that involve many dimensions for Dr. Brystol, and sometimes they become what the British would call 'sticky wickets.' And when they do, I have a myriad of colleagues who live for that sort of thing while I try to stick to the intelligence side of the business." *Occasionally that even works*, he thought.

Now it was Menlo's turn to shift in her chair, as though she was changing persona in some way, and then she leaned in over the table, hands clutched together in her lap. "As you've already noticed, my husband, Tom, is a Special Operations soldier in the United States Army. He deployed to Iraq in 2006 and to Afghanistan in 2009. Now he is on his third tour. Afghanistan again; this time I think he is in Western Helmand Province."

"Herat or Ziranj?" Dawson asked. He knew both areas well.

"Just outside of Ziranj," she replied. "Do you know that area?"

"As well as I ever want to," Dawson replied evenly. "Interesting assignment."

Menlo drew in a breath at Dawson's words, as though he confirmed something she had already suspected. "Why do you say that?" she asked. "Please be frank with me."

"Listen, Carolyn," Dawson said, "Ziranj is, in and of itself, not a bad place. It's a reasonably good-sized city with commerce, better than average infrastructure for Afghanistan, and relatively quiet from the standpoint of IEDs, snipers, car bombs, and the like. But as you probably already realize, Ziranj sits right on the border with Iran. One of the biggest official highways between the two countries crosses the river there at the border. There are refugee camps, a lot of traffic and trafficking, and the local officials, well, let's just say they conduct a lot of unofficial business. The second Marine Expeditionary Force ran the place when I was last there, so if you had told me that your husband is a captain in the Marine Corps, I wouldn't have thought twice about it. But Ziranj has been pretty quiet for some time, and your husband isn't a Marine. He's a soldier. So what's a soldier doing in an AO, an area of operations that has only been controlled by the US Marines? Secondly, your husband isn't just any soldier. He is a thrice-deployed combat veteran and a light colonel in the Army's Special Forces. As an experienced and obviously competent guy in his niche, he's out of place in that part of the country—unless they have something particularly suited to his skills that he is assigned to do."

"Such as?" she asked.

"Speculating aloud about that won't help either of us, Carolyn." Dawson paused. "Did your husband—"

"Tom," she interrupted again.

"Yes, Tom. Did Tom *tell* you he was in Ziranj?" Dawson asked.

"No, not exactly," she replied. "A friend of his, another soldier named Jimmy Fitzpatrick, mentioned to his wife that Tom was headed that way a few weeks ago when he was home on leave. He's gone back now, I think."

"Hmm. Like I said, it's interesting," Dawson said.

"Yes," Menlo replied, "it is especially interesting now. I expected to hear from Tom well over a week ago. He told me he was headed out on an excursion—he's normally stationed up in Kabul—and that he would be back in a few days. That was almost three weeks back."

Dawson leaned back in his chair and thought about that. Three weeks. An awful lot could go wrong in that part of the world in three weeks. He didn't like the sound of this at all, but he kept his face impassive.

Menlo continued. "Any thoughts?"

"As I said, I don't think it's useful to speculate," Dawson said. It was all he could come up with, and it was the truth.

Menlo shifted gears. "Ben, exactly what is it that you do for the Foundation? I know you report to Kenneth directly, but no one seems to know exactly what it is that you do for him. Even Margaret seems to know little or nothing about your actual work. I know you have a very high clearance level, higher than mine, I think, and mine is a Top Secret. And here, at the Foundation, I mean, we are encouraged to ask very few questions, which I normally respect, but in this case I would really like to know."

Dawson didn't like the way the conversation was heading. "Carolyn, I can't tell you that in any detail. The fact that Dr. Brystol hasn't already told you, I'm sure, makes that clear. But you're right about my clearance level so even if Dr. Brystol told you, I wouldn't be able to confirm or deny it." He paused, but saw that Menlo was not intending to interrupt or challenge him, so he went on. "At a general level, I am Dr. Brystol's 'gofer.' I go for this and go for that whenever he asks me to. I am also the Foundation's liaison into a few specific US government agencies." Again Dawson paused, and again Menlo offered no response, so he continued. "I am curious about why you're curious."

"I understand from Kenneth that you've spent a good deal of time in the Middle East," Menlo replied. As Dawson's eyes narrowed a bit, she interjected: "Don't worry, he didn't share any details. He just told me that you are well connected in that part of the world and are a *very* resourceful man."

"Ah," Dawson said. He was gathering data, but thus far little information, and that usually made him impatient. "So is there something in particular that you are looking for help with?" While he couldn't see her hands directly at this point because they were hidden in her lap behind the desk, he could tell, from observing the muscles along her forearms, that she was squeezing one hand with the other, and then alternating hands. She was nervous or under stress about this part of the conversation. He thought he knew where she was headed, and he was about to find out whether he was right.

"I'd like you to help me find Tom," she said. "I believe he is in trouble, and if he is, I want you to help him."

Bingo! Dawson thought. But it was his turn to wait silently while Menlo provided additional information.

She continued: "I've talked with Kenneth, and he is willing to make certain that you come out whole in terms of compensation, and willing to set aside your normal work priorities for a short time. But ultimately he says this is your decision. I imagine that this sort of thing is not your normal assignment, though. As we discussed, I don't have a very detailed understanding of what it is you actually do."

"I appreciate your position," Dawson responded after a moment of consideration. "However, I'm sure you understand that whatever I do, this is not typical. Also, I really prefer to get my work direction from my boss. I'm a little disappointed that I'm not hearing about this first from Dr. Brystol." Menlo began to interrupt, but Dawson held one finger aloft just for a moment, and she relented politely. Her face clouded over, as though she saw an important opportunity fading away. "But I'll take that up with him. I suspect he thinks I'll be more likely to agree after understanding the personal angst involved, and having a face rather than just a name behind the request. He's probably right about that part." The dark clouds forming across Menlo's expression dissipated just a bit. "But I do have one or two questions for you, and those are: Did Brystol recommend that I help you with this, or did you approach him? Also, what have you already tried?"

Menlo leaned forward, crossing her arms atop her desk. "Fair enough. Kenneth and I were talking about Tom's situation after our staff meeting last week. While I can't recall the exact conversation, I remember that he suggested, after hearing about Tom's interval of non-communication, that I have a private chat with you. I wasn't exactly asking him to intervene, just looking for advice. Speaking with you was the best advice he said he could give me."

"Got it," Dawson replied.

"As to what I have already tried, I have reached out to Tom's CO, talked with the wife of Tom's friend who mentioned that Tom was headed to Ziranj, and tried the normal family support numbers. I've hit a wall of silence each time." At this point Menlo sighed and leaned back, arms still crossed. "I really wanted to pull General Garvin aside today after the presentation and ask him for help, but Kenneth was pretty emphatic about that being the wrong approach. To be completely candid, I'm still not comfortable that I should have allowed that opportunity to slip away. I don't rub shoulders with officials at that level often, and it seemed like the perfect opportunity. But Kenneth insisted, and I am in no position to argue."

Dawson thought about that. He could understand both sides: From Menlo's perspective, the opportunity to pull a member of the Pentagon brass aside, especially when she was cast in such a favorable light, would seem to be divine providence. But, as Dawson knew, whispering in the ear of the wrong general officer almost always creates a lot of activity without a great deal of productivity. Indeed, even well-intended inquiries and direction often proved catastrophic in such cases, as each level of information dissemination and activity between the general officer and the front line interpreted what they were hearing. And that didn't even consider the potential involvement of intelligence leaks and bad actors. Over his time in the military and in the intelligence community outside of the military, Dawson had seen it a thousand times. On balance, Dawson concluded, Brystol had probably given Menlo good advice. "What did his CO say?" Dawson asked.

Menlo frowned. "He wouldn't say much of anything, really. He told me he couldn't discuss details of ongoing operations and that he was sure I would hear from Tom as soon as Tom was free to communicate with me. He couldn't or wouldn't tell me when that might be, or even whether he was talking about weeks or months. It just wasn't consistent with how things have been between Tom and me during his deployments. I can tell something just isn't right."

Dawson had heard this kind of statement many times. It was designed to stall until the matter became obvious—either because the deployed soldier communicated again and the matter was resolved, or because the soldier was officially reported lost or killed in action.

"OK, I think I understand. I need to talk to Dr. Brystol about this before I tell you whether I can attempt to help you. I say 'attempt,' because no matter how that conversation comes out, I can make no promises. Even if I engage on this target, I have no idea what I'm going to find. I can only promise that I will talk with Brystol and get back to you within twenty-four hours. Fair enough?" Dawson stood, signaling that he was ready to end the meeting. He knew this wasn't the commitment Menlo had been looking for, but it was the best he could do for now; she would just have to live through twenty-four hours awaiting his decision. "I know this is very difficult for you. I just need to make absolutely sure before I can tell you whether I can be of any help. I'll get back to you as soon as I can."

Menlo stood slowly. "Fair enough," she said through a weak smile. "Just text me or call my office. I'll break free from whatever I'm involved in." Dawson stuck out his hand and liked the fact that she had a good strong handshake. Over the handshake, Menlo met his gaze and said: "I know I am asking a lot, Ben. But I really need help."

"I understand; I truly do," was all Dawson could say in reply. Then he turned and left her office just as her eyes began to tear up.

CHAPTER 4

As he exited the building, Dawson pulled his cell phone out and thumbed a number. In his address book, the name listed was Tom Bradley - office. The name was fictitious, but a lot of calls occurred between Dawson's phone and that number. On the other end of the line, the phone rang once and then was disconnected. About thirty seconds later, Dawson's phone buzzed and he hit "Accept." The voice on the other end of the line was mellow and seemed unperturbed at the lateness of the call. "I was just about to call you. How was the party?"

"A fluid funding frenzy," Dawson replied, pleased with his spontaneous outburst of alliteration. "Have time for a chat?"

"Of course, Benjamin," came the reply. "Usual spot?"

"That would be fine," Dawson said. He pressed the "End Call" button, replaced the phone, and headed for his rental car. Dawson found it easier to use rental cars, and as long as Brystol was footing the bill, it was a great way to accomplish several objectives. It permitted him to drive many different makes and models during any given month, made it extraordinarily difficult for bad actors to install listening devices, locating devices, or other more lethal surprises, and he found he enjoyed the variety. This week it was a gray Buick LaCrosse.

It took about forty minutes for Dawson to reach the Rock Quarry Tavern in Silver Springs. He liked the atmosphere for meetings like this. A tavern in a basement made being seen and overheard unlikely, especially with spur-of-the-moment rendezvous. This late on a week night it wasn't too noisy, and Dawson spotted Charles Jennings within a few seconds. Jennings had staked out a booth around the corner from the door where he could see anyone entering before they would see him. He was a cautious man and at nearly seventy, the value of that characteristic had been amply proven. Tall and slender with silver hair, a matching mustache, and "cheater" spectacles that he was using to peruse the wine list between seemingly casual glances at the door, Jennings looked like a Harvard professor in a dapper tweed jacket. Dawson thought that if he had only had a pipe the image would have been perfect. Dawson's former boss, Jennings was a deputy director in the National Security Agency. He was also a close friend and distant family relation of Dr. Kenneth Brystol.

"You said you were about to call me?" Dawson said, sliding into the booth across from Jennings.

Jennings smiled in reply: "You're always in such a hurry, Benjamin. Life is too short to hurry so much. I have ordered your usual, by the way, along with a glass of the Bordeaux for myself. Would you like anything to eat?"

"Sorry," Dawson said sheepishly. "You're right, of course. That was abrupt of me." Dawson paused as his "usual" was delivered to the table, and ordered an appetizer: chips and artichoke dip.

When the server retreated, Jennings responded. "Yes. I need to chat with you about the little problem you had on your recent excursion into the desert. You were, of course, correct; there is a leak. There can be no doubt that the mission was compromised, given the specificity of the response and the extremely limited number of people on our side who were read in on your trip. There is something else as well." Dawson listened as he nursed the iced tea before him, what Jennings had called his "usual." It was a long-standing point of amusement to Jennings that Dawson almost invariably chose a bar as a meeting place, yet had never been much of a drinker. Dawson had explained to Jennings that he not only learned more that way, but he actually *remembered* some of what he's heard the next morning. While at NSA, it had earned him the status of standard designated driver. Dawson's other favorite locations were cathedrals. They were typically empty during weekdays and offered plenty of privacy. Dawson often hung around after those meetings for a few minutes and just enjoyed the quiet.

"Some of the ISAF folks got back to the site last week and discovered a few artifacts from that little dust-up. The reason you were so effectively engaged out there was that the combatants were MSS, Ministry of State Security. Evidently a highly skilled force with their tactical training focused on Middle East operations."

"China? Ah, of course," Dawson said. "Stands to reason that China would be involved. Between their ongoing efforts to extract everything from copper to barium in that part of the world, and their new-found determination to build a global naval presence, it makes perfect sense. What was found?" Dawson was just curious.

"Among other things, ISAF found the remnants of a gas-operated feeder from a Chinese variant of the AK-47," Jennings replied. "While not conclusive in itself, between that and a few other items, there really isn't much doubt."

"Interesting," Dawson said. "I didn't see that coming, but I probably should have."

"Don't be too hard on yourself," Jennings said, clearly reading Dawson's mind. "You couldn't have known that they had that information. We certainly didn't know back at the office, and for that matter, still don't know exactly how much was compromised and more importantly—"

"By whom?" Dawson finished the sentence for him.

"Precisely," Jennings responded quietly, "and that, my boy, is why I was calling you. Now then, why were *you* calling *me*?" Jennings returned to sipping his Bordeaux.

"I have been approached by Dr. Menlo with a request to locate and possibly rescue her husband," Dawson said flatly. "Apparently, at the behest of Brystol. Certainly with his blessing, it seems. I haven't spoken with him directly about it yet."

He could see the mental gears turning in Jennings' head. Finally Jennings asked him, "What are your thoughts?"

"Well, the temporal element of this is interesting, isn't it? And then there is the erstwhile connection between all of these apparently unconnected events."

"Yes," Jennings replied. "Your instincts are still quite sound, Benjamin. I believe these events are indeed connected, but of course the question is *how*. Let's explore that. In reverse order of probability, here are a few scenarios: 1) Tom Menlo is the leak. His wife spilled sensitive information via pillow talk, and your mission was compromised. Of course, the timeline doesn't work there, because even if LTC Menlo is a prisoner somewhere, he can have only been in enemy hands for a few weeks. So if he was the traitor, he would have had to be on the payroll of the other side for longer than that. It also presumes that his wife would spill the beans, which seems unlikely from what I know about her. Then there is a more probable scenario: 2) Dr. Menlo is herself the traitor. This would of course let LTC Menlo off the hook, if indeed he is still alive to worry about such things."

"And there is a hybrid of those two theories," Dawson said. "Carolyn Menlo could have revealed the nature of her work with no intended malice out of sheer professional exuberance, wanting to share this stunning scientific breakthrough with her husband, whom she trusts implicitly—and probably for good reason. Then either the colonel turns or is persuaded through blackmail or extortion or some other means to yield what he knows. But of course in that scenario we still have the open question of how the other side gained such specific information about the mission. Not even Dr. Menlo herself had that information."

Jennings picked it up from there. "And then there is the very real possibility that it has nothing to do with the Menlo family at all. Purely bad actors and normal espionage. This of course opens up a wide range of possibilities. Are the traitors in our military environment, in the Foundation, or in both? And at the same time, it doesn't help to resolve the problem faced by the Menlos—a missing husband and father in one of the most dangerous areas of the planet."

Dawson, swallowing a dip-laden chip, added: "And the overarching problem, of course, is that the technology is at risk and we don't know how serious our exposure and our vulnerability are."

"And that, my boy, is the problem in a nutshell," Jennings smiled. "But it sounds to me as though you believe there is, indeed, a connection between the colonel, the doctor, and the information leak. Is that true?"

"It just feels that way somehow, but I honestly can't put my finger on why. A hunch, I suppose," Dawson said.

"Hmm," Jennings murmured, "your hunches have served us well over these last years. I am inclined to recommend that you go with it."

"OK. I'll see what I can do," Dawson responded. "This is all pretty tenuous."

Jennings was finishing up his Bordeaux, and sighed. "Well, I have every confidence in you. I'll speak with Kenneth tomorrow, and between the two of us we shall find a way to make sure that whatever you need to do is adequately funded. Just please be careful, and as always—"

Dawson once again finished Jennings' sentence for him. "Remember that technically I am just a hired contractor now, and there are limits to what anyone can—or will—do to back me up. Is that about right?"

Jennings smiled. "You can always come back to the agency you know."

"Thanks, Charles," Dawson said, rising from his seat to leave, "but I can't afford the pay cut."

Jennings shook his head slowly and locked eyes pointedly with Dawson. "We both know that's nonsense, Ben. The fact is you're a consummate, unmitigated, and unapologetic patriot. You'd do what you do gratis if you thought it was necessary. In all my years around this very jaded community, you are damned near unique, and in the best possible ways."

"Well, Charles, if I really am unique in that respect, then we're all in trouble." With that Dawson shook hands with Jennings, wished him a good evening, and made his way out of the bar.

As Dawson walked away, Jennings muttered to himself, "You couldn't be more right."

* * * *

The next morning, Dawson asked Brystol for a slot on his calendar, and as was typical, Brystol made a spot for him within an hour. By nine a.m., they were sitting together in Brystol's office. A well-kept secret at the Foundation was the general state of disorder that was Brystol's inner sanctum. Papers, books, and periodicals were everywhere, and Brystol's visitors frequently needed to move stacks of papers off of chairs in order to find a place to sit. Today was an exception, Dawson noticed, as he had no trouble finding a seat.

"Margaret has been housecleaning again," Brystol complained, observing Dawson's look of surprise as he entered the room. "I have told her repeatedly that I cannot abide people rummaging through my things. I know they often seem disorderly, but I always know where everything is." At this Dawson raised a skeptical eyebrow. "Well, generally anyway. Now it will take me weeks to recover so that I can find everything again," Brystol harrumphed. "Anyway, you didn't come in to listen to me complain about my little organizational challenges. I suspect you've spoken with Carolyn Menlo?"

"Yes," Dawson replied. "I understand you'd like me to assist her in locating her husband; is that correct?"

"It is," Brystol responded. "As you know, Doctor Menlo is a critical element—the lynchpin, really—of our Salacia program. Anything that distracts her could be a real problem, especially now. The scaling of this technology is absolutely critical, and if something should happen to impair her performance, the program would be thrown into serious jeopardy."

Ah, yes. Far more profit motive than loyalty to the woman who delivered the world-changing technology into your hands, Dawson thought, but what he verbalized was: "I understand. The last time we chatted about the Foundation's 'Top 10' projects, Salacia was pretty near the top of our priority list. Is that still true?"

"Yes, that's still true. I'd say it vacillates between number two and number three right now, but because we are nearly into a pilot deployment, this one takes priority. I doubt it will eclipse Angelia anytime soon, but it is certainly further along, and therefore more critical to our immediate future, than Synapse, Gnosis, Icarus, or any of the second-tier programs. Several have some intriguing possibilities, but it is far too soon to depend upon them."

This entire conversation left Dawson stunned the first time he was exposed to it. Most R&D organizations would be staggered by the implications of a world-changing technology. The mobile phone, for example, was a world-changing technology. But it required cell towers, repeaters, optic fiber backbones, and basically a world of infrastructure to bring it to a level that approached its full capability.

The Foundation worked on no less, but rarely more, than ten projects at a time that required no such infrastructure. They were all potential world-changers, and when fielded they all held the promise of nearly overnight transformation. Salacia was a classic case. These programs usually required massive R&D funding, the best minds in their respective fields, and—more often than not—government clearances due to their potential impact. A program like Salacia was irresistible to the military and intelligence communities because it offered an undeniable edge for as long as they could maintain the secrecy of the technology that enabled the device. Funding would flow in rivers, even in the current world of military spending cutbacks. Programs like this made the Foundation, which was a foundation in name only, a very profitable enterprise.

"All right then," Dawson said, "I need some clarity around your expectations here. I'll start looking, but as you know I'm not terribly selective; what I find is what I find. How much do you want to know?"

"I don't need any 'operational details,' as you would put it. Just inform me when you encounter something that has a direct impact on the Foundation, and keep me apprised of significant outcomes."

Brystol was being his usual evasive self, Dawson observed. "Significant outcomes?" he pressed. "Such as whether the lieutenant colonel turns out to be dead or alive?"

"Yes," Brystol responded, "exactly that level of detail. Nothing that would prove inconvenient, should I be required to confirm or deny it in a deposition one day."

"Any other unusual limitations?" asked Dawson.

"No specific constraints come to mind. You know the Salacia timeline, Ben. It would be helpful to get this matter behind us sooner rather than later, no matter the fate of the good colonel. Of course we are hoping for the best, but either way Carolyn will need to get this behind her in order to focus over the next six months." Dawson tilted his head a bit to one side in response. Brystol said: "Oh, I know I sound very callous. But you understand the magnitude of what we're talking about here. None of us is worth the failure of any one of the Foundation's programs, including me." Dawson didn't bother even thinking about that one. He knew that without Brystol the Foundation would be gone. It had less to do with the actual scientific prowess of Brystol or his staff than it did with his connections and reputation throughout the military-industrial complex. His ability to command the attention and garner financial support of that community was unmatched.

"In that case I'll take care of a few things here and then get under way. I'll need an initial deposit of $250,000 in the normal account, and about fifty thousand in Euros. The Euros I'll need in cash. I'll let you know when I require the rest. This may involve a team," Dawson said, standing to leave.

Brystol stood as well. "I'll have Margaret get that done for you today. Good luck, Ben. I'm looking forward to seeing you back here again in one piece when this matter is resolved." In spite of Brystol's avarice, Dawson believed him. Brystol was not a malicious man, and to a point he could be quite generous both financially and in terms of personal loyalty. But Dawson knew that there was a clear line beyond which those loyalties did not extend— he was determined to remain inside that line.

Dawson's next stop was Menlo's office. Carolyn's administrative assistant asked Dawson to wait while she summoned her from the lab, but again Dawson's impatience kicked in. He asked the admin to tell Menlo that he would meet her outside the building in the small gazebo near the employee parking area, which was more convenient to his own departure and, Dawson reasoned, adequately secure as a location to speak privately about this matter.

Menlo nearly arrived ahead of him. She hadn't been kidding; she must have walked out of the lab as soon as the call came in from her admin. She seemed reluctant to look him in the eye until she was very close, and Dawson suspected she was fearful he would not agree to her request. He surmised that Menlo was a woman at the end of her rope and that he was the only remaining option in which she had some confidence, the one on whom she was pinning her hopes. Even with Dawson's particularly colorful history, it was a sobering position. He found that he genuinely liked this woman, and wanted to help her if he could. Now that the mission was sanctioned—well, unofficially sanctioned—he would do his best to try.

After she had a chance to catch her breath, Dawson looked her in the eye and said as evenly as he could: "I'm going to do what I can." As soon as the words left his lips, before he could say anything else, she threw herself into his arms. He immediately cursed himself silently for having arranged this chat in public, and so close to the very building where she was so well known. *How could I be so stupid?* On the other hand, he couldn't help but return the hug. He knew she was hurting, and he could imagine how much. He had no handkerchief—*who carried them these days?* he wondered—and felt helpless when he saw the stream of tears flowing down her face. She was still wearing a smock from the lab, and used its sleeve to wipe her face leaving a smudge of mascara across her cheek.

She actually looked for a moment as though she might collapse, and he gently guided her over to the gazebo and deposited her on the wooden bench. The gazebo was designed to shelter commuters from the rain until friends or family members or carpool drivers picked them up in the evening, so mid-mornings usually left the area pretty deserted. Dawson glanced around and saw that no one appeared to be watching. After a moment and an abject apology, which Dawson brushed off politely, Menlo calmed down.

Dawson began again. "Take your time, Carolyn, because I need your mind to be clear. There are several things you need to remember, and I want you to memorize them rather than writing them down. So take a few breaths, and listen carefully to me for a minute. When you're ready, I'll tell you what you need to memorize. OK?"

She nodded, sniffed, and said, "Of course. Go ahead."

"All right," Dawson continued. "As this effort gets under way, I know you are going to be wondering how I'm doing and what's going on and if there is any news. But because we don't know yet what we're dealing with, I won't be in any position to tell you those things without putting you, myself, and possibly even your husband at risk. Unfortunately, as I hope you can appreciate, I don't know how long this is going to take. It could stretch to thirty days or more. I'm guessing not much longer, though. Are you with me so far?"

"Yes. Go on."

"Beyond that, the mere fact that I'm now engaging in this activity will put you and your son at risk if things have already gone sideways. I don't believe that risk is serious or imminent right now, or I'd be advising you to take precautions. More about that in a minute. Right now, though, I'd like you to go on about your work and your life at home just as you normally do. Don't alter your normal routine, don't tell any friends or family members that anything is going on, and don't do anything overt like having a new alarm system installed at home or pulling your son out of school or out of sports, etc. Just go on about life as you normally would. Understand?"

"I understand you, Ben," Menlo replied, "but I have to admit that you're scaring me a little." It was obvious to Dawson that she wasn't stretching the truth. *In her situation,* he thought, *anyone would be scared.*

"I'm sorry about that, but I'm just laying out the course of action that I know from experience is likely to be the safest path for you. The other day you asked me to be frank. Now I need you to trust me, for all of our sakes—yours, your son's, and Tom's most of all," he said.

"I understand," she replied, and Dawson could only hope that she did.

He went on. "I need you to identify a family member or trusted friend with whom you could stay if something should go wrong. Odds are you won't have to do that; this is an emergency backup plan, but still it's important. I would prefer that the friend or relative be someone outside this area—at least a county away, and preferably outside Virginia. But someone you trust completely, and not the friend who is married to Tom's friend—the soldier you told me about. Can you do that?"

Menlo thought about it for several seconds, and then nodded. "Yes, I have a sister in Atlanta. I could go there," she said.

"Perfect," Dawson replied. "Please write her name and address down for me." He fished a small spiral notebook and pen out of his pocket and passed them over. "Also, please write down the name of Tom's friend, the one who passed along the information about where Tom was headed."

Menlo did as she was asked without hesitation. "Obviously," Dawson said, "don't share this plan with anyone. If you need to execute it, don't tell anyone where you're going or where they can reach you. You call in to work only when you have to, and never stay on the line for more than thirty seconds if you do. OK?"

Again she nodded and said: "OK." She closed the notebook and handed it back to Dawson, who pocketed it immediately.

Again he went on. "All right, now here is what you need to memorize. First of all, I want you to remember the email address: bradley.comms@gmail.com. Got it?" She repeated the address. "OK, then," Dawson continued. "What is your son's first name?"

"Andy," she said.

"All right, then," Ben replied, "when you log in to that account, the password will be andymenlo. No caps, all lowercase. Got it?"

Again she nodded, and repeated: "bradley dot comms at gmail dot com, password andymenlo, all lowercase. Got it."

"Great," Dawson said. "Now, when you log into that account, open up the folder called Drafts. Whenever I can, I will get a status message into that folder for you." She looked at him quizzically. "I know," he continued, "I said that I won't be able to tell you what is going on, and that's still true. What you will see in these messages will be very brief, and I have a little pneumonic device for you to use. Here's the device: MENLO. M stands for 'Moving. You may not hear from me for a few days.' E stands for 'Engaged. I have found Tom and am trying to get him back to you.' Now if you get that message from me, bear in mind that Tom may no longer be alive. If that is the case, I'll try to get his body back to you. I'm sorry to be so brutal, but I just don't know of a less painful way to put this, and I don't want you to necessarily get your hopes up when you see that status."

He paused and let that sink in. After a few seconds he continued: "N stands for 'Normal situation. Mission proceeding, but nothing meaningful to report.' L stands for 'Leave now!' This is the distress signal, Carolyn. If I leave that message for you, do not wait until the end of the workday, the end of the school day, or lunchtime. Just go. Pick up Andy and head for your sister's place. Wait there until you hear from me or from my proxy. You'll know my proxy when he introduces himself. And finally, O stands for 'Over.' If you get that message, my mission is concluded, and I am on my way back. I'll do everything I can to make sure that it's with your husband. So that's it: MENLO. Now, you run through it for me, please."

She repeated the letters and their meanings, and Dawson was convinced that she understood.

"That's great. Now, when you see my messages, they will be comprised of the word MENLO and a single digit. If you don't see the word MENLO in all caps, the message is not from me. I don't anticipate that, but you just never know. The digit will represent the letter in our pneumonic device that I am communicating to you. So, suppose you see a status that says: ME3NLO. What is my message?"

"Normal," she replied without any hesitation.

Dawson said: "Good—now suppose it says MENLO4?"

"I leave immediately for my sister's house," Menlo replied.

"Excellent," Ben said. "You have it. The word MENLO will *always* appear, and it will *always* be in all caps, and *always* be in the correct sequence, but the single digit can be anywhere adjacent to the word—in front of it, within it, or after it."

Dawson paused again and let this all sink in. "I realize this is a lot to remember …" and Carolyn Menlo actually smiled for the first time that day.

"I studied Latin as an undergrad," she said. "Believe me; I'll have no trouble remembering this." At that, Dawson returned the smile.

"There is one thing I'm still wondering about, though," she continued. "You said I would know if I ever met your 'proxy', but how can I be sure?"

Dawson thought about that for a minute. Then he replied, "Tell you what. If that day should come, ask the man who presents himself for the password, and wait for him to respond. If he responds with anything other than this phrase, it's not my guy." Then he leaned in close, and bent over to whisper in her ear, "There is no password."

Menlo shivered as Dawson straightened back up, "Will that work for you?" he asked.

Looking up at him from the bench, her smile returned. "Yes," she said quietly, "I think that should work perfectly." She laid her hand on his arm. "Thank you."

"You're welcome," Dawson replied. "I'll let you get back to work then. I've got several things to do. I'll be in touch, starting tomorrow, as we arranged." Menlo rose, and it seemed to Dawson that she stood a little straighter this time. The tiny lines around her eyes had softened a bit, too. As he began to turn away, Dawson said, "Oh, a couple last things."

"Yes?" she said, pausing as she was stepping down from the gazebo onto the sidewalk. "You'll want to take a look at that mascara as soon as you get inside," he replied.

"Oh! Thanks," she said, already dabbing at it with her sleeve. "What was the other thing?" she asked, casting a self-conscious glance down to see if something else was out of place.

"You smell *very* nice, Dr. Menlo. Your husband is a very fortunate man," Dawson said and disappeared around the nearby row of junipers and headed toward his Buick before Menlo could respond.

CHAPTER 5

The morning following his meeting with Menlo at the gazebo, Dawson squinted into the blinding sunrise as he drove along 495 into Old Alexandria. It was just before seven a.m., and he decided he had plenty of time to pick up a bagel and a mug of hot tea at the local Einstein's. He then walked the remaining blocks to the Shock 'n Aw Gym, and up the stairs to National Martial Arts. There he found exactly what, or rather who, he expected working out on the wooden dummy.

When Dawson approached, Max Kelly stopped and dropped his hands to his sides. "Hey, big guy!" he exclaimed through a wide grin, arms held wide for a bear hug. Kelly's skin glistened with sweat and he had grown a beard and let his hair grow so long that he looked like Grizzly Adams.

Dawson held up his hand in a halting motion and then stuck it out for a handshake instead. "Whoa! I'm headed in to work. I can't walk around smelling like you all day." Not many people could talk to Kelly that way, but Dawson topped that very short list.

Kelly had been a Navy SEAL in the days before it was a household name. A few years later, Dawson and Kelly had been together through NSA training. But gradually, Kelly became angry and disillusioned with all the politics. If he couldn't "kick ass and take names," he wanted no part of it. These days he ran a security agency comprised of six employees, all but one of whom were former Special Forces of one ilk or another, with the exception of an assistant named Boxer and the woman he referred to as his "main squeeze," Lily. Lily Gerard was a martial arts legend in regional circles, and a trained investigator. Formerly a member of the Boston Police Department's Organized Crime Unit, she was a top-notch personal bodyguard who fit in beautifully whether the client required refined cocktail party participation or accompaniment for a grueling hike along the Appalachian Trail. She was a fiery redhead, stood five feet six inches tall in her bare feet, and still turned heads at age forty-four.

"I figured you'd be here," Dawson said.

"Regular as clockwork," Kelly replied. The two men were alone in a relatively isolated room, away from the windows overlooking Hooffs Run Drive.

"How's business?" Dawson asked. "And more importantly, how's Lily? I can see that other than losing a step or so, you're doing all right."

"Ah, looking for a sparring partner? Think you can finally take me?"

"Oh, no," Dawson laughed. "Even in your condition, you'd beat the crap outa me." At that point, the much vaunted Lily Gerard entered from a side door leading from the women's locker room.

"And you'd deserve it, you scoundrel! What do mean staying away for so long? Too good for your old friends?" She strutted up, wrapped her arms around him, and planted an enormous kiss on the side of his face. As always, she smelled wonderful. At some point, Dawson couldn't remember exactly when, he'd discovered the fragrance was called Sand & Sable. It just seemed to suit Lily Gerard somehow.

"Hey!" Kelly complained.

"Hey yourself!" Dawson responded, grinning broadly. "If you ever start looking like her, then sweaty or not, you can hug me any time."

"If he starts looking like me," Gerard said, "it will be time for *all* of us to pack it in. But seriously, Ben, what's been keeping you away? You got a girl or something?"

"Of course not!" Dawson said through a melodramatically pained expression. "There will never be anyone for me but you, Lily. I just keep waiting for you to see the light and drop this guy." He would never admit it, even under pain of extreme torture, but there was a kernel of truth to what he said. His marriage hadn't been a happy one, and once his wife got sick and then after she died of cancer, he'd sworn off women completely and concentrated on doing his job. But Lily Gerard … well, she was … *no!* Thinking that way about Lily would've been the same thing as putting a knife through his friend's heart.

"Hey, I'm standing right here you know," Kelly pouted.

"Why?" she asked, striking a coquettish pose. "I'm girl enough for *both* of you!"

"Why do I get into trouble every time I'm around you two?" Dawson asked no one in particular.

Kelly tried to respond, but Gerard cut him off. "Trouble is what you live for, Ben Dawson, and you know it. If we weren't cut from the same cloth, we wouldn't love you so much." She crossed her arms and leaned casually against Kelly as though he were just another wall. He may as well have been; he didn't react one iota to compensate for her weight. "So if you didn't come in to work out or spar, I assume you're here on business?" Gerard asked.

Dawson was so pleased to see his old friends again that he'd nearly put it out of his head for a moment. Now he was forced to return to reality, and switched back into work mode. "Yes, as a matter of fact, I am," he replied. "I have a personal security detail gig and it will require at least a two-person team, more likely three. You'll be a better judge than me."

"Ha, I doubt that," Kelly said, "but tell us about the PSD, and we'll talk it over."

Over the next thirty minutes, Dawson explained what he had in mind. He needed a personal security detail assigned to both Carolyn Menlo and her son Andrew. It could be up to thirty days, he estimated, but probably not longer. He would pay one and a half times their going rate and a twenty-percent bonus if everything went well and they all came out whole at the conclusion of the engagement.

"How serious are the bad actors here?" Kelly asked when Dawson finished.

"I think we're dealing with Chinese MSS, and possibly even rogue US operatives. Professional, well trained, and merciless would be my best guess."

"My, my," Gerard smiled, "you are just chock-full of good news today, aren't you?"

Dawson smiled back at her. "You know I never have easy stuff, Lily. This could be uneventful or an all-out firefight rolling down the freeway in broad daylight. I simply have no idea. But I wouldn't ask you two if it wasn't important, and you both know what the word 'important' means when I use it. Absolutely no hard feelings if this kind of thing isn't your cup of tea any more. None of us is getting any younger."

At this remark, Kelly groused and said: "I'm still benching 225, Ben, how about you?"

Gerard just looked at him and said: "We'll be all right, Ben. Just you be careful. It sounds to me like you've drawn the short straw here. Now are you sure you don't want this Menlo woman to know that we're there? It could be pretty comforting if she is really scared."

"Oh, she's scared all right," Dawson said, "and she ought to be. I think she's a fighter though; there was something I could see in her eyes. Still waters run deep kind of thing."

At this, Kelly nodded knowingly but Lily cocked her head slightly, and her right eyebrow arched. She folded her arms and continued listening. "But I don't want her acting differently, instinctively looking around for one of you every time a car backfires. It would give you away, and then you wouldn't be as valuable to her. So no, I think it's better if the surveillance is transparent—that is, unless you guys have lost your touch."

"Oh, I think we can handle this all right," Gerard said, making eye contact with Kelly just to be sure they were in agreement. They were.

"So I've given you the name, address, sister's address, work hours, Andy's school schedule, contact password, and so on. Is there anything else you need from me to get started?" Dawson asked.

Kelly frowned and exchanged glances with Gerard. "Can you think of anything, Lily?" he asked.

Gerard thought it over and shook her head. "No, I think we've got it, Ben. We'll take good care of them. You just focus on the mission and don't worry about them; we've got 'em."

"That's a relief; thank you," Dawson responded. "Now, I've got one last thing. This is completely illegal, Lily, so if you'd rather I speak with Max alone about this...."

"Don't you start with me, Ben Dawson," she warned.

Dawson shrugged and went on. "All right. I need some heavy-duty surveillance on a soldier working in the DC area. Dr. Menlo thought this guy was back in Afghanistan, but he's in Crystal City 2 these days. I want everything—text messages, voice communications, the whole nine yards. I only need it for about a week, but I have no warrant."

"What's the name?" Gerard asked.

"Major James Fitzpatrick," Dawson replied. "I need the system running tomorrow—the earlier the better."

"I'll get on it as soon as I finish up here," said Kelly.

"OK, then," Dawson said. "I'll be on my way."

He shook hands with Kelly again and turned to get a departing hug from Gerard, but she was already three steps toward the stairs. "I'm going to walk Ben out," she called to Kelly. "I'll be right back." Kelly just waved at them and returned to work on the wooden dummy.

"So I have question for you," Gerard said as they ambled down the rickety stairway.

"Shoot," Dawson responded.

"My question is this," Gerard said, turning to face him, basically trapping him with her face mere inches from his on the narrow landing between flights. "Are you in love with this woman?"

"What? What are you talking about?" Dawson stammered.

Gerard moved closer. When she was almost nose-to-nose, looking him dead in the eye, she finally said, "Listen to me. I love you, you know I do." She paused for a moment, and Dawson's heart hammered in his chest. "But you men seriously don't have the brains God gave a snail when it comes to women. I know you have no idea what's going on in here—" she poked him hard in the chest without ever breaking eye contact "—but *I* do. It's written all over your face. 'Still waters,' huh? Give me a break. You don't even know whether this woman is a straight shooter or a bad actor. For all you know, she could have done her husband in, or he could be in cahoots with her and lying in wait to ambush you somewhere." She moved her index finger from his chest to the middle of his forehead, and almost hissed the words: "So get your head in the game. Not your *heart*, buster, your *head*. You need to be all there for this little party, you understand me?"

Dawson knew she was as serious as a heart attack. "I understand," he croaked.

"You'd damned well better. If you go out there and get yourself killed, I am going to *kick your ass!*" She spat the words at him with such utter ferocity that Dawson was speechless, which, as it turned out, was just as well. By the time he found words again she had vanished back up the stairs and out of sight. As the thudding in his chest subsided, he tried to understand what was going on, and then decided that whatever this massive ball of confusion he was feeling meant, it was going to have to wait. Gerard was right; he might not survive even if he was completely focused. He almost certainly wouldn't survive if he was distracted. But Carolyn Menlo? Sure she smelled wonderful, and sure she was smart and beautiful and … maybe just being attracted to a woman at all meant he was finally ready to get back in the game. After all these years. He stood in the stairwell a moment more. Sand & Sable. He breathed in and thought of Lily Gerard back upstairs with his old friend. "This is ridiculous," he said aloud and turned and headed back downstairs.

Dawson's next call was to Jennings. He called from a coffee shop across the street from the gym. After he got through the standard protocols, Dawson said: "I'm sending you a request for a package delivery. Need it today, if possible."

"Understood," Jennings replied. "Will be standing by. Out here."

With that, Dawson logged in with his cell phone and placed an email in the draft folder of an email account, similar to his instructions to Menlo. "Need introduction to TM's CO. Need jackets on TM and Major James Fitzpatrick, Army. Usual delivery location."

Finally, Dawson thumbed 1 on his speed-dial, and after a couple of rings, heard a familiar voice at the other end of the line.

"Winger here," the gruff baritone announced. "What's up, Boss?"

Dawson couldn't help smiling whenever he heard the voice of his old comrade. "How are you, Billy?"

"Aw, you know—I'm still standing, but getting a little bored. I hate it when I start to feel myself rusting up. You hear about something interesting?" Winger, a former Delta Force operator who later joined NSA, worked in Kabul and Baghdad through the "noisy" period between 2003 and 2009, left the agency after nearly a decade to marry, and then regretted the union almost immediately. The marriage lasted only a year, but Winger didn't leave NSA under good terms. He had been working freelance contract assignments for the CIA and FBI ever since.

"I'm going back in soon, was looking for a little help," Dawson responded. "Interested in replenishing your retirement fund?"

"Roger that!" came Winger's voice. "Same destination?"

"Not exactly, but close," Dawson replied. "Next AO to the left. We'll also need at least one other operator. Probably a week or two on the ground, and in K&R, kidnap and ransom mode."

He heard Winger emit a soft, low whistle. "Those guys don't like us much these days, Boss. I'm gonna have to wear my steel underwear."

"Yes, indeed," Dawson said.

"Say, you know, I think I know someone who might be interested in this gig, if you're game. You know him, too."

"You mean Kelly?" Dawson asked. "He's already on another job."

"Naw," Winger replied. "I know Kelly is a great operator, but he's mostly doing domestic stuff these days. The guy I have in mind is Jim Romero."

"Jim Romero … Do you mean *Chief* Romero from our excursion a few months back?" Dawson asked.

"That's the guy," Winger replied.

"He would be *outstanding!*" Dawson said. "But is he available? That soldier saved our bacon back there in Helmand."

"Funny thing," Winger retorted, "that's exactly what he said about you!"

"Last I knew he was on active duty," said Dawson.

"He retired about five weeks ago," Winger said. "Actually he called me because he was looking for work. I told him that I didn't have anything at the moment, but I was going to point him to you anyway."

"Billy, he would be *perfect*," Dawson said. "Ask him to come along and I'll meet you at that dive you're always hanging out in. Can you make 1800 hours?"

"Absolutely. I'll see whether Chief is available, and if he is, I'll bring him along," responded Winger.

Later that afternoon, Dawson entered a little place called Jimmy's Grand Irish Pub on King Street in Old Alexandria. Oscar, a Santa Clause look-alike, was the long-standing bartender at Jimmy's. Seven days a week, he seemed never to leave his post behind the bar, and had been there for longer than Dawson had been frequenting the place. How he was hooked up with the Jennings crowd, Dawson had no idea, but he had been Dawson's most frequented "drop" for several years. Oscar nodded to him as he took up a stool, and shortly appeared with Dawson's usual—an iced tea with lots of ice and two packets of Splenda. As he deposited the glass on a cocktail napkin, Oscar mumbled, "Candy was in lookin' for ya earlier."

Dawson nodded. "Thanks, Oscar." He took a couple of sips of his tea while looking over the few patrons, then meandered back to the men's restroom. It was a single occupancy toilet, so the door could be locked from the inside. Once inside, Dawson pulled a nickel from his pocket and squatted down in front of the sink. There were two slotted screw-like fasteners just under the lip of the sink, which—even if one happened to be looking under there for some reason—would appear to the observer to be an access panel to the P-trap and water lines. In fact, when Dawson turned each one a quarter turn, the panel fell forward on hinges exposing the cypher lock of a small safe. He pressed the appropriate five-digit code and removed a manila envelope.

When he opened it, he found Jennings had provided what he asked for: bio information on both Lt. Colonel Tom Menlo and Major James Fitzpatrick. Menlo had served with distinction, earning a number of medals and commendations including the Defense Distinguished Service Cross and the Bronze Star. He had attended West Point and entered Ranger school. After becoming a Special Forces member, he had served three hitches, one in Iraq and two in Afghanistan. It looked from the cryptic notations in his record as though Menlo had been involved in several black ops missions during his deployments. Married, one child, spotless record.

Then there was Fitzpatrick. While he did not appear to be in any particular trouble, Fitzpatrick's service record showed no signs of distinction, and his performance ratings were consistently in the "meets expectations" range. At first Dawson could not, from the two service records, see where the two men had crossed paths, or what they had in common. "Oh, there it is," Dawson said aloud. They had been living in the same military quarters in Kabul. That had to be it. He folded the envelope in half length-wise and slipped it into his jacket. Then he replaced the cover over the safe, and returned to the bar. When he finished the tea, Dawson left two dollars on the bar, waved at Oscar, and left Jimmy's.

CHAPTER 6

Like a mirror, the small man-made lake behind the office complex situated off Fairview Park Drive in Falls Church, Virginia, reflected the spring blossoms of surrounding trees. It provided an idyllic home for the occasional deer, geese, and other water fowl in the area. Occupants of surrounding office buildings strolled around the lake on breaks, ate lunches on benches along its shores, and generally took pride in their lake and in the local flora and fauna it supported. All the occupants, but one. A chain smoker, he took countless daily smoking breaks, standing at the edge of the lake and lighting up, finishing his cigarettes and then flicking the butts into the lake.

Other office workers seethed as they watched the man, who seemed to take great pleasure in seeing how far out into the lake he could make the cigarette butts sail, sparks cascading off in the air, before they descended finally into the water below. Over time, the nasty, decomposing butts accumulated in the surrounding reeds and even poisoned some of the ducks. Vociferous complaints from neighboring businesses did nothing to curb the man's habits, but did result in the engagement of a landscaping service which now appeared twice a week to keep the lake pristine. Cost, apparently, was not a prohibitive matter. The neighboring business people still regarded the habit of the daily smoker to be outrageous and disgusting, but had no choice except to relent.

Today, the smoker had not been out to cast his traditional butts into the lake since early morning. This wasn't the result of any capitulation, however;

he was badly craving nicotine, and it was adding to his already foul mood. But he was trapped in a meeting within a secure, soundproof room in the basement of the low, sprawling glass and rust-colored metal building and not even a restroom call had been made all morning.

The sign along the drive to the building proclaimed "Computer Services Corporation" in bright red lettering, and the name on the man's US passport was Donald Brewer, but his real name was Dong Biwu and the Computer Services Corporation was a front for a satellite office of the foreign services directorate of the Chinese MSS, Ministry of State Security. Brewer, or Biwu, was a primary operator in the clandestine operations, and facing him across the conference table was Lee Teng-hui, the MSS Station Chief for Washington, DC.

Although their underground conference room was surrounded by sound-deadening material lining the ceiling and walls as well as electronic surveillance countermeasures, the two men spoke in near-whisper level tones, and there was no mistaking the severity in their Mandarin exchange. Biwu had just completed a very short description of the situation, which was basically that MSS had learned of a new weapons technology under development by the US government that could be debilitating to the burgeoning Chinese military capability.

Teng-hui was not impressed. "I don't care what exotic technology you believe the Americans are developing. Those almost always turn out to be ghosts, and I cannot afford to chase ghosts here. I have already sent a very direct message to your director in Beijing. You have been operating for months in my area of responsibility without my knowledge, and this cannot be tolerated. We have many important objectives here, and we have years— decades, even—invested in achieving those objectives. We have relationships and operatives that have taken entire generations to build. I will not permit those to be compromised because of some rumors which you cannot even verify." While his language was direct and his intention was to scold, he was having no visible impact on Biwu.

Biwu was the son of an American father and a Chinese mother. His father was an adventurous manufacturing sales representative who had moved to China in the 1950s, fallen in love with a low-level ministry clerk, and married her. Their marriage had been happy, but Biwu's father was injured in a freak traffic accident, and, although he survived the initial trauma, he succumbed to his injuries and died the following day. Biwu was four years old at the time, and by the time he was ten, he didn't even remember his father.

But remember him or not, Biwu was the spitting image of his father. He had inherited his father's western look, a gift for languages, and his natural athletic prowess. In his late teens, he was recruited into MSS and then accepted into a "special" educational indoctrination program. In return, Biwu's mother received privileges and special treatment at work, better-than-average medical care, and although their life in China was modest, they never lacked for anything. Biwu's mother was never permitted to know the exact nature of her son's work, of course, but she knew he worked for the national government, and was very proud right up to the day of her death from lung cancer just two years earlier. At the time of her death, Biwu had not seen his mother for more than three years, and he didn't bother to return for her funeral. His work consumed him.

Throughout his indoctrination, Biwu had been brainwashed to believe that the decadent society of the West produced an overweight, dull, and lazy populace who had been so incredibly blessed with natural resources and intelligent—with a special emphasis on Chinese—immigrants that they had risen to prominence in the world almost in spite of themselves. He was educated by instructors and taught from texts that emphasized the role of Chinese slave labor in building the US railway system in the 19th century, the victory of Chinese-backed guerillas in the Viet Nam conflict, and similar anti-American propaganda.

By his twenty-fifth birthday, Biwu was a skilled assassin who boasted a Stanford bachelor's degree in political science with a minor in history. His English was nearly flawless, but he was carefully cultivated to remain perfectly fluent in Mandarin as well. Now in his thirties, Biwu had spent more than half of his life in North America and he had risen steadily through the ranks of the MSS by executing increasingly complex missions that required intricate planning, the ability to engage effectively with the local populace, especially business people, and utter ruthlessness. He blended in seamlessly among the North American population, and with his high-quality, forged US passport, he knew he was being groomed for big things and was well regarded among the senior leadership at MSS. So it was not surprising that, while he appeared impassive, he was mentally reviewing a number of ways he could make the angry man before him disappear.

"Yes, I have already heard from my director," Biwu said. "He has asked me to please avoid killing you if possible. You are free to check with him when you return to your office." At this, Teng-hui sat back in his chair and fell silent. No one at MSS would make such an outrageous assertion if it was untrue. Clearly, if the MSS had to choose who was more expendable, Teng-hui was their choice. Apparently, he was not as well connected as he thought. This changed the situation dramatically.

"Very well," Teng-hui responded, "then what can I do to assist you so that I may be free of you as soon as possible?"

"I want a list of all of your deepest cover assets in the Washington, DC area. I also need their employee records, with clear indication of what information and business or government personnel to which they have access."

"You cannot have that!" Teng-hui exploded. "You have no idea what you are asking. You are risking everything we've worked for all these years!"

Biwu smiled for the first time that morning, but it was a very unpleasant smile. He could not wait to be rid of Teng-hui and to take a smoke. "There is no question I will have it by noon tomorrow," Biwu said quietly. "The only question is whether you will give it to me, or whether I will come to your office and get it myself after you are no longer in a position to grant requests from *anyone*."

Teng-hui stewed for a minute, and then capitulated: "Come to my office at noon, then. I will have it for you," he said. With that, he started to rise from his chair.

But Biwu wasn't finished with him yet. "I don't think you quite understand," he said. "I want the files in my hands, here, by noon tomorrow. It's your choice, Teng-hui. If you do not deliver them to me, then make sure you enjoy a very nice lunch tomorrow, because it will be your last."

Teng-hui was seething, but turned and left abruptly before he made things worse. He was never treated like this. How *dare* this upstart—no matter how lethal or how connected he might be—openly threaten the most powerful station chief in North America? The situation was ludicrous and utterly unacceptable. *I did not arrive here by acting as the lamb,* Teng-hui thought. *I am a lion. And I will not allow some jackal to steal away with the fruits of my labor within his slobbering jowls!*

When he had stomped his way up the stairs and out to his car, Teng-hui called his assistant. "Tell Fengche I wish to see him in my office before five p.m. today," he said, and abruptly disconnected the phone. The word *fengche* is mandarin for "windmill" or "pinwheel." In this case, it meant windmill, and it was a nickname acquired by the man's fighting style. Whether he used weapons or his own body, he left an impression in the mind of the observer that he had just seen a windmill, a blur of motion impossible to break down visually into discrete movements, as though it was a set of fan blades whirling toward his opponent. For the opponents, it never ended well. As it turned out,

Fengche was near the office anyway, so he was already waiting when Teng-hui arrived.

Once the door was closed, Teng-hui wasted no time getting to the point. "I have an unofficial assignment for you. It will pay twice your normal fee. I want you to watch for a likely opportunity and when it comes, use that opportunity to arrange the untimely death of this man." Fishing in his drawer for a file, he plucked it out and dropped it with a flourish in front of Fengche.

When Fengche opened the file, he glanced lightly at its content, then the name caught his eye, and he frowned immediately. He leaned forward and read the two pages in the folder line by line. Then he closed it slowly and leaned back in his chair. "Three times, not double," he said. "This man will be hard to kill, which you already know."

Teng-hui had to think hard about that. He could, with some effort, cover the double fee in his annual operating budget. But a triple expenditure for an unsanctioned kill order against one of his own agency's operatives would end his career. In fact it would almost certainly end his life—if it was ever uncovered.

Finally, his hubris and damaged pride won out. "All right," he said, "triple. Just do it, and do *not* leave any evidence behind. If you fail, it will be the end of us both."

Fengche sighed, and stood. He looked Teng-hui in the eye, and said, "It will be done."

"Fine," Teng-hui replied. "One third of your fee will be deposited today, and the balance when your work is complete."

"I was planning to return to Iran to complete our interrogation work," said Fengche. "Is this more important?"

"I would not say more *important*," said Teng-hui. "But more *urgent*, yes."

"Very well, our work in the desert can wait a few days," Fengche replied. He bowed slightly, returned the file to Teng-hui, and left.

CHAPTER 7

At eight o'clock the following morning Dawson drove to the closest Metro stop, parked his rental car, and jumped on. About forty minutes later he was disgorged at the Pentagon. Every time Dawson returned to the Pentagon, it struck him just how dramatically things had changed since September 11, 2001. Pylons everywhere, guards with M4 carbines at the top of the escalator bank, and even the Metro stop had been walled off. Pedestrians now had to walk outside and pass through a guard station before entering the actual building. There were other changes, too, he knew, especially related to prevention of cyber attacks. It would never be the same, not even close.

When Dawson cleared the escalators and wound around behind the bank, video rental kiosk, and other shops, he headed for the ramp that took him up to the third floor of the E-Ring. In an office suite located behind a cipher lock facing out onto the courtyard, Dawson was greeted by a receptionist who asked him to state who he was there to see and the nature of his business.

"I'm here to see General Banks. My name is Dawson, and he is expecting me."

"Please have a seat," she said, and pushed a button on her console. Then she spoke into her headset. Not quite thirty seconds later, a very business-like young female lieutenant rounded the corner briskly and stuck out her hand. "Mr. Dawson?" she asked.

"Yes, Lieutenant, that would be me," he replied.

"I'm Lieutenant Dubey," she said. "Please follow me to see the general." Dubey ushered Dawson down a long hall and past several small offices. A few were empty, but most were filled with junior-level officers, elbow-deep in paperwork and computer monitors. Near the end of the hall, they passed a conference room occupied by a colonel and a major. Dawson couldn't see either of the men's names, but he noticed they were seated across from one another and that the colonel looked much more relaxed than the major. A new assignment or a dressing down? Either way, Dawson didn't envy the major.

After a brief knock, Dubey ushered Dawson into an expansive windowless office with a large desk and a massive conference table that seated twelve. The tabletop was tempered glass, and beneath the glass rested what could have been no less than two hundred "coins" bearing the logos of various military and DOD organizations. It was striking.

Seeing Dawson appear in the doorway, General Banks leapt to his feet and rounded his desk in two long strides. The general was an impressive man himself. Six foot four inches tall in his bare feet, a black man hailing from Texas, Banks was heavily muscled, with a booming bass voice. Today he was smiling from ear to ear. "Ben Dawson, you old rascal!" he proclaimed, ignoring Dawson's outstretched hand and swallowing him up in a bear hug. "I haven't seen you since Baghdad ... 2007, right?"

"Yes, Sir. That's right. Those were the days, Sir. You and me and LTC Hickman. I think you logged more air time over MND-B than any other general officer in the United States Army. Those were interesting times, and I was always grateful you allowed me to tag along."

In those days, Banks had been a one star and his AO, area of operations, had encompassed the Multi-National Division/Baghdad, which included all of Baghdad, including the infamous Sadr City. They were dark, difficult days with car bombs exploding every forty-five minutes on average by Dawson's own estimates, and soldiers getting blown up by IEDs, improvised explosive devices, in Humvees every day. A West Point graduate and brilliant historian, Banks was simply the most impressive general officer that Dawson had ever encountered in his career—and that included every level up and down the chain of command.

"Ha! What nonsense!" Banks laughed. "Don't let him fool you, Lt. Dubey; this man never 'just tags along.' Best intelligence operator I ever worked with. You should have seen him at this old meatpacking plant when we were...." but then he caught Dawson's eye and remembered this wasn't a social call. "Well," he broke off, "those are stories better suited for another day, and around a good cigar," he said. "Lieutenant, would you please close the door?" Banks waved Dawson over to the conference table and sat down with him there, the men facing each other across the corner.

"So I understand from our friends over at NSA that you need to borrow one of my men?" Banks asked him. He was all business now.

"Yes, that's right, Sir," Dawson answered him. "Major James Fitzpatrick. I will need him for a month or so."

"What can you tell me, Ben?" Banks lowered his voice, even though they were in a closed room, signaling his understanding that whatever was said would remain between the two men.

"One of his personal friends has gone missing, Sir," Dawson explained. "A Spec Ops light colonel named Tom Menlo. I want to borrow the major to help me while I look for him. Major Fitzpatrick knows him and that could prove very useful."

"Hmm," Banks said. "I'm sure what you say is true, Ben, and I've already signed the papers detailing him to NSA and to your care specifically—which is not technically legal now, you know, with you being a civilian contractor. So I'm not trying to make a decision on whether you get him. You've got him, and it wouldn't have taken a call from the SecDef's office to make that happen. You could have just asked," Banks paused. "But there's more to it than that, isn't there?"

"Why do you ask, Sir?" Dawson said.

Banks sighed, took a deeper-than-usual breath, and then went on: "Well, here's the thing, Ben. His CO has been keeping an eye on this soldier for several months now. He began to observe odd behaviors in the major while they were deployed in Kabul last year. Just little things; he could never really prove anything. But often when things went wrong outside the wire—like an important operation thwarted by an ambush or IEDs, he noticed that Fitzpatrick had been taking a stronger-than-usual interest in the mission planning, paying close attention to the comms and satellite feeds in the NOC, the Network Operations Center, that sort of thing. They were at end of tour before anything solid was surfaced, but, as I said, his CO has been watching him. With all that said, are you still interested in taking him along?"

"Yes, Sir, I am," Dawson said. "I have some suspicions of my own, and I need to determine whether they have any merit. Just a hunch really, and I could be completely wrong, but I have to find out."

Banks grimaced a bit while nodding his head in agreement. "Well, if we do have a problem, I want to know. I'd hate to think we lost soldiers over there because of a bad actor on our own team," Banks said gravely. "He's all yours."

"Thank you," Dawson replied. "If it's all the same to you, I would like to see his CO first, though."

"Makes sense," Banks said. "I'll set it up. Just wait right here." With that he got up and left the room.

About two minutes later, Lt. Dubey reentered the general's office and asked Dawson to follow her. She ushered him to one of the empty offices along the hallway, where he found General Banks and a full bird colonel. It was the same colonel Dawson had glimpsed as he walked by the conference room earlier. "Colonel Jack Breecher, this is Ben Dawson. Ben, this is Colonel Breecher. I have instructed him to give you any information you request. If I don't see you again before you pop smoke, good luck. I'll be looking forward to hearing from you when the mission is over. In the meantime, if there's anything else you need...."

"I understand, Sir. Thank you," Dawson said, and turned to Breecher as Banks closed the door behind him.

"Good to meet you, Colonel," Dawson said.

"Likewise Sir," Breecher responded. Jack Breecher looked to be in his middle forties, sporting short salt-and-pepper hair and horn-rimmed glasses. "General Banks seems to think very highly of you. He didn't give me any details, though. Just said you worked with him in Iraq."

"Yes, that's true," Dawson said, "but most of our activity was classified, and what wasn't classified mostly amounted to me watching the general smoke those cigars he loves so much. Not much worth telling there, I'm afraid."

"Well," Breecher observed, "he says you're the best G2 guy he's ever worked with, and that's pretty high praise coming from General Banks. So I understand that you'll be borrowing Major Fitzpatrick for a while?"

"Yes, that's true as well," Dawson replied. "I have some investigating to do over in the desert, and I am hoping your man will be able to help."

Breecher responded: "I hope that's correct. Most of Major Fitzpatrick's work during his deployment in Afghanistan was done at ISAF headquarters in Kabul. He did get outside the wire occasionally, but worked primarily in Operations Planning. Never spent much time interfacing directly with the locals."

ISAF stood for International Security Assistance Force, and Dawson was familiar with where it was located in Kabul. "Ah. Yes, that's what I wanted to ask you about," he said. "Do you recall any occasions where Fitzpatrick would naturally have spent time alone with any Afghan officials or non-official

Afghan citizens during his tour?"

Breecher seemed to be turning this question over in his mind. "I don't think there was a lot of opportunity for that," he said. "Hadn't really thought about it before, but there were a couple of times when he specifically asked me to detail him over to another AO so that he could help with special duties. Once was in Marjeh and the other time was in Delaram ... no, wait—that's not right. It wasn't Delaram, but it was somewhere out west like that...."

"Was it Ziranj, perhaps?" Dawson asked.

As soon as he said it, Breecher's eyes widened and he slapped his thigh. "Ziranj!" he replied, "That's it exactly! How'd you know that?"

"Just a hunch," Dawson said.

"Quite a hunch!" Breecher said. "Well anyway, both times he had been requested by some Spec Ops officer to support a COIN operation in a very bad neighborhood, if you know what I mean."

"Yes, I know what you mean," Dawson said. Counter insurgency efforts, or COIN, entailed convincing locals to turn against the Taliban and were often messy. "I spent some time in Marjeh back in 2009 and 2010. Noisy place."

"Yeah, I hear it was IED Central during those days," said Breecher. "Anyway, the whole thing was classified—almost all of the COIN stuff was like that—so I wasn't privy to the details. Seems like it had something to do with handing out cash to some of the locals who were playing both sides, trying to get them to come over. Some of the spooks ... sorry, no disrespect intended. Some of the intelligence guys were starting to call it 'reintegration' in those days. I think it was some State Department guy's idea. I heard later that the whole thing backfired; a lot of bad guys took millions of dollars and then either sold us out or just disappeared with the dough."

Dawson knew about the Reintegration Program. While it had occasional successes, most of the results were indeed pretty accurately depicted by Breecher. "Do you happen to know who the Spec Ops officer who requested Major Fitzpatrick for those assignments was?" Dawson asked.

"No, Sir," Breecher replied, "but if you'll give me five minutes to get to a SIPR,"—secure Internet protocol router—"line, I'll find out for you." Dawson said he'd wait, and Breecher excused himself.

True to his word, in just under five minutes he was back. "The request came from a one-star named Scott. I asked about him while I was on the phone with CENTCOM, but apparently he is now deceased. They said it was a post-retirement accident and since he was then a civilian, they didn't have any more details. The team's lead operator in both cases was Colonel Tom Menlo.

I asked about his status, too, but they said they don't have that information, which is, of course, a crock."

"Interesting," Dawson said. He figured if US Central Command, CENTCOM, didn't have or wouldn't give out information on Menlo to Breecher, they didn't have it.

"Interesting indeed. The only way they wouldn't know Menlo's status is if he was AWOL or something, and this guy doesn't sound like the type."

"What do you mean?" Dawson said.

"Well, Sir," Breecher continued, "every Special Operations guy I've ever known is pretty disciplined. They roughhouse and can hold their liquor and all that same as the next guy. But they are not the kind of soldiers who go out drinking and fail to show up for duty the next day."

"Yes, that's true," Dawson replied. "That's been my experience as well. So, Colonel, what specialized skill made Major Fitzpatrick such a valuable asset to the Special Operations folks?"

"I wish I knew," Breecher replied. "I tried asking that a couple of times, and I was basically told to mind my own business. It was loud and clear, so I stopped asking."

"Interesting," Dawson said. "What does the major do in his normal posting?"

"Communications officer," replied Breecher. "He speaks Dari and passable Pashto, which made him useful when we got into a bind at a shura someplace and either needed a translation or needed a better skill than the local terps (interpreters), could provide."

"Did you run into that a lot?" Dawson asked. Shuras were meetings with elders or local government officials, and it was routine for local terps to be used as translators.

"Well, what we ran into mostly was a situation where the commander on the ground would speak to the terp, and it would be something pretty short like, 'Have you seen Hassan today?' and the terp would turn to ask the local Afghans, but he would say fifteen or twenty words. It was as though he was not only asking the question, but giving the locals some coaching about how to answer. After a few of those things, you just start to wonder about the terps, if you see what I mean."

"Yes, I've seen the same thing many times," Dawson responded. "So you would call in Fitzpatrick at that point?"

"Yes, Sir," Breecher said, "for a while anyway. After a few months, though, it seemed to me that it got to the point where he was worse than the local terps."

"Really?" said Dawson through a frown.

"Yeah, I know it sounds kind of ridiculous," Breecher replied, "but it was like an Afghan local would be talking to Fitzpatrick for two minutes solid, and then Fitzpatrick would turn to us and translate that entire two minute speech as three or four words. It just didn't feel right."

"Did you ever challenge him on it?" Dawson asked.

"I tried a couple of times, and he was pretty evasive, and then it seemed to get better, and then our tour was over, and I guess I didn't really think any more about it," said Breecher. "The fact is, Sir, if you hadn't sort of walked me down memory lane like this, I probably wouldn't have thought any more about it."

Dawson sat silently for a few seconds, and then said: "One more thing, Colonel. General Banks told me that you mentioned something about the major acting suspiciously around the NOC."

"Oh yeah, there was that," replied Breecher. "It might have been nothing, though. It just occurred to me, on toward the end of our last deployment, that whenever Major Fitzpatrick showed up in the NOC during a sensitive or dangerous operation, he was like a bad luck omen. Almost every time, the team involved would report they were under fire or had rolled over an IED or something like that. It was a little unsettling. Twice we had to send out a QRF to rescue our patrol, and in one case we had to call in an Apache. Almost like the enemy was testing our reaction time or something."

Dawson thought about this, and said: "But again, no real evidence that he was directly involved, right?"

"That's right," Breecher replied. "If I'd seen any evidence, I'd have rolled him up. Anyway, then we were recalled, and there wasn't anything else I could do anyway. I figured it was probably just an overactive imagination on my part."

"In those cases you're recalling, would Fitzpatrick have had access to the patrol planning?" Dawson asked.

"Just about any of my staff could walk in and out of the planning sessions at will," Breecher said, clearly now excoriating himself mentally, "so the answer to that question would be 'yes.'" His visage was crestfallen.

"Don't be too hard on yourself, Colonel," Dawson said. "We don't know that he's guilty of anything yet, and even if he is, well, I've been in enough of these situations to know that you guys have your hands full. Doesn't sound to me as though you had anything actionable."

"No, you're right about that, Sir," Breecher said, "but I should have tried to develop something. I just never put it all together."

"Well," Dawson said, "if it's all right with you I'd like to meet the major now."

"Of course, Sir; I'll bring him right in." Breecher replied.

While he was waiting for Breecher to return with the major, Dawson stood quickly and removed a small metal box from his pocket. He extracted a remote, self-sticking wide angle video capture device about the size of a marble and stuck it on the wall just under and behind the edge of the conference table, then returned to his seat.

A moment later, Breecher ushered in the major with an air of professionalism and after introductions, prepared to excuse himself. "Before I leave you gentlemen alone, I just want to make certain that we are all on the same page," said Breecher. "Sir, I have made it clear to the major that for the duration of his detail with you, he reports directly and only to you. You will have his complete and uncompromised loyalty and service. Correct, Major?" he asked Fitzpatrick.

"Correct, Sir," Fitzpatrick barked out. "I am reading you crystal clear." Fitzpatrick then looked at Dawson. "I am all yours, Sir." Dawson turned to Breecher and shook his hand.

"Thank you, Colonel. I'm sure we'll be fine," Dawson said.

"Yes, Sir," Breecher responded. He closed the door gently behind him on the way out, leaving Dawson and Fitzpatrick alone.

"Have a seat, Major," Dawson said, and both men sat. "Tell me, how well do you know Lt. Colonel Tom Menlo?"

Fitzpatrick's eyes shifted upward for a second, and then came back level with Dawson's. From time to time as he spoke, though, he glanced down and to his left, as though pausing to gather his thoughts. "Well, the colonel and I bunked in the same building in Kabul. So we shot pool together, had lunch or dinner together from time to time, that sort of thing."

"Did you talk with Colonel Menlo about his family at all?" Dawson asked. At this point, Fitzpatrick shrugged. "Yeah, some I guess," he said. "He told me he was married and had a son. His wife is some kind of scientist here in the DC area."

"Hmm," Dawson said, and then leaned in slightly: "I need to know about that," he said. "I want you to think carefully about this, and tell me every detail you remember. I'm trying to build a character sketch of Colonel Menlo, and any detail you can remember is important. Let's start with his wife. What do you remember about Ms. Menlo?"

"Let me think," Fitzpatrick said, appearing to focus hard, "I think her name is Carol or Carolyn. Carolyn; yeah, that's it. Carolyn. She is a doctor of some kind, I believe...."

"Medical doctor?" Dawson interjected.

Again, Fitzpatrick hesitated. "I don't think so, but I'm not sure. I don't remember Tom ever saying anything that caused me to think that she was a medical doctor. I think she does some kind of research. Sorry, I just don't know that much about her."

"So you never met her?" Dawson asked.

"Oh, no. I never met her," replied Fitzpatrick.

"And you don't know anything about her research? Colonel Menlo never said anything about either the nature of her work or who she was working for?"

"No, Sir. Not that I can recollect."

"OK, thank you, Major," Dawson said. "Now let's turn our attention to the colonel himself. What was he working on when you were rooming together up in Kabul?"

"Well, of course a lot of what he did was classified. So while I had a Secret clearance, I had no need to know. Also, a lot of his work would have required a Top Secret or higher classification, so he couldn't have shared that with me anyway."

"I see," Dawson replied. "So what *did* he share with you about what he was working on?"

"Well, he just said he was supporting COIN activity most of the time," Fitzpatrick said. "Sometimes he'd say things like 'I'm catching an 0200 flight tonight over to FOB Price, so I won't be around for the poker game,' or something like that."

"Where did he most often seem to be headed on those trips?" asked Dawson, wondering if Fitzpatrick would name any other forward operating bases. "Well, he didn't tell me all that often," responded Fitzpatrick. "I would say mostly he went to Kajaki, Kandahar, and Gereshk just based on what I heard."

"Any idea where Colonel Menlo is right now?" Dawson asked pointedly.

"No, Sir. Not really. I haven't heard from the colonel for some time," Fitzpatrick replied.

"That's odd," Dawson replied, "because your CO tells me that you were detailed to Special Operations at least twice, reporting directly to Colonel Menlo."

Beads of perspiration began to break out along the major's upper lip, even though the room was an even seventy degrees. "Oh, that," Fitzpatrick choked out, "that was a while ago and totally unrelated. Yeah, a couple of times I was detailed over to Special Ops for translation-related services. It wasn't anything exotic, Sir. Just communications with locals when the terps on the ground were considered inadequate to the task or considered to be potential security risks."

"Was there any special subject matter that came up more than once, or were they just support for ground patrols and shuras?" Dawson asked.

"It was routine stuff, mostly," Fitzpatrick said. "I think he—I mean Colonel Menlo—asked for me mostly because he knew me and knew I was pretty good at the local dialects. If he was doing secret stuff, which I assume he must have been at least part of the time, being a Spec Ops guy, I wasn't involved in those things. My work was pretty routine."

"OK. A couple of other questions: first of all, did you ever personally handle, or observe Colonel Menlo handle, large sums of money, either US dollars or Afs, while you were working over there?"

Now the beads of perspiration weren't beads at all; they were small puddles. "No, Sir."

"Not once? No backpacks filled with cash, anything like that?"

"No, Sir, I did not," Fitzpatrick responded. "Is there some money missing, Sir?"

Dawson thought a second about this. He was certain that, with all of the cash being moved around, especially as a part of the Reintegration Program, there was undoubtedly a substantial amount that went missing along the way or was unaccounted for, especially when it left US hands and moved through intermediaries such as the ANP, the Afghan National Police. So he decided to wing it. "Yes," he said with deliberately ominous overtones, "there is. Last question for the moment: what can you tell me about the Reintegration Program?"

There was clear hesitation on Fitzpatrick's part. "I've just heard rumors, Sir. I was never involved with it."

"That's very interesting, Major," Dawson replied. "The Reintegration Program, most of which is no longer classified by the way, distributed over eleven million US dollars through Regional Commands, Provincial Reconstruction Teams, and Joint Task Forces in 2011 alone. Before it was over, it seemed to me that almost everyone knew about some aspect of it, and a lot of people were handling money. I'm surprised you never encountered it."

"No, Sir," Fitzpatrick responded, "I never did."

"And did you ever hear the word 'Salacia' before?" Dawson asked.

"No, Sir," Fitzpatrick responded, "I have no idea what that is."

"All right, Major, I understand—" At that moment, Dawson's phone buzzed. He thumbed a couple of buttons on the phone, and stood. "Sit tight; I need to take this call, but I'll be right back," he said.

"Yes, Sir," Fitzpatrick replied. Dawson slipped into the adjacent office, an anteroom off the office they were in. He pretended to close the door loudly behind him, but deliberately allowed it to spring back open just a bit. He had already engaged the small remote video cam in the outer office, and now lifted the handset from the desk phone in front of him.

Without bothering to dial an extension, Dawson began to speak into the headset. "This is Ben Dawson returning the general's call as requested," he said. Dawson was trying to speak just loudly enough to be heard as a muted voice in the next room, and it appeared to be working. On the screen of his mobile device, he could see Fitzpatrick paying rapt attention. As he continued to speak, Dawson could see him stand and very quietly take a couple of steps toward the door that stood ajar between them.

"Yes, Sir," Ben continued to speak into the handset, "I'm with him now. I just stepped out to call you back. It is as Army Intelligence suspects; something is wrong here. I provided the major with several opportunities to come clean, and he bypassed them all. We know the information about Ziranj came from him, and a number of other pieces of intelligence. Yet he repeatedly denied knowing about Colonel Menlo's deployments, Reintegration, or the colonel's family members. He even pretended that he wasn't sure what Ms. Menlo's first name is."

Dawson paused for effect. "No, Sir, I'm not ready to have him taken into custody yet. I want to give him some more string, and see whether we can learn any more from him first. But there's no question about it. With the other evidence we have, there is more than enough to convict him of treason. I'm sorry, Sir."

Dawson took another pause, as though he was listening intently to a voice at the other end of the line. "Yes, Sir. I will keep you apprised every step of the way." At this point, he could see on his phone screen that Fitzpatrick was returning quickly to his chair and trying to resume a nonchalant posture.

Dawson waited a few seconds, then shuffled about a bit to make some noise and returned to the outer office and sat down again across from Fitzpatrick. "All right, Major," he said, "I think I have what I need from you for now. I appreciate your candor."

"Certainly, Sir," Fitzpatrick replied, "no problem at all. Where do we go from here?"

"Ziranj," Dawson replied. "We lift off for Dubai tomorrow night out of Dulles on a commercial flight, and should be in Ziranj sometime this weekend." Dawson could almost see the blood drain from Fitzpatrick's face.

"Ziranj?" Fitzpatrick asked.

"Yes," Dawson replied. "Pack a Go Bag. We may be gone a while, and you'll want to warn your wife that you'll be completely off the grid for most of that time—possibly for several weeks."

"But how will we do that, Sir?" Fitzpatrick said, clearing his throat. "I mean, ISAF has drawn down over there now to an advisor status. What kind of mission is it?"

"Well, the truth is I can't tell you much about it until we're on the ground. But I think you should know that we're going to try to recover important US assets, and we'll be operating covertly much of the time in hostile territory. I owe you that much. Major, this is a dangerous mission, and you should make sure that things are in order at home."

Fitzpatrick swallowed hard and said, "I understand, Sir. Thank you. So we meet at Dulles tomorrow night, then?"

"That's right. Your travel orders are on their way to your home now via FedEx. I'll see you tomorrow night. Sorry about the short notice, Major. Obviously, this is considered a matter of national security, so speak to no one about it, other than to tell your wife that you are deploying for at least thirty days, perhaps longer, and comms will be intermittent, perhaps nonexistent, after we launch from Dubai."

"Yes, Sir." Fitzpatrick stood. "I'll see you at the gate," he said, and excused himself.

Dawson retrieved the tiny video capture device and replaced it in the metal box in his pocket. Then he walked down the hall to Lt. Dubey's office, poked his head in the door and, seeing her at her desk, asked, "Is the boss still in?"

"Yes, Sir," Dubey replied, "I think he's just about to leave for the day, though. Meeting up on the Hill. Do you need to see him?"

"Yes, just for a couple of minutes," Dawson said.

Dubey walked around her desk and down the remainder of the hall. She pecked at General Banks' door and stepped inside, closing the door discreetly behind her. A moment later she came out and beckoned Dawson with a hand gesture to join her. When he arrived in Banks' office, the general was putting papers into his briefcase and preparing to leave. "Come on in, Ben. I only have a minute, I'm afraid, but I'm all ears."

"Sir, I wouldn't normally do this, but I'm about to give you half-baked intel because of the timing here. I just pulled a ruse to convince Major Fitzpatrick that I know he knows more than he is telling me, and that I am about to confirm he's a bad actor. I will send you confirmation in the form of a voice mail saying I have positive confirmation on the matter we discussed when I have it. If I do not send that to you by 2400 hours on Sunday, then I was wrong or at least I have no proof, which should amount to the same thing in your eyes, Sir. I'm telling you this now because things are going to move very quickly soon, and I'll be off the grid. If things go sideways, and I don't make it out, I'd want you to know what I know."

Banks stopped what he was doing and focused on what Dawson was saying. "I understand, Ben. I will stand by for your confirmation. If it comes, do you need me to do anything?"

"No, Sir," Dawson replied. "We'll be airborne at that point anyway, headed to our target destination, and you cannot know anything about that. It's just that if I am no longer able to report...."

"Roger that, Ben. I got it. I'll be praying it doesn't come to that. What about his CO, Colonel Breecher?"

Dawson had already thought about that. "Solid as a rock, Sir, as far as I can tell."

The general resumed his preparations for departure. "Well, Ben," he said, "I've known you to be many things, but a bad judge of character isn't one of them. And for what it's worth, although I'm naturally biased with regard to my own men, I feel the same way. Breecher is as good as they come."

Dawson smiled and said: "Good luck on the Hill today, Sir."

"Ben, they'll never know what hit 'em."

CHAPTER 8

As soon as he cleared the perimeter of the Pentagon, Dawson sent a text message to both Kelly and Gerard: "Should be some good music on the radio tonight."

Within a minute, Gerard responded: "We're listening now. All the classics. XO."

Dawson responded: "Excellent; thanks! Could you have someone drop off what you have at 1600 hours? I'll swing by the Shock 'n Aw and pick it up then."

Again the response was nearly immediate. "One of us will be there." Dawson took the Metro back to his condo, only to head out again, driving this time. He stopped at the National car rental office and swapped out his Buick for a blue Chevy Malibu, and drove toward Winger's favorite dive, a place called Ireland's Four Courts on Wilson Boulevard in Arlington. He was pleased to find Winger and Romero both at a small corner table nursing beers.

"I can't tell you how happy I am to see you, Chief," Dawson said after greetings were behind them.

"Well, I feel the same way, Sir," Romero said. "I was looking for work anyway, after hanging it up. Twenty-four years was enough for me, though I'm sure there are some things I'll miss."

"Are you married, Chief?" Dawson asked.

"No, not exactly, Sir," Romero replied. "My wife Sadie passed a few years back—breast cancer—and I just don't think I'd ever be completely comfortable with anyone else. We were together a long time, since high school, in fact."

"I am sincerely sorry to hear that, although it makes the nature of this job a bit easier to saddle you with. How many years were you together?"

"Twenty-six years, Sir. Twenty-one as an Army wife. They just don't come any better than that." His voice broke just slightly on the last sentence.

"No, Chief, I don't think they do," Dawson said softly. He turned to Winger. "Did you tell Chief how much you manage to extort out of me for these little jobs?"

"I figured you'd want to talk about that privately."

Dawson just waved dismissively and said, "Chief, the pay for this assignment is the same for both you and Billy, here. I pay $30,000 a week plus expenses."

Romero looked as though he could be knocked over with a feather. "Thirty K a week?" he said. "Are you serious?"

Winger smiled broadly. "He's good for it, Chief. That's my rate, and he's never failed to come through on it."

Dawson looked Romero in the eye and said: "You'll earn it. This is, as you know, extremely serious business. If we make it home, there will be a one-week bonus, and I pay a full week for any partial weeks we work. If you want health insurance or life insurance, I have no objection, but I don't provide it, so you'll have to get your own. I asked you about your marital status only because I have found that these missions don't often work well for married men. The risk is just too high, and the stress on loved ones at home can be debilitating over time. None of these engagements we get involved in are low-risk, and there's a real possibility of a lethal outcome on every one of them. You saw that for yourself when you helped us out over in Helmand. I expect this next project to take around a month. It could be as short as a couple of weeks, but it could also be six or eight weeks. The first week's pay will be deposited in whatever account you'd like in advance—tomorrow morning in fact—by me. No company name on it, just a cash deposit. Our assignment begins at Dulles at 2000 hours tomorrow. If all that is acceptable, a copy of your travel plans will arrive at your home tomorrow morning via courier. OK, I'm going to pause now and take a breath. Before you respond, Chief, do either of you have any questions?"

"Where do I sign up?" Romero asked.

"You just did," Dawson replied. "And if you two are finished with those beers, I'd like to take you for a little drive." Five minutes later the three were ensconced in Dawson's Malibu and headed down the 495. During the drive,

Dawson filled them in on the details.

When he was finished Winger said, "Boss, do you really think it's wise to take Fitzpatrick along just as though there's nothing wrong? I mean we're going to have to watch him like a hawk."

"You're right," Dawson replied. "He's a proven liar, and I think he knows a lot more about Menlo's location than he's saying. I also believe he's going to try to blow our mission before we ever get on that plane tomorrow night."

"So you've taken precautions, right Boss?" Winger asked hopefully.

"Yes, I have taken precautions, Billy," Dawson replied. "I think I can keep him off balance through the trip over, but once on the ground I don't know what we're going to find. At that point, we watch him, we watch each other's 6, and we improvise when necessary. I like to be much more structured about my missions, but this one is loose and fraught with known risk, not to mention what we don't know. I have a contact in Ziranj from the old days who I trust. But she doesn't know yet that we're coming so we may have some staging time there, and then you know how getting into the right situation for an insertion can be. We could go in hours or we could wait for weeks."

Dawson looked in the rearview mirror to make eye contact with Romero. "Chief, what are you thinking?"

"Well, I think the element of this mission that sounds a little dubious, if you don't mind me saying so, Sir, is that we don't even know *for sure* that Menlo is where you *think* he is."

"You're right about that, Chief. I've got a little intel but it's sketchy. Mostly I'm working on a hunch here. The fact that China is up to its eyeballs in industrial espionage has been an open secret for more than thirty years, and they get better at it every year. We know now that they were trying to get the material we removed in Helmand several months back. You saw that one up close and personal, although we didn't know with certainly who it was until some weeks later. Also, our friends over at CIA have been saying for almost a year that high-level cooperation, uneasy though it is, has been established between MISIRI, Iran's Ministry of Intelligence and National Security, and the Chinese MSS. In light of their longstanding love/hate relationship with Russia, this is a potentially disruptive development. Cooling relationships between Iran and Russia have had Iran looking for help with their nuclear program and other similar initiatives from other sources, such as the North Koreans. But the North Koreans have had little to offer, and in fact seem to be coming out ahead on that particular barter with Iran. As a result, what seems to be developing now is a relationship where Iran is trading whatever they can get to China for assistance with their nuclear, biochemical, and other ambitions. The material we retrieved in Helmand enables technology that would provide an almost unimaginable leap forward for the embryonic Chinese Navy. When you put it all together, there are just too many nearly connected dots for all this to be a coincidence."

"So how does Colonel Menlo figure into this?" Romero followed up.

"I've been wondering about that too, Boss," Winger contributed. "What's that particular intersection in this multi-dimensional Venn diagram you're building?"

"Huh," Dawson grunted, "that's pretty good, Billy. It's a much better mental model of this problem than I had come up with. I need to think about that on the plane. But to answer your question, I don't know. Several theories come to mind; one is that Colonel Menlo is a mole. Seems extremely unlikely to me. There is nothing to bring that about that I can find in his history or his work file. But if he was, he could have defected and be working for the Chinese now. That scenario only works if he knows about the material we extracted. He has one possible source of that information: his wife."

Dawson stopped long enough to glower at an incompetent driver, and then continued. "So here's one scenario: Menlo learns more than he should from his wife about the nature of the material and the potential application. He tells his Chinese handler, who in turn passes the G2 up the line to MSS. The MSS realizes that they have no way to get the material without the Afghans' cooperation or at least tacit approval. The Afghans have been trying to get food, medical supplies, even clean water and other goods in across the border at Ziranj for years now, but the Iranians, who couldn't care less about the plight of Afghans, by the way, have only been allowing materials to trickle across the border. So the Chinese MSS strikes a deal with their new-found Iranian friends. China will provide the technology Iran needs for their nuclear program if Iran will provide the technology for Salacia, and support their efforts to get the materials needed from Helmand Province."

At this point, Dawson paused to let them consider what they had heard thus far. Seeing that they were still tracking him, he continued again: "Who knows the most about the various pieces of the puzzle? Colonel Tom Menlo. So when Menlo is in Ziranj, they bring him across the border into Iran. Now they have several ways to go. They can actually keep Menlo and maybe get him over to China to get whatever last details they can get out of him. They might even use him to try to persuade his wife to defect, too, and join him over there. Or they may just kill him after they have whatever they can get from him. I think waiting to see whether he can get any more information from his wife is a non-starter; too distant an opportunity and it doesn't deliver the material to them unless they can find some more of it somehow. Given the tons of earth and debris sitting on the location where that mine was, I think that's a remote possibility. So this is not my highest probability theoretical variant."

"Whew!" Romero said. "Do you guys think like this all the time? I'm getting kind of dizzy back here!"

"Naw," Winger responded, "most of the time we just play poker. Which reminds me, Boss, don't I still owe you forty bucks?"

Dawson thought about it, and said: "You know, Billy, I think you do. Kuwait, right?"

"Right. I had no US currency, and as I recall, you weren't particularly fond of the Kuwaiti currency...."

"I just hated constantly doing the conversion," Dawson interjected.

"Well, anyway, I still owe you forty bucks," Winger replied. "So what was it you were asking, Chief? Oh yeah, I remember. Do we think like this all the time? Answer is no. And so, Boss, I know you don't want to drive around talking to us all night, which means you probably ought to tell us the 'theoretical variant,' as you put it, that seems most likely to you."

"I'd be interested to hear that myself," Romero agreed.

"OK," Dawson replied, "so most of what I said before still goes. My personal judgment is that Carolyn Menlo is a straight shooter and so is her husband Tom. I think the bad actors are Fitzpatrick and whoever he is hooked up with. If I were a betting man, Fitzpatrick is tied up with either the Iranians or, more likely, some bad actors in the Afghan government. My personal guess would be ANP. I don't think he has the moxie or the personal grit to be more connected than with the police. In addition—and here is the part I didn't cover in my earlier scenario—if the technology-related leak isn't the Menlos, then it is someone else, maybe more than one someone else—close to the technology. I attended Dr. Menlo's demo of the new Salacia technology a few days ago, and the audience included Brystol, some of his staff, Menlo's technicians, and about a dozen dignitaries and military brass. I'd be willing to bet that beyond Fitzpatrick, the other spy or spies were in that room with me. I have a hunch or two, but I haven't figured out how to snare them just yet; still working on that. And Fitzpatrick may not even know who it is—or they are. Although he must realize there are other operators securing that information. So when you pour all of that into the machine, framed by the China—Iran—

Afghanistan model I described earlier, the result is what I believe to be the most likely scenario."

This left the car silent for a minute. While Winger was still working his way through that mental maze, Romero issued a low, soft whistle from the back seat. "Well, Sir," he said, "the most important pieces I've gotten out of this conversation so far are these: number one, we're about to launch tomorrow night into Afghanistan and probably Iran looking for a guy we believe to be a good guy who has been captured or killed, so time is not our friend. Number two: the guy we're taking with us is strongly suspected of being a spy or a traitor and was likely involved with whatever happened to the man we're looking for. And number three: the traitor or spy we're taking in with us is who we are depending on for translating between us and the locals on the ground, so if he says the wrong thing, like 'Kill these Americans,' we won't know it."

"Well, you got *most* of that right," Dawson said. "But Winger here is passably competent at Dari, and made his way through Kurdistan on some kind of Pashto, so I think we have that base covered. We just don't want Fitzpatrick to know that."

"Now that does make me feel a little better about this," Romero responded, sitting back in his seat. "Man, this is gonna be some trip."

When the briefing was over, Dawson dropped Winger and Romero back off at the Four Courts and he headed toward the Shock 'n Aw Gym. When he got there, he found that neither Kelly nor Gerard had arrived yet. While waiting, Dawson remembered Kelly's chide about how many pounds he could bench press and, since no one else was on the machine, Dawson walked over and moved the pin to 180 pounds. In street clothes, Dawson had no intention of doing a workout; he just wanted to test himself to see how much ground he'd lost since the time he'd really worked on his physical strength. He managed to get 180 up for five reps and decided that he wasn't going to try any harder. At least he knew where he was. There was a time when twenty-five reps at 180 pounds was part of his standard workout routine, but those days were gone.

"Well?" Kelly's voice boomed through the room as he swaggered through the door. "How'd you do?" Casting a glance at the weight bank, Kelly said, "Well, 180 isn't awful for a little guy, I guess, but you used to be better. You're slipping, Boss."

"Ha," Dawson responded, "you're telling me. You'll have to push me around in a wheelchair one of these days." Stepping away from the equipment, Dawson asked, "So what do you have for me?"

"Come on," Kelly replied. "You can use my office." Dawson followed Kelly downstairs, outside, and around the corner into a small nondescript brick building that merely had a street number on the outside. The exterior of the building gave no indication of the heavily fortified and insulated operations inside. It was a small company in terms of employees, most of whom were contractors, so there wasn't a lot of office space required. There were just a few offices, a couple of conference rooms, and a NOC. An armory and a walk-in safe were in the basement.

When they reached his office, Kelly pulled a small recorder from his pocket and laid it on his desk. "I'll be just outside when you're done," he said. "This place is pretty secure, but even so I'd use those headphones." A pair of noise-cancelling Bose headphones was already sitting on the desk. "Some pretty sensitive stuff here, and I know you. You're going to want to listen for background noises, voice intonations, and that kind of thing."

Dawson smiled. "Thanks, Max. This is perfect," he said.

"I won't have it any other way," Kelley said as he pulled the door closed behind him.

Dawson pulled on the headphones, plugged them into the speaker jack on the recorder, and hit play. Each conversation was date-and-time stamped with a synthesized voice. The first entry was stamped the previous day, about ninety minutes after Dawson's conversation with Fitzpatrick. *He must have gone out for lunch yesterday,* Dawson thought, and smiled.

The synthesized voice also said: "Telephone conversation between caller (297) 406-3341 and (525) 233-1233."

"Hello?" It was an unfamiliar voice at the receiving end of the line. The number was a US number, but there was no doubt, based on the delay and the tinny sound of the voice that the handset was several time zones away. Based on his experience with hundreds of similar calls, Dawson was pretty confident that the handset was somewhere in the Middle East. "This is Scotty," Fitzpatrick's voice said. "We have a problem."

"We cannot discuss problems on this line," the distant voice replied brusquely. "I will send someone to speak to you. Where are you now?"

"That's the problem," Fitzpatrick's voice, tightly wound, responded, "I'm in DC now, but tomorrow night I'm leaving, and I'm headed toward *you!*" There was a long silence.

"Please stand by," came the reply. Even though there was a "please" in the sentence, it was clearly not a request. In a moment, the voice returned. "Go home; someone will be there in an hour." The connection ended. When the call was ended, Dawson could hear a string of expletives erupting from

Fitzpatrick as he ended the call on his end.

The next entry was tagged an hour and five minutes later, and rather than telephone numbers, it listed an address, the name of Major James Fitzpatrick, United States Army, and an unknown individual. Unknown individual was described by the synthesized voice as male, estimated to be thirty-five to forty-five years old, Caucasian, with black hair and brown eyes, weighing 175 pounds and five feet seven inches tall. The conversation was a capture from some form of electronic eavesdropping device. Based on the clarity of the sound, Dawson guessed it was an electronic bug rather than a remote amplifying device, but he didn't really care how it had been done; it was just professional curiosity.

Fitzpatrick opened the conversation. "Listen, I have a job. I can't just take off in the middle of the day without somebody noticing. Fortunately, I'm transitioning today to a new boss, so it worked out this time. Anyway, we've got a real problem here."

"Please stick to the facts, and be brief," his guest replied coldly.

"OK, the facts are these," Fitzpatrick said. "First of all, I was suddenly reassigned yesterday to some spook named Ben Dawson. Don't know anything about him personally, but from the way the brass is treating him, I'd say he's pretty hot stuff at the Pentagon. He is building a team for a recovery operation in Afghanistan and maybe even Iran, based on what he would tell me, which wasn't much. He just said he is after US assets, and wouldn't say what—or who—those assets are." It sounded to Dawson as though the guest could be writing things down as he listened to Fitzpatrick.

"Secondly," Fitzpatrick continued, "they know there is money missing from the Reintegration Program, and they have evidence that links it to me. They are getting ready to prosecute me for treason, but they don't think I know that. They want me to take them back into Ziranj, help them find whatever it is they're looking for, and then bring me back here just to throw my ass in jail. I don't know exactly what I'm going to do yet, but coming back to that scenario just isn't in my plans. I mean, I realize you guys don't give a crap, but I have to come back tonight and tell my wife that life as we know it is about to end."

Again, a cold flat response came from the guest: "Major Fitzpatrick," he said, "it does not serve you well to become so emotional. Please stick to the facts. I can only help you if you give me the facts clearly and briefly."

Fitzpatrick basically ignored him. "Right," he practically spit back at his guest, "like you, or anybody else, can actually make this go away."

"Is there anything else, Mr. Fitzpatrick?" the guest asked.

"Geez, isn't that enough?" Fitzpatrick asked incredulously. "Well, as a matter of fact there is," he continued, his ire rising to a higher level than his prudence. "These guys want to know why I was passing along information about where Colonel Menlo was, and to whom. That means they realize my wife was involved in passing that information along, which was stupid. It was stupid of me even to mention it to her, since I wasn't even supposed to know. But she had no idea she wasn't supposed to know, and now she's implicated, too."

"I see," said the guest, with a shade of additional attentiveness in his voice, Dawson thought. There was something odd about the accent in the guest's voice, almost imperceptible, but it was there. He couldn't quite nail it down, but it just struck him as out of place, or not within the framework of what he was expecting, somehow. It was aggravating, but he let it go and focused on the content of the conversation. The guest asked, "Do you know why they were asking about Colonel Menlo?"

Fitzpatrick responded: "I assumed it was the whole Reintegration connection, but now that you mention it, I don't know. That reminds me, though, do you guys know about something called Salacia?"

Suddenly, Fitzpatrick had the full and undivided attention of his guest.

"What did you just say?" he demanded.

"Salacia. Dawson asked me about something called Salacia. I didn't know much about it, but Dawson's not the kind of guy who asks questions randomly. He was looking for *something*, I just don't know *what*. And for that matter, I don't *want* to know. I have enough trouble. Do you realize I still haven't spent a dime of my share from our little enterprise over there? I've been waiting for things to settle down, and now it looks like it's all not only heating up again, it's *on fire*. I'm going to have to liquidate and relocate, and I need to do it the minute I get back from this little excursion—maybe even before that if I get a chance."

"Major Fitzpatrick, this is important," the guest said. "Please focus. Exactly what did Mr. Dawson say about Salacia? Try to remember his exact words."

"Sure, I remember exactly. He said, 'Did you ever hear the word *Salacia* before?' I said 'no.' I'm not sure he believed me, though. But I really *don't* know anything about it except that it's some super-secret thing Menlo's wife is involved in." This seemed to calm the guest down a bit.

"Very well," the guest replied. "Could you wait for a moment, please, while I step outside to make a short phone call? I understand your situation now, I think, and wish to see whether we can help you."

"Absolutely! If you can get us out of this mess somehow, that would be an incredible relief," Fitzpatrick responded in near disbelief. Dawson heard the sound of the Fitzpatrick's door opening and closing. A moment later he could hear the unmistakable clinking and flowing sounds of Fitzpatrick pouring himself a tall one. Then about eight minutes went by, which was pretty excruciating; Dawson was beginning to think the recorder had stopped or there was some other problem when the sound of the door was audible again.

"Major Fitzpatrick," the guest said reentering the room, "I believe we have a solution. What time will your wife be home from work this evening?"

"About 1800 hours," Fitzpatrick replied, "maybe 1815. Why? What have you got in mind?"

"My employer believes you could continue to be a very valuable asset to us, and he is willing to make you an offer," he replied. "He would be willing to relocate you to another country where you and your wife would be safe and comfortable. She would have no need to work outside of your home, but would be free to do so if she would like to. If you agree, you would be given new identities, and you would earn a handsome salary for, we shall say, 'consulting' work. I have been directed to ask you to meet my employer with your wife this evening so that he can extend the invitation in person and discuss specific arrangements. He understands your timetable, so he has encouraged me to move quickly. Are you able to do this? He will, of course, provide you both with dinner, over which you can discuss the details."

Dawson could only imagine what Fitzpatrick was thinking. First, he knew Fitzpatrick's wife would likely blow a gasket and that the major would have to make her see there really was no alternative. Would he tell her they were both now targets of a federal investigation involving grand theft, conspiracy, and even treason? Would he tell her they had to run or would never see freedom again? Could he convince her this was their only way out, and they were incredibly fortunate to have it? Dawson felt sorry for Fitzpatrick's wife. She had no idea what a bombshell she'd walk into after her workday was over.

"Sounds good," Fitzpatrick said. "Where should we meet for dinner?"

"My employer has invited you to his estate for dinner this evening," the guest said. "Here is his address and a handwritten set of directions. I trust that you can make out my handwriting?"

"Yeah," Fitzpatrick replied, "I've got it; clear as a bell. What time should we be there?"

"Would eight p.m. be acceptable?" asked the guest, suddenly exuding grace and kindness.

"Perfect!" Fitzpatrick replied. "Tell your boss we'll be there."

"Very well," the guest responded, as he was making his way to the door. "I know he is very much looking forward to meeting both of you, and I believe he will be able to assist you in explanations to Mrs. Fitzpatrick. He is very good at this sort of thing."

With that, just as Fitzpatrick was replying: "Great ..." Dawson could hear the door closing as Fitzpatrick's guest left the house.

"Darn it!" Dawson said to himself. If only Fitzpatrick had read the address aloud. Well, there was undoubtedly more ahead. Dawson readjusted himself in the chair, and continued listening. The next conversation was indeed between Fitzpatrick and his wife. It was far less helpful than Dawson had expected, though. Basically, Fitzpatrick didn't have the backbone to spill the beans and clearly determined that he'd prefer to do that with the help of their new benefactor. He just told her that he had a pretty amazing job offer and wanted her to go with him to dinner at the employer's estate as soon as she could make herself beautiful. She complained for a while about being tired from work and about the short notice, but eventually was a good sport about it. They were out the door before seven. That was the last recording on the device.

Dawson switched it off and removed the headphones. Kelly was waiting outside when Dawson opened the door. "Figured you'd be finished about now," he said. "What'd you think?"

"Before I answer that, Max, I have a couple of questions. First, are there no other recorded audio or video clips after that one?"

"None," said Max. "I wish we'd had an opportunity to bug the wife's car, but we never got one, and that's apparently the vehicle they took to see the employer."

"Second question: no one returned to the Fitzpatricks' house last night?"

"You didn't ask for physical surveillance, Boss," Kelly reminded him, "and frankly we've got our hands full with the Menlos as it is. We'd have had to pull in some contractors. But all electronic surveillance indicates that they never returned to the house and never communicated by phone after they left the house about 1900 hours."

"Well, in that case," Dawson said, "I'm guessing that Major Fitzpatrick is already dead."

* * * *

Since his conversation with Dawson, Fitzpatrick had felt like an elephant had been sitting on his chest, and for the first time since then, he allowed himself to breathe easier. He hadn't had the nerve to tell his wife about their situation. It was better to spin it as a great opportunity for a new job, a new life. He didn't know who he was going to meet, but he had no choice but to grab the opportunity—or take the risk. The intermediary with whom he had worked in Afghanistan—the man to whom he had placed the call that brought his "guest" to his home earlier—had always paid off before. There was just over a half million dollars hidden in his brother's attic in cold hard cash as a result of their beneficial relationship. Of course, that was another thing that his wife didn't know about. His brother knew nothing about it, either. He was just storing a few of Fitzpatrick's old deployment clothes in footlockers up there as far as he knew. In fact, his brother had almost certainly already forgotten about them; he never got up into his attic anyway.

The drive from the Fitzpatrick home to the address of the estate provided by Fitzpatrick's guest was estimated at forty-five minutes, according to Fitzpatrick's onboard GPS system. It was almost a straight line into the Virginia countryside, followed by a winding three-and-one-half-mile stretch of private road over a small river and onto the estate. The drive out had been relatively uneventful, and the countryside was increasingly beautiful as it disappeared into the fading sunlight. As they were approaching the estate, Fitzpatrick noticed that the woods along the passenger side of the car stopped abruptly, revealing a spectacular view over what appeared to be an ancient rock quarry, with the floor of the quarry now filled by a gorgeous lake. Just before the bridge leading to the estate, Fitzpatrick pulled up to a little guard house that stood aside a very substantial, though ornate, wrought-iron gate.

"You folks must be the Fitzpatricks," the guard said as the driver's side window was opening.

"Yes, that's right," Fitzpatrick replied.

The guard was an older man, Fitzgerald figured for about sixty years of age. His hair was silver, and he sported large, 1960s style eyeglasses with thick lenses. His mustache was a prominent feature beneath a bulbous nose. As they spoke, a second guard, this one looking as though he might be the first man's son, ambled out from the guard shack and walked in front of their headlights, over to open the heavy iron gates.

While both of the Fitzpatricks were watching this in anticipation of entering, the first guard withdrew a Mac-10 machine pistol from beneath the window and fired the entire magazine of .45 caliber bullets through the driver's side window and into the Fitzpatricks. Just a few rounds were perfectly adequate to complete the job, as there was almost nothing left of either of their faces after the initial spray, but the attacker really enjoyed firing the gun and rarely had the opportunity. So, while his nephew finished opening the gate, the man indulged himself as he finished up the magazine, basically shredding the bodies of both husband and wife.

"Yes, sir, Jimmy boy," the guard called out to his nephew, "you just can't beat the old Mac-10. As long as you remember to hold down under the barrel so she don't raise up on ya, this here is the absolute, ultimate weapon. I just love shootin' this thing!" With the gate now fully opened, the nephew walked over to the car and used his foot to push the major's body marginally out of the way.

"Geez, Uncle Bob," he said, "that dang gun is all you ever talk about." He shifted the still-running Chrysler out of park, and directed it over the side of the bridge. The car did exactly as several other vehicles had done before; it nosed over the edge, and the weight of the engine pulled it into the 150-foot abyss below. Then the guard emerged from the guard shack, handed his nephew one of two push brooms, and the two of them set about cleaning up the splintered glass and other debris, eventually sweeping it off the edge of the small bridge as well.

* * * *

Concluding his discussions with Kelly, Dawson thanked him for the intel on Major Fitzpatrick and asked him to watch the news over the next few days to see if they—or either of their bodies—surfaced someplace. He had a hunch they wouldn't, at least not for many years. He also asked for an update on the PSD/surveillance team covering Carolyn and Andy Menlo. That report was better; it seemed Dr. Menlo and her son had stuck to their normal routines, just as Dawson had hoped. *This ought to make Brystol happy anyway*, thought Dawson. *As long as she is still on the job, she is moving Salacia forward.*

CHAPTER 9

Teng-hui had initially decided to have one of his staff deliver the personnel files to Biwu. But after thinking about it, more accurately *stewing* about it overnight, he decided that he would do it himself. He told himself there were two reasons justifying his decision. First, he wanted to retrieve the files that were not retained by Biwu for his own purposes; he had to minimize the exposure of his operatives to the greatest extent possible. Second, Teng-hui wanted to find out whatever he could about what Biwu was doing in North America, and especially in his area of responsibility. If he could also determine what the best opportunities would be for Fengche to assassinate Biwu, it would be a wonderful bonus, but he supposed that would be too much to hope for. Fengche would likely have to do that groundwork himself.

When Teng-hui arrived at Biwu's office, he was greeted matter-of-factly by the administrative assistant, and taken to the same basement-level conference room where he and Biwu had met the previous day. He was not offered tea or even drinking water. It was humiliating for a man of his stature, and Teng-hui knew it was deliberate. He was seething, but determined to remain impassive. Six or seven minutes went by before Biwu entered the room.

He was all business. Without any greeting and without even looking Teng-hui in the eyes, he ordered, "Show me what you have." In response, Teng-hui opened his briefcase and extracted a stack of manila folders about one inch thick. There were twenty-four folders, each of which spelled out the identity, placement, and primary assignment of the operative. It was an impressive group. Biwu understood why Teng-hui was so fiercely defensive of this information. It represented decades of work and sacrifice, and contained the crown jewels of China's anti-American espionage. Operatives ranged from officers in some of the largest industrial and financial institutions headquartered in Virginia and the District of Columbia, leaders in the most prestigious American universities, and of course government offices at local, state, and national levels. Biwu thumbed through them, committing the ones he found most interesting to memory.

Finally, after he had been through them all, he set three of them aside and pushed the rest back at Teng-hui. "These three are of interest to me right now," he said. He tapped at the top folder. "What do you know about this individual at the Brystol Foundation?"

"That operative was recruited as a teenager, while she was studying at Berkley," Teng-hui replied evenly. "Her fiancé at that time, a Chinese student who was an activist in the Viet Nam era, was killed in a scuffle with the police. She is one of our most valuable assets, owing to her access to the most critical research underway in the United States. Her reputation and credibility within the Brystol Foundation are beyond reproach. She is particularly valuable to us right now because of several projects under way at the Foundation."

"Good," Biwu responded. "You will set up a meeting between me and this operative at the Foundation. I wish to see the facility, and I have matters to discuss with her."

"But that is impossible!" Teng-hui protested. "The security at the Brystol Foundation—"

Biwu interrupted, "Yes, I see your point. All right, Teng-hui, just instruct her to come here then, tomorrow at three p.m. Can you manage that?"

"Yes," Teng-hui replied sullenly, "she will be here."

Biwu moved to the second folder. "And this one?" he asked.

"Ah," Teng-hui responded, "another excellent operative. As you can see, he is embedded at a position within the United States Department of Defense that gives him exceptional visibility of the most important development programs and military initiatives. He is one of the first people to be aware of changes in priority and support. He is also—"

Biwu interrupted, holding up one hand with an expression of both dismissal and disdain. "Is he involved in Salacia?" Biwu asked.

Ah, so this is all about Salacia, thought Teng-hui. "Yes, he is. He attended a Salacia demonstration at the Brystol Foundation earlier this week. Normally, he could strongly influence decisions about funding and support for these programs, but he has made it clear that in this case the demonstration of capabilities is so compelling that the Americans will pursue it aggressively with no accommodation for resistance."

"I see," Biwu replied. "That is very interesting. Here is what you will do: contact this operative tomorrow and ask him what the impacts would be if Dr. Menlo should be withdrawn from the Salacia Program. I will need an answer to that question the day after tomorrow. Do you understand?"

So he thinks that I work for him now, Teng-hui thought. *Well, that will come to an abrupt end, and very soon!* "Very well," he said. "I will bring his response to you the day after tomorrow."

"One other thing, Teng-hui. When I see you in two days, you will bring me whatever information you currently have, as well as whatever information your organization can gather, about an American operative named Ben Dawson. I want everything, but I am especially interested in his connection to the Brystol Foundation and to the Salacia Program."

"We have an extensive dossier on Mr. Dawson," said Teng-hui. "I will have it updated and bring it to you."

"Very well, then," Biwu said. He gathered up the two folders about which they had just spoken. He pushed the third folder back toward Teng-hui, and said as he rose to leave the room, "It may also interest you to know this operative is already dead."

"What?" Teng-hui exclaimed, rising to his feet. But it was too late; Biwu was already gone.

* * * *

Back at his office later that afternoon, Teng-hui met with Fengche again. "Biwu will be meeting with one of our operatives tomorrow afternoon at three p.m. at Biwu's office," he said. "Sometime after that meeting, naturally, Biwu will be leaving the building. I have no interest in telling you how to do your job, Fengche, but since I happen to know this, you might be able to use it to execute your assignment."

Through half-closed eyes, Fengche said, "I will drive out there tonight to survey the area; it may work, but I don't know yet. I would like to get this over with and get on to the matter in Iran. The American we are holding there won't last much longer."

"I understand," said Teng-hui. "The sooner the better, for both of us. Biwu could cause great damage to our ongoing intelligence-gathering operation, and he knows far too much about our network of operatives now." *And I am also very eager to see him dead,* he thought.

The following day, Biwu spent most of the morning in the basement conference room because the cursed landscaping people were running their grass cutters, weed-eaters, and filtration pumps around his normal smoking spot behind the building, and the noise was mind-numbing. They had even chosen to replace the spring flowers with fountain grass for the summer, and so they had basically blocked him from the lake with their digging.

While in the basement, Biwu suffered the added hardship of requiring his laptop computer rather than the desktop unit, and he hated the smaller keyboard and monitor. By noon he was not in a charitable mood. The afternoon meeting occurred as Biwu had requested. At precisely three p.m., a female figure emerged from a nondescript five-year-old Ford Taurus and entered Computer Services Corporation's front door. The security cameras would be of little value if someone ever reviewed them, since the woman wore loose-fitting clothing, ordinary shoes, large sunglasses, and a long headscarf. About the only distinguishable features were that she was of average height and Caucasian. Not even her age could be effectively estimated by those who observed her. She was clearly experienced with tradecraft, and this was not the first time she had effectively disappeared from view. Biwu's conversation with her was not lengthy.

"Tell me about Salacia," Biwu demanded.

The woman leaned forward and said, "I can't begin to tell you everything I know about Salacia, and even if I could, you would hardly be qualified to understand it." This was not a response Biwu expected. He assumed he was not making himself clear, so he leaned across the table and slapped the woman hard across the face, knocking her from the chair. Then he resumed a casual posture in his seat, and repeated the question. The operative recovered slowly from her position on the floor, struggling back into her chair. Biwu's response made several things clear, among which was his lack of concern over her value to MSS.

"What specifically do you want to know?" she asked.

Biwu decided he would accept that question. "How long will it be, at the current development pace, until Salacia is ready to deploy?"

The woman thought about that for a moment, and then said, "The current schedule reflects a pilot vessel trial run five months from yesterday. If that one-month trial run is successful, a fleet-wide deployment gets underway sixty days thereafter. This presumes that both parties—the United States Department of the Navy and the Brystol Foundation—agree to terms and conditions of a contract."

"Is there some reason to believe that the two parties will not agree?"

"No," she responded.

"Are there any technical challenges that pose a serious risk to the program today?" Biwu continued.

"No technical risks remain which are likely to prohibit the program from attaining its scheduled milestones. There are certain lower level risks such as fiber optic lens adhesion, which could result in cost impacts, but those are also relatively minor."

Biwu thought about this more a full thirty seconds, frowning and turning the implications of this in his mind. Then he said: "Is there anything that you personally could do that would delay the program, and if so, for how long could it be delayed?"

The operator considered this carefully. She didn't dare to respond as she wanted to, presuming that another slap or possibly worse would be Biwu's response. She finally replied: "No action that I take now could delay the program for more than a few days, perhaps a week at most. And any action I take will almost certainly expose me as a spy."

Biwu sighed. *These operators are so tiring,* he thought, *they all think only of their own safety. How did our organization become so weak? It must be all this privileged western lifestyle.*

"Tell me," Biwu said, "this exotic material that was retrieved a few months ago. How critical is it?"

"No other known substance is capable of splitting the laser-emitted light in the manner that will result in the catalytic reaction required to produce the Menlo Bubbles. In other words, it is absolutely key to the technology."

"Is the material well guarded?" Biwu continued.

"The material is under armed guard in multiple locations at a security level similar to the level currently in place at America's nuclear power plants. The weakest security is at the Foundation itself."

This was not the news Biwu was hoping for. "Where can we get that same material?" he asked.

"No one knows," the woman responded. "The only known source was plundered by Ben Dawson's team, and the surrounding area was destroyed. It would take the equivalent of an extensive archeological dig to relocate the source of that material, and even if that occurred, it is unlikely that more would be found. The geological causes of this situation are quite complex."

Biwu knew this was a lame attempt on the part of this spoiled woman to make him feel stupid, and he was tempted to hit her harder this time. But he wanted to keep her unbruised if possible so that she could return to the Foundation tomorrow without suspicion, so he let it go.

"One more question, and you may go," Biwu said. "If your life and the lives of your family depended on your ability to get this technology out of the hands of the Americans and into my hands, what would you do?"

The operator thought about that for a long time. Finally, she responded: "I would destroy the Foundation facilities, recover the materials from the wreckage, and start the program again in Shenzhen."

"That is most interesting!" Biwu said, and even smiled just a little at the thought. "And if the program had to begin again, how long would it take to reach deployment?"

Again, the operator took a long time to consider. "I would estimate, with the information I have at this stage of the program, that it would take four years to establish a similar program in China and get to a deployment capability," she said.

"Very well," Biwu said, "you may go. Tomorrow you will return to your normal duties." At that point, he rose and left the room. He had the rough outline of a plan formed in his mind. He would need to ask one more question of the Directorate at MSS before he initiated any action. It was a bold plan, and if exposed it would set China—US relations back by two decades. In fact, it was not inconceivable that it would result in war, though Biwu thought that unlikely. He decided to send off an encrypted message to Beijing, and then call it a day. He would think through more of the details over dinner.

It took about thirty minutes for Biwu to develop the message and get it through encryption. It was already five a.m. in Beijing, so once the message was sent there was really nothing more to do until morning. He needed a cigarette, and then he would think about getting some dinner on the way back to the condo. One thing about these Americans, he grudgingly admitted to himself, was that they did know how to cook.

He strode out onto the path behind his building and lit up his first cigarette since lunch time. The cooling evening, the sinking sun, and the nicotine all helped to persuade him that it hadn't been a totally unproductive day. Sometimes, though not often, Biwu almost convinced himself that when some big assignment concluded he would be offered a cabinet position or at least a high-level post in the Directorate where he could simply oversee other operatives and stop all the travel, the intrigue, and the killing.

But those self-deluding thoughts came infrequently now, and he faced the fact that almost everyone in his profession dies an untimely death, many of them at the hands of their employers. *In fact*, he thought, *if I am successful and China develops this Salacia technology well ahead of the rest of the world, it will only escalate the political conflicts, making people like me busier than ever.* Biwu took one long last drag from the cigarette, and as he did so, he noticed a man standing across the pond, just staring at him. As he flicked the glowing cigarette butt out toward the water, Biwu thought, *I think I have seen that face—*

KA-WHOOM! An enormous fireball sprang from the area of the cigarette while it was still in flight. The leaking natural gas pipeline that had been nicked carefully by Fengche while posing as a landscaper that afternoon had filled the area along the lake and adjacent to the building with gas, and the burning embers of the butt provided the perfect spark to ignite the whole area.

The explosion was spectacular, knocking Biwu backwards into the sliding glass door of his office and onto the ground. Only the fact that the glass was actually bullet-resistant polymer kept Biwu's body from being hurled through it. However, that was less than fortuitous. Biwu was covered with burns over his exposed skin. His eyebrows and a few inches of the hair around his face were gone, as were most of his clothes. His face and hands had taken the worst of it, and now looked like shriveled birch bark. The doctor who admitted Biwu to Fairfax Metro Hospital forty-five minutes later was uncertain about whether he would live at first, but after a more detailed examination, reduced his status from "critical" to "serious." Still, the prognosis was at least several months of recovery and physical therapy, almost certainly to be punctuated by two or three rounds of plastic surgery.

As soon as Fengche observed the medics loading Biwu into the ambulance with Fairfax Metro painted on the door, he left Falls Church and headed for the Brystol Foundation research center. Having scouted the location before, he had already identified a likely spot to wait. He parked his Lincoln Navigator and extracted a Nikon DSLR with a 400/800 mm zoom lens from the cargo bay.

Sitting in his passenger seat with the window down, he had less than twenty minutes to wait before Dr. Menlo emerged from the front entrance and walked along the sidewalk perpendicular to his vehicle and about thirty meters away. She paid no attention to any unwanted observers as she passed, and instead was repeatedly checking her watch and chewing her lower lip with that classic "I'm late for an appointment" look. Sharp close-up images were quite literally a snap. Fengche followed Menlo, driving at a safe distance all the way into Vienna, where she retrieved her son Andy from the Wien Private Day School. Here matters were even easier, since Andy had a soccer game after school, and Fengche could pose as just another proud father snapping images of his son out on the field. By seven that evening, Fengche had all the images he needed.

About twenty meters away long the sidelines, Lily Gerard was posing as one of the soccer moms in attendance, also taking photographs. In a light windbreaker and blue jeans, with her hair pulled back in a loose ponytail, she fit in perfectly. She waited until the play on the field had moved in his direction, and took the opportunity to shoot several images of Fengche. The enhanced SD memory card in her camera wirelessly uploaded the images to her smartphone, and seconds later they were being reviewed by Max Kelly in the rented Ford Expedition parked behind Fengche's Navigator.

"Not bad, Ansel Adams," Kelly quipped through his radio into her earbud.

"Well," Gerard replied quietly through a grin, "I guess he is a type of wildlife at that."

"I still say we were lucky to get ahead of him," chided Kelly. "That was taking a chance you know, using the alternate route to beat them both here instead of sticking with the target. Menlo was technically uncovered for almost thirty minutes."

Gerard sighed heavily. "All right," she conceded, "next time we split up. But this time it worked out, and he has no idea we tailed him to get his picture while he was getting theirs. And as I said, the fact that he was shooting her with a camera rather than a carbine when I spotted him meant that he wasn't out to get her—today, anyway. Otherwise he would already be in the trunk of my car."

"Hmm," Kelly responded, "I've got nothing but confidence in you, sweetie, but this is one big dude, and his moves are fluid. I'm not at all sure you could get close enough to tase this one."

Gerard shrugged deeply, seemingly at no one in particular: "You know me; I'm not picky. I'll just shoot him if I need to."

Kelly squinted and rubbed his temples. "Yes," he admitted, "I know that. By the way, speaking of splitting up," Kelly said, "I already called Boxer to swing by and drop off your car. You can stay with the target. I'm going to see if Boxer and I can follow this wildlife specimen of yours back to his cage."

"Great idea. Just be careful," Gerard replied.

"Oh sure," Kelly retorted. "*Now* you talk about being careful! Ha!"

* * * *

From the soccer field, Kelley and Boxer stayed a generous distance behind Fengche, who seemed to be oblivious that he might be under surveillance, or else uncaring. Kelly continued to follow Fengche and passed his Navigator as it pulled into the parking lot of a Walgreens on Wilson Boulevard in Arlington. After circling the block and finding the Navigator still parked there, Kelly sent Boxer in with instructions to buy condoms or something and see what he could see. Boxer, as always, shrugged and did as he was told. Boxer was a long-time junior member of Kelly & Gerard Enterprises, LLP. He had no military or law enforcement background. He was a street kid in his early twenties who had cleaned up his act after Kelly had seen him in the gym one Saturday morning and had taken him under his wing. But, as Kelly pointed out to Gerard, he was a smart kid who followed orders and showed potential. Gerard had looked at Kelly in that funny way of hers, all skeptical and patronizing, and replied: "OK. I think a hobby would be good for you, Max. He looks like a hobby to me."

When he returned to the Expedition, Boxer said, "He's getting a prescription filled at the pharmacy while he waits for his photos to be printed."

"The pictures he just took tonight?" Kelly asked.

"Yeah, I think so," Boxer replied, "and he's getting two copies of each, all of them five-by-seven-inch prints."

"Now isn't that interesting," Kelly mumbled to himself. Twenty minutes later, Fengche emerged from the Walgreens and climbed back into the midnight blue Navigator. "Very nice, very nice indeed," Kelly said aloud, admiring Fengche's vehicle as it headed out into traffic. About twenty seconds later, Kelly started up the Expedition and resumed his follow-the-leader routine.

About ten minutes went by, and just as he was thinking that Boxer had been uncharacteristically quiet, Kelly heard him say, "Hey Boss?"

"Yeah?" Kelly responded.

"What should I do with these?" he said, holding up a shiny new box of Trojan condoms.

Kelly blinked at him a couple of times and sadly shook his head, once again speaking aloud but talking to himself. "Holy cow. All this time I've been telling Gerard how smart you are!"

At seven forty-five p.m., Fengche pulled into the parking garage at Fairfax Metro Hospital. Carrying the small bag from Walgreens, he walked into the main entrance, stopped at the reception desk and asked a question, and then made his way to the bank of elevators. Kelly followed him as far as the lobby, then sat down and picked up a magazine and pretended to read.

On the sixth floor, Fengche left the elevator, walked past the room he was looking for, number 604, and then sought out the most distant restroom on the corridor. Once in the restroom, he found a stall with a baby changing table and locked himself inside. On the changing table, he emptied a small bottle of Digitalis tablets that he had just obtained using a prescription issued by one of the doctors on the MSS payroll. He used the bottom on the container to grind all of the tablets into a fine powder and scrape the powder into a little pyramid. Using the Walgreens receipt as a scoop, he retrieved almost all of the powder and carefully poured it into the open end of a syringe he removed from his pocket. Stepping out of the stall, he checked that the restroom was still empty and then stepped to the sink. He filled the syringe up with tap water and shook it vigorously until he was satisfied that the powder was fully dissolved. Then he attached a needle and placed the loaded syringe carefully in his jacket pocket.

Just before leaving the restroom, he placed the Walgreens bag and the crumpled receipt in the paper towel waste bin and lit the receipt with a cigarette lighter. He left the restroom immediately and, as nonchalantly as he could, made his way back to room 604. Just as he was approaching the room, a soft feminine voice announced over the hospital PA system that visiting hours were coming to a close in five minutes. Fortunately for Fengche, and for any nursing staff who might have been attending Biwu at that time, the room was empty except for the patient. And just as Fengche had anticipated, Biwu was sedated, with an IV already dripping medication into his left arm as it hung from one of the ubiquitous chrome IV trees.

It took Fengche less than thirty seconds to empty his syringe into the port along the line running from the IV bag into Biwu's arm, and return to the hallway. He was already in the elevator when the fire alarm sounded, and by the time he reached the front doors, he was engulfed in a throng of people pouring out into the parking lot.

It wasn't easy, but Kelly managed to maintain the visual connection with Fengche all the way back to the parking garage, at which time he had to hustle to get to his Expedition before it was lost to view. With fire trucks and other emergency vehicles closing in from every direction, pandemonium had ensued and that slowed everything, including the egress of Fengche's Navigator. Ultimately, that made the difference and Kelly was able to stay on him.

From the hospital, Fengche headed northwest. By the time he merged from the 495 onto 267 West, Kelly knew he was headed for Dulles Airport. "Holy crap," Kelly said to Boxer, "I'll bet you fifty bucks he heads for the international terminal."

"You know I can't afford fifty dollars," replied Boxer, "not on what you pay me." It took another forty-five minutes of running around the parking garages and terminals, but Kelly's hunch turned out to be right on the money. He watched as Fengche checked his bag, and the sticker clearly said DXB. Fengche was headed to Dubai, and Kelly had a feeling he was on an intersecting course with Ben Dawson.

Wasting no time, Kelly pulled out his phone and dialed Gerard. "Lily, Ben's got a problem. Where are you?" he said.

"I'm sitting outside and down the street from our target's residence right now, but I'm wherever you need me to be as soon as you tell me where that is," she replied, jerking erect and turning the key in her ignition.

"Whoa, girl. Just stay put for a second and let me tell you what's going on," he said. Lily turned the ignition off again, and listened as Kelly filled her in. Her first response was: "Max, we have to get a message to Ben before he gets on that aircraft."

"Exactly," Kelly replied. "Boxer says that he transferred the laptop over to your car. Is that right?"

"Yes, but it's in the trunk," she shot back, "stand by." Kelly could hear the entire episode and almost see it in his head as Gerard fished around for the trunk release—she always took forever finding that button—then flew out the door, violently unzipped her backpack, ripped the laptop from its moorings, and slammed the trunk in spite of her need for quiet, finally jumping back into the car. Then he heard the familiar chimes of the Windows startup process, and a quiet, desperate string of expletives and prayers. Although this often appeared to work miracles for Gerard, Kelly could never figure out the reasoning with that process. After a couple of seemingly years-long minutes, she had her laptop up and was logging onto her Internet account. "Thank God we sprung for the wireless Internet connection," she said. "I *told* you—"

"Yes," Kelly interrupted, "you certainly did, and you were right. Now if we could please focus."

"OK, OK, OK, OK, Okaaaaaayyyyy," Gerard whispered. "I'm into the mail account, and alongside the drafts folder I am adding a folder titled, 'Friends from the Gym.'"

"I like it!" Kelly smiled. "You got imagination, Lily. I always said that."

"I thought it was my legs you were always talking about," she replied, "but I believe someone mentioned something about focusing."

Kelly cleared his throat. "Right. OK, so we need to put a Word doc in that folder with a file name that is today's date and time. You need to embed a couple of photos of the guy along with a warning to watch his 6. Tell him we think he's carrying photos he took this evening of both of our targets, but that our targets are still secure."

"Got it," Gerard responded, "but slow down. No one can type as fast as you talk. I just hope he finds this before he gets on the aircraft."

"I'm working on that now," Kelly said. He was just sending a text message off to Dawson that said "Check your email."

CHAPTER 10

News of Biwu's death traveled at the speed of light between DC and Beijing. By five-thirty a.m. DC time, Teng-hui had already fielded two calls. The upshot of those calls was that until specific facts were known, the organization would proceed as though it was an accidental death. Between the events at the office and the subsequent fire at the hospital, details were hard to pin down. Teng-hui was now back in full control of MSS activities in his AO.

Of course, Teng-hui realized, this was a double-edged sword. The upside was that Teng-hui could operate with a comparatively high degree of autonomy; it was likely that the security of his operatives would remain intact, and neither he nor his operators would be subjected to Biwu's abuse and humiliation. The downside was that now Teng-hui was entirely accountable for wresting the Salacia technology from the hands of the Americans. While that came with a few additional degrees of freedom in terms of his operating capabilities, the penalty for failure was huge.

Teng-hui decided that he needed to do two things: first, use this crisis as an opportunity to expand his political prowess and the powers of his office, and second, build a feasible mitigation strategy that enabled him to shift the blame to someone else, should things go wrong. He decided to pull in another operative who could be called on for black operations, specifically, in this case, operatives for whom kidnapping and murder were merely aspects of their job description. He needed contingency plans, and he needed them quickly.

With Fengche headed into the Middle East, Teng-hui decided to pull in a private contractor that he had worked with before. Private contractors were not always as reliable as direct employees, but their motivation was clear—money—and one never had to worry that their loyalties would change in the middle of an operation because anyone failing to complete a job would likely never work in their profession again and would just as likely be assassinated themselves.

At this point, with his newly expanded authority, Teng-hui was far less concerned about blowing his budget than he was with blowing this assignment. He spoke into the intercom, and his assistant appeared immediately. "Get me Bi-shou," he told her. "I need her today." She bowed respectfully and retreated, silently closing the door behind her.

Next, Teng-hui called in his chief of operations. Jing-ti was only thirty-four years old, but was an exceptionally clear thinker. He had earned advanced degrees in business and mathematics, as well as an undergraduate degree in sociology. Still unmarried, he was an attractive young man who paid attention to his appearance and his health. He had many female companions, but was focused far too narrowly on his career to allow any of those attachments to become binding. His organizational skills were very strong. He was respected by the other members of his staff, and was influential around Washington when important matters were to be decided on Capitol Hill. He had good instincts about which opportunities would be best exploited through bribery, which by threats, and which by blackmail. He was not afraid to employ whatever means were necessary. He was not a hands-on operator and would probably shrink from killing someone himself, but he had no reservations about ordering someone else to do it. He showed every sign of growing into a brilliant strategist one day. Teng-hui thought it might be time for Jing-ti to grow into a new area.

"Sit down," Teng-hui directed Jing-ti when he arrived in his office a few minutes later. The young subordinate had thoughtfully brought in his leather portfolio and pen, and was prepared to take notes if required. "I have an assignment for you," Teng-hui continued. "This will almost certainly be one of the most challenging opportunities of your career. I need you to develop a plan for the acquisition of one of the most important technologies since the invention of the atomic bomb."

He watched Jing-ti as he spoke. At first, the serious young man frowned behind his stylish Varvatos eyeglasses, and began to open his portfolio to capture notes. But then, as he grasped the import of the matter before him, he decided against it and closed the portfolio, leaning forward and listening with rapt attention as Teng-hui outlined the events leading to their current position. Teng-hui spared no detail in his description. Then he turned to what he needed in terms of planning.

"I need the following from you, Jing-ti, and I need it in forty-eight hours: an overarching plan with a detailed timeline and resource requirements for the acquisition of the Salacia technology. I don't care what means you use, and there is only one primary constraint—do not precipitate a full-scale military conflict between the United States and China. Beyond that, do not embarrass me or diminish my credibility in the eyes of MSS or the government of China. It would be beneficial if, in the course of obtaining this technology, the actions taken also destroy or severely delay the development of this technology by the United States or any other country. The target for obtaining the technology and implementing whatever steps are required to debilitate the development of the technology in any other country is ninety days from now."

Teng-hui paused to ask whether Jing-ti had any questions.

"No, Sir," he responded. "I understand perfectly."

"Very good," Teng-hui said. "At the close of business tomorrow, I want you to show me the detailed project plan, including required resources and timing. I also want you to be prepared to execute the plan if I find it to be adequate. Jing-ti, I understand you are a very intelligent young man, and I am entrusting a—quite literally—history-making program into your hands. I have great confidence in your ability to develop and oversee this most ambitious activity. We have an operator inside of the Brystol Foundation who can provide you with whatever information you require about the technology and the current program timeline. I will introduce her, and make her contact information available to you. Please be judicious about using her. It has taken me over a decade to get her into this position, and we hope to continue to benefit from that investment for many years.

"However," Teng-hui continued, "especially with Fengche out of the country, you will need assistance with the more delicate aspects of this program. And so I have reached out to a most experienced and competent outside contractor to assist you in those matters. She and whomever she chooses to employ for that purpose will be at your disposal. She will be here to speak with me sometime today, and I will introduce you. Do not leave the office today until you have met her. Her name is Bi-shou. To be very clear, you may place every confidence in Bi-shou for elements such as kidnappings, assassinations, extortion, and blackmail. I have used her many times, and she has always brought me the end result I required. She works primarily in the DC vicinity, but has also done work for me in other parts of North America and once in Europe. For this work, there is no one better, except perhaps Fengche; I would not like to have to decide which one would survive if they were at war with one another."

"Sir," Jing-ti said, "there is still one matter here that is very unclear to me. Understanding better may affect my planning."

"Oh," Teng-hui responded, "and what is that?"

"I know little of the events surrounding the capture of Colonel Menlo of the American Special Forces. Since Fengche has been overseeing that effort for you, and I know that you have great confidence in him, I have not asked you about it before now. But if it is involved here in some way…."

"Ah, I understand," Teng-hui replied. "You are correct; it is perfectly appropriate, and I had planned to cover that with you today in any case."

Teng-hui folded his hands into a steeple shape on the desk before him and began his explanation. "As you know, one of our most highly placed operatives in the current American administration is Ralph Simons, who is responsible for overseeing funding associated with US military programs. As it turns out, one of the many contacts Simons made as he was coming up through his various government posts was a young US Army soldier named James Fitzpatrick. I will not go through all of the details about how this contact was cultivated into a partner in some of our ongoing operations, other than to say that relatively small payments were required to bring him into the fold. Over time, we were able to manipulate Fitzpatrick into a close living quarters arrangement with Colonel Menlo in Kabul. His assignment was to learn all he could about the ISAF Reintegration Program, and become involved in it to the maximum extent possible. Are you clear about what I have said thus far?" Teng-hui paused to ask.

"Yes, Sir. Please continue."

"Very well," Teng-hui said, and went on. "As you already know, Simons realized the opportunities that existed within the Reintegration Program to surreptitiously funnel money away from the Americans and the Afghans for other purposes. The very nature of the program made it an exceptionally easy target for such activity. And any accountability challenges were able to be covered over by Simons and the other MSS operatives who report to him in that department. However, as one of the US Army officers overseeing the Reintegration Program and reporting on its successes and failures, Colonel Menlo became suspicious of the distribution of funds out of the Reintegration

Program. We are not absolutely certain on this point, but I suspect Colonel Menlo was somehow made suspicious by Major Fitzpatrick. It may have simply been Fitzpatrick's constant pushing to become involved in the Reintegration Program or it may be that Fitzpatrick let something slip in his conversations with Menlo. We may never know, but that is one of the things that Fengche intends to discover."

Again, Teng-hui paused. This time he pressed the intercom button and requested tea for himself and Jing-ti. He waited a moment until his administrative assistant appeared and distributed two china cups with saucers, placed a silver serving tray with milk, sugar, and a tea pot on the conference table, and retreated silently from the room.

"All of this talking makes me thirsty," he remarked and then continued. "As things progressed, Simons and other MSS operatives were able to work with Afghan officials to see that funds were diverted away from the program. Along the way, it became obvious that while he was an increasingly valuable source of ground-level intelligence, Fitzpatrick was also becoming a liability. The more involvement Fitzpatrick had the better, as he deliberately mistranslated during transactions with mid-level Afghan officials and pointed any suspicions in the wrong directions. Over time, however, Menlo became increasingly suspicious of Fitzpatrick, confirming whatever Fitzpatrick may have said or done to alert Menlo in the first place. Eventually, Fitzpatrick altered his translations in a critical meeting in Ziranj, and Menlo had a plant in the room that was able to provide him with transcripts of both the accurate translation of the Afghan side of the conversation and the one Fitzpatrick had altered. He confronted Fitzpatrick, and told him that he was about to request a full investigation."

"Please excuse the interruption," Jing-ti interjected, "but about how long ago did this occur?"

"It was about two years ago," Teng-hui replied.

"And yet it has taken this long for the Americans to become suspicious," commented Jing-ti. "How can so much time have elapsed?"

"Between the work done by Simons and the other MSS operatives, and the complicity of Afghan officials, we were able to keep Menlo from producing any credible evidence other than the transcripts he had from the meeting in Ziranj," explained Teng-hui. He took a drink of tea, cleared his throat, and continued, "But Menlo would not give up."

"Finally," he continued, "several months later and just before his current deployment, Menlo found a sympathetic ear in the office of the US Inspector

General. That official called Major Fitzpatrick in and offered to forget the evidence of his complicity if Fitzpatrick would provide information they could use to break open the swindling operation in Afghanistan. Fitzpatrick, thinking uncharacteristically quickly, convinced the Inspector General's office that he knew only about the activities occurring on the western side of Afghanistan, and emanating from Ziranj. He provided contact information and some details which, of course, were half-truths and lies. The primary contact he provided was our own Fengche, who had an alias and local support structure in that region as a result of our other work there."

Teng-hui took another drink of tea, and then continued his explanation. "Fitzpatrick promised to reveal the truth behind the plot. But as soon as he had the designated meeting place and time in Ziranj, he provided those to me. This enabled Fengche to set up an ambush, resulting in Menlo's capture in Ziranj and movement across the border into Iran. While this process was going on, Fitzpatrick became concerned that he himself might be killed to silence him—something that, in truth, we had intended to do in Ziranj when he landed there to 'assist' Menlo. But then Fitzpatrick offered up some intriguing new information. He pointed out that Menlo was the husband of a top research scientist back in the US, and might be useful to provide leverage to get that information—perhaps even the technology itself. Once we put the pieces together and discovered that the technology involved was Salacia, the potential opportunities there rapidly eclipsed the value of simply eliminating Colonel Menlo. So now we need to see what we can discover about Salacia from the colonel that our own operatives may not already know, and potentially leverage the fact that we have the colonel as a tool—perhaps to persuade Dr. Menlo to sabotage the program or even defect to China."

Teng-hui took another drink, this time emptying his cup. Jing-ti quickly but gracefully responded by retrieving the tea pot and replenishing Teng-hui's cup, and then his own. When Jing-ti settled back into his chair, Teng-hui concluded. "You are of course free to make use of any of these approaches. However, I caution you that Fengche reports Menlo's physical health is deteriorating. His physical condition is quite serious, as our Iranian friends are not especially kind to active duty American armed forces these days. Therefore, making use of the colonel may not be an option for much longer. We are arranging for some medical attention for him in his current location, but it is fairly rudimentary. We must keep his presence and our involvement very well concealed, as you can see."

As Teng-hui and Jing-ti were preparing to wrap up, Teng-hui's assistant tapped at the door and timidly stuck her head inside. "Excuse, please," she begged, barely looking up at her boss, "Bi-shou say she be here in fifteen minutes."

"Ah," Teng-hui replied, "excellent." His assistant, looking very relieved, diminutively edged back out of the room and closed the door gently. Teng-hui was smiling broadly, something Jing-ti could not remember ever witnessing before.

True to her word, Bi-shou appeared at Teng-hui's office thirteen minutes later. "I was only a few blocks away," she explained as she entered the room. Jing-ti, who was rarely all that impressed by members of the opposite sex, could barely keep his jaw from dropping. He had encountered everything from professional women in the DC party scene who were looking to land a promising up-and-comer like him to multi-thousand-dollar-a-night call girls, but this woman was practically smoldering. Some of the effect, he realized, was the exceptionally well-appointed designer suit and shoes, but her personal magnetism far outweighed all of those things. *She would be stunning even in a dirty T-shirt and blue jeans*, he thought. Suddenly, Jing-ti, one of Washington's most eligible young bachelors, was absolutely undone.

Bi-shou was very shapely, tall for an Asian woman, and in superb physical condition. Jealous rivals sometimes referred to her as an "Amazon." She was physically strong, but had also developed great stamina in conjunction with her physical strength. Her demeanor bespoke self-confidence and professionalism, but the relatively short skirt and lower-than-typical neckline also demonstrated her willingness to deploy the full array of her considerable assets in pursuit of her objectives.

Bi-shou's parents had been mid-level Chinese diplomats. They worked out of the embassy in Washington, DC when Bi-shou was born, giving her the advantage of dual citizenship. When she was a teenager, her father died as a result of a heart attack while riding home from work on the Metro. Her mother returned to China as Bi-shou entered Harvard, where she studied political science. While she loved the lavish life style, the parties, and the clothes, she developed a disdain for America's perception of its own exceptionalism, and its inherent belief that America is somehow ordained by God to occupy the dominant position in the world. The fact that American English had become the pervasive language of business across the world was particularly irksome to her.

Bi-shou had developed skills around assassination during her college years. When she studied abroad, she trained with MSS in the mountainous region of mainland China, punctuated with "field exercises" where trainees were overseen by veteran MSS operators as they murdered various targets, moving to harder and harder targets over the years of their training, so by the time she graduated from Harvard, she was accomplished with an array of firearms, bladed weapons, and her bare hands as well as various toxins. She also had some knowledge of light ordinance such as rocket-propelled grenades, and construction of both military grade explosives such as C4, and more primitive devices such as pipe bombs and pressure cooker bombs.

At the age of thirty-three, Bi-shou decided that she would become an independent contractor. By that time, she had built an enviable base of contacts and clientele from freelance work, and had no trouble earning six figures from each assignment she completed. A few had even reached the seven figure category. MSS tried to discourage this, sending out teams three times to convince her to return to their workforce or kill her. She killed them all, the last team comprised of three of the MSS' best operatives. At that point, the organization determined that the best way to deal with Bi-shou was as a private contractor and, while it was more expensive for them, they eventually realized that it offered them significant advantages as well.

Since that time, Bi-shou continued to spend most of her time in the United States. She worked for MSS, but also accepted assignments from outsiders as long as they were not in direct conflict with the interests of MSS. She preferred up-close work: a syringe on the docile body of a lover, or a small caliber pistol with a silencer were her most common methods. She had developed a close community of several other assassins and thieves. These contractors rarely turned away offers to work with Bi-shou, because her work was lucrative and because of the cache of her reputation. Consequently, Bi-shou was in the enviable position of doing the work herself when it was in her specific area of interest, while contracting out what she deemed to be too messy or was simply more than she could handle because of other commitments.

Teng-hui rose to his feet, another first in the eyes of Jing-ti, and bowed slightly in response to the deeper bow of Bi-shou. "Bi-shou, thank you for coming so quickly. I would like to introduce you to my chief of operations, Jing-ti." Jing-ti followed Teng-hui's example, bowing slightly. Teng-hui noticed that as Bi-shou turned and moved two steps closer to focus her attention on Jing-ti, the young man looked unnerved and his cheeks reddened slightly.

Bi-shou was accustomed to similar reactions, and handled it with her normal grace, saying: "Ah, Jing-ti. It is my honor to meet you at last. I have heard about you for some time, and now I understand why Teng-hui has such great confidence in you." She bowed deeply as well, and it seemed to Jing-ti that she must have lingered there for just a second longer in order for him to enjoy the benefits of that plunging neckline. He caught a whiff of her perfume, and it was somehow both fresh and intoxicating.

Bemused and feeling just a twinge of jealousy, Teng-hui waved Bi-shou to a seat, saying, "Please sit down."

Bi-shou perched there like a lioness, a serene look on her face, as though surveying her pride of cubs. "How may I be of service to you?" she asked softly.

Teng-hui cleared his throat. "Bi-Shou, we are about to enter into an enterprise related to the acquisition of a specific and extremely important technology under development here in America. As a result, some actions may be required of the type that you and your colleagues normally perform. Jing-ti will be leading that endeavor and will be your primary contact here in our Directorate for this engagement or series of engagements. The work will not extend beyond ninety days from now, but during that time Jing-ti may need to call on you for these services with very little lead time."

Bi-Shou frowned just slightly at this, and replied: "You know, Teng-hui, from our work together in the past that I require some time to prepare for the work that I do. Preparation comprises a great deal of the reason that I am successful in so many cases where others are not." She then turned her attention again to Jing-ti. "It will be to our mutual advantage," she smiled at him, "to alert me as soon as you become aware of what you will need me to do, and when. Some things take longer to prepare for than others. For example, if I will be entertaining 'guests' for a long time, then preparations must be made for their housing, security, and sustenance. If you require that these guests be compelled to provide some particular information, then I will need to arrange for special accommodations, medical staff, and so on. On the other hand, depending on the individual involved, if it is simply an accidental death that you require, that is less difficult and usually requires less preparation."

Jing-ti was impressed with Bi-shou's command of the organizational aspects of her work, but more impressed that she was able to describe kidnapping and murder with such detachment. She could as easily have been describing the development and sale of office buildings. "Of course," he said.

Bi-shou turned once again to Teng-hui. "You are familiar with my normal fee structure. How shall we handle payment for this series of engagements?"

"I shall have $500,000 deposited into the normal account by close of business tomorrow as a retainer. As you require additional funds, Bi-shou, please present Jing-ti with your typical invoice for professional services and related expenses, and we will have the funds transferred within one business week. For all matters related to this project going forward, please work directly with him." Both Jing-ti and Bi-shou recognized that this arrangement was no mere organizational consequence; it was a way for Teng-hui to develop a firewall to protect him in case the operations should go badly. It presented Teng-hui with a way to maintain what the American politicians called "plausible deniability."

It had not worked so well, in the end, for the American President Nixon following his Watergate debacle. But for many who followed him, the technique had met with greater success. Bi-Shou believed the events surrounding the debacle in Benghazi, Libya, in 2012 was one such case.

As she had watched the misdirection and suppression of information following those events unfold, she was struck by the comparatively primitive capabilities of her own government in these areas. The Chinese government merely shut down the Internet, blacked out broadcast news channels, and essentially resorted to the same measures that they had employed in the 1950s. In America, however, because of the relative freedom of the press and freedom of speech, government officials had become more sophisticated, confiscating ever-larger portions of Americans' incomes in the form of direct and indirect taxes, using those funds, campaign contributions, and political favors to pay for the cover-ups and media misdirection that they needed.

In the end, the American methods were far more elegant. Bi-shou knew that many of her Harvard professors would have been pleased with her understanding of these events. But she also knew that in the end, many Americans understood these things implicitly; they were merely complacent. She had learned to appreciate the American circus entertainer P.T. Barnum who had famously remarked, "You will never go broke by underestimating the intelligence of the American public." Barnum had understood well the art and power of misdirection and "giving the people what they want." Bi-shou thought that Mr. Barnum would have made a great American politician, and could have taught Chinese government leaders much about handling their citizenry.

"Very well, then, gentlemen," she said. "If there is nothing else you need from me today?"

"No, I believe that is all we require today," Teng-hui said, rising to his feet. "Jing-ti will be in touch just as soon as he has a clear understanding of how he expects these events to transpire." With that, Jing-ti moved to the door and opened it for Bi-shou's exit.

She turned to him as she approached the door, bowed again, and said: "I look forward to a long and happy partnership, Jing-ti."

When Bi-Shou had left, Jing-ti turned back to Teng-hui and said: "Will there be anything further?"

"Just one thing more," Teng-hui said. "Tomorrow morning you have an appointment for breakfast at a restaurant in Falls Church with the operative I mentioned earlier, our most senior operator at the Brystol Foundation. I have asked her to meet us in order to provide you with background on the man who is our most challenging adversary in this matter, as well as any other matter involving technologies under development at the Brystol Foundation."

"Dawson?" Jing-ti asked.

"Yes," Teng-hui said. "You must understand your adversary, Jing-ti, as you well know. In addition, she will be able to help with a better understanding of Salacia. I shall expect to hear from you when your plan is complete."

"Yes, Sir," Jing-ti replied, and left the room. He had an enormous amount of work to do.

CHAPTER 11

Dawson arrived at the airport earlier than Winger and Romero, so while he was waiting he logged on to the Bradley email account and left a message for Carolyn Menlo: "M1ENLO." He also noticed the "Shock 'n Aw" folder that had been deposited by Gerard. Opening the file, he saw the embedded photos of Fengche, Gerard's brief description of what had transpired, and the warning that he was likely on the same flight. His furrowed brow gave way briefly to a smile when he saw that the note was clearly from Gerard rather than Kelly. It was signed with an "XO." Dawson pulled that last line off, and then copied the email from Gerard into a folder in another account for Jennings. He named the file: "Who_Is_This" since he had no idea who the assassin was.

Winger and Romero arrived about thirty minutes later. He showed the photos to them as they stood off in a corner before starting through airport security. "So here is the guy we are looking for," Dawson said. "Let's watch for him during the boarding process. I don't believe for one second it's a coincidence he's headed into the region around the same time we are."

Winger shrugged. "Suppose we see him. How do you want to play this?"

"Well," Dawson responded, "we really don't know what he is up to. Given what's transpired so far, he may not be targeting us at all. In fact, he might conceivably be headed where we are for entirely different reasons. If he is looking for any of us, it's almost certainly me. So I think the thing to do is find out what he does when he sees me. If he demonstrates that he's oblivious to me, and to us, then I think we start observing *him*. Does that make sense?"

They both nodded. Dawson thought the two of them made a pretty good team. Winger was clearly the senior guy here, but Romero seemed fine with that. He was more of the "take orders/execute orders" type than the "give orders" type. While Winger was taller and more agile, with a deep tan and long black hair, Romero was stockier with a ruddy complexion and closed cropped hair that was more gray than black. Winger's bearing was prone to adopt some swagger, while Chief was all tenacity and determination. "OK, then gentlemen, I'll see you in Dubai," Dawson said. "Until then, we don't know one another." They split up and headed in different directions, with Dawson going through TSA screening first. After emerging from the screening process, he headed for the United Airlines lounge. Romero and Winger went their separate ways, but ultimately ended up going through two different screening lines at nearly the same time. When they emerged, Romero headed for the gate area and Winger headed for one of the bars along his concourse.

About fifteen minutes later Dawson's phone chimed, signaling an incoming text message from Winger. "Found our friend in the bar," it said. Dawson took one more drink of his tea, grabbed his carry-on bag, and walked out of the lounge. When he arrived at the Firkin & Fox Bar, Dawson spotted Fengche immediately. He charted a course to the bar that would take him directly in front of him, and between him and the television he was absently watching. Before he did, he made sure that Winger saw him as well. If things got ugly, he wanted Winger to be alert and ready to respond.

Dawson walked slowly in front of Fengche to the bar, ordered his usual, and retreated to a booth along the wall, his back to Fengche. He fished around in his carry-on, pulled out a copy of the Wall Street Journal, and scanned the brief synopses of the paper's contents. Then he turned to the stories he was interested in, read them, finished his iced tea, stood, and left the bar. Winger watched Fengche closely during the entire exercise. Although Fengche clearly saw Dawson as he walked directly in front of him, he exhibited no interest at all—no flash of recognition, no momentary change of focus on him, or visual tracking of Dawson at all. Winger reported he had a very high level of confidence Fengche was not after Dawson. As they had discussed, that shifted the odds in their favor. Dawson, Winger, and Romero could each observe Fengche, and if they did a good job, learn the purpose of his trip. If Dawson's hunch was right, Fengche might even lead them to Menlo. And as Winger told Romero, "Dawson's hunches are pretty damn good."

The flight to Dubai was uneventful. Dawson and his team were all in separate seats, and for the entire fourteen hours Fengche showed absolutely no interest in any of them specifically. He did look wary on occasion, but no more so than any other competently aware business person traveling into the Middle East. As they were nearing the end of the flight, Dawson typed a text message to Winger, saying "Stay with him and then I'll see you at our hotel."

As soon as they were on the ground and had a signal, Dawson sent the message. As he was walking into the customs area, Winger's reply came back: "Roger that."

Once out of the airport, Dawson and Romero each caught separate taxis to the Millennium Hotel and checked in. Again, Dawson relied on a text message to both Romero and Winger, simply stating his room number. About fifteen minutes after he was in his room, Dawson was joined by Romero. About thirty minutes after that, Winger arrived. He sat on the end of the desk and said, "He's at the Hyatt a few blocks from here. Just staying one night."

"Any idea what room he is in?" Dawson asked.

Winger grinned. "You must think I'm slipping, Boss. Yeah, he's in the North Tower, room 738. I followed him into the elevator, rode it to the sixth floor, double-timed up the stairs quick enough to see his door closing."

"Would he recognize you again?" Dawson asked.

"I don't think so," Winger replied. "He never paid much attention to me or any of the other people in the elevator; never spoke at all."

"Hmm," Dawson mused. "Still, it's best to take no chances. You two both check back out of here and take up residence at the Hyatt. Follow him whenever he goes out. We need to understand what he is up to. I think it's interesting he isn't staying at the Palace or one of the other high-end properties in town."

"Yeah, I wondered about that, too," Winger replied. "Money doesn't seem to be a problem for him—he flew first class over here—but he seems inclined to keep a lower profile now that he's on the ground." Before they broke for dinner, Dawson arranged communication schedules and made sure the men had enough cash to ease whatever red tape they might encounter as they followed Fengche.

The following morning, Dawson caught his flight to Kabul. When he arrived, he was greeted by a local private security operative from Axis Security, a company Dawson had worked with many times before. Axis wasn't as large as many of the other companies working in the region, such as Aegis and Triple Canopy, but they had been there since 2003 and had a solid reputation. Dawson had been pleased with the way they handled things on prior assignments, so he was happy to work with them again and gratified to see an Axis operative waiting.

The company was under contract to several organizations, including NSA, CIA, and other agencies. But when he was on an assignment for the Brystol Foundation, the arrangements were made through Brystol's office— probably by Margaret—and Dawson never had to think about how invoices were handled and paid. The operative introduced himself as Robin McCall. He smiled perpetually, wore Oakley sunglasses, and was clearly in great shape. He seemed to know the terrain well, and Dawson noticed that he had good situational awareness. McCall drove Dawson directly to the US Embassy compound in an armored Toyota SUV.

Dawson was escorted into an 18,000-square-meter "unclassified annex building," and into the office of a one-star US Army general officer named Lyons, Colonel Tom Menlo's commanding officer. Dawson noticed that they had not entered the building through the main lobby. He was badged through a side door by the security operative, and the staff sergeant on duty there asked the operative only one question: "Is this Mr. Dawson?" Learning that it was, he looked over Dawson's credentials, handed him a white visitor's badge, and buzzed them through. McCall excused himself after making introductions to the general and then retreated to a waiting area near the building's lobby.

Lyons was a soft-spoken man who struck Dawson as competent and to the point. He motioned Dawson to a chair at his conference table and took a seat facing him. Dawson opened the conversation by thanking the general for his time, and assuring him that what he learned would be handled with the greatest of discretion.

"Mr. Dawson," Lyons said, "I've been ordered to make any and all information about Colonel Menlo's current mission available to you. I have been assured the highest levels of command have complete confidence in you, and that's good enough for me. In addition, Colonel Menlo is not only my responsibility, he is one of the finest young officers I have ever led, and I am extremely eager to see him safely returned. I'll do whatever I can, and I appreciate your assistance."

"Thank you, Sir," Dawson said.

"Now, while we have some assets in that area, as I'm sure you understand, my hands are tied operationally once I am outside my AO. Even inside my AO these days, things get dicey very quickly when we have to resort to firearms, especially relating to civilians."

"Yes, Sir, I understand," Dawson said. "I'll do all I can, but like you, I'm somewhat limited. My activities are primarily intelligence related, and not as much along the line of firefights. That's more your territory in Spec Ops."

Lyons smiled and thought, *Yeah, well I hear another story,* but he let it go. Dawson had a sort of transparency and quiet confidence that Lyons liked. Dawson struck him as a guy who under-promised and over-delivered.

"So tell me what happened, General," Dawson said. "What is Menlo's mission, what were his mission parameters, when did he leave, when were you expecting to hear from him, and so on."

Lyons wheeled his chair backwards and retrieved a file folder from a battered metal filing cabinet with a combination lock on the front. He placed it on the conference table, turned it 180 degrees, and slid it across to Dawson. "This is the colonel's file. You're welcome to read through it while you're here; take as long as you want. I would prefer that it remain here, though. As to his mission, I believe you already know that Menlo was involved in a review of the State Department sponsored program called 'Reintegration.' The Reintegration Program basically paid local Afghan leaders, both legitimate and informal leaders, who were perceived to be on the fence as far as the battle between the Taliban and the official Afghan government went, to swing to our side. A lot of people considered it out-and-out bribery; some considered it to be the cost of doing business in Afghanistan. The bottom line, though, and I doubt that anyone was really surprised by this, is that money started disappearing in larger and larger quantities. At the same time, more and more Russian arms and increasingly lethal munitions were beginning to flow into Afghanistan and into the Taliban's hands. It became increasingly dangerous for our people, and that's when I began to get involved."

"How long ago was that, Sir?"

"The money started disappearing in larger quantities almost two years ago," Lyons replied. "I started to get involved about a year ago, and I brought Menlo in on this about six months ago. As I'm sure you realize, Mr. Dawson, everything takes longer over here than it does almost anywhere else."

"I've certainly heard that said many times, Sir," Dawson agreed.

Lyons raised an eyebrow. "You don't believe it?"

"I didn't say that, General. But I will say I've heard that said many, many times and not just in Afghanistan. Also in Iraq in 2006 and 2007, and in Africa in 2008 and 2009. I think it's true as far as it goes. But at the end of the day, in my experience, it comes down to leadership and priorities and perseverance."

"Well," Lyons admitted, "it's true that those are often in short supply in these situations. In any case, Colonel Menlo is an energetic and passionate guy, maybe a little green yet about working with the locals and understanding boundaries. I was a little uncertain about allowing him to undertake this latest mission, but ultimately decided to let him go. Menlo was involved in a firefight a few months back with some Taliban thugs down in Khost Province. He pursued a couple of particularly bad actors through Paktia and up into Wardak. At that point, he discovered an operation that appears to be moving arms shipments including AK-47s, RPGs, and some of the small explosive device components we've been seeing in suicide bombing vests, car bombs, and roadside IEDs along the Ring Road from Iran."

Dawson knew the Ring Road referred to 2,200-kilometer two-lane road network circumnavigating Afghanistan, connecting major cities from Mazar and Kabul in the northeast, Kandahar in the southeast, Farah and Ziranj in the southwest, and Herat in the northwest. It has extensions that also connect substantial cities such as Jalalabad, Lashkar Gah, Delaram, and several others. It is by far the longest stretch of paved highway in Afghanistan, and one of the longest in that region of the Middle East.

"Of course," Lyons continued, "the entire western border of Afghanistan is infested with Iranian spies and Taliban sympathizers. The locations where a major highway supports traffic between the two countries, such as Ziranj and Herat, are probably the worst for highway-based trafficking of illegal substances and weapons. But the truth is that most of the stuff seems to be coming across the border near but not on the actual highway. And the Afghans have their hands full just trying to keep the legal stuff, ranging from water to oil, coming across. Iran has a stranglehold on a lot of it, as you may have seen from the trucks backed up on the borders."

"I've seen the long line of trucks, especially tankers, backed up and waiting to get across the bridge from Iran down in Ziranj a number of times. I've also suspected that the refugee camps along that corridor make great Taliban recruiting grounds. People who are desperate make easy recruits."

"Exactly!" Lyons exclaimed. "And that's where Menlo was headed. We had reports of Taliban recruiting, accompanied by handsome payoffs, from the area around Ziranj. We also suspect that the border along the shallows of the river there was a source of entry for increasingly large shipments of arms and explosive devices. Menlo had been working on a series of leads for about three months that led him to that area, and the dots he was connecting indicated that another soldier he had known from up here in Kabul had been up to his elbows in the whole mess."

"Fitzpatrick?" Dawson asked.

Lyons nodded. "Major James Fitzpatrick. Menlo hadn't been able to make the case, but he was getting close. Then something happened that spooked Menlo. As he was trying to close in on him, Fitzpatrick asked him right out of the blue if his wife was the same Dr. Menlo who was working on a program called Salacia. Menlo had heard the name of the program from his wife, which was natural, but a breach of protocol nonetheless. I understand Salacia is a black program even now. So Colonel Menlo was shocked to have someone outside the chain of 'need to know' come up with this out of nowhere. At that moment, he knew Fitzpatrick was connected with people who were involved with more than embezzlement of funds. Whomever Fitzpatrick was working with was deep inside the military/contractor system, and was looking for extremely highly classified information. Fitzpatrick was cagey about it, of course; he kept saying things like he imagined people would pay a lot of money for even incidental information about programs like Salacia. Menlo said that Fitzpatrick was always saying things like 'There's a lot of money to be made in this part of the world right now, Tom. Everybody's here, and everybody's got their own agenda. It's just a matter of understanding who is looking for what, and putting the right people together so that both parties get what they need.'"

"Sounds like Menlo is a pretty good intel guy," Dawson remarked.

"Well, that's certainly not what we trained him for," Lyons said, "but there's some truth in what you say. He doesn't seem to mind working alone, keeps information to himself, and spots potential trouble a mile away. Still, I'd rather you guys wouldn't steal him until we're done with him here."

Dawson smiled. "I understand, Sir." He just hoped Menlo came out of this alive. "So the colonel went to Ziranj when?"

"He left about six weeks ago," Lyons replied. "At first, we received normal reports, all very cryptic, of course, but what we were expecting. But for the last three weeks there's been nothing."

"When did you expect to hear from him?"

"The normal interval is no less than weekly. You know how it is when you're working on something like this. He may not have been able to report on an exact day or at an exact time, but we certainly should have heard something by now," Lyons said.

Dawson nodded. "Did you have any kind of monitoring device on his person?"

"He had a Blue Force Tracker with him, modified to boost its signal. But you have to recharge the batteries every couple of days, and it's bulky. Plus, it only has a range of a few miles. But it's basically a radio-based panic alarm and beacon, and as far as we can tell it was never triggered. Once it's engaged, you can't turn it back off remotely. It has to be retrieved and returned to base for deactivation. In retrospect, I shouldn't have allowed him to do this alone and I probably should have waited until I could get better equipment for him. But we are where we are."

"What can you tell me about how the colonel traveled and where he was last seen?"

Lyons opened the file, flipped through a couple of pages and said, "Colonel Menlo arrived on our Thumper flight at 2205 hours on the twenty-ninth. He checked in with the Deputy Chief of Mission who runs the Provincial Reconstruction Team out of the State Department, and bunked there at the PRT for the first few days. He checked out with one of the local terps at 1930 hours on the third, and neither of them was seen again. They were riding in a beat-up old 2003 Toyota, and the car was found the following morning near the Ring Road about two klicks from the border. There was some blood in the front seat but it wasn't Menlo's. At this point he's missing, but there has been no ransom demand and neither his personal effects nor his service weapon have been recovered. The locals aren't talking of course, and our informants in the area have come up dry."

Dawson thought about this. "State would have had an address for the terp on file," he said.

"Yes, they did. But when the PRT sent a team out there the terp's family was gone. The neighbors aren't talking. They just say one day they were there and the next day they were gone. Can't be entirely true, though, because the place is empty. Cleaned out. Not that they would have had much, but still it would have taken several hours to get it all cleared out."

"How about the other terps and the supervisor on site at the PRT?" Dawson asked.

"I did speak to him, but frankly it's a very loose organization over there," Lyons replied. "They don't have much. Basically, he tells me that the young man, a kid really, I think, about twenty years old, is a good kid. Never caused any trouble, provided quick and accurate translations, and rarely complained. The supervisor sent another terp out to the house when he didn't show up for work, and the family claimed that they hadn't seen or heard from him since the day he left with Menlo. The supervisor thinks they were telling the truth. And then, of course, they disappeared."

"Got it," Dawson replied. "That's all of my questions, Sir. Is there anything else about this that I ought to know?"

Lyons thought about it for a moment, and said, "No, I don't think so. You now know everything that's relevant, I think. By the way, you're not going out there alone, are you?"

"No, I have a team."

"Well, I want Menlo back, but I'd advise you to be careful," Lyons said. "On the Iranian border, especially now after the drawdown, we have very limited capability. And of course you realize that if you *go* in after him, we can offer no assistance at all."

"Understood, Sir," Dawson replied. He rose to leave, and passed the Menlo file back over to Lyons. "Looks like a very good soldier," he said. "I'll do everything I can."

"I appreciate that," Lyons said, returning the folder to his lock-protected file drawer.

Lyons stepped around his desk, opened his door and gestured to McCall, who was still stationed at the end of the hall waiting for the men to emerge. McCall whistled softly as he escorted Dawson back through the security checkpoint, surrendering the visitor badge and walking on to the SUV. Driving through the outer perimeter checkpoints onto and off of a local military base is always a tedious experience, "a TSA airport security checkpoint on steroids." Speed bumps made it impossible to exceed ten kilometers per hour. Iron gates hinged to concrete bases inhibited traffic further. Then there were ANA, Afghan National Army, and US troops handling long rods with mirrors and bomb-sniffing dogs that inspected each incoming vehicle. End-to-end, it was a deliberate and arduous process.

After about ten minutes, McCall pulled out into Kabul traffic and headed toward the private security compound leased by Axis Security. The compound was about thirty kilometers northeast of Kabul. It wasn't large as such properties go, but was about two acres of ground with two buildings, a high wall with razor wire along the top, and never less than two armed guards at the gate. One of the buildings operated as apartments for paying guests, and the other was used to house Axis personnel.

Dawson had stayed there before, so McCall was brief with him about the security arrangements. Nonetheless, he covered them again. Not only was it his job, but McCall was clearly a man of method. He reviewed the drill for compound under attack, where the weapons were kept, what the radio codes were, how rapidly they could expect assistance in the event it was needed, and so on. Dawson had heard it all before, but he still found it comforting. After he settled in, Dawson logged on to check for messages. There was nothing from Winger and Romero yet, which did not surprise him. However, there was a message from Jennings indicating Axis would have a package for him "soonest." Not sure precisely what "soonest" meant in that context, Dawson shrugged it off and walked over to the security building for dinner.

The buildings were very similar—1960s vintage brown brick-and-stucco structures with flat roofs. The building occupied by Axis operatives and staff was most easily differentiated by the many antennae bristling from the roof. Each was three stories and had been the property of wealthy foreign industrialists in years gone by. As such, they were equipped with generator farms, modern electrical systems, and western plumbing. The compound was near the foot of the mountains, and the buildings on the compound were the only tall structures within a mile. The nearest road was paved, but it was only one lane and it ended about a kilometer beyond the compound.

The Axis operator building boasted an especially spacious kitchen and dining area, and the kitchen staff arrived every morning in time to prepare breakfast and remained through after-dinner cleanup each evening. The chef did a great job, and Axis staff members always ensured the food was prepared from fresh local produce, minimizing the danger of contamination, either intentional or unintentional.

Dawson was pleased to see that the evening meal was starting with a tomato-based vegetable soup, and there were platters brimming with locally produced "foot bread." The soup was always delicious, with flavor combinations that were unlike the varieties that existed in any other location. Dawson took a seat around the massive dining room table with several of the Axis operatives and two other guests. One guest was a *Wall Street Journal* reporter, and another was a DOD civilian contractor conducting a survey of electrical power needs across the region. Dawson was trying to decide whether to ask for a second bowl of soup or move on to the entrée when the outer door opened and McCall burst into the room. The look on his face told Dawson that his decision about the soup had just become moot.

"Gentlemen, we have a developing situation. I have an operative coming in hot. He's about seven klicks out and being pursued by two other vehicles. Shots fired and it looks like we may have to repel the pursuers as they are coming in. I'd appreciate it if you would follow the protocol we rehearsed. You two gentlemen"—McCall pointed to other two guests—"downstairs immediately, please. Mr. Dawson, can you assist me topside?"

Dawson was already out of his chair, muttering something about hoping the soup wouldn't be cold by the time this was finished, and halfway up the stairs by the time McCall caught up with him. "How do you know there aren't other vehicles behind the first two in pursuit?" Dawson asked.

"We have surveillance cameras set up along the road at a few critical points," McCall said. "There's just the two."

"Good enough!" Dawson smiled. They stopped at the large closet that was fitted out as an armory on the way, to pick up weapons, goggles, vests, and gloves.

When they reached the roof, Dawson took up a prone position along the wall where McCall directed him. He could see that Axis had deployed one of their armored SUVs to take up an ambush-enabling flanking position behind a nearby farm's out-building, out of sight from the road. One Axis operative was standing inside the vehicle, perched through the open sunroof with an M16. A driver and one other operative were inside the SUV.

It was less than a minute before the Axis vehicle appeared, flying down the road at what Dawson estimated to be about eighty kph. There were indeed two pursuit vehicles, the first an old Ford Ranger pickup truck and the other a beat-up Toyota sedan with blacked-out windows. Dawson couldn't help thinking that the pursuers should have known better. They were chasing an armored vehicle into what they should have realized was going to be a dead-end road out here at the foot of the mountains. If the pursuers thought they were driving the vehicle into a trap, they were mistaken; what they were doing was running into an ambush.

As they approached, the Axis SUV screeched to a halt while turning abruptly to the right, effectively blocking the road. The driver flung open the door and rolled out to the pedestrian door within the gate and into the compound, bullets whizzing around him as they barked from the pursuit vehicles. He flung himself through the doorway, and one of the gate sentries slammed it immediately behind him. Seconds later, as the pickup truck passed the farm building across the street, the Axis SUV pulled out from its location behind the out-building and drove to a position blocking any retreat.

The two pursuit vehicles were essentially trapped between the compound wall, a deep ditch on the opposite side of the road, and Axis vehicles in front of and behind them. At that point, the Axis personnel waited to see whether the pursuers would stop firing, since they had little hope of actually hitting anyone. It would have been the smart move, but Dawson surmised these were not very smart people. They poured out of the vehicles, three from the Toyota and two more from the pickup, took cover around the vehicles and in the ditch, and kept firing.

All were wielding AK-47s, and none were hitting anything worth hitting although they were chewing up windows and masonry quite a bit. After about thirty seconds, when it became clear that they weren't going to stop their assault, McCall signaled the team to return fire. It wasn't much of a battle on these terms. The Axis SUV rooftop gunner and the two other SUV occupants focused primarily on the pursuers in the ditch, while the operatives positioned on the rooftop focused on those who were firing from behind the open doors of their pursuit vehicles.

As they were all doing the shooting-and-ducking routine, Dawson was still wondering at the utter futility of this approach by the pursuers. Bullets were spraying chunks of masonry up into their faces as they rolled away and then back into position again to fire; more than once Dawson was glad he had grabbed goggles from the armory on his way.

Then he noticed one pursuer climbing into the bed of the pickup. The man shoved aside some pieces of wood and canvas and lifted out a RPG (rocket-propelled grenade) launcher. This changed the game, Dawson realized, and the episode back in southern Helmand Province came flooding back to his mind. He wished he had his portable laser again.

To his right, he could see that McCall had just noticed it, too, and was beginning to reposition his weapon, but Dawson was already on it. "I've got it," he said loudly enough for McCall to hear, and squeezed off a two-round burst. It struck the assailant center mass, and sent him spinning backward over the wall of the truck bed, leaving the RPG lying in the bed of the truck.

Within a few minutes, the firefight was over and the Axis compound had added an RPG launcher to the undeclared elements of their armory at the compound as well as a half dozen AK-47s that were deemed adequate to keep for potential future use. The balance of the weapons was set aside to turn over to the ANA or ANP if they ever showed up to ask questions, but Dawson guessed Axis probably wouldn't ever hear from either the army or the police.

The bodies of the assailants all looked to be men from that region, likely Afghans, Pakistanis, or Iranians. Men in their twenties and thirties, none of whom looked well fed, and none of whom looked like armed forces regulars. Based on appearances, they might have been Al Qaeda but could as easily have been local thugs. But of course local thugs would have had little reason to travel in two separate vehicles in pursuit of what was obviously an armored SUV holding no apparent cargo of value.

When Dawson descended the stairs after handing over his M16 and unspent ammunition for cleaning and storage, he found the driver of the newly returned Axis SUV waiting for him. "I have a package for you, Sir," he said. He handed him an unmarked envelope and then excused himself to provide McCall with an after-action report. Dawson asked the chef whether he could have another bowl of his excellent vegetable soup, and sat down again at the dining room table and opened the standard size insulated manila envelope.

After he'd finished his soup and verified that he wasn't in anyone's sightline, he extracted the envelope's contents, which turned out to be a single eight gigabyte flash drive. He pocketed it long enough to finish the rest of his meal, and then retreated to his room to plug it into his laptop. Jennings had sent him a file with the information available on Fengche, and at last Dawson had a name for the man Winger and Romero were tracking. The bad news, though, was that once again someone had enough inside intel to know that important information was being sent to Dawson. It was unclear whether they knew exactly what that information was, but Dawson thought it likely.

Life in Afghanistan was cheap, but it seemed improbable someone would try to stop the delivery, expending men, munitions, and vehicles unless they believed the information was important enough to pay a significant price for its interception. *No*, Dawson decided, *someone on the inside discovered this package was on its way to me and went after it specifically.* He was feeling better about his hunch all the time; Fengche was on his way to Colonel Tom Menlo.

Fengche had been a soldier in the Peoples Liberation Army's Special Forces since the late 1990s, when it was known as the Guangzhou Military Region Special Forces Unit, the first such unit of the PLA that was capable of air, sea, and land-based operations. At the end of three years, he was transferred to the Chengdu Military Region Special Forces Unit, dubbed "Falcon," which specialized in target location, airborne insertion, sabotage, and offensive strike. It was during this time that he acquired the nickname Fengche, based on his fighting style.

After nearly a decade in Special Forces, he was recruited to the MSS and provided with a diplomatic service title in order to afford him diplomatic immunity and other privileges associated with his new position. Fengche had never married and appeared to be utterly devoted to his work. He was rumored to be a heavy drinker, but that was his only documented vice, and there was no record it had ever interfered with his work.

Recent reports indicated Fengche was known with high levels of confidence to be responsible for the assassination of more than a dozen people since joining MSS. The number of kills attributed to him while a member of the Special Forces was more than twenty. He was described as highly proficient in hand-to-hand combat and light weapons, and while he had demonstrated competence with explosives, he seemed to prefer close-in work and favored bladed weapons and breaking necks. Fengche's father had been a regular military officer who had been disciplined for excessive drinking and violent behavior. He held primarily lower level posts and never saw any action on the front lines.

Now in his late thirties, Fengche stood six feet three inches tall and was comprised of 210 pounds of solid muscle. He was a reasonably intelligent man, but it appeared his interests were few. Over the last several years, Fengche had worked much of the time in the Middle East, which had afforded him unprecedented opportunities to hone his lethal skills and develop new ones. Most recently those skills involved interrogation methods. There was some evidence to suggest he had observed the interrogation of Afghan soldiers and civilians by the Taliban, and even a few American soldiers in Iraq by Al Qaeda and in Afghanistan by Taliban operatives. He had been described as ruthless and bloodthirsty.

But Dawson would have been surprised to learn the extent of what was *not* contained in the file. Fengche had some ideas in store for the young colonel when he encountered him again, and was eager to get back to that work. He was very mistrustful of the Iranians guarding Menlo and he needed him alive in order to experiment with these new approaches. But first of all he would try the photos. Americans were softies, he believed, and he suspected that when he confronted Menlo with the very recent photos of his wife and son, Menlo would immediately cave. Even if that was true, of course, Fengche would proceed with the torture. It was his hobby now, and rapidly becoming his greatest passion.

After reading through the materials on Fengche, Dawson sat down with McCall and arranged for a flight into Herat. Then he placed an email in his account for Winger and Romero communicating Fengche's name and a few other details. At the same time, he picked up a message from Winger indicating that they were on the move, tracking Fengche through a series of commercial flights, busses, and other dubious transport mechanisms.

It took Dawson forty-eight hours to get on a flight. It was a military bird, and Dawson chose not to pull rank but rather travel "Space-A," as space is available after all military personnel are aboard, to begin lowering his profile as he grew closer to his destination. He drew a few weapons from the armory at the Axis compound, including a smoke grenade and the best of the AK-47s captured from the Taliban assailants a couple of nights earlier. He put all of his gear in a standard black plastic foot locker, and kept only Go Bag articles in his backpack. It was a long, hot trip, stopping at Mazar-i-Sharif for refueling en route.

At Herat, Dawson was met by another Axis operative named Paul McCartney—no relation, he claimed, to the famous musician though he was clearly a Brit. McCartney moved him into the Herat compound for one night, and the next morning helped Dawson make the bulk of his transformation into a generic businessman. There were a fair number of business people from Europe and even America strewn around Afghanistan by then, with the ISAF drawdown well behind and the opportunities for exploiting local resources such as pomegranates, cotton, marble, and especially poppies returning to exportable levels. Fortunately, Dawson was already deeply tanned and familiar with the local garb. He had the all-too-common crows' feet around his eyes from many months of squinting into the blinding Middle Eastern sun, and with several days' growth of beard, he could blend in reasonably well as long as he didn't have to speak. If the conversation got past a simple greeting such as "As-salamu alaykum," he was helpless.

From the Axis compound in Herat, Dawson placed a message in the drafts folder of his email account for Winger and Romero alerting them that he planned to be "on target" by 2300 hours, then jumped in a late model but well-worn pickup truck decked out with layers of Afghan accoutrements such as lacey seat covers, velvety fringe, and an incredibly gaudy paint scheme. With weapons close but invisible to anyone outside the vehicle, McCartney and Dawson departed for Ziranj. Since most of the trip was along the Ring Road, it proved fairly uneventful, though traffic backups resulting from donkey carts and similar obstacles frequently slowed them down.

About a mile from the border, the Ziranj City Center was comparatively clean and modern. While not advanced in terms of technology, the city benefited from a reasonably consistent flow of electricity and clean water. Axis had no compound in Ziranj, but arrangements had been made for Dawson and his team to stay for a few days at a local hotel. The International Hotel in Ziranj was adjacent to the city government building, housed many foreign business people, and had only been the victim of a car bomb on one occasion. Along the southern section of the eastern Iranian border, this was the best Dawson could do for accommodations.

Because of its proximity to the border, Ziranj benefited from a great deal of travel-related business, although well over half of it was illegal. As such, security was difficult. There were Iranian refugee camps around the outskirts of Ziranj, especially at the bridge over the Khash River just north of its confluence with the Helmand River. These camps were comprised of tent cities, filled with people milling about and simply sitting or lying on the ground. Periodically, Afghan authorities came through and forced them all to leave, but, having nowhere else to go since their expulsion as illegal immigrants in Iran, they returned almost as soon as authorities looked the other way.

All in all, the situation reminded Dawson of the narrator's voice-over at the opening of the famous Humphrey Bogart and Ingrid Bergman movie, *Casablanca*. A great many people passed through Ziranj, and not all of them left the area alive. An appropriate bribe got Dawson into the hotel under an assumed name with no inconvenient documentation requirements or questions. As he settled in, he reflected on his odds of success and hoped he'd beat them one more time.

CHAPTER 12

Teng-hui and Jing-ti were seated across the table from the MSS's Brystol Foundation operative. She occupied the same chair from which Biwu had sent her sprawling just a few days earlier, but her comfort level was certainly improved. The purpose of the meeting was to bring Jing-ti up to speed on their most dangerous adversary in the acquisition of the Salacia technology— Ben Dawson—so Jing-ti could properly account for him in his planning. The operative had come directly from her job at the Foundation, and seemed eager to get finished with the interview and get back to her own affairs.

Teng-hui could see that she had worked very hard to overcome the faint bruising left from Biwu's blow, and silently cursed the arrogant bully again even though he was already dead. Although Teng-hui had no particular affection for this agent, she was *his* operative and should never have been treated this way by anyone other than him. Biwu had paid for his insults with his life. The only thing about the entire affair that made him even angrier than Biwu's insolence was the fact that the cowards in Beijing—his own superiors—had backed Biwu rather than himself, a loyal and productive member of the party and of the MSS for more than twenty years. *One day,* Teng-hui swore, *I will find a way to repay each one of you.*

With introductions out of the way, Teng-hui explained the purpose of the meeting and asked his operative to provide an overview of the available facts about Ben Dawson. She drew in a deep breath, crossed her long and angular legs, and began. "Benjamin Lee Dawson was born in Chandler, Arizona, at the Good Samaritan Hospital on September 29, 1967. He is the son of James and Martha Dawson, both of whom are now deceased. He has no siblings, and no living relatives with whom he maintains an ongoing relationship. He is five feet eight inches tall, weighs approximately 180 pounds, and is in good health. He has brown hair and brown eyes, and has no discernible distinguishing scars or tattoos. Mr. Dawson earned a bachelor of science degree in mechanical engineering from Arizona State University in 1990 and a master's degree in technology management at the University of Phoenix while employed as a systems engineer at McDonnell Douglas Helicopter Company in Mesa, Arizona, in 1994."

After pausing to determine whether either Teng-hui or Jing-ti had any questions, she continued. "On September 12, 1993, Mr. Dawson married a colleague from his workplace, Janice Miller. They had no children, and according to materials from Mr. Dawson's clearance interviews, the marriage was not a happy one. In October of 1995, Janice Dawson was diagnosed with pancreatic cancer."

"In December that same year, Ben Dawson took an extended leave of absence from his employment and cared for her until the time of her death the following July. The period surrounding his wife's death, particularly after her death, was a period of significant change for Mr. Dawson. He was convinced by a former college classmate and friend named Max Kelly to apply for an analyst position at the National Security Agency. Mr. Kelly was, at that time, a respected member of the agency and a somewhat storied field operative. Mr. Dawson's analytical skills, technical background, and affinity for hot, arid climates eventually provided him with an opportunity to work with Mr. Kelly on several assignments in the Middle East. Although we have few details about these assignments owing to their classified status, it is known that Mr. Dawson was proficient with a wide array of weaponry by that point. He had studied martial arts throughout his adolescent years, and this combination of skills and experience made him a very effective operative. Between 1997 and 2012, Mr. Dawson was promoted several times. By 2012, his official title was Special Projects Director."

Again she paused, waited for questions, and receiving only stares from Teng-hui and Jing-ti, she continued. "We know he has personally participated in dozens of altercations and firefights, and to our knowledge he has never been injured beyond bruises and abrasions. His opponents in these altercations rarely have a similar experience. While he is not naturally aggressive, Mr. Dawson has a remarkable ability to survive such encounters. In 2012, there was a significant dispute over the handling of some intelligence assets in Afghanistan involving Mr. Dawson and Mr. Kelly. Again, we have almost no detail, but the conflict appeared to be one of the many long-standing confrontations between Chief of Mission staff members at the US State Department and the US Department of Defense. Mr. Dawson and Mr. Kelly consistently align themselves with the military in such matters, and this one evidently reached the level of the Secretaries of Defense and State before it was finally resolved. A significant outcome from the debacle was the forced resignation of Mr. Kelly and the voluntary resignation of Mr. Dawson."

Finally, Jing-ti broke the responding silence by asking: "How did Mr. Dawson become involved with the Brystol Foundation, and with Salacia?"

"Someone in the NSA recommended Mr. Dawson to Dr. Brystol when he left the agency. It was evidently someone Dr. Brystol has known for many years, but we do not know who. Dr. Brystol was having difficulty with an Air Force research program related to quantum computing. He believed that a team was working in the Soviet Union exploring the same area of research and had made a breakthrough that had the Brystol Foundation team at an impasse. Mr. Dawson and his team infiltrated the Russian facility and retrieved the required information without alerting the research team. As far as we know, they are still unaware that it was stolen. Dr. Brystol offered Mr. Dawson a generous retainer and a bonus-based compensation arrangement for additional work, and Mr. Dawson accepted. That is how he became involved with the Foundation."

"Most impressive," Jing-ti admitted.

"Now," she continued, "I will explain how Mr. Dawson became involved with Salacia. About a year ago, the Salacia Project team determined they were ready for the application of the final element required to enable their device. It is an extremely rare element that exists only suspended within a crystalline structure that is known to have been unearthed only three times. This element is unique because of the way it fractures beams of light as they pass through the crystalline material. But even with the correct material, which—as I mentioned—is extremely rare, the crystal must be ground with extreme precision into a circular lens, which is then attached to the end of a glass fiber that is roughly the diameter of a human hair. It is this part of the device that is catalytic in combination with the laser that creates the chemical reaction resulting in the effect known as Menlo Bubbles.

"About," she closed her eyes and thought for a moment, "twenty years ago, I believe, a Russian excavation company discovered it when they were searching for uranium in southern Afghanistan. They had no use for it at the time, and the nearby uranium mine was depleted and abandoned several years before the Russians were driven out by the Taliban. The rare element was not located in the mine itself, but in one of several exploratory shafts created in the process of looking for a suitable uranium deposit. Although the location was known to the Russians, since it was of no use to them, they made no great effort to conceal the information. Again, Dr. Brystol turned to Mr. Dawson for assistance. Mr. Dawson led an extraction team into Afghanistan and retrieved the only remaining known material in existence. It has now been divided into three sections for security. One is at the Brystol research building under the care of Dr. Carolyn Menlo, and the other two are at different and separate locations. Only Dr. Brystol is aware of those locations and how the material can be retrieved."

"When did you discover that Dawson was going after the critical material?" Jing-ti asked.

"About a week before he left for Afghanistan," the operative replied.

Jing-ti looked at Teng-hui and said, "This is the mission that failed a few months ago?"

Teng-hui nodded curtly. He returned his gaze to his operative. "Please continue."

"There is little more to say. Mr. Dawson is now engaged to locate the husband of Dr. Menlo, and although I do not know precisely where he is right now, I know he has engaged the Axis Security Company to assist him somewhere in the Middle East." A knowing look passed between Teng-hui and Jing-ti that contained elements of both understanding and trepidation. If Dawson was in the Middle East and looking for Colonel Menlo, he would likely encounter Fengche. The outcome of such an event could not be known in advance, and it was a factor Jing-ti would have to consider in his planning.

Jing-ti asked, "You said Dawson has no family members to whom he speaks. Does he have close friends?"

"He has many professional friends and contacts in both government posts and private security companies," she replied, "but we have no information that leads us to believe he has close friends. He has had no significant romantic involvement since his wife died. He seems to be closest to William Winger, and two other individuals from a private security company, Max Kelly and his partner, Lily Gerard." At this, she paused, and seemed to be considering something.

Finally, Teng-hui said, "What is it?"

She seemed to resurface from some feat of deep recollection. "Probably nothing. I just remembered an event, immediately following the Salacia demonstration several days ago, when Dr. Menlo spoke with Dawson for what I believe was the first time. I'm not sure what I saw there, but I thought there might be something…. No. Please excuse me. It was probably nothing at all."

"Hmm," Teng-hui replied. "You have been a valuable member of this organization for a long time, and I have never known you to notice something that was not worth noticing. Are you sure it was nothing?"

"I'm sure," she said. "It was nothing."

"He turned to Jing-ti. "Do you have any further questions?" he asked, but he was already rising to his feet.

"No," Jing-ti said, "I believe I have what I need."

Then Jing-ti turned to the operative. "Thank you. You have been extremely helpful. I shall be in touch if I should need to speak with you again."

The operative nodded, rose, bowed slightly, and left the room.

At the end of their working day, about six p.m., Jing-ti asked Teng-hui's assistant to alert him that the plan was ready. About five minutes later, he received a responding call from the assistant relaying a message from Teng-hui: "You are to set up your presentation in the conference room downstairs, and be prepared to brief me in the morning. I will be there at 0900."

Well, at least I can get a full night's sleep then, Jing-ti thought. He had been up for forty-eight hours working on the plan and participating with Teng-hui in meetings and interviews as well as gathering information from his own sources. He was physically and mentally exhausted. Teng-hui recognized this and, although he had neither particular affection for Jing-ti nor any genuine interest in his well-being, he did need his chief of staff to be mentally alert to present his plan. Teng-hui had no time for stumbling about, and this was far too important to leave in the hands of a man who was mentally exhausted. The planning was complex and it must be done thoroughly and competently.

The next morning, when Teng-hui arrived in the conference room, he was very surprised to find that six of the largest high-definition flat screen monitors he had ever seen had been mounted adjacent to one another, basically covering the wall from within a meter of the ceiling down to less than three meters of the floor. The conference room table had been moved toward the opposite wall, where it was still fully accessible but afforded a view of the entire array of monitors. On the table were not only the normal tray of hot tea and muffins, but also a wireless keyboard and mouse. "Most impressive,"

Teng-hui admitted to Jing-ti as he took a seat at the conference table.

"Good morning, Teng-hui," Jing-ti responded, bowing.

"Personally, of course, I prefer a paper-based PERT chart timeline."

"Yes, I understand that. I did begin to prepare my presentation in that form, but I almost immediately realized that certain features of this plan made an electronic display a better choice. I believe you will see what I mean as we get into the presentation."

"Well," Teng-hui sighed, "I did tell you to spare no expense. It looks as though you were listening to that part of my instruction, in any case."

His assistant had poured tea into ornate cups for the two men and added one teaspoon of honey to Teng-hui's cup. As soon as she bowed and excused herself from the room, Teng-hui took a sip and said, "Proceed."

Jing-ti began to work the wireless mouse and keyboard before him. The room lights dimmed significantly, and the wall monitors came to life. The presentation was timed to the required ninety minutes without questions, but with the probing along every dimension that Teng-hui did, it took nearly four hours to complete. The plan was indeed intricate and complex. But beyond the complexity of the plan, Jing-ti had built contingency plans—plans within the plan—to cover significant points where he anticipated that the outcome of events was very uncertain. The activities were laid out in a giant flow chart, divided into "swim lanes" showing the role of major players such as Fengche, Bi-shou, Ben Dawson, and others. Then there was a lane devoted to the group of minor players who performed critical tasks. Lines and arrows stretched between the boxes on the flow chart, depicting the chronological order of the events as well as the dependencies: which events would trigger which other events.

"You see," Jing-ti said as he was wrapping up, "as events occur, this method can compensate for differences between the baseline plan and actual events. If something takes longer than expected, or an outcome is different, the critical path, the longest string of events, shifts to reflect that change automatically and advises us of actions to be taken. For example, if Fengche should fail to extract the information and leverage he needs from Colonel Menlo, this path in the plan is automatically activated. If Mr. Dawson discovers our plan for obtaining the crystalline material anywhere along this timeline, this other activity is then initiated by Bi-shou, and so on. We can monitor and adjust continuously. But no matter which combination of these events occurs, the critical path for this plan never extends beyond sixty days. Although you indicated that my target was ninety days, I believe it can be accomplished within sixty. Even if the plan is off by twenty-five percent, it still gives us ample time."

Teng-hui admitted to himself that it was a work of art, and, although this was an admission he would never make to Jing-ti, he could never have done it himself. It was not only brilliant, but nearly foolproof. And if it all worked as planned, the Salacia technology would be theirs within sixty days. Instead of professing his admiration, he shook his head slowly. "I am not such a strong believer as you are in the power of systems and artificial intelligence," he said. "I admit your plan looks very good, Jing-ti. I am impressed by your diligence and attention to detail." Jing-ti beamed. "However," Teng-hui continued, "I believe your confidence is too high and reflects some immaturity on your part. No system has ever fully predicted or accounted for the actions of human beings. We are unique combinations of emotion, intellect, morality, self-interest, loyalties, complicity, and courage. Yours is a good plan, perhaps a better plan than I could have developed even with more time. But it is not foolproof, and no matter what your critical path is telling you, I am telling you no plan is perfect. When this is behind us, if Salacia is ours, then you will have great opportunities ahead of you, Jing-ti. But beware of overconfidence. It has brought many great men to ruin, and you would not want to be the next one."

The expression on Jing-ti's face was now very serious. "No, Sir, I would not," he said.

"And one other thing," Teng-hui continued. "In making this plan as solid as it is, you are spending a great deal of money. You have a small army of operatives, costing more than two million US dollars, many of whom are contractors, which introduces significant risk, and more than one million US dollars on equipment from electronic communications to weapons. I realize this may vary depending on the contingency plans that must be invoked. But the resources of MSS are not unlimited, and such a spending profile will come under scrutiny in Beijing. I currently enjoy some latitude with MSS headquarters because of recent events, but the shelf life of this new degree of freedom is short, and we must produce results. So if we extend beyond ninety days after this level of expenditure and do not manage to acquire the Salacia technology, it is likely *neither* of us will survive."

At this point, Jing-ti's face was ashen. That was the result that Teng-hui was looking for. "Very well, then," Teng-hui said. "Assemble your resources and get under way."

CHAPTER 13

"Rebecca," Dr. Carolyn Menlo said without lifting her eyes from the microscope, "would you ask Joan to come in here, please? I think we have a problem." About twenty miles from where Jing-ti and Teng-hui were just concluding their meeting, Menlo was at work in her laboratory at the Brystol Foundation.

"Sure," Rebecca, Menlo's assistant, said. A few minutes later Joan Wu, Menlo's top optics and optic-borne energy researcher appeared.

Wu was a petite Asian woman who fit the stereotypical portrait of a scientist. Thick glasses, a white lab coat, sensible shoes, and a serious expression were all elements of the image that came to everyone's mind when they thought of her. Born in the United States, she was a first generation American who graduated with honors from MIT with degrees in physics and electrical engineering. She had already been at the Brystol Foundation for three years when Menlo joined the organization, and had been working on Icarus, another of Brystol technologies. Icarus had hit a snag that was outside her area of expertise, and Wu had complained to Brystol of boredom. Not wanting to lose one of the most gifted researchers in her field, he offered to move her onto Menlo's team when Menlo arrived, assuming Menlo would be thrilled for the opportunity to be supported by such a talented expert. He had been right. The two women had hit it off immediately, and Wu had become Menlo's most trusted and valued team member. Wu was a single mother of two, and her two girls, Gillian and Kristi, bracketed Menlo's son Andy in age. The two researchers had socialized outside of work on many occasions, and since their children all liked one another, the situation made for pleasant outings.

"What's up?" Wu asked, breezing into the room. "Rebecca says you came across a problem?"

"Take a look at this." Menlo stepped back from the microscope and allowed Wu to replace her.

Wu adjusted the eyepieces to support the uneven strength in her own eyesight, and refocused the device. "Hmm, I see," she said. "The adhesive is failing. We need to achieve a tighter and cleaner adhesion between the surface of the lens and the surface of the fiber it's attached to."

"Exactly," Menlo confirmed. "This is the last piece of the puzzle. If we can just make the adhesive work, the entire system is finally sound."

Wu was quiet for a moment and then brightened. "I have an idea," she said. "Give me just a couple of minutes to check something." With that, she walked briskly out of the room.

When she returned, she was wearing latex gloves and carrying a fresh strand of fiber coiled up in a petri dish and a small tube of liquid. Seating herself at the microscope again, Wu carefully removed the old strand of fiber and threaded the new piece into position. Using tweezers, she gently and carefully removed the tiny lens from the end of the old fiber and used a solvent-saturated cloth surface to remove the remaining adhesive. Dipping a needle-sized probe into a single drop of liquid from the tube, she touched it to the end of the fiber. Then she very carefully attached the lens, holding it in place for a few seconds with the tweezers. "Give this one a try, and let me know," Wu smiled at Menlo. "I've been working with a different adhesive, something I picked up from a friend at JDS Uniphase. If this works, it will give us much better fidelity and resistance to deterioration in humid, saline-laden working conditions."

"And what is this mysterious new adhesive?" Menlo asked.

"I'll tell you if it works," Wu smiled, "OK?"

"You're impossible!" Menlo said. "But all right. I'll have Rebecca run it through trials this afternoon and let you know." As Wu turned to leave again, Menlo said, "Glad to see that black eye of yours is healing, finally. I know you said Kristi pelted you with a whiffle bat, but I still think you probably just gave someone else the same kind of lip you give me, and they walloped you."

"You wish!" Wu chuckled, heading out the door.

As Menlo watched her leaving the lab, she noticed the large wall clock near the door and said: "Uh-oh. I have a lunch appointment in ten minutes. Rebecca, will you take over here and get the trials under way please? I'll be back as soon as I can."

"Sure," Rebecca replied, walking over from another work station. "I've just been setting up the device for insertion of the new fiber-and-lens combination over there. We should be well under way by the time you get back."

"Thanks," Menlo said, and walked rapidly out of the lab, down the hall, and toward the elevators.

CHAPTER 14

Winger knocked quietly on the door of Dawson's room at the International Hotel in Ziranj about two hours after Dawson settled in. Their route, following Fengche into Ziranj, had been different than Dawson's, but equally circuitous. Winger was wearing local garb and looked a little tired, Dawson thought, but well.

"Chief and I never bothered checking into the hotel," Winger said. "We're laying low out in the farm country along the river. Fengche is holed up in a compound out there, and we've been keeping eyes on. I think they're getting ready to move soon. They just had a couple of guys show up who are definitely out-of-towners. I'm thinking Iranians. If I were a betting man, I'd bet that these guys are here from Iran to take Fengche back in with them."

"If you were a betting man, huh? How much did you say you owed me?" Dawson laughed. "Well, I never bet against you unless I'm sure of my hand, and I'm not sure of anything right now except that it appears Fengche isn't wasting any time. It seems to me we should follow both paths as long as there are three of us. Now I'm wishing we had brought along a fourth operator, but we are where we are. Why don't you go ahead and take a shower while you're here and grab a drink, then swap out with Chief so he can do the same. You guys probably shouldn't shave, so you look as much like locals as possible. Looks like you're already dressed for the occasion."

"Yeah," Winger said, "picked these up along the way. Locals are always happy to trade their old clothes for cash."

"It helps if you speak the language," Dawson said. "If I offered a local a handful of cash and asked him to take off his clothes, I'm sure he'd probably think I had something else in mind."

"Ha!" Winger guffawed. "Now I'd like to see *that*!"

While Winger showered, Dawson thought about how to proceed, and by the time Winger emerged, he had the primary elements of a plan. "So here's what we'll do," he said. "You and Chief continue to follow Fengche. Stay back enough to avoid detection, but stick with him if you can. I'll go ahead with our planned crossing method. If we are both successful, we'll rendezvous at specified GPS coordinates. Now as to the coordinates, here's how we handle those."

Out of his bag, Dawson produced three "burner" phones, subscribed to the MCI, the Mobile Communications Company of Iran, network. "Don't turn these on until you need them, and shut them off as soon as you're finished with your transmission. Otherwise they turn into homing beacons. If things go sideways, of course, the opposite is true. Turn it on, send a 911 text, and leave it on. I'll try to find you from that. Our burner numbers and an independent Gmail account are in the contact list. When you figure out your destination, text me the coordinates. I'll check in every hour on the half-hour, and one of you do the same. Don't worry if I'm offline for a few hours here and there to sleep, but otherwise I'll be checking in on that schedule. Understood?"

"Makes sense," Winger replied. "And if we find we can't follow Fengche across the border?"

"Ping me on the cell, and I'll get you in by our planned route if I can," Dawson said.

"Got it," said Winger. "Now I'd better get back and relieve Chief. We're about ten klicks out."

* * * *

It turned out Romero never had the opportunity to get in town to shower at the hotel. By the time Winger returned, night was falling and things were heating up at the adobe hut Fengche occupied. Winger slipped quietly through the open area around the farmhouse, careful to ensure the lone sentry outside didn't have a line of sight that could enable him to be seen. The group inside included Fengche, the two men Winger had identified as likely Iranians, and another man Winger figured was the transporter, essentially a local smuggler.

When Winger slipped up behind Romero, he was still lying on the ground where Winger had left him, peering through a pair of night vision equipped binoculars that were propped on top of a flat rock. "Glad you're back," Romero whispered. "I need to pee."

"Man, I would think so by now," Winger replied. "I'm planning to spell you so you could go in to the hotel and get cleaned up."

"There's not gonna be time for that. These guys are getting ready to pull out. Their transporter is here, and I'm pretty sure they're just waiting for dark. It will be full dark in a couple of hours, so we'll need to be ready to go. The good news is there's no vehicle. They're going in on foot." Winger settled in behind the binoculars, and Romero slipped away to relieve himself.

* * * *

As soon as Dawson realized Romero wasn't coming, he surmised that things were likely moving and decided he'd better get moving himself. He directed McCartney as they drove the old pickup through town to a small compound located on the east side of a secondary road, about five kilometers south of the main city. The compound looked like a half-farm, half-industrial site—which was, Dawson knew, precisely what it was. The sign on the wall alongside the ancient, rusty iron gate merely said "Women's Center." The old man attending the gate was clearly not there as a deterrent of any kind; he merely opened and closed the gate when people or, on rare occasion, a vehicle required passage.

Dawson had met the woman who operated this facility several years earlier, and managed to provide her with some assistance related to harassment by local Taliban thugs. Her name was Najia Koofi. Dawson had been in Ziranj for a completely unrelated reason, and Koofi was just getting her business started. Situated on an abandoned cotton-production site, the facility housed eight or ten women at the time, all war widows or women whose husbands, under the auspices of Sharia Law, had beaten their wives so badly they were disfigured or maimed.

Koofi provided the women with a place to live, food, and basic medical care. In return, the women worked. They either worked with the farm—growing vegetables and fruits, milking goats and raising chickens—or sewed clothing from donated materials in the small sewing building. Proceeds from the clothing and whatever surplus food they produced supplied the women with clothing, medical care, and electricity.

As they parked in front of the main building, Dawson could see that the number of people living in the compound had grown substantially. There were a few children now as well, and off to the side he could see a rudimentary playground area with a couple of swings and primitive teeter-totters.

When Dawson appeared in her doorway with his customary Afghan greeting, "As-salamu alaykum," the petite forty-something woman behind her desk, toiling over a column of figures in a small ledger, looked up at him as though she were seeing a ghost. Realizing at last who she was seeing, she abandoned her work and practically tripped over her own feet getting around the corner of the desk to greet him.

"Mr. Dawson!" she exclaimed. "It is wonderful to see you. I never thought I would ever see you again in this life!" Dawson had held his hand out to shake hers, but she swept it aside and wrapped herself around him in an unfettered hug. This behavior was not only uncharacteristic for Koofi, Dawson knew, but a horrendous taboo for Afghan women in general. The fact that he was seeing her with her head uncovered would have been a travesty for most of the women of the region. When she pushed back away from him, he could see that his tunic was spotted with her tears.

The office contained a basic wooden desk, a small plastic table, and two once-white plastic chairs. "How are you, my friend?" Dawson asked.

"Allah has been good," she said. "We have many more families here now. Almost twenty! And now there are some children. We are even thinking of starting a small school. What you did for us, it was truly a blessing from Allah. We would never have survived. We owe you so much, and now you are here, you must come see for yourself."

"Najia, we've been all through this," Dawson reminded her. "I did very little. It is *your* courage that these women see every day. It is *your* idea and *your* faith that keeps this dream alive. All of us who know you are so very proud of *you*." As Dawson knew all too well, the odds stacked against Koofi were truly overwhelming. Afghanistan's literacy rate hovered around twenty percent for adults, and for women it was less than half that.

Just two years before, Dawson had come across Koofi as she defended her enterprise against a combination of local government officials and Taliban sympathizers who advocated the most brutal aspects of Sharia Law in the areas surrounding Ziranj. He had managed, as a part of his work at that time, to develop a friendship of sorts with one of the local ANA commanders. Over the years, Dawson had discovered that many in the army were good men, devoted to cleaning up the Afghan government to the extent they could, at least in their respective locales. He had much less respect for the ANP, whom he found in many cases to be little better than criminals themselves.

Having worked closely with the ANA on a border security issue as a part of preventing the loss of some intellectual property, Dawson's team was able to not only close down the IP smuggling operation that included several ANP personnel, but also establish a partnership with Ahmadi, the ANA commander. This arrangement involved Dawson sending along about two hundred US dollars a month, automatically transferred from his personal account into the account of the commander in a Jordanian bank. The commander used the funds to pay off local ANP officials to leave the Women's Center alone, and to pass along any information they came across about people making trouble for the Center or for Koofi. For two years, as nearly as Dawson could tell, the partnership had been working. Koofi knew nothing of the ongoing arrangement. All she knew was that Dawson and his team had taken out the people who had showed up at the Center's gates every week demanding money and harassing the women.

Under the oppressive influence of the Taliban, women were mere property. Even the behavior Koofi had exhibited since Dawson's arrival moments before would have merited death by stoning in such circles. To open and operate a school, especially if that school taught girls how to read and write, was inviting real trouble. He knew that even when ISAF was operating at its peak within the country in 2011 and 2012, eighty-seven percent of women surveyed by international health care workers reported domestic abuse. The majority of schools built by international forces during Operation Enduring Freedom began closing behind the departing backs of phased-out foreign forces in 2012. There were reports of schoolgirls poisoned and beaten, head teachers assassinated, and classrooms firebombed. The majority of girls didn't stay on after fifth grade, and nine out of ten fifteen-year-old girls remained illiterate. Under such conditions, people like Koofi exhibited superhuman courage to keep the hope of future equality alive in the hearts of Afghan women.

"I would be honored to see it all, Najia. But before we walk together, I must tell you I am here seeking your help," Dawson said.

But before he could continue, she interrupted, "Anything I have is yours, Mr. Dawson, anything at all."

"Thank you, Najia, I know you mean that," he said. "You are among my very closest friends." Dawson did not understand, he reflected later, the impact of those words. They meant more than gold to this woman who had sacrificed so much and been shunned by so many. "But what I need from you is something you may not even be able to do. I need help finding someone who knows about a captured American soldier. I believe he is being held in Iran."

She stepped back one pace and gazed at him steadily. "Did someone send you to rescue him?" she asked.

"Yes. His wife and young son," Dawson said.

"Yes," Koofi responded with a wan smile, "I should have known. Is this soldier being held near Ziranj?"

"I believe so, but I am not certain. He was taken from here just a couple of months ago," he said.

"Please," she said, "wait here," and she pointed to a chair. "I will be back in two minutes." With that, she swept out of the room and closed the door behind her.

When she returned, she was accompanied by a pretty young woman, a girl really. She appeared to be about fourteen and was carrying a tray with a carafe of hot tea, a small container of brownish crystallized sugar, and two cups. Dawson noticed that the girl was missing two fingers of her right hand. "Thank you, Fawzia," Koofi said.

The girl looked up at Dawson and smiled, and then continued smiling as she turned her gaze to Koofi, saying, "You're welcome, Ma'am," and padded silently from the room.

As Koofi poured tea for them both and then sat in the other plastic chair in the office, she told Dawson: "Fawzia fled to me after losing her fingers. Her father died several years ago fighting the Taliban. Her older brother, Mohammad, had been involved in skirmishes with them as well, and then joined the ANA. After they found out who he was, the Taliban targeted his family. They raped and then killed Fawzia's mother, and took the two fingers from her. They told her they would be back for two more each time they encountered her brother. She has been with me for over a year now, and is a delightful girl. She is like my own daughter. And as you can see, she is studying English."

"Quite successfully, too," Dawson remarked. "That's the first time I've ever heard an Afghan of either gender use the word 'Ma'am.'"

"Now, back to the help you need," Koofi said. "I have sent for a friend of mine, a medical doctor, who I believe may be of assistance. He is Dr. Mohammad Heidari, and his work takes him across the border into Iran frequently. He knows many of the people who know about such things. I trust him, Mr. Dawson. He has helped me many times with the women and children here, even when it was unsafe." They finished their tea, and Koofi caught Dawson up on the progress they had made at the Women's Center. Then she escorted him around the compound, introducing him as her "great friend," and an "instrument of Allah."

Dawson counted at least eighteen women, spanning a wide range of ages, and a half dozen children at various places. The buildings were all vintage 1950s, but had been well kept. There was one building which was a dormitory, one that was a kitchen/dining room/office, and one that was the workshop with twenty-four sewing machines. Then there was an outbuilding that served as a barn, a fenced-off yard containing a few goats, and another small fenced-off area with about a dozen chickens and a small chicken coop.

On the west side of the barn, where it was not easy to see from the street or anywhere else in the compound, was a garden that was large by Afghan standards, and several fruit trees. The garden provided some corn, watermelon, squash, onions, beans, sugar beets, and eggplant. The trees included apricot, pomegranate, and apples. As Dawson knew, they could have made the equivalent of several thousand US dollars each year if they had simply used the ground for poppy and hemp, but the sale of such crops would have brought unwanted attention from the Taliban. The compound had running water, a small generator, and even grid-based electricity for most of the day each day.

In light of the political and economic situation, Dawson thought Koofi had done a remarkable job, and he told her so as they walked back toward her office. She smiled up at him and said, "I thank you for saying this, Mr. Dawson. It has been very much work, but I am happy for these women and their families. But now I am faced with a very big decision, and I do not know what to do."

"Oh?" Dawson asked. "And what is that decision, Najia?"

She sipped her tea quietly for a moment, and then said, "You remember the army commander you worked with when you helped us two years ago? Kaurosh Ahmadi?"

"Yes, of course I do. Why do you ask?"

Koofi's cheeks flushed as she swallowed hard and continued. "He is a good man. He stops by every two weeks or so and checks to make sure we are well. Sometimes he even brings us things—a bag of flour, a roll of cloth for our sewing, things like that. And I think he has told people that he has a special interest in us here. So people do not make trouble for us. Do you see what I mean?"

"Yes," Dawson said, wondering where the conversation was going. "Like you, I believe Commander Ahmadi is a good man."

At this, Koofi stopped abruptly and turned to Dawson. "He has asked me to become his wife."

"Oh, I see," Dawson said, as the ramifications of this situation began to unfurl in his mind. "That is, well, I guess I should be offering my congratulations. Whether you decide to accept or not, it is an honor to be asked for your hand in marriage by such a man, is it not?"

"Yes, it is," she said. She looked into her tea cup. "I am very flattered, especially at my age, to be asked such a thing. It is unusual to have a man ask me personally, instead of asking a family member to answer on my behalf. It is very special."

"Do you *want* to marry him?" Dawson asked.

She looked up at him and then off into the distance. After a moment, she looked back at him and held his gaze. "I do not know. He is honorable and respected, and I shall not receive such an offer again, I am sure. And I think he would continue to offer me some support and protection for the Women's Center here. But he is already married to a woman who has been a good wife to him for many years. I would be his *second* wife. I know you Americans do not understand this, but it is a very ... *pichida* ... how do you say ... ah, complicated. Yes, it is a very complicated thing."

Holy cow! Dawson thought, *I have absolutely NO idea what to say here!* The concept was certainly not a new one. He knew Islamic men could marry several wives if they could afford them. But a situation in which someone who was a friend of his, a person he cared about and respected, was considering entering such a polygamous relationship as one of multiple wives ... well, he had absolutely no idea how to respond. Finally, he simply said, "Najia, do you love him?"

She looked up at him with an odd expression, and, before she could respond, McCartney walked up along with the old man who had been tending the front gate when they arrived. McCartney had been sitting with the old sentry at the gate house and had obviously gotten to know him at least a little.

"Sorry to interrupt," McCartney said, "but Sabah here says he has a bit of an urgent message for the lady." At that point, the old man began speaking in Dari.

At length, Koofi turned to Dawson and said, "My friend Dr. Heidari will be here within the hour. He can help you with the search for the American soldier."

Dawson wondered: *Did the situation just get better or just get worse?* But to Koofi, he smiled and said, "Thank you, Najia. I hope this does not put you in any additional danger."

"I trust Dr. Heidari completely," she replied. "You will see. He, too, is an honorable man." This brought Dawson back to their earlier discussion about Commander Ahmadi, and made him very happy for the current distraction from that conversation with his friend.

"How long have you known this doctor?" Dawson asked.

"I knew him before I became involved in all of this," she replied, "since I was in my early twenties. He was a friend of my father's—they studied medicine together in Kuwait—but he was kind of an unknown, a mystery, I think you would say. He was never married that I know of, and I don't really know where he lives. He works in a clinic in Ziranj, but also works in clinics in Herat and I think also in Zabol and Zahedan in Iran. His mother was Iranian, I think. He's older now, almost sixty, but still he travels between his clinics. We were fortunate Sabah was able to get through to him so quickly. They were finishing up for the day, and the doctor said he would come immediately."

Dawson hoped the doctor would arrive soon. Darkness was indeed falling, and he wondered how Winger and Romero were doing.

CHAPTER 15

About three kilometers upriver, Winger and Romero came to a small bridge that seemed to have been built for a railroad that never arrived. They'd been following Fengche and his two companions for over ten kilometers. Dressed in local garb and carrying their primary weapons slung under loose-fitting Tumbaan tunics, they skirted refugee camps and construction sites, avoiding people and lights. With the rest of their equipment in ordinary draw-string sacks, they looked common enough to avoid suspicion even if seen.

There were no railroad tracks over the bridge, and it was only wide enough for a single vehicle. It seemed to Winger, as he watched Fengche's transporter scramble up the hillside to approach the guard shack, that motorcycles and "tuc-tucs," the three-wheeled vehicles fashioned locally from motorcycles to support transport of local produce, were the only vehicles that could possibly make use of such a narrow passage. On the Afghan side of the bridge, there was a single ANP pickup truck, one of the many thousand dark green Ford Rangers used by the Afghan National Police for patrols and transportation.

Romero held up two fingers, and Winger nodded. Through night vision binoculars, Romero could see only two ANP types at the bridge, one walking around and smoking outside and the other tipped back in a chair inside the guard shack, probably asleep. He wasn't moving. They watched the transporter clamber up onto the unpaved roadway and walk into sight of the guard. If the guard was startled, he didn't show it. He merely moved the AK-47 from its sling to hold it casually in his hands. He didn't bother to alert the other guard that someone was approaching.

A quick conversation ensued, which clearly involved the price of looking the other way while the transporter did his job. The Americans watched as a price was agreed on and funds changed hands. Then, while the transporter waited, the guard with whom he had negotiated roused his sleeping companion, and the two men climbed into their pickup truck and drove about half a kilometer up the road. It was a classic case of looking the other way. The transporter then walked across the bridge, which took him about five minutes, and repeated the process on the Iranian side.

Winger and Romero could see that the Iranian checkpoint was more modern. It looked as though it might even contain a telephone and electric lights. However, the same kind of two-man checkpoint team was deployed there, and the transporter was able to achieve the same result with the handover of some funds. The two guards simply walked some distance away from their post, broke out either cigarettes or joints, and started puffing away.

"The way the world works," Winger whispered. He and Romero both knew it was probably the safest method for everyone involved. By not seeing who or what was being transported, the guards would have no details to trip over if questioned later. Whether saving their skins, getting a handsome bribe, or accommodating a transporter who was well connected, looking the other way was probably the best way for the guards to stay alive. Fengche's party, signaled in by the transporter, followed his earlier path. They climbed along the bank and came out somewhat closer to the bridge itself, and began a rapid hunched-over walk across the bridge.

By this time, Winger and Romero were in position about thirty meters behind them, moving in the soft sandy earth along the riverbank and staying as close to cover as possible. When Fengche's party was almost across the bridge, the Americans followed in their tracks. As they reached the other side, one of the Iranian guards started to turn back to resume his duties. He caught a glimpse of the men moving off the bridge, but, luckily for Winger and Romero, must have assumed he hadn't waited long for the transporter's party to cross because he immediately averted his eyes again. Neither he nor his companion looked that way again for an additional five minutes, by which time Fengche's party, with Winger and Romero in silent pursuit, were long gone.

* * * *

Dr. Heidari's 2005 Iranian-made Paykan sedan pulled through the gate of the Women's Center. The driver's side door creaked open and the elderly gentleman climbed out and headed for the main entrance. Heidari was a pleasant enough looking man with little hair left on top of his head, but a long scraggly beard with more gray and white than black left in it. He wore small, round glasses, and one of the lenses was cracked along one corner. He seemed a serious man, but smiled warmly when he saw Koofi.

The next ninety minutes were spent in Koofi's office, with Dawson getting to know Heidari and explaining what he needed. Dawson showed Heidari a photograph of Colonel Menlo, and a photograph of Fengche. "You are indeed fortunate to know our dear friend Najia," Heidari said after listening quietly and then carefully considering Dawson's request for help. "There is no amount of money that would cause me to take such a risk, but because you obviously mean so much to her, I will help you. And I am in an unusual position to do so, because I am the doctor who provided medical care for your soldier."

Dawson sat back in his chair. It seemed like an impossible coincidence, but when he thought about it, Heidari was a traveling physician who covered clinics on both sides of the border. He was exactly the type of medical help someone like Fengche would look for.

Heidari continued, "Two men, including this man," he said, pointing to the photo of Fengche, "approached me as I was leaving the clinic in Zabol several weeks ago. They said they had an injured friend who badly needed attention but could not be moved. I told them I did not do such work. I have had bad experiences with going out into the countryside, especially here in Afghanistan. Iran is much safer for me, but there is still some danger. But *this* man," he pointed to the photograph, "made it clear to me it was not a request. He said I would be well paid, but that I had no choice. I was going with them." He shrugged and continued, "So I went. The building where he is kept used to be a tractor repair shop. It is about twenty kilometers north of Zahedan, almost exactly west of the point where Pakistan borders Afghanistan."

"Zahedan?" Dawson asked.

"Yes," the doctor said. "I knew this was some kind of trouble, because Zahedan is a major city. They have hospitals and even an airport there. It would be easy to get good medical care if they had money."

"So do you believe you could find that place again?" Dawson asked.

"Oh, I have no doubt of it," Heidari replied. "I would like very much to help this man. He is in great pain, and they do not care. They allowed me to treat his wounds, because they required stitches, and he had lost a great deal of blood. But they would not allow me to use any medicines to help him with the pain. I was able to apply some topical treatment around the wounds before I did stitching, but that was all. Otherwise I was only able to administer antibiotics to reduce the chances of infection. They were not feeding him properly, either, which is what he needs to replace the lost blood and repair the damaged tissue. I would like to get him to a hospital and treat him properly."

"Did it look as though they had been torturing him?' Dawson asked.

"No, not at that point," Heidari replied. "But he would not have been able to withstand it. He was too weak."

"What kind of wounds did he have?" Dawson asked.

"He had a bullet wound in his torso here," Heidari said, pointing to his side. "It was not bad. It missed vital organs and passed through his body. But he also had a wound from a blade, which caused me some concern. It was a greater risk of infection because the blade had nicked his lung. His breathing was labored and there was internal bleeding. I managed to get the bleeding stopped, and made it possible for him to relieve himself. But he had to have fluids and be kept clean. They had a woman who was helping with those things. I think she lived close by."

"If I can get to him, do you think he can be moved?" Dawson asked.

Again, Heidari shrugged. "If he has been provided with food and water, if his wounds did not become infected, and if he has not been injured further," he replied. "But if any of those things has happened, he is probably already dead."

Dawson thought about that. If Fengche really was headed to Colonel Menlo, which seemed apparent now, Menlo must still be alive.

"Did they ask you to come back to check on him?' Dawson asked.

"No," Heidari replied, "and they made it clear that if I ever told anyone about this visit they would kill me. But I have been threatened many times in my life, Mr. Dawson, and I am getting to be an old man. Still, I had no reason to mention it to anyone before now."

Dawson was quiet for a moment, then he looked at the old man. "Doctor Heidari, I know this is a very difficult thing, but can you help me get across the border into Iran, and to this location?"

The doctor didn't hesitate. "Yes," he replied. "I can do this. I am a doctor, and I will do it for the patient and for Najia. But if I help you, we must go tonight. I must be in Zabol in the morning. Also, the crossing guards I know best are on duty at night. In the daytime, this will be much more difficult, maybe even impossible."

"I can be ready in ten minutes," Dawson said.

"Absolutely not!" Koofi exclaimed. "We have prepared dinner for you, and you will both eat before you undertake this journey. I will not let you go on an empty stomach!" Dawson and Heidari looked at each other, and acquiesced. Dawson was hungry anyway. In his bag he had a half dozen Clif Bars, removed from their commercial wrappers and encased in airtight bags. They would keep him nourished in a pinch, but they were no substitute for a hot meal. He knew it might be a while before he had another such offer.

An hour later, Dawson found himself in the back seat of Heidari's sedan, wrapped in a blanket. Heidari had hung a bag of saline solution from a shirt hanger, with the plastic tube taped to his arm rather than attached to a needle. It wouldn't fool anyone who inspected it closely, but made it look very official in a medical way, Dawson thought. The bulk of Dawson's weapons were under his tunic and beneath the blanket, but he had a few items that had to be stowed elsewhere. Heidari concealed these beneath his own medical supplies as best he could.

As they approached the checkpoint, Heidari said, "Now, Mr. Dawson, if they speak to you, which I do not expect, just keep repeating 'Inja dard mikonad.' Say it as though you are in much pain, so your accent will not be noticeable. Understand?"

"I think so," Dawson replied. "Inja dard mikonad. What does it mean?"

"It means 'it hurts right here,'" Heidari explained, "and believe me, when I explain why I am transporting you for medical attention, they will not want to see where 'right here' is."

Dawson smiled at this, and began groaning and repeating the phrase through clenched teeth.

As it turned out, although it added to the effect, Dawson never needed the phrase. The first checkpoint required the customary bribe, and Heidari was moved to the front of the line owing more to the size of the bribe and the familiarity of the man than to the perceived medical emergency. The border crossing guards never did more than glance at the prone figure in the back seat of the familiar sedan. At the Iranian side of the checkpoint, it took a bit longer. This wasn't because of any suspicion, but because an oil tanker had finally run out of fuel waiting in line and, as a result, stopped all ingress and egress for more than an hour. It struck Dawson as ironic that a truck full of oil was helpless without a tank of gasoline. The Iranians were more careful, stamping Heidari's paperwork, but never bothering to try to get adequate passport information from the patient. Few Afghans had an official passport, and usually an adequate bribe allowed medical emergencies to pass with little trouble.

As soon as they were away from the checkpoint, Dawson checked the time and turned on his Iranian cell. He went to the drafts folder of the Gmail account and alerted Winger and Romero that he was in country and en route to the target destination. He would have liked to share more, but knew it was too dangerous. He would have to await their reply and hope for the best. It was midnight as they were drawing near their destination. Dawson asked for Heidari's cell number, and committed it to memory. He didn't want to enter it into his own burner phone in case it was discovered later as it would have been impossible for Heidari to explain what an American operative was doing with his cell number should it be found on him.

When they arrived at their destination, Dawson could see the building Heidari had described was one of a long string of unfired brick buildings, many of which had roll-up metal doors that acted as storefronts. The doors were also the only pedestrian access. There were no windows on the ground floor. A few of the buildings had two stories, and those buildings had windows in the second-story walls, front and back.

One of the two-story buildings still sported a faded sign depicting a tractor that looked to Dawson like a knock-off of a red Massey Fergusson. It had the distinction of having both a roll-up metal door for the repair area and a pedestrian door which likely led to an office. It was still deep in the night, and there were no lights in any of the buildings. There were also no street lights, and trash was strewn along the barely paved street.

"When you were here before, did you notice whether any of these buildings were unoccupied?" Dawson whispered to Heidari.

The doctor thought about that for a moment, and then said: "That one on the end, I think," he replied. "I remember because the metal door was jammed and clearly broken, just as it is now. It had obviously been unused for a long time. There may be others as well, but I did not notice."

"I'll grab my things and let you move on to your rounds, Doctor," Dawson said. He reached over the seat and patted Heidari on the shoulder. "Thank you very much for your help."

Heidari popped open the trunk, and Dawson quietly fished his remaining equipment from the medical supply containers. Then he slipped quietly along the roadway to the building Heidari had pointed out. Heidari slowly drove away, not engaging his headlights until he was almost a kilometer in the distance. The street was deserted. Eerily quiet. The only sound of life was the distant bark of a dog somewhere past the other end of the line of buildings.

Dawson quickly pulled on night vision goggles and knelt to scan the interior of the building with the broken door. Heidari was right; there were no signs of life. The building looked as though it had once been a motorcycle and bicycle repair shop, but it had clearly been unused for years. Dawson slid his equipment bag under the metal door and then rolled in behind it. With the aid of his night vision goggles and an occasional illumination from his tiny lanyard-borne flashlight, Dawson set up camp in a corner of the building least visible from the outside. The building had a concrete floor, but was dirty and smelled of oil and animal feces. Once set up, he scouted for another way out of the building and found a small air vent in the back of the structure that looked as though he could get out of it if he had to. He peered out the window. There wasn't much to cover his escape once he was through the opening, though. He didn't like it, but it was what it was. Then it was time to check his phone.

* * * *

About twenty kilometers north of Dawson's position, Winger and Romero were driving south in a newly acquired jingle truck, a large farm truck extensively "pimped out" with gaudy paint jobs and ostentatious accoutrements draped over every visible surface. Jingle trucks originated in Pakistan, but rapidly became popular across many Middle Eastern countries in the 1990s. They became known as jingle trucks because of the jingling sound from the many chains typically hanging from their bumpers. It was not a vehicle that either Winger or Romero would have chosen, but when it became clear the transporter escorting Fengche's group had a Mercedes waiting for them, it was the expeditious choice. It was nearby, easily hot-wired, and likely to attract little attention in that part of the country. Nursing it along the road at more than forty kph was a struggle because it was badly out of alignment and wobbled dangerously when faster speeds were attempted.

Nonetheless, using no headlights about half of the time, Winger was able to keep the tail lights of the Mercedes in view. Romero checked the cell phone at 0230 hours, and saw the text from Dawson. It outlined his position and said, "In building with broken door." As nearly as he and Winger could tell, they were getting very close to the coordinates Dawson had provided.

Romero typed back: "Inbound. ETA fifteen mikes." When they saw the Mercedes turn left onto the destination's street, Winger continued on past

Dawson's location and began to look for a place where the truck could be hidden from view. It took over thirty minutes because there weren't many good choices, but Winger finally located a small gorge that provided some obscurity. Pulling the truck off the road, he could get it far enough down the decline to prevent all but the very top of the vehicle from being seen from the roadway. Someone would have to be looking for it to see it from there. Then Winger and Romero grabbed their equipment bags from the back of the truck and headed back on foot to find the building with the broken door.

Dawson saw Fengche's Mercedes pull up and three occupants roll out. He watched as Fengche pulled a bag from the trunk of the car before the three men went inside. Then one came almost immediately back out and stood in the street smoking a cigarette, leaning back against the wall. A dim light went on for about five minutes. Fengche stepped outside again and urinated along the street as he spoke to the man who was smoking. Then they both went back inside, and about a minute later the light went out. About fifteen minutes later, he saw Romero, followed a minute later by Winger, approaching his building. *So far so good.*

CHAPTER 16

The testing of Salacia with the new adhesive in place was well under way when Menlo returned from lunch. She studied the resulting efficiency of the laser as exhibited in the tank, and couldn't believe what she was seeing. She was still studying the results when Wu walked through the door, smiling from ear to ear. "I think you owe me dinner!" she called out, still walking across the lab.

"Joan, this is amazing!" Menlo replied. "How did you ever come up with an adhesive that yields this clarity and resistance to thermal variation? I've never seen anything like this in the lab."

"Well," said Wu, "like I said, I have a friend, Vickie Albota, in the R&D lab up at JDSU in Ottawa. I called her up and asked her whether she could share the chemical formula of an adhesive for the attachment of a crystalline lens to the end of an optic fiber. They do that stuff all the time up there, splitting beams of light with prisms and mirrors to redirect signals inside router switches for commercial customers. Anyway, she said, 'No, I can't.'"

"Well, then, how did you get it if she wouldn't share it with you?" Menlo asked, brow furrowed.

"I didn't *have* to," Wu beamed.

"You didn't have to? Then how—"

"I didn't have to because what she uses, and what you are seeing here, is the result of applying a commercial off-the-shelf adhesive."

Menlo crossed her arms across her chest. "So you're telling me that this adhesive, which looks to me as though it's yielding an optical transmission performance level improvement of nearly fifteen percent—"

"14.912%, to be precise," Wu interjected.

"OK, 14.912%, and it is actually something I can buy at Home Depot?"

"Sure, if you want to drive that far," Wu replied impishly. "But Walgreen's is closer. It cost me $2.99 for enough to do about forty lenses."

"What *is* it?" Menlo demanded.

Wu laughed. "It's cyanoacrylate, $C_5H_5NO_2$."

Menlo knew Wu was purposefully making this excruciating, and enjoying every moment. "Cyanoacrylate …." Menlo turned it over in her mind. "Wait a minute. You're kidding me, Joan. You're telling me this is *Superglue*?"

"Bingo!" Wu laughed.

Menlo was astonished. "Superglue! Holy…."

"Exactly," Wu said, "and I'm thinking of Italian for dinner. Portabellos in Arlington, maybe?"

"Yes, I'd say you've earned dinner, all right," Menlo replied. "Is there any reason to think the adhesion won't be durable over time?"

"None that I can foresee," Wu said. "Nancy said they use it all the time. And get this, the anionic polymerization actually gets stronger in the presence of water, even water vapor, and the fact that salt water is involved seems to have no impact on the process at all."

"Unbelievable." Menlo shook her head. "I don't know if it would even have occurred to me … *ever*."

"Ah," Wu smiled, "I like the sound of that. Sounds like job security to me."

"Tell you what," Menlo said. "We were going to meet over at Lake Fairfax Park with the kids on Saturday anyway, right? Why don't we just bring them all back to my place afterward, leave them with a sitter, and go on to Portabellos from there? That will give us a chance for a quick shower at my house between the park and dinner. We can order pizza for the kids as we head out the door."

"Sounds perfect!" Wu replied. "You're on—and you're buying."

An hour later, Menlo stopped by Brystol's office. "Hi, Margaret. Is he still in?" Menlo asked as she came through the door.

"Oh, yes, dear. He's in. But let me check to see whether he is in the middle of something." She punched her intercom button.

"Hello again," she smiled into the phone. "Dr. Menlo is here and would like to see you for a moment." She paused and listened. "All right, then. Thank you." She replaced the receiver and looked up at Menlo. "You can go right in, dear," Margaret said. Menlo opened the door and stepped inside. Brystol was seated at his desk, digging through a stack of papers, apparently in search of something.

He looked up briefly and a smile flickered across his face: "Yes, Carolyn, let me guess, you'd like to do lunch all over again and get dessert this time?" Brystol chuckled.

"No, but you're close. Actually I stopped by to tell you that I'm buying dinner this weekend for Joan Wu."

"Oh?" Brystol stopped looking through his papers now and appeared to be completely confused.

"Actually, *you're* buying Joan dinner this weekend. I'm putting it on the Foundation credit card." She smiled. "Joan just solved the last significant technical problem in the Salacia system. It was the problem we had with lens adhesion."

"Incredible!" Brystol said. "How did she do it? Some kind of diffusion bonding process?"

"No. The amazing thing is that she discovered a commercial off-the-shelf adhesive which not only does the job, but enhances optical performance characteristics by fifteen percent."

"That *is* worth dinner— and a nice bonus as well."

"I'm going to pass that along," Menlo warned, "and you know Joan. She's not likely to forget it come end of the year. Anyway, there's nothing stopping us now. I'm going to call our folks at Norfolk tomorrow, and get the field trial fit-ups started. We are definitely on our way."

"Outstanding!" Brystol said. "Absolutely outstanding!"

As she left Brystol's office, she closed the door behind her and Margaret said, "Congratulations, dear! I couldn't help overhearing since you left the office door open. I must say that is wonderful news."

"Thank you, Margaret," Menlo replied cheerfully, and headed back down to the lab.

The next two days were a blur, with calls made to start production and prepare for fit-up of the full-scale Salacia system on a Ticonderoga-class vessel, the USS Vicksburg. When they were designed, the Ticonderoga-class had the most powerful electronic warfare equipment in the US Navy, as well as the most advanced underwater surveillance system. As such, they were equipped with sufficient energy to pilot the Salacia system for initial runs, though sustained operation at peak performance would require some bolstering of the power plant and power translation mechanisms.

Ticonderoga-class vessels are multi-role warships. They can utilize their Mark41 vertical launch systems to launch Tomahawk cruise missiles, striking strategic or tactical targets, and fire long-range standard antiaircraft missiles for air defense and against anti-ship missiles. They're also equipped with LAMPS III helicopters and sonar systems, enabling them to perform antisubmarine missions. This versatility made them an excellent proving ground for Salacia, and if the system worked as demonstrated at full scale, the next such deployment would likely be an aircraft carrier. Once full-rate production was under way, Menlo's team would switch over to address the application of Salacia to submarines and underwater drones. Underwater vessels offered unique challenges, but Menlo was confident they could be surmounted. Still, as each day went by without further word from Dawson, her worry—and her level of distraction—grew. She had checked the Gmail account faithfully twice each day, but no additional word had arrived since the "We are moving" signal. She tried to put it out of her mind and concentrate on her work, but every day with no word made that a bigger challenge.

* * * *

While Menlo arranged contractors and suppliers, and managed the assembly and installation crews at Norfolk Naval Shipyards, Jing-ti made his own arrangements from a Starbucks about thirty kilometers away. He and Bi-shou were seated at a corner table in the coffee shop with the frenetic buzz of the bustling morning commuters engulfing them. Their choice of location was designed to make eavesdropping very difficult if someone had been attempting it. Bi-shou was striking in a tight short-sleeved gray cashmere sweater and a single strand of pearls, her hair swept back in an opal clasp on one side, and falling in luxurious curls from the other. Jing-ti, as always, was impeccably dressed in a charcoal Armani suit and fringed wing-tips. They made an attractive pair—a typical DC power couple.

"My information is that Menlo has completed her system and, with all the technical problems solved, it is time to obtain her services on a full-time basis," Jing-ti said. "I need you to mount operations to do that sometime over the next week, the sooner the better. I believe it will be easier to gain Dr. Menlo's cooperation if we have her son Andrew in our care as well. I have made arrangements for their housing and management on one of the Diayou Islands, and we should be prepared for them any time after next weekend. I also need you to obtain at least one-third of the crystalline material that was acquired by the Brystol Foundation. Our information is that it is stored onsite, at the Foundation."

"So, our arrangement is that you want me to kidnap Dr. Menlo and her son Andrew," Bi-shou said. "I presume you want them unharmed?"

"Yes," Jing-ti replied.

"And you want me to provide their housing and life support for some period of time after they are abducted?"

"Yes," he said again.

"And do you plan to transport them to the island yourself, or do you want me to take care of that for you?"

"I have that taken care of," Jing-ti said. "I just need to know where you have them so I can pick them up for transport."

"And you expect this pickup to be made within two weeks from today?" Bi-shou asked.

"Yes," Jing-ti replied again, "but prepare for an additional week just as a contingency."

"Of course," Bi-shou replied.

"Do you know whether either Dr. Menlo or her child have any medical conditions or other factors that demand special care or treatment, or specific dietary needs?"

"None were listed in our files, but I would not consider that a guarantee. Is this research that you can do?"

"Of course," Bi-shou said, adding coquettishly: "In your case, Jing-ti," she practically purred, "please consider me to be a *full-service* provider." Before he could even think of a way to respond, she continued: "Is there any specific day you would consider a drop-dead date for the abduction?"

"No, not precisely," he said. "My plan has a window of time for this task which opened with the completion of the last technology enabler for the system. That occurred two days ago. The task must be completed before the window closes, and that is triggered by Dr. Menlo's completion of this phase of the program."

"And what is the *next* phase?" Bi-shou asked.

Jing-ti thought about this for a moment, and said: "I'm not sure you need to know that, Bi-shou."

The beautiful assassin leaned closer, her fragrance enveloping Jing-ti in an intoxicating fog, and spoke softly through an exaggerated pout, "You don't trust me, Jing-ti? You *should*. I will soon be holding your most precious objects. Your 'crown jewels,' so to speak," she said suggestively.

"Very well," Jing-ti relented, even though in the back of his mind he knew better. "The next phase after surface vessels is submarines and underwater drones. It is entirely possible, with the help of Menlo and the critical materials, for China to come abreast of the Americans—perhaps even surpass them with the deployment of their own technology if we are extremely fortunate. But if they are able to surmount the challenges of applying Salacia to underwater vessels, it will be decades before China achieves parity, if it is ever achieved at all."

"Ah," she sighed, resting back again in her chair. "I see. And so really there is no great urgency. Even if the abduction does not happen for even a month or longer, it will not matter except that it will delay the start of Dr. Menlo's services on your behalf."

"That may be true, but then again it may not be," Jing-ti replied. "There are other events in motion right now that could impact the doctor's frame of mind and our ability to influence her. They are transpiring elsewhere, and I have limited control over them. In order to mitigate the risk of those events taking an unfortunate turn, the sooner this abduction occurs the better."

"This has something to do with Dr. Menlo's husband?" Bi-shou asked. It was more of an observation than a question, but they both knew she was right. And they both knew that Carolyn Menlo's state of mind and willingness to cooperate would be greatly influenced by whatever happened to her husband. For the sake of their country—and their own lives—they hoped whoever was handling Colonel Menlo would not fail.

CHAPTER 17

About twelve hours before the rendezvous at Starbucks, things started to heat up on the other side of the planet. Dawson, Winger, and Romero were exhausted. Since Dawson was confident Fengche and his men were sleeping, he decided that given the arduous activity that lay ahead of them, the best way to take advantage of that lull in activity was to get a few hours of sleep themselves. It would be irresponsible to undertake the next phase of the operation if they couldn't keep their eyes open. So they took turns on sentry duty while the other two slept. By 0515 hours, they had each got at least three hours.

They awoke to the muffled tone of Dawson's wristwatch beeping. Each of them downed a bottle of liquid energy and ate a Clif Bar while reviewing their game plan. When they were all suited up and ready to go, Winger led the way. Romero backed him up, followed by Dawson.

Outside the building Menlo and Fengche were in, the sentry was sitting on the ground at the base of the wall just outside the door. He was sound asleep, chin on chest. Winger slipped up alongside the man and killed him with a single knife thrust, his left hand over the man's mouth to prevent an outcry. It left him in nearly the same position, so aside from the growing pool of blood around one side, he wouldn't likely attract immediate attention.

Romero scanned the interior of the first floor with a fiber optic device equipped with night vision technology. He snaked it around the edge of the window so it maintained a very small profile, and then held up two fingers. There were two bad guys on the first floor, and both appeared to be asleep. Winger slowly pushed down on the crude door latch, and began to push open the door. About halfway, the door creaked and Winger stopped. As Romero watched, one of the men stirred. He roused himself, shook himself awake like a large wet dog trying to dry off after a swim, and stumbled wearily toward the door.

Romero figured the man was likely heading outside to relieve himself. He signaled Winger, who backed up one pace and flattened himself against the wall. The door swung open, and the man stumbled outside. He stood just outside the door for what seemed to Romero to be an eternity, stretching himself. Then it seemed to occur to him that there should be a sentry there. He glanced down, saw the dark figure of the man still in a sleeping position against the wall, and muttered a *Hmpf* to himself, turned to walk a few paces and take care of his intended task. Two steps along the wall he was confronted by Romero, who struck him in the throat with the butt of his rifle and finished him with his knife as he fell into a heap on the ground. *Two down. How many more inside?*

They entered quickly then, knives resheathed and rifles trained. There was indeed one man left on the first floor. He proved surprisingly responsive for a man just awakened in conditions of near darkness. He appeared to have heard the second man fall, and was rolling to his feet and shouting. He pulled an old, stockless AK-47 up and began to fire. He had made no real attempt to aim beyond merely pointing and spraying, so although the noise and debris shower was impressive, no rounds struck Winger or Romero, both of whom were inside by that time.

They had entered, Winger high and Romero low, and immediately fanned out to the sides, crouched and looking over the tops of their rifles through night vision goggles. Winger returned fire first, and since the newly awakened man had not had time to seek cover, he toppled over backwards with a choked scream, careening over a small table with a few dishes and some radio gear. There was a narrow wooden staircase in the northeast corner of the structure, where Winger and Romero could immediately hear movement and muffled shouting overhead.

The room they had entered had clearly been the office of the defunct tractor repair building. The man they had just killed, and his two companions outside, had been sleeping on pallets on the floor. There was a small gas stove in one corner, and a sink with a water faucet, all of which had clearly seen better days. The windows were just gaping holes in the walls—no glass and no curtains. There was one window in the front, where Romero had been surveying the interior, and one in the back. There was also an interior door, which served as the point of egress between the office area they occupied and the larger space where tractors had been repaired. The door was closed and locked.

Upstairs, Fengche and his remaining team member had been asleep on the only two actual beds in the building. The sounds below awakened them immediately. Fengche's companion, an Iranian criminal and former soldier who had moved on to kidnapping, smuggling, and strong-arm robbery, grabbed his AK-47 and headed for the stairs. Fengche looked around and realized that descending the stairs with the other man would be foolish, likely suicidal. He grabbed the only other firearm in the room—a twelve-gage Remington shotgun with slugs, which certainly would not have been his weapon of choice—and headed for the window. He dropped quietly to the ground after squeezing through the opening, and ran to the front door.

Dawson entered about five seconds after his two companions, and although he, too, heard the noises coming from above their heads, he moved immediately toward the door that led to the larger repair facility. He had just taken up a position to the side of the door, back to the wall, and was reaching over to pull down on the lever to open the door, when the first burst of gunfire erupted from a figure on the stairs. The figure leapt from somewhere at the top of the stairs onto a point near the bottom step.

Although dawn was breaking, it was still dark and there was no way to discern and evaluate specific targets. Without night vision goggles, the man on the stairs fired in an arc from his waist, spraying the room at chest level to the men on the ground floor. Romero was in the best position to return fire, and his first shot struck the man in his left thigh. Romero was revectoring his weapon for a center mass shot when Fengche crashed through the door.

Startled by the sound, the split-second distraction caused Romero's second round to hit the man's shoulder, sending him spinning to the floor two steps below. By that time, however, Fengche had discerned Romero's position. Fengche fired and struck Romero in the rib cage, the bullet glancing off of Romero's flak jacket and cracking two of his ribs as it knocked the wind out of him and sent him sailing backward onto the floor.

Winger spun away from the stairway to face the front door. Fengche moved deeper into the darkness, away from Winger. But with his night vision goggles in place, Winger had little trouble with the darkness. He immediately fired a three-round burst, striking Fengche with two of the rounds. The first impacted Fengche's right arm, rendering it useless. The second round fractured the bone just above the ball-and-socket juncture and drove him back into some old wooden furniture, which splintered beneath him as he fell.

Fengche was still conscious, but without the use of his right arm, his options were few. Just a couple of meters from his left hand, his companion's AK-47 lay on the floor. He lunged for it, which took him out of Winger's sightline behind the overturned table and other furniture. Winger moved to his left to gain another line of fire when he heard Dawson squeeze off two rounds from his position near the door. Neither of those shots struck home, though, as he had no better firing line than Winger. Dawson just wanted to ensure Fengche's options were limited.

The man shot on the stairwell, now bleeding heavily from the thigh and the shoulder, begin inching his way toward the small pile of armaments stashed next to one of the pallets on the floor. His fingers closed around an Nr20 C1 fragmentation grenade from the one of the dead men's cache. Fengche saw the man's movements, understood what he was trying to do, and flattened himself behind the table and debris pile, covering his head as best he could with his remaining working arm. The man, breathing heavily, pulled the pin, tossed it over the debris pile onto the floor, and rolled away as best he could.

"GRENADE!" Winger shouted as he wheeled and dived behind the remnants of what was previously the sales counter. Dawson instinctively fell to the ground, turned his face to the wall, and drew himself into a fetal position. The only cover he had was the remains of an old tractor engine block.

The concussive force of the explosion within the small room was enormous, and Romero felt as though a baseball bat had just slammed into his already fractured rib cage. Shrapnel grazed his left shoulder, and left him bleeding from four separate wounds. But the bleeding wasn't too bad; the cracked ribs were still his most serious injury, even after the grenade blast. Behind the counter, Winger had escaped the worst of it as shrapnel had ripped into the counter, but hadn't penetrated. Dawson wasn't so lucky. Largely unprotected, fragmented masonry and machine parts had blasted into him, and he was bleeding from multiple pockmarks on the left side of his face. Although the shrapnel missed his eyes, he looked like he'd come down with a severe case of bleeding chicken pox. Except for the loud ringing in their ears, all of them were basically deaf for an hour or so.

Fengche took advantage of the confusion and pushed himself up from the floor using the AK he'd picked up. He sprayed the room as he staggered out through the front door. His clip ran dry just as he rounded the corner of the building. So he dropped it, yanked open the car door, and fell hard into the driver's seat of the Mercedes. Romero struggled to his feet and had made it to his knees when Winger swung out from behind the counter, aiming for the man who had tossed the grenade. Still dazed, it took him about thirty seconds to get into a clear firing position, but a head shot finished the man off. By the time Winger made it to the doorway, Fengche was speeding away in a cloud of dust. Winger turned away, reentered the building and checked on Romero's condition.

Dawson pulled a balaclava from his cargo pants and wiped the blood from his face. Then he pulled himself to his feet and tried the door again. With a hard tug, the lock gave way, and it swung open with a rusty squeak. The repair area had a dirt floor, a workbench along the far wall, and an old overhead jib crane on a pedestal. One light bulb hung from a poorly insulated wire near the back of the room. Old parts and tractor carcasses were strewn about on the ground. In the center of the room was a broken-down wooden shipping crate that looked as though it had initially contained tractor repair parts. It was covered with blood and urine, and in a heap lying next to it was Colonel Tom Menlo.

Menlo was filthy, naked, and barely conscious. Dawson knelt beside him and checked his pulse. It was still strong, and his breathing was steady. Dawson pulled a bottle of water from his bag, and poured some into Menlo's throat. He also had several baby wipes in a Ziploc bag, and he used some to quickly clean the areas around Menlo's eyes, mouth, and ears. It seemed clear that the Iranians had Menlo's restraints attached to the end of the jib crane, and were using it to hoist him up where they could administer beatings. The marks around his neck and the heavy bruising, along with the fact that two of the colonel's fingernails were missing, indicated the interrogation had been aggressive. *Damn!* Dawson had seen worse, but this still made him cringe. *The general public has no idea,* he thought for the hundredth time, *what it costs us to keep these animals away from our shores and from our families.* The family photo from Carolyn Menlo's office flashed through his mind. The staggering contrast between that image and the one he saw before him was beyond his ability to communicate, but he knew those who had seen these things could never erase them from their memory.

Dawson propped Menlo up and kept slowly dribbling water into his mouth. Menlo coughed, doubled over in pain, and then seemed to recover a bit. After a few moments, Menlo's eyes focused and found Dawson's face.

Dawson called out to Winger, and after asking about Romero's status, told him to find clothes for Menlo. "If you can't find anything," he said, "take them off of the guy you just shot out there. He looks about the same size."

Then he turned back to Colonel Menlo. "Can you speak?" Dawson asked. Menlo tried. He could only manage whispers, but he was able to form words. The important thing was that he was conscious and lucid enough to understand what was going on. Dawson quickly explained that they were there to get him back home, but that they were going to have to move quickly and without support. Menlo blinked, nodded that he understood, and tried to push himself up. The colonel was putting on a brave show, but Dawson knew Menlo wasn't going anywhere under his own power.

When Winger returned, he had some clothes from the upstairs bedroom that were comparatively clean, as well as Fengche's bag. With a scowl, Dawson threw aside the implements of torture Fengche had brought along, noted the photos of Carolyn Menlo and Andrew, and found other items such as a cell phone that might be useful later. While Dawson helped Menlo dress, Winger left at a trot to get the jingle truck. Grimacing as he went, Romero was able to walk, and between Dawson and Romero, they had Menlo at the door of the building by the time Winger returned with the vehicle. They got Menlo into the back of the covered truck and started down the road. In order to attract as little attention as possible, they jettisoned the bulk of their personal protection gear and reverted to relying on their local garb.

A few people in the area poked their heads out of other buildings and peered cautiously at the strangers loading a sick looking man into the truck. Dawson and Winger looked at each other before climbing in: *The clock is ticking!* It was just a matter of time—perhaps even minutes if one of the locals had a working cell phone—until authorities were told about the gunfire, the explosion, and other odd activity going on at the end of the street. Beyond that, as light continued to dawn, someone would notice the dead men, if they hadn't already seen them.

As they drove, Winger and Dawson donned their balaclavas, and set their weapons on the floor between them within easy reach. They headed north, backtracking over their path from the previous night. Twice they passed police vehicles, but both were headed south. Neither of them had a siren or flashing lights engaged. However, as they approached the border crossing, they could see that security had been tightened from what Dawson had experienced when entering the evening before. The checkpoint was abuzz with police cars as well as the normal contingent of Iranian guards. On the Afghan side, the situation appeared normal. Clearly, the Iranians had been alerted and were expecting trouble.

Dawson considered multiple approaches, weighing the odds of success for each. The main factor working against them now was time. Colonel Menlo had to be provided with competent medical care soon or they would likely lose him. Romero's injuries and his own were less severe, but infection was a strong possibility for *all* of them under these circumstances. There was no way to bribe their way through this situation in broad daylight and with all of the additional firepower. They would certainly be arrested, incarcerated, and executed. If they simply rammed the police vehicles and were successful in forcing their way through the checkpoints on both ends of the bridge, the Afghans would be in pursuit and the outcome would be only slightly better. They drove past the checkpoint, turned onto the first road they encountered that headed inland, and found a place to pull off the road that offered some visual cover. There they parked the vehicle and thought about what to do.

Finally Dawson struck on a plan. "Billy, how about this?" he said. "Suppose we don't use the checkpoint. Suppose we drive over to that little airfield just north of Zabol and borrow an aircraft?"

Winger emitted a long, low whistle. "Well, partner, I got to admit that is one ballsy plan. I don't think anybody would see that coming. But where exactly would we put this borrowed aircraft down? I mean assuming we get it off the ground here —and I don't know if you recall, but my piloting skills are pretty basic—we'll have a worse problem with the Afghan authorities pursuing us from the airport than we'd have if we broke through the checkpoint over there."

"You're right," Dawson agreed. "I never was a big fan of airport security anyway. No, I think we'll need to find an alternative landing strip someplace. And someplace close at that. We don't want to be any higher than we have to be, and we don't want to be airborne for a minute longer than we have to be. It just makes us a target."

"Roger that," Winger replied. The two men sat there for another minute, lost in thought, and finally Winger said, "You know, Ben, my nine-year-old niece has an expression that just about covers this situation."

"Really? Dawson responded. "What would that be?"

Winger looked at him and said: "Holy moley, guacamole!" Both of them burst out laughing. A moment later, Winger started up the stolen jingle truck once again and pointed it northwest. "Let's go borrow us an aircraft!" he said.

The local airport just a few kilometers north and east of Zabol was fairly modern, with a working control tower, ground-based radar, and enclosed hangars for private aircraft. There was significant commercial transport business as well, with both fixed-wing and rotary aircraft using the field. As the jingle truck approached the parking area, Dawson could see a Russian Mi-8T helicopter, circa 1992, inbound.

"What's the useful payload of an Mi-8T?" Dawson wondered aloud. Following Dawson's view, Winger caught sight of the helicopter.

"About forty-five hundred pounds, fully fueled," he said. "That would be just about perfect if we could get it." He broke out in a grin. "Man, timing is everything."

"Can you fly one of those things?" Dawson asked.

"Maybe," was Winger's disheartening reply, "but why would you want *me* to fly it? There's already a pilot in the cockpit."

Dawson thought for about two seconds, and laughed. "Billy, I *do* love the way you think! Here's what we're going to do."

Five minutes later, the jingle truck was parked near the chain-link fence surrounding the employee entrance to the airport hangar area. Dawson swung out and briefed Romero on what they were going to do while Winger found the security camera aimed at their section of the fence line. He quickly climbed the fence and repositioned the camera with a jerk so that it would produce a blurry motion for just a second or so, and still showed the fence, just a *different* part of the fence. It wouldn't fool anyone for long, but it would likely buy them ten or fifteen minutes, maybe longer if the guard monitoring the security cameras was less than vigilant. Then he scrambled back down the fence and hooked one of the chains draped from the truck frame around the bumper to the padlock on the pedestrian gate that stood about ten meters away.

The small pedestrian gate was designed to permit private aircraft owners access to the hangar area, and Winger thought it was likely to be the weakest point along the security perimeter. Putting the jingle truck in reverse, they saw the padlock hold together as the frame around it came apart. Dawson and Romero had Menlo out of the back of the truck by the time Winger came around to assist. He grabbed the rest of the gear they intended to take, stuffed it into a single bag, and tossed the bag on the ground just inside the gate.

Then, when the others were safely inside the gate and moving toward the nearest hangar, Winger pulled the jingle truck back out into the parking area. He stuck the end of his balaclava into the opening of the gas tank and used an old disposable lighter that had been rattling around on the dashboard of the truck when he stole it to ignite the end of the cloth dangling outside. He walked as quickly as he could without drawing attention to the edge of the lot, and then trotted casually to the opening in the fence they had just created.

About the time he reached that gate, the jingle truck exploded in a ball of black, smoky fire. Less than a minute later, another vehicle parked in the adjacent position also went up. As diversions go, Winger thought it was pretty spectacular. By the time Winger caught up with the other men, Dawson had spotted the position of the Mi-8T, where cargo handlers were still unloading the freight from its rear door. An orange forklift was backing carefully out of the aircraft with the last stack of material, two pallets of boxes with one stacked atop the other, and leaning precariously.

"Sitrep?" Winger said, asking for a situation report as he trotted up to the remainder of the group.

"That's the last of the cargo," Dawson replied, giving the situation report. "I think the pilot is planning to take off again without refueling. Must be flying out of a nearby field. Herat, maybe."

"Sounds likely. These things can only fly three hours or so on a tank. Still, it's good that he's already got fuel."

"Roger that," Dawson said. He handed Winger an orange plastic vest he had just stolen while they were waiting for him. Dawson was already wearing one. Winger put it on, and Dawson explained: "These are just to confuse observers, if there are any, long enough to get us out onto the tarmac and over to the bird. I don't have vests for Chief or Menlo, so they're going to stay right up close behind us. The colonel is in rough shape, so Chief is going to have to basically shoulder his weight as we walk. Chief's cracked ribs are going to make this an experience to remember."

"I'll be all right, Boss," Romero interjected through teeth that were already gritted against the pain.

"We need to go slow enough for them to keep up behind us," Dawson said to Winger. "You keep your eyes moving, because I'm going to keep my face pointed mostly down. After the shrapnel hit us, my face looks like hamburger so I'm planning to keep it averted to avoid drawing attention as much as I can. Everybody got it?"

Romero and Winger nodded, and Menlo, who hadn't spoken since they got him off the truck except the occasional grunt or moan, looked like he might pass out at any moment. He was pale as a ghost, and Dawson knew he didn't have much time. "OK, then," Dawson continued. "Billy, I'll carry this end of our gear bag, and you grab the other end. Lean in, like it's full of heavy stuff instead of just a few rifles, and we'll look as though we are carrying a bunch of tools or something. That should help to confuse any observers. OK, let's go!"

With that, they started moving toward the helicopter. They had closed about half of the distance to the bird when the pilot, who was helping the copilot/cargo master button things up in the cargo bay, spotted them. His expression was confused, but not alarmed, which was exactly what Dawson was hoping for. It allowed them to close most of the remaining gap. The first time the pilot really knew something was amiss was when Winger and Dawson, followed closely by the other two men, stepped onto the lowered tailgate and walked up the ramp into the cargo bay.

As soon as he was past the end of the tailgate, Winger produced his M9 and pointed it directly at the pilot's head. Dawson followed Winger's example, training his gun on the cargo master. Both men froze. Winger, who was the only one of the team who spoke a little Russian, pointed at the tail ramp behind the group, and said, "затворять," shut up. The pronunciation was close enough that the cargo master got the message immediately. Winger looked at the pilot, whose hands were up, and he nodded stoically. "Do you speak English?"

"Yes, some leetle," the pilot replied.

"We are going for a ride," Winger said, and waved the pilot forward with his pistol.

Dawson joined the pilot in the two-man cockpit, clambering in behind him and strapping into the copilot position. The cargo master was waved to a seat on the webbing along one side of the cargo bay after he had closed up the ramp, and the helicopter lifted off while Winger was still strapping in. Dawson instructed the pilot to stay low and head toward Ziranj. The pilot did as he was told, in spite of the fact that his radio was crackling with objections to his uncoordinated departure.

Dawson was relieved to see no inbound fighters, and realized their actions were likely to be viewed as a relatively benign infraction of flight safety rules in this part of the world. Also, Afghanistan had no air force, so they were unlikely to meet with any significant resistance for barely entering Afghan air space. The flight itself only took about thirteen minutes. While airborne, Dawson quickly updated the status in his drafts folder for Carolyn Menlo with "MEN2LO : MENLO4." This double message was designed to alert Carolyn Menlo that he had recovered her husband, and direct her to leave immediately and head for the relative safety of her sister's home in Atlanta. He would have liked to alert Kelly and Gerard that he was advising their target to flee, but he simply didn't have the time to do it. They were going to have to adjust.

Then Dawson sent a text message to McCartney from Axis, saying: "Coming in hot with injuries. Landing at the madrassa close to our recent point of departure. Need assistance." In truth, he had no idea whether McCartney could be there on such short notice, even whether he was in the area or had returned to Herat. The spot Dawson directed the pilot to land was a location where he had spent some time a couple of years earlier, looking into the smuggling trade.

When the pilot set the helicopter down, Dawson pressed a wad of currency into his hands. The cargo master opened the front door, and as he was doing so, Dawson said to the pilot: "As soon as we are off the ramp, you lift off. I don't care where you go from here, but lift off right away. Do you understand?" The pilot looked at the wad of bills, looked back again at Dawson, and nodded vigorously, giving Dawson a "thumbs up" sign. *The stick got us here, now we'll see how the carrot works,* Dawson thought.

CHAPTER 18

About a kilometer and a half to the west of the helicopter's makeshift landing site, two ANP police trucks were parked in front of a local farm produce vendor. The six policemen were taking a break and sharing a watermelon selected from the vendor's inventory. When the Mi-8T came into sight, it startled them. Such commercial aircraft were rarely seen in Ziranj and never without prior consultation that would flow down from the provincial governor's office. It was a little like a bulldozer rolling down a quiet American neighborhood street. Adding insult to injury, the helicopter's prop wash blew copious quantities of dirt and debris onto their freshly cut watermelon slices. The policemen were not pleased. They threw their watermelon unceremoniously to the ground, jumped into their pickups, and wasted no time in an effort to get to the landing site.

The fact that the helicopter ascended again so quickly might well have kept the situation from coming undone if the ANP had not been so close. Unfortunately, the first vehicle arrived on the scene in time to see the Dawson's team as they moved into the madrassa. Several things were very wrong with that image, including the fact that one of the men was obviously wounded or very ill, and they were carrying a large bag with them. Why such men would have emerged from a helicopter in this location only to enter a madrassa was itself a mystery. Afghan civilians only traveled on helicopters at the level of provincial and national government officials, and even that was very rare—

usually when they were guests of foreign governments. The ANP captain who was the senior man among the group decided to investigate further.

The madrassa was unoccupied at the moment. It was used for elementary education, focused on local boys ages six to fourteen. Education wasn't a top priority in the outer reaches of Ziranj, nor in any other non-metropolitan area of Afghanistan, so the fact that the place was empty wasn't surprising. Once inside, they moved Menlo to a corner and helped him on to the floor. Dawson started to put the equipment bag behind him and lean him back against it when Winger moved to the only window just in time to see two ANP trucks pull up outside and a couple of very agitated looking policemen climb out.

"Damn," Winger said.

Hearing the combination of arriving vehicles and Winger's gesticulation, Dawson curtailed his efforts to make Menlo comfortable and retrieved his and Romero's rifles from the bag instead. Winger signaled for Romero to replace him at the window, while Dawson flattened himself against the wall just inside the door. Winger moved to the door, leaned his rifle against the wall just inside the door, and stepped outside to meet the two policemen stomping up to the building, AK-47s at the ready. Two additional policemen were more slowly exiting each of the trucks as well. One was riding in the back of each vehicle. One of the trucks had a primitive but serviceable tripod mounted in the bed, and it was fitted with an AKM assault rifle and banana clip. The other truck bed was occupied by an officer with an RPG-7 rocket-propelled grenade launcher. Winger thought: *This could get really ugly, really fast.*

He was right.

Winger did his best to be nonthreatening and acquiescent to the policemen, smiling and referring to them with great respect. They were unmoved. They kept getting closer and closer to Winger, who insisted that they were only here to make repairs on the building at the request of the provincial governor. The ANP captain wasn't buying it. He kept demanding to go inside, and finally attempted to push Winger out of the way. That movement was the last one that was clear to most of the other policemen. Suddenly, the captain was on the ground and off to the side of Winger, and he wasn't moving. The other officer who had been immediately behind the captain was trying to pull his rifle up into a position to shoot Winger, but Winger stepped in and prevented the maneuver, simultaneously pulling his M9 from inside his tunic and shooting the officer in the right temple.

At this point Romero opened up from the window, and Winger dived back through the door. Dawson slammed the door behind him, and all hell broke loose. Within seconds, the man with the AKM assault rifle was making toothpicks out of the wooden door in front of Dawson. Two of the other policemen had taken cover behind their vehicles, and were firing from there. Romero could probably keep up with them until he picked them off, Dawson thought. But the big problem by far was the fourth guy, the one who had dived into his truck bed to arm his RPG-7.

"We gotta move, Boss!" Winger said.

"I know." Dawson wished he had another hand grenade like the Nr20 used against them earlier, but he was out of luck. What he did have was an L83A1 smoke grenade. He thought he might need it for identifying a landing zone in the event an air rescue was required, but they weren't going to need an air rescue if they couldn't get out of the madrassa alive.

There was a light breeze coming from the west. That could be helpful, if he could land the thing properly. "Chief," he yelled over at Romero, "cover me while I try to give this a toss. Billy, get the colonel ready to move. We're going around to the back of the building."

He rolled across the doorway in front of the shredded wooden door, and positioned himself beneath the window. When he saw that Winger had Menlo up in a fireman's carry and his weapon ready, he nodded to Romero and then pulled the pin of the smoke grenade. Romero opened fire aggressively and Dawson popped up long enough to throw the grenade. He thought it had fallen short at first, but it bounced and rolled, eventually stopping directly under the upwind vehicle where it detonated. A massive plume of purple smoke blossomed, completely enveloping the downwind vehicle in which the policeman with the RPG was positioned. The combination of choking and lack of visibility basically took that man, and the other officer who was taking cover behind that vehicle, out of commission.

Romero focused his fire on the other truck, and by alternating between the two policemen there, was able to hit the man wielding the tripod-mounted assault rifle. As soon as that happened he shouted to Winger, and Winger followed Dawson out the front door and around the building to their left. Dawson had the equipment bag, Winger had Menlo, and Romero was right behind them. Dawson and Romero alternated covering the team's 6 as they scurried along the side of the building to the back.

By the time they reached the back of the building, they realized that still another ANP truck had arrived. More police officers were about to join the fray. The dismounted officer from the first group had moved out of the smoke and got into position to fire on them. Bullets ricocheted off the wall, splintering stucco closer and closer to Romero and Dawson. As soon as they got behind the building, Dawson saw what he had been looking for: the opening to a karez. It wasn't easy to spot among the old partial structures left over from decades of abandonment and piles of debris and weeds, but there it was.

For thousands of years, communities in Afghanistan have depended in many areas upon ingenious systems called karez to move water for drinking and irrigation. They are basically underground canals that tie together individual wells in order to move water so it resists evaporation. Many of these canals are large enough for humans to move through, and some were even bombed by the Russian military when Afghan resistance fighters hid in them during the Russian occupation in the 1980s.

Back when Dawson had been working on the smuggling problem in Ziranj, his team had come across this particular karez, which is why he'd remembered the location of the madrassa. If it was still passable, Dawson thought it could be their way out. The last time he was down in it, the karez was large enough for human passage. If it hadn't been clogged up, he knew they could reach a series of similar well structures about a kilometer away. He pointed the team toward that opening, which looked like a small cave in the hillside behind the madrassa. Winger went in first, dragging Menlo behind him. He got the colonel about twenty meters in before laying him down and returning to the opening to cover Romero and Dawson as they followed.

Romero made it next, but by the time Dawson was just few meters away, the policeman with the RPG was back in position. Dawson dove inside, hit the ground, and curled around his rifle in a quarter-turned forward somersault. Just as he was rolling back onto his feet, the man fired and the RPG slammed into the wall next to the opening. Rolling through the somersault was the last thing Dawson remembered.

The force of the blast further opened the mouth of the karez, momentarily obscuring the area with smoke and debris from the blast. It threw everyone inside to the ground. Winger suffered from a second round of hearing loss, but never lost consciousness. He belly-crawled to Dawson's position and pulled him further back into the opening in the earth. Then he and Romero, realizing that with Dawson either unconscious or dead they couldn't move much further, took up protective positions as close to the opening as possible. Romero crawled to a point where he could peer up over the top of a dirt mound.

Through the clearing smoke, he could make out the policeman with the RPG refitting his weapon. He saw him stand and move into a crouch, preparing to run a short distance to his left. He was clearly trying to find a way to fire deeper into the karez. Ignoring the bullets now thudding into the dirt in front of him, Romero brought his rifle up to a resting position on the mound. Two seconds … three seconds … and the RPG operator started running in a low crouch to his new position. He had about twelve steps to cover, so Romero had less than five seconds to get off his shot before the target was gone or he was hit himself by incoming fire. *No point in worrying about incoming*, Romero knew. He blocked it out, steadied his breathing, and squeezed off a two-round burst. He struck the man in the head, ending that threat until someone else could pick up the weapon and take over. No one else seemed eager to replace him.

Winger had gone to work trying to pick off the officers who were firing on Romero. He knew there were at least two from the sounds involved, but he could only actually see one of them. After a couple of minutes, he decided their only hope of getting through this with Menlo alive, and perhaps Dawson if he wasn't already dead from the blast, was to get outside and flank the remaining ANP officers. He needed another distraction, but they had no other smoke grenades, and he had no line of sight to the RPG so there was no hope of exploding the ordinance there with a carefully placed shot. He scanned the area for anything else that might be useful to create a diversion.

Winger thought he could barely hear more gunfire somewhat further away, but his hearing was down to about ten percent of normal, so he paid no attention to it or anything else except the immediate threat. He finally decided that he would try to make it to a small pile of dirt and weeds that had been dug from the karez over the last year or so. It was perpendicular to and about twenty meters from the opening, on a vector parallel to the back wall of the madrassa. He signaled to Romero, attempting to get him to understand that he was about to run directly across his line of fire.

As a part of their training, special operations personnel such as Delta Force operatives are trained extensively in close-quarters combat. Operators such as Billy Winger and Max Kelly were not only expert-level marksmen at the target range, they also trained in aspects of armed combat such as shooting while running, and picking off enemy targets who are feet—or even inches— away from their hostages. However, it had been many years since Winger had been through the Delta Operator Training course, and he knew his chances of making this run were slim. He had almost no chance at all of inflicting any pain on the enemy unless and until he was in position behind the dirt pile. Nonetheless, Dawson's original scheme to travel through the karez and escape safely from there was simply impossible now. The only choice was to fight their way back out through this phalanx of ANP. Before taking off, he looked back at Dawson and Menlo one last time. No change there. He met Romero's gaze, counted to three on his fingers, and sprinted out into the open.

As soon as he cleared Romero's line of fire, Romero was in position again and prepared to cover Winger. He got lucky. Winger's run was enough to draw the attention of one of the ANP officers, who stood to a crouch in order to get off his shot. Once he crouched, Romero had a clear line of fire and executed another head shot, toppling what was left of the man over backwards.

The second of the two ANP officers was in a much better position. Standing behind the cover of a partial wall left behind from some former structure that had been long-since demolished, he could stand fully erect and remain completely hidden from Romero's view with the exception of his rifle barrel, which was tracking Winger as he ran. Romero tried to draw a bead on the rifle barrel itself, a practically impossible shot, when he heard the bark of another weapon. He saw the barrel jerk upward and then fall harmlessly to the ground. Around the corner of the madrassa, Winger, who had just flopped into a prone position behind the debris pile, and Romero saw a British issue helmet atop the goggled face of Axis operative Paul McCartney.

CHAPTER 19

It was early Saturday morning, and Carolyn Menlo was looking forward to a day of distraction with her son and Joan Wu's family at the park, and then a leisurely dinner with Joan. Still in her pajamas and sipping her first cup of coffee, she popped open the browser on her home PC and checked for any status update in the Gmail account from Dawson. She nearly dropped her coffee when she saw the new entry: "MEN2LO : MENLO4." It was the best and worst news she could have gotten. Dawson had found Tom and was bringing him out from wherever he was. But now he perceived that she and Andy were in danger, and she needed to flee—*immediately*.

Fortunately, Dawson's instructions about this eventuality had been crystal clear. She had bags packed for both herself and Andy. All she had to do was dress, get Andy moving, throw their bags and computer cases in the car, and they'd be on the road. It would be a long drive, over ten hours if they stopped often, mostly along Interstate 95 and then 85. She had driven it a few times, and while it was long and better suited to two drivers, she knew she could do it alone.

She managed to get Andy up and into the car in twenty minutes, a speed record for the ten-year-old, who had never been a morning person, and in less than thirty minutes they were headed down the road in the family's late model Lexus hybrid. She would need to stop and get Andy some breakfast before long and replenish her caffeine supply, but the most important thing, she knew, was to get on the road.

When she was safely out of town and on the interstate, she used the vehicle's onboard phone system to call Joan Wu. She knew this violated Dawson's instructions, but she just wanted to make sure Wu wasn't hustling to get her girls dressed and fed and all spun up about a big day at the park when she and Andy wouldn't be there. She also really needed to ensure that the week's meetings with suppliers, contractors, and staff from Norfolk were covered.

Joan answered her cell brightly, saying: "Are you already on your way? I thought we had decided on eleven?"

"Good morning," Menlo replied. "No, unfortunately, I'm not. I'm calling to let you know that I can't make it today, Joan. Something has come up: an illness in the family. Andy and I are headed out of town right now. Sorry. It looks like our celebration is going to have to be pushed out a week or so."

"That's too bad," Joan replied. "The girls were looking forward to it almost as much as I was."

"Me, too," Menlo said. "It just can't be helped, I'm afraid. We're likely to be out of town for several days, and I'm not sure exactly how long this is going to take, actually. Can you cover my meetings for, well, I don't know, at least the first half of the week?"

"Of course," Wu said. "Is everything all right? This isn't something about Tom, is it?"

"No," Menlo lied, "I almost wish it was. Just need to visit my sister for a while. I'll be back before long."

"OK. I'll cover your meetings and email you if there are any emergencies. Otherwise just assume everything is fine. We have more than enough to keep us productive until you return."

"Thanks," Menlo said. "Please tell your two amigos"—Steve Hoffman and Paul McCallister, the other two members of the Salacia team—"about this as well, but I'd prefer that all of you keep it under wraps. No need for anyone else to know."

"I understand," Wu replied. "Family business is personal. We'll keep a lid on it. Just let me know if there's anything I can do before you get back."

"Thanks, Joan. I will. And thanks for understanding. I wish I'd known sooner, but this just came up."

"No worries," Wu replied, "as long as you remember that this defers rather than cancels your commitment to buy me dinner. Which reminds me, I'll cancel the reservation at Portabellos for tonight, too."

"Thanks. You really are a life saver," Menlo said, and signed off.

* * * *

When Menlo backed out of her garage and pulled onto the street, Boxer had been turning over his night-shift duties to Gerard. Gerard had been handling daytime surveillance on Menlo; Kelly was doing the five-to-midnight shifts, and Boxer was covering midnight to six a.m. Boxer and Gerard were both using rental cars, and turning them in for new ones every three days. Kelly preferred pickup trucks and SUVs, but was following a similar pattern of vehicle swap-outs. Owing to the early hour on a Saturday, and the fact that she was headed the opposite direction from the direction that she normally took when departing for work, Gerard was immediately wary. She and Boxer began to follow her in their individual vehicles, swapping out every few miles so as to be less conspicuous. Finally, when they saw that Menlo was pulling onto the interstate highway, she dialed Kelly and explained what was going on.

"Sounds like Ben issued a warning order. She must be popping smoke," Kelly said.

"Yeah, that's why I'm calling," Gerard replied. "If that's true, I'm likely to need more than Boxer when we run into trouble."

"Roger that," Kelly said. "Think she is headed for her sister's then?"

"That would be my guess," Gerard replied.

"OK," Kelly said. "I'm going to pick up Ron on my way, and I'll catch up with you as fast as I can."

Ron Meriwether was another member of the regular staff at Kelly & Gerard Enterprises, LLP. He hadn't been assigned to the Menlo engagement, so all he knew was that it was a PSD, a Personal Security Detail, assignment. Meriwether was a retired Special Operations guy who shared Kelly's penchant for staying in top physical condition. A six-foot-two black man, he was quiet and thoughtful with an easy smile and very different on-duty and off-duty personas. After retirement from government service, he'd gone back to college to study Shakespearian literature using the earnings from his part-time work with Kelly and Gerard to offset his educational costs. Now pushing sixty, he still moved with grace and confidence, though his knees had given him trouble over recent months. Kelly wasted no time picking him up and getting on the highway.

* * * *

Within ten minutes of the completion of Menlo's call to Joan Wu, one of Jing-ti's technicians called him at his desk and relayed the information. As soon as he received the information, Jing-ti picked up his phone and notified Bi-shou cryptically, saying that his personal doctor was traveling to see her sister and was en route via automobile. Jing-ti's plan called for the abduction of Menlo if Fengche failed to gain adequate leverage during his work with Colonel Menlo in Iran, and that trigger had just been pulled. It now seemed that Fengche had been unsuccessful. Further, although Fengche didn't know Dawson, this sounded like Dawson's work to Jing-ti. If it was, then Dawson was on the other side of the planet and that created a window of opportunity for Jing-ti to abduct Dr. Menlo without his interference.

Bi-shou's team had been setting up to abduct Menlo and her son at the park later that day. As such, they had a secluded safe house prepared for maintaining the two with adequate security and life support arrangements. Now, however, with Menlo leaving town, she had to adjust her plans.

Bi-shou was an extraordinarily well-organized, well-financed, and an effective leader. A woman of intense passions, she was also fully capable of shutting all vestiges of mercy and compassion off as though they were faucets, and bending the will of her subordinates to her own. Within her organization, there were just a few dedicated full-time staff members; all of her other operators were independent contractors.

She used a group that she referred to as her "tier-one" operators most frequently, and trusted them enough to share more information about the nature of their assignments than she would with any of the others. Her stable of tier-one operators included a dozen people: five women and seven men. For this assignment, she had engaged four of her tier-one team for the abduction, and she had four additional tier-two operators contracted for the security and life support actions at the safe house. They were prepared to be called in at any time.

Along with her staff, Bi-shou maintained access to a Cessna Citation fixed-wing aircraft, a MD902 helicopter, and two armored land vehicles: an armored Ford E-350 van and a Toyota Land Cruiser. Her weapons armory was extensive, and she provided weapons as necessary for her tier-two operators; her tier-one operators provided their own, but Bi-shou made certain that they met minimum specifications and that the operators had an adequate supply of both weapons and ammunition before she engaged them.

Bi-shou looked at the map, verified the route and departure time frame, and decided to initiate her plan. She made calls to engage four of the tier-one operators that were previously briefed in, directing them to meet her at the local airport where her helicopter was hangared. She also alerted her security and life support contractors that their services would be required later that evening, directing them to open the safe house and prepare to receive Menlo and her son. She then called one of her tier-two operators, and engaged him to retrieve the armored van and start driving south on I-95, then southwest on I-85 toward Charlotte. En route to the airfield, she called the pilot and directed him to file a flight plan for a municipal airport near Charlotte. She also directed him to arrange two SUV rentals for them, to be picked up at the airport.

At the airfield, Bi-shou met up with her operators. She ran through a quick equipment list and refreshed the plan as the pilot was checking out and spinning up the helicopter. She had decided to deplane with her operators at Charlotte and do the abduction along the road somewhere in that vicinity. Out on the open highway, she thought, Menlo should be an easy target.

* * * *

Andy slept for an hour in the back seat, and when he woke they were approaching Fredericksburg, Virginia. Menlo pulled into a local Waffle House where they had breakfast and then got back on the road. She was relieved to see Andy was content to play with his Nintendo and didn't complain about the long car ride.

About eighteen miles south of Fredericksburg, Kelly and Meriwether caught up with the other two vehicles in the surveillance team traveling down the highway. Almost immediately, Boxer pulled off the highway long enough for Meriwether to transfer from Kelly's truck to Boxer's car. Then they quickly resumed their path and got back into position on the highway. Gerard took the first point position approximately one mile ahead of Menlo. Boxer and Kelly traded off getting close enough behind Menlo to keep her in visual range. Essentially, they had Menlo bracketed as she traveled down the highway none the wiser.

By the time they made it to Greensboro, North Carolina, Menlo and her son were both hungry again. She pulled off at a Chick-fil-A south of Greensboro on I-85, and persuaded Andy to leave the game in the car long enough for them to go in for lunch. The meal and bathroom breaks took about forty minutes, during which Gerard grabbed lunch for the team at the Chick-fil-A drive-thru. After a brief additional stop to refuel, Menlo got back on the highway and resumed her journey toward Atlanta.

Bi-shou and her team landed in Charlotte well ahead of Menlo's arrival.

They drove their rented SUVs out to the hangar area, and transferred their equipment from the aircraft to the vehicles. Then the two SUVs, both Chevy Trailblazers and each containing two of Bi-shou's tier-one operators, got on the road heading north to intercept Menlo. Bi-shou returned to the helicopter and waited while refueling operations were completed. Then the aircraft ascended again and began to travel slowly north, up Interstate 85. The pilot spotted Menlo's Lexus between Greensboro and Lexington. Not wanting to alert Menlo, the aircraft continued northward, veering away from the interstate and setting down in a large open field that was at least a mile from the closest farmhouse. Bi-shou figured that, with the current rates of speed, they needed to sit tight for a few minutes before checking on Menlo's position again.

* * * *

Kelly was on point when Bi-shou flew over, and, while he noticed the aircraft, he wasn't alarmed by it. Gerard and Meriwether noticed it as well, but since they were well behind Menlo, the aircraft was already veering off its interstate-hugging path, and they saw no reason to pay much attention to it, either.

However, when the same aircraft reappeared less than an hour later, this time tracking the interstate again and headed south, it definitely caught their attention. As soon as it came in sight, Gerard was on the radio: "I don't like the way this NOTAR keeps showing up," she said. They all knew NOTAR was short for "No Tail Rotor," a tail rotorless design of the MD902. The lack of tail rotor makes the helicopter safer and substantially quieter than other similar models.

"I was just thinkin' the same thing," Kelly responded immediately as the aircraft was flying over his position. "Doesn't seem threatening. No gunners hanging out empty doors or anything like that, but it's just too much of a coincidence. Let's tighten up our formation. Ron, you and Boxer go on up there with Lily and move in a bit closer. I'm going to drift back some, too. This bird could be doing some kind of recon. Lily, I know Ron's packin', because we moved his equipment into the back seat when he transferred over to Boxer's car from my truck. What are you carrying?"

"I've just got my nine here in front. The rest of my stuff is in the trunk, but it won't take me long to get to it if I need it," she said. She reached into her shirt pocket, plucked out a ponytail holder, and stuck it between her teeth.

Then she used both hands to pull her hair back into a ponytail as she steered the car with her knees.

* * * *

Bi-shou alerted her teams in the SUVs, and when she confirmed they were in position, she directed the pilot to return to the municipal airport from which they had come. That was the expected rendezvous point where Menlo and her son would be transferred to the armored van for transport to the safe house. The van was still about an hour out, but she wanted to be there when her team arrived from the highway with Menlo.

At the Route 64 ramp, a few miles northeast of Lexington, the two Chevy SUVs were idling and pulled onto the interstate as Menlo passed. The first of them accelerated until it was in front of Menlo's car, and then pulled into her lane slowing gradually as the second SUV pulled up alongside Menlo in the left lane. Kelly, about a quarter of a mile ahead of Menlo, saw what was coming next. "They're going to move her off the road to the right. I'm getting off at the next ramp. That's gotta be where they are trying to take her."

Menlo also realized what was happening. The two SUVs boxed her in as they approached the exit for Old Raleigh Road, and the SUV in the left lane moved inexorably to the right, exactly as Kelly had predicted. She checked the rearview mirror to see if Andy noticed anything, and gripped the steering wheel.

As they approached the ramp, Meriwether instructed Boxer to accelerate until his front bumper was inches from Menlo's back bumper. As Menlo was moved up the ramp, the front SUV accelerated again, wheeled in front of her, and forced her to slam on her brakes.

Bi-shou's plan had been for her operatives to sandwich Menlo's car between the two SUVs, haul Menlo and her son out, and be on their way west on Route 64. Instead, they now had Menlo's car and another vehicle between the two SUVs. Another vehicle still approached the rear SUV from behind, and wheeled to a stop across the roadway. About that same time, the operators in the lead SUV saw that the Ford Expedition in front of them had stopped, backed up, and was now turning to block the road in front of *them*. Almost simultaneously, Kelly opened his door and jumped out with his M4 pointed at the lead SUV as Meriwether followed suit alongside the second SUV. Gerard popped her seatbelt loose, pulled her nine millimeter from its holster, chambered a round, and thumbed off the safety as she ran for Menlo's car.

Bi-shou's operators were professionals, and they had no intention of disappointing her. But she had not told them to expect company, and they were definitely not prepared for a confrontation. They had one shotgun in each vehicle in case of an emergency, but their primary weapons were nine millimeter pistols, and the bulk of their equipment included zip-ties, hoods, and blankets to cover their captives while en route to their rendezvous point. They were in unarmored rentals, trapped between three other vehicles, and facing a vaguely understood number of opposing forces who were clearly better armed than they were. The driver of the first SUV decided to try ramming Kelly to flee the scene. Kelly immediately shot out both front tires, and shook his head gravely while returning the aim of his M4 to the driver's head. "Out of the car and on the ground!" he shouted.

In the second SUV, the two occupants had different ideas. The passenger side occupant, who was closest to the Menlo car, pushed open his door and lifted his pistol toward Meriwether. Meriwether, however, didn't get off a shot because Gerard dropped him before he could even get his weapon leveled. The driver flung himself out of the SUV on the other side, pulled open the back door, and racked a round in his shotgun. He stepped backward into the ditch, ducked down and raced toward the back of the SUV. As soon as he emerged from the cover of the vehicle, he was firing. If Boxer hadn't ducked, he would have died immediately. As it was, the twelve-gauge slug obliterated both front windows but passed straight through. Meriwether returned fire with his own M4, and the operative in the ditch went silent. With both occupants of the rear SUV out of commission, he moved forward to assist Kelly with the one in front.

As the firefight raged outside, Menlo and her son sat staring, frozen with shock and fear. Gerard ran to the Lexus and motioned for Menlo to roll down her window all the while keeping her weapon leveled at the occupants of the front SUV as Meriwether approached it. Menlo hesitated, but under the circumstances, she decided that cooperating with the people who had guns facing *away* from her was probably the right thing to do. "Dr. Menlo," Gerard said, "nice to meet you. I'm Lily Gerard. That's Max Kelly up there, and Ron Meriwether on the move. We're friends of Ben Dawson, and we've been keeping an eye on you for him."

"Oh," was all Menlo could say in response.

"If you'll move over, Ma'am," Gerard continued, "I'll get you out of here."

Menlo unfastened her seat belt, climbed over her console, and buckled in again on the passenger's side. Gerard re-engaged the transmission of Menlo's

Lexus, nursed it around the other vehicles, and back onto the road. She drove back up onto Old Raleigh Road and continued west. After a couple of miles she turned right again, and headed north toward Route 64.

When they were about five minutes down the road, Menlo finally spoke. "What's the password?"

Gerard turned to her and smiled. "There is no password." She chuckled.

"Why does that make you laugh?"

"Because Ben always thinks he's so clever. I mean, who would use that? It's just, I don't know, so *corny*, I guess. It's typical Ben Dawson."

Menlo smiled and sank back into her seat. She took a deep breath and started to breathe normally. She turned around and reached out to her son who clasped her outstretched hand. "Doing OK, buddy?"

"I think I need to go to the bathroom," he said, eyes still wide.

"I'm on it," Gerard replied. "There's a rest stop just a few miles up the road. We'll be there in no time."

CHAPTER 20

Back at the failed abduction site, Kelly and Meriwether finished gagging and zip-tying the two operators who were still breathing. They each pulled on latex gloves, and then used balaclavas to blindfold the men before moving them into the back of the first SUV. The two operatives looked around fifty years of age and of indeterminate ethnic background. Both were swarthy men with close-cropped hair and mean, snarling expressions. They each wore cargo pants, heavy work boots, and loose-fitting shirts.

Kelly walked over and spoke with Boxer, while Meriwether threw an old plastic tarp and Kelly's equipment bag in the back seat of the SUV, then climbed in. After giving Boxer instructions about cleaning up the scene, Kelly drove the SUV away while Meriwether kept the men in back covered with his pistol. They were fortunate that additional cars had all stayed up on the interstate, and no one had tried to venture down the Old Raleigh Road during the twenty minutes that it took to recover and get Menlo out of the area.

Kelly drove about two miles and pulled onto an old, overgrown gravel road. He followed it to where it ended, where he had seen an old, falling-down barn and a couple of rusting-away pieces of farm equipment. Kelly and Meriwether shepherded the operatives into the barn, and while Meriwether covered them, Kelly rearranged the zip-ties such that one operative was tied to a central pillar of the barn, and the other was restrained tightly to the internal fence of a horse stall. He retrieved a couple of small plastic bags containing ear plugs from his equipment bag, and jammed the foam plugs into the ears of both men.

Meriwether moved to the door and posted himself as a sentry. Kelly went to work on the operative restrained to the fence, working the small blade of his Leatherman tool under one of the man's fingernails. The screaming went on for about thirty seconds, and the man looked to Kelly as though he was on the brink of passing out. At that point, Kelly pulled the earplugs out of the man's ears and began to ask him questions.

Within five minutes, he knew that the operator's services had been engaged by Bi-Shou, who the other operators were, and when and where they were scheduled to deliver Menlo and her son. He asked for, and immediately was provided with, the contact phone number and payment methods used. The payment method was a blind drop and was probably useless. But the phone and backup number were valuable. He borrowed a ball-point pen from Meriwether and carefully wrote those down in ink on his forearm. They would have to be checked out later.

Then he jammed the earplugs back into the man's ears and repeated the same process with the other operative. The second man provided essentially the same details as the first, verifying in Kelly's mind that he had the truth. Kelly finished up and called out to Meriwether, who brought in the plastic tarp and then returned to his post just outside the door.

Kelly pulled a sound suppressor out of his equipment bag and screwed it onto the end of his pistol. He made sure the plastic tarp was properly positioned, and then moved to one side and shot the man who was tethered to the fence through the temple. Then he moved quickly behind the dead man and cut through the zip-ties, allowing the operator's body to fall neatly onto the tarp. He threw the remaining bits of zip-tie onto the tarp, and then dragged the tarp across the hay-covered dirt floor to reposition it in front of the second operator. There he repeated the process.

When both bodies and all of the other artifacts including bits of zip-tie were on the tarp, he called Meriwether in again. The two men wrapped the bodies up tightly in the tarp, one lying on top of the other to make for the smallest possible area to roll into the tarp. They secured the tarp around the bodies with duct tape from Kelly's equipment bag. Then Kelly backed the SUV into the barn. He and Meriwether hoisted the body-filled tarp onto the tailgate, and shoved it inside. Then they closed the tailgate, looked around one more time to make certain they had left no unnecessary traces, and returned to the SUV.

Driving down the old road to make their way back to the highway, Kelly asked Meriwether: "Bother you any that we took those two out?"

"Some people just need to be killed," Meriwether replied. "I understand that. But I wonder...."

"Yeah?" Kelly asked. "You wonder what?"

"I'm pretty sure Dawson wouldn't approve," Meriwether replied.

"Well, you're probably right about that, Ron," he said. "That's why I don't tell him. And one smart thing about Ben is that he knows better than to ask questions he doesn't want answered." Meriwether configured his face in a tight-lipped smile and nodded, continuing to look straight ahead. "The same is true for Lily," Kelly continued. "She doesn't have the stomach for this kind of thing. I'm not *fond* of it either, here on US soil especially. But at times like this, it's about the only way to get answers fast enough for them to do any good, and like you said, some people just need to be killed."

Kelly and Meriwether drove back past the abduction site. Kelly's truck was pulled off onto the shoulder of the road, as was the SUV with the two flat tires. Boxer had managed to get the other operators' bodies in the trunk of his car and had driven away as instructed. He had also kicked the broken glass off of the roadway with his feet as best he could, and retrieved the spent cartridges from places that were in plain sight. There would be no concealing the battleground from a trained forensics team of course, but the objective was to keep any such attention from being drawn to that location in the first place. Kelly jumped into his truck and started north. Meriwether followed in the SUV with the two operators' tarp-shrouded bodies in the cargo area.

Kelly and Meriwether drove about three and a half hours, eventually winding their way back into the countryside, where Kelly finally pulled up in front of an old gate, padlocked shut with a heavy, rusted chain, and marked with a faded No Trespassing sign. Boxer was already there waiting. Kelly left the truck idling while he jumped out and unlocked the gate. He shoved the gate back out of the way, revealing two tracks looping off into the distance. Then he jumped back into the truck and pulled inside, turning the vehicle so that the front of the SUV was facing the fence line. Boxer pulled up behind the SUV and transferred the two bodies from his trunk into the cargo bay of the SUV, atop the tarp-wrapped bodies of the other two operators. Boxer knew that he was going to lose his car as a part of this operation, and that Kelly would make sure that their little company covered the cost. With the blood, fiber, hair, and other forensic evidence undoubtedly all over the vehicle by now, setting it on fire or dumping it into a lake were the most likely options.

With that, Boxer was posted at the gate as a sentry. Kelly steered his truck forward, following the bumpy overgrown path. The old tracks went on for more than a half mile, ending at a small farmhouse with a newer equipment shed that had a larger footprint than the house. The house was a safe house owned by Kelly & Gerard, and it was rarely used. Gerard had only been to the place once, shortly after it was purchased three years earlier.

Kelly and Meriwether drove around behind the farmhouse, and over to the edge of what appeared to be a small private landfill. They turned off their vehicles, and Kelly walked back to the equipment shed while Meriwether pulled the bodies and then the tarp out from the back of his vehicle, allowing them to drop with heavy thuds onto the ground.

Meriwether heard an engine start up in the distance, and after about five minutes, saw Kelly driving toward him in a seventy-five horsepower John Deere tractor with an end-loader on the back. As he approached Meriwether's location, he turned to his left and dumped several heavy paper bags of lime from the end-loader on the ground. Then he continued on to the area of the landfill. He stopped near the edge and used the end-loader to scoop bucket after bucket of soft earth from the ground.

When he had created a hole about seven feet deep, he pulled on a face mask and dragged the first bag of lime over to the freshly dug cavity in the earth. He cut the end open with his Leatherman tool, and dumped the lime into the hole. Then the two men dragged each of the bodies over to the pit, and dumped them unceremoniously into it. Following each body, another bag of lime was deposited. Finally, Kelly remounted the tractor and filled in the rest of the pit.

Meriwether, Kelly, and Boxer spent the remainder of that day recovering the other SUV from the abduction site, getting a roadside assistance truck from the local car dealer out to replace the tires, getting the two vehicles washed and refueled, and returning them to the National rental car lot at the airport. While he waited for the tires to be changed on the SUV, Kelly logged into the Gmail account used for communications with Dawson and added a folder. He named it with the current date and added a note that reported an interrupted abduction of the target and her son, that they were both safe, and that the operators involved had been engaged by a female of Chinese descent named Bi-shou. Then he listed the contact numbers the operators had provided and logged out.

CHAPTER 21

Gerard engaged the cruise control in Carolyn Menlo's car and headed toward Old Alexandria. "I'm taking you two to my condo until we sort out what the safest place is for you," she told Menlo.

"OK," Menlo said, calmer, but still shaken.

Gerard knew it was back into the lion's den in some respects, but it was only temporary. In addition, she and Kelly hadn't really had an opportunity to think through what to do in this eventuality. She considered the situation and ran through the options in her head. First, while this particular set of operators was now out of commission, the person or agency that engaged them wasn't, and that meant Menlo and her son were still in grave danger. From her own experience as a policewoman, she understood that no law enforcement agency had unlimited funds to provide indefinite protection for the Menlos. Second, she didn't relish having to explain to the police that they had defended the Menlos with firearms without enlisting the aid of local law enforcement, and she knew that merely leaving the scene of such an altercation was not entirely legal. Third, she didn't know what Kelly had decided to do after she left. And fourth, she was afraid to ask. Although she loved Kelly and trusted him with her life, she knew there was something troubling going on deep inside him. He'd been going dark, as she called it, more and more often, and she knew operations like this one could trigger dark episodes. Finally, she had accepted an assignment from Ben Dawson to protect Carolyn Menlo and her son, and that was something she didn't feel comfortable relinquishing to anyone—including the FBI, which is the agency that would almost certainly be called in. Not even Dawson knew where the leaks were that had landed them in this situation, and they could very well exist in federal law enforcement agencies, including the Bureau. While she didn't have any illusions she could do a better job than the appropriate agency *if that agency was uncompromised*, she couldn't be absolutely certain about that. So the best course of action, in her judgment, was to hold onto the Menlos at least for a while.

"Clearly," Gerard continued, "you're going to need looking after, and right now we're not sure who we can trust. I don't want you to feel like a prisoner, but I strongly advise you not to call anyone because your cell signal can enable your location to be pinpointed. So please turn the phone off unless you're using it. In fact, if you don't have any strong objection, since your line may well be monitored, please just use my phone if you really need to make a call. As soon as I can get back into my office, I'll get you a burner, I mean a disposable cell phone, and you can use it. OK?"

"I think so," Menlo responded. "I wish I could talk to Ben," she said quietly.

"Quite frankly, I do, too. Listen, I know what you're thinking—at least I know what I would be thinking if I was in your position," Gerard said with another reassuring smile. "I'd be wondering who this woman is you are riding with and whether you should trust her. So all I ask is that you reserve judgment until we get to my condo. As soon as we settle in, I'll pull out some photo albums with pictures of Ben and Max and me in them. I think you'll find it easier to believe that we're friends after that. In fact, now that I think of it, there are even a few on my walls. Of course," she said with a wistful sigh, "I was younger and thinner in those days."

"Thank you," Menlo said. "Actually that does make me feel better."

They drove in silence for a while and then Menlo said, "So how did you meet Ben Dawson?"

"Oh, gosh, now that's a long story, but I guess we have some time, right?" Gerard said, all the while wondering *Why do you want to know?* Gerard had been involved with Max Kelly for a long time, but she'd always had what she jokingly referred to as a "soft spot" for Ben. A soft spot that sometimes turned into a painful ache, but one she vigilantly kept locked down tight so neither Max nor Ben would notice it. "The fact is, I didn't really meet Ben; I met Max. I'd been with the Boston Police Department for several years, worked pretty hard to make detective, did several stints of undercover work with Vice and the Organized Crime Unit, and eventually got an offer to move into OCU."

"That sounds like a pretty demanding job, especially for a woman," Menlo said.

"You're right about that," Gerard agreed. "I worked my"—she remembered there was a ten year old in the car—"my rear end off for years in martial arts, kickboxing, and strength training at the gym to develop the stamina and strength I needed. Then there were the exams for each grade as I worked my way up in the department. I even went back to school at night and got my bachelor's degree. So anyway, I was following a money-laundering operation from drug dealers that led right to some foreign politician who was posted in DC. So I'm running surveillance one night at the hotel where this guy was staying. Hookers and drug money were running through his room like a river. I file for a warrant to go in after the scumbag, and get turned down cold. He had diplomatic immunity."

"So I'm about ready to throw my badge and weapon down on my boss's desk, and he knows it. He was a good guy, and he'd always had my back. So he says to me, 'Lily, you've been working too hard.' I was ready to turn and walk out when he rolls forward in his chair and gets right up in my face and says: 'I want you to go to lunch. Do it right now. Go to the Korean barbecue on the corner of E Street and Washington. You know which one I'm talking about?' I did, of course, and I told him yeah, but I didn't understand. I remember saying, 'Listen, I don't even *like* Korean food.' He looked at me like he couldn't believe how slow I was to catch on, and then I got it. He was sending me to meet someone, but he didn't want to say that out loud. Anyway, I went to the restaurant, told the manager of the place that Blake—that was my boss—had sent me, and I was supposed to ask for the table he gives Blake whenever he comes in. So they show me to a table, and I order a drink and start looking at the menu. I'm just about to give up on the whole thing when I look up from the menu and there is Max Kelly. He looks, for all the world, like that character from the old TV show, *Grizzly Adams*. The last kind of person I'd expect my boss to send me to meet. I had an uncle like that, kind of a mountain man type." She smiled and chuckled. "I loved that guy to death."

Gerard changed lanes, passed two slowpokes in recreational vehicles, and re-engaged the cruise control as she continued. "Anyway, it turned out Max was working for the National Security Agency in those days, and corrupt foreign dignitaries committing crimes in the United States was something he was tackling as a part of a special joint task force with some other agencies. I think one of them was Interpol. In any case, I told Max what I had, and how I was stymied and about to throw in the towel at work because I had the guy dead to rights and couldn't do anything about it. Max looked at me with this knowing, 'It will be OK' smile, and said, 'Give me a week before you do that, Lily. If things don't work out, then you can resign at the Boston PD and come to work with me, where you'll be appreciated.' Or something like that. I immediately trusted this guy. I know it sounds stupid. I don't trust a lot of people and almost *no one* immediately, but Max was just *different*. Anyway, I did trust him and it all worked out." She cast a glance over her shoulder to make sure Andy was occupied with his Nintendo, then said, "The bad guy ended up dead of an overdose on his own drugs, and his entire organization was rolled up. It was a major bust. Turns out his organization spanned three countries."

The afternoon was wearing on, and Gerard said, "Let me know when you want to stop to get something to eat or use a restroom. We still have over an hour to go."

Menlo checked with her son, and then said, "I think we're all right for now. If it's all the same, I think I'd prefer to just get there. I'm still a little nervous about being out in the open, I guess, after this morning."

"I'm not surprised," Gerard said. "No problem. When we get to my place we can just order in."

"Can we get pizza?" Andy piped up from the back seat.

"Whatever your mom says is OK by me," Gerard laughed. "We do have a great brick oven place near my condo that delivers."

Menlo smiled and leaned her head back against the headrest. "That would be fine," she said. In the back seat, Andy pumped one fist in the air and went back to his DS game. "So, back to your story. As you said we've got an hour to go, and I still don't know how you met Ben."

"OK," Gerard continued, "as I was saying, I met Max first. Well, when you meet Max, you're drawn into this kind of vortex, a special clandestine community of people who have been or still are what they call 'operatives' or 'operators.' They're almost all former military Special Ops of some kind. You know, Delta Force, SEALs, Army Rangers, and so on. Many of them followed up their military time with work for the CIA, NSA, Homeland Security, or one of the other agencies that have need of their specialized skills. Max happened to be especially close to three guys—Billy Winger, Ron Meriwether, and Ben Dawson. At first I'd run into them at the bar when I met Max for a drink, but then when I finally got fed up with the police department about eighteen months later, I left and went into business with Max. We have our own company now, and we do quite a bit of personal security work. There's only a half dozen employees, but we do pretty well. We started to take some work where these other operators were involved, and sometimes subcontract with them when we need added arms and legs. So as time goes on, I see more and more of these buddies of Max's. And I came to understand that Ben Dawson is a lot different from the rest of them."

"Really?" Menlo asked. "How is he different?"

Gerard considered that for a bit. She didn't really know how to answer. There was some part of her that took pride in talking about Ben and another part that wanted to keep him to herself. Besides, if, as she suspected   there was something going on between Ben and Carolyn Menlo, she ... well, she didn't know how she felt about that. Finally, she took a deep breath and let it out slowly before she continued. "Well, for one thing, he's smarter. I mean it's pretty amazing what this guy knows and knows *about*. For example, I heard him talking Shakespeare one night with Ron Meriwether. Now, Ron is studying Shakespeare in college, and he's no dummy. But I could just tell from the conversation that Dawson was telling Meriwether things he'd never heard or thought about before. It turned out Dawson had actually spent some time in Shakespeare's hometown—Stratford, I think he said. He'd gone on vacation over there all by himself just because he was interested in his work. And that's another thing about Ben. When he feels strongly about something, he *does something about it*. He *engages*, you know? He doesn't just form an opinion based on what other people say or what he reads. He goes *after* things. I admire that."

"That is interesting," Menlo said sincerely.

"Also," Gerard continued, "Ben is not former military. In fact, out of that entire band of crazy people I've been talking about, Ben is the *only* one who isn't former military."

"Except for you," Menlo reminded her.

Gerard's eyes widened. "You know, you're right. Except for me. I hadn't thought about that." She continued to turn that over in her mind until Menlo spoke up again.

"Is it important, the military background?"

"Well," Gerard replied, "I guess it's about respect and trust. Ben has spent years working shoulder-to-shoulder with the military in Iraq and Afghanistan, and with politicians and officials in several countries. But more important to guys like Max," she said, "is the fact that he didn't have to. He did it because he *chose* to do it, to help the military out or to do something that other people just couldn't do. I don't think Ben particularly *likes* working in those places; he does it out of a sense of duty to his country, and loyalty to the people he works with. It's incredibly dangerous work, and Max tells me all the time that Ben has spent more time 'outside the wire' than a lot of the soldiers and Marines stationed on the big bases there. Recently, he's been spending time in other places too, of course, but something about this project of yours got him back into Afghanistan again. Since then, things have heated up and he seems to be in the middle of quite a storm. Just like the old days, but maybe more so. And none of us is getting any younger."

"I understand what you mean," Menlo said. "I can tell you, though, that without Ben's contribution, my project would have ground to a halt. We had gotten as far as we could go, so his work a few months ago was absolutely pivotal. In a small but very real way, Ben's work is enabling us to make history. He's quite different from most of the people at the Foundation. We all have egos the size of Kilimanjaro—many of which are justified, of course—but Ben's contributions are more ... I don't know. He puts everything on the line, and I don't think many of us would do that—at least not deliberately," she said, obviously reflecting on her current situation. She was quiet for a moment and then she peeked around her seat to check on Andy who was still concentrating on his game. She turned back to Gerard. "There's no end to this, is there?"

"What do you mean?"

"I guess it just dawned on me." She was quiet again and Gerard let the silence stretch out. Finally, Menlo said, "I guess I thought once the technology was fielded, there wouldn't be any danger. But now I'm not so sure. As long as we've got such a profound technological lead, the desire for stealing the technology isn't going to go away."

Gerard looked over at the researcher. She was married to an army colonel. Surely she didn't think danger stopped at the water's edge.

"I don't want to live like this indefinitely. Looking over my shoulder and expecting the next kidnap attempt at any moment," Menlo said. "How does Ben do it?"

"Do what, exactly?" Gerard responded.

"How does he live with the danger in his work?" Menlo replied. "He must get threatened all the time. Doesn't he have a family to worry about?"

"Oh, I see what you mean," Gerard replied, but thought: *No I really don't see what you mean.* Menlo's husband was on his third deployment. Surely he'd talked to his own wife about living with danger. *Is she fishing for personal information on Ben?* "The answer is 'no', actually. He doesn't. Ben was married for a few years, but it was an unhappy marriage, and his wife died several years ago—cancer, I think. I don't think he has been involved with anyone since."

"Well," Menlo said, "while I certainly see the advantages related to his work, it must be a pretty lonely existence for him."

Gerard shrugged and said, "Well, it's not as though he hasn't had opportunities. He's just all about his work right now. You must know something about that, right? Your husband seems to be deployed a lot of the time, and that can't *all* be mandatory."

"You're right about that. Part of it with Tom, I think, is the curse of being good at what you do. Tom's bosses always loved his work, and as a result, a lot of the brass asked for him to work on their teams, and eventually to *lead* their teams on bigger and bigger projects. But a lot of it for Tom is patriotism, too. He really loves this country, and when I see his eyes light up it's always around his next deployment, and how important it is to national security or the defense of the United States. It's his passion. And as much as I ..." then she cast another quick glance toward the back seat "... as much as *we* both miss him, I came to realize that keeping him from going would mean keeping him from his purpose in life. It would be like telling me I couldn't be a scientist. It would make life pretty hollow." She sighed heavily. "So I let him go and pray he comes back safely again each time, and Andy and I do the best we can. But yes, you're right; I *do* know what it's like to lead a lonely life."

The conversation itself was getting pretty dangerous, and Gerard wasn't sure she wanted to know any more about Carolyn Menlo's lonely life—especially if she was, as Gerard suspected—thinking that Ben Dawson might be the perfect guy to step in when her evenings were particularly empty. She decided it was a good time to change lanes in terms of their conversation as she was changing lanes again while driving. "So why don't you tell me *your* story. How did you become Dr. Carolyn Menlo, super scientist?"

"Hmm," Menlo responded. "My story is not nearly as interesting as yours, I'm afraid."

"Ha!" Gerard chuckled. "You mean it's not as *long*. That's all right. Still over half an hour to go, and I have nothing else to do."

Menlo spent the next twenty minutes outlining her life story. Born in California, educated at Cal Poly and then grad school at MIT, she had been introduced to Tom Menlo who, it turned out, was not a Neanderthal like she had thought all soldiers must be. One thing led to another, and soon they were trying to make their separate careers work. She'd had offers from several of the national labs and some heavily VC-backed start-ups, but one day, in her last semester at MIT, the dean introduced her to Dr. Brystol.

"Did you know about the work of the Brystol Foundation already?" Gerard asked.

"I had never even heard of him or the Foundation," Menlo said. "The dean actually excused himself from his own office and left us alone there. That was my first clue about the importance of Dr. Brystol."

"So he recruited you," Gerard said. "Impressive."

"I don't know about recruit. He started talking about my research, and Kenneth—I mean Dr. Brystol—finally said something like, 'I have some bad news and I have some wonderful news. The bad news is that this new technology you've discovered and nurtured up to this point has been deemed to be potentially critical to national security. Effective immediately, you won't be allowed to publish any additional information about it.' Of course, I was outraged. It was *my* idea, and it was *my* work that brought it to life. I was determined to see it through, and I didn't care what the government, the faculty at MIT, or *anybody* else had to say about it. But Dr. Brystol saw that coming a mile away, and was already prepared with what he had referred to as the 'wonderful news.' He told me I would not only be able to continue working on the new technology, but that I could have my own lab and hire my own staff. Whatever funding I needed up to a multi-million dollar annual budget was mine as long as I continued to be successful. The specific application of the technology was one that would not have occurred to me immediately, especially a military application. In fact, one of the key elements didn't come out of my work at all—it came out of some alternative energy work being done about that same time by Brystol Foundation researchers. They were working on automotive propulsion systems, believe it or not. Anyway, as it all turned out, I think it's a great compromise. The new technology doesn't harm anyone and still contributes to our national defense in a huge way. It will eventually be commercialized, of course, and when that happens—even though it may be decades from now—I hope to become a wealthy woman, as the original patents are in my name. That is, of course, assuming I live to collect the royalties from the technology one day."

"I'll do what I can to make sure that happens," Gerard said. "So will Kelly and Ben. And I don't pretend to be particularly insightful when it comes to gambling, but I will say this much: I'd never bet against Ben Dawson."

"So, if you don't mind my asking," Menlo said, "are you and Max Kelly a couple?"

"A couple?" Gerard replied. "Now that's an interesting way to look at it. Max and I are, well, kind of inexplicable, I guess. Max is an extraordinary man in some ways. We are business partners in the firm of Kelly & Gerard Enterprises, LLP. We often 'date,' I guess you'd say. He sometimes refers to me as his 'main squeeze.' But we're not married, not engaged, and have no plans to do either."

"That's interesting," Menlo said. "So, is there something between you and Ben then?"

The smile that spread across Gerard's face was a sheepish one that she fought against in vain. "No," she sighed, "although I keep telling them I'm woman enough for *both* of them."

Menlo looked at her and thought: *I don't think she's kidding … not kidding at all.*

Gerard continued, "But the thing about Max is that he has a dark side. Sometimes he actually scares me, and I'm not easy to scare."

"From what I've seen, I certainly agree with you there! You were so calm back there when … you know," Menlo said.

"It's my training. And I'm not saying I think Max would ever harm me," Gerard said, "but bad guys—well, I don't think there's much Max wouldn't do if he thought it was necessary—or even just a good idea. Or convenient. I've never said this to anyone before, but I don't think I could be married to Max. Hmm … I don't think I've even said that to myself."

Gerard stopped at a light and then turned down the street, nearing her condo. Pulling into the driveway, she looked at Menlo and smiled. "Home sweet home. At least for a while."

CHAPTER 22

When Fengche sped away from the small group of buildings where Colonel Menlo was held, he was bleeding badly from his shoulder. The pain from that wound coupled with the one in his arm were almost enough to cause him to black out. It took him fifteen minutes to find a clinic, and it was almost miraculous that he made it before he bled out. He staggered through the door and collapsed in the waiting area only to wake up two days later in the Imam Khomeini Hospital in Zabol.

After he regained consciousness, the hospital staff alerted a representative from the Chinese consulate who arrived at the hospital thirty minutes later. The consulate staff member was also a member of the MSS, and he arrived prepared to debrief Fengche and get the results of the debriefing off to both the MSS department director in Beijing and Jing-ti in Washington, DC as soon as he had them. It took about ninety minutes to gather the information from Fengche, get back to the consulate, and get it out on a secure line. Fengche was scheduled to remain another week in the hospital before he could be released. In the meantime, the governments of Iran and China were engaged in some interesting discussions about how a Chinese national with clear ties to the US came to be shot up and bleeding in Iran with no record of his entry into the country. It was not a good day for the Chinese ambassador.

* * * *

On the other side of the planet, Bi-shou was also not having a good day. In fact, it had been a less-than-stellar week. She had met the armored van at the municipal airport in Charlotte, and waited for her operatives to arrive with Menlo and her son. When they didn't arrive on time, she radioed them without success. She directed the pilot to spin up the helicopter again, and as soon as they were ready, they lifted off. But by the time they were over the site, everyone was gone. There were a couple of remaining vehicles, since Kelly's team had not yet returned to retrieve them, but there were no signs of life.

Bi-shou's anger was almost palpable as she signaled the pilot to return to the airport. She was not accustomed to failure; she really couldn't afford it in her business, in fact. This would be viewed as a sign of weakness, and an indication that she was beginning to decline in her capabilities and reliability. She knew that could only lead to disaster. When she landed at the airport, she fired off a message to Jing-ti, apologizing profusely and vowing to recover Menlo just as quickly as possible if he would only give her another chance. She almost choked on the words as she typed the message; her hands were shaking with rage. *I hope the operatives are dead, because if they aren't dead now, they will be when I find them.*

Jing-ti was stunned when he received Bi-shou's message. Bi-shou came with the highest recommendation from his boss, and seemed exceptionally competent. Her track record with Teng-hui and with MSS was impeccable. *Until now,* he thought. But the worst aspect of this situation was that Bi-shou was the fallback plan to gain leverage with Menlo should Fengche, another historically revered operator, fail. Now the primary plan and the fallback plan had *both* failed. The critical path of his elaborate and detailed plan was completely broken.

The only thing Jing-ti could come up with was to abort this plan, and move to the least desirable option: capturing Menlo's three subordinates, Wu, McCallister, and Hoffman, and perhaps assassinating Menlo when she surfaced again. This was an extraordinarily messy approach. The sheer risk management aspect would be almost impossible to accomplish. Furthermore, the fact that neither Fengche nor Bi-shou had proven successful would likely cause Teng-hui and his superiors in Beijing to lose confidence in Jing-ti's ability to plan and execute critically important matters such as this one. Jing-ti had no doubt that he was standing on a precipice, with his career hanging in the balance. Teng-hui, when he became aware of this, could well push him over the edge in an effort to save himself.

* * * *

Back in Ziranj, Ben Dawson was slowly regaining consciousness. His head felt as though it had been caved in with a baseball bat, and he actually saw stars when he opened his eyes for the first time. As this personal constellation cleared from his vision, the first thing he saw was the face of Najia Koofi. She was a bit blurry for a moment, and then he felt the prick of a needle in his right arm, and he drifted back off to sleep, feeling the soft hand of Koofi resting gently on his forehead.

After several more hours, he awakened again. This time his head only protested with a dull ache, his ears were no longer ringing, and his vision was clear. He didn't recognize the room, but knew it must be Koofi's bed in which he lay. Dressed in a long white tunic and nothing else, Dawson was covered by a sheet. A very light blanket lay over the sheet where it would warm his feet.

Dawson laid there for some time, staring at the ceiling and trying to paste the shards of his memory back together. After about forty minutes, it came rushing back. He attempted to sit up in alarm, realizing how tenuous the situation had been and wanting desperately to know the status of Menlo and his team. That abrupt repositioning was a mistake, and the resulting pain actually caused him to cry out in response.

Within seconds, Koofi was at his side again. She sat on the bed beside him, speaking gently while pressing a cool wet cloth to his face and forehead, alternating the position of the damp cloth between rinsings in a shallow bowl of water on her bedside table. He started to speak, but Koofi gently placed three fingers to his mouth, and spoke herself instead. "Let me speak first. I think I can answer many of the questions you have and save you the energy of asking them. You are still weak. Doctor Heidari has been treating you. He says that you are going to be well again soon. You should be able to walk a little tonight or tomorrow. Your friends are all well. Mr. Winger is waiting down the hall. You should know he would not leave your side until you were well on your way to recovery. He even slept on the floor here in this room for two nights to protect you in case the ANP should find us, but they did not, and that has all quieted down. It has been three days since you arrived."

Koofi laid the washcloth aside, poured water into a glass from a plastic bottle, and held it to his lips. "Now drink a little," she said. "We must not allow you to dehydrate."

The water helped, and he tried to speak. It was very scratchy at first, but he managed to croak out, "Colonel Menlo?"

"I will call Mr. Winger in," Koofi replied, "and he can tell you all these things. Do you think you are strong enough for that now?" She took the water glass away, set it on the table, and used the damp cloth to wipe a few remaining drops from his lower lip and chin.

At that point, Dawson realized that in spite of his circumstances, he had been bathed and shaved. Someone, presumably Koofi, had cared for him as well as if he had been in any American hospital, perhaps better. "Yes, I think so," he replied. Koofi began to rise from her place at his side, but then seemed to change her mind. Settling back again, she turned to him and placed her hand gently behind his neck. It felt cool and soft. She leaned in slowly then and kissed him. Gently, but with the fullness of intent and meaning. When she pulled away, she said nothing but her eyes were glistening.

Dawson also said nothing, but in his case it was owing to having absolutely no idea what to say. Koofi was an attractive woman, but Dawson simply had never considered her in a romantic light. Still, there was no denying the stirring she had invoked with that kiss. It was like entering an alternate reality for him. Koofi rose, smiled and said, "We will talk later." With that she left the room, and a moment later Winger appeared in the doorway.

"So, back in the land of the living, are you?" Winger asked through a broad smile.

"I think so," Dawson replied. "I haven't figured out quite how, though," he admitted. "How about catching me up?"

"Sure thing, Boss, if you're up to it," Winger said. He dragged a rickety old wooden chair over from the corner of the room and set it on the floor next to the bed where he could be heard even when speaking quietly. He put the back of the chair facing Dawson and straddled it, crossing his arms and leaning them on the top of the chair's back.

"Najia tells me that you're asking about the colonel, so I'll start there. Colonel Menlo has been transported to Landstuhl Regional Medical Center just outside Ramstein Air Base in Germany. As you know, I think, it's a damned fine hospital and it's the only US Medical Center in Europe. I've been promised he will get VIP treatment there, and initial reports are that he will make a full recovery."

"How did you manage that?" Dawson asked.

"I didn't," Winger replied. "McCartney did. In fact, McCartney saved our bacon." He went on to recount the events that had brought them to where they were.

McCartney had been returning to Herat when his text message from

Dawson arrived. He had turned around immediately, but between the often treacherous roads and the fact that he was uncertain about the exact location of the madrassa Dawson had been referring to, it took him some time to find it. When he arrived, he was following the third ANP truck that appeared just about the time Dawson's team was diving into the karez behind the madrassa. Because they weren't expecting him, McCartney had the advantage of surprise and the advantage of a flanking position. He was able to take out the remaining ANP personnel and get Romero, Dawson, Winger, and Menlo out before additional ANP arrived. After conferring with the Axis office in Herat, it was decided that the best approach would be to airlift Menlo through Herat and on to Germany.

"Dr. Heidari was able to get you stabilized here," Winger said, "and give Chief some basic treatment, but as you know there's really not much you can do about cracked ribs except let them heal on their own. Anyway, McCartney and Chief got the colonel up to Herat by car, and McCartney got 'em both onto a military transport from there. That took some string pulling, but as soon as Axis communicated to the Foundation about what was happening, they got to the right people who contacted the Pentagon, and from there it was pretty smooth sailing."

Dawson thought about that for a minute. "Sounds like McCartney pulled us out of the fire," he mused.

"You can say that again, Boss," Winger replied. "I know your plan was to get out of the firefight using that karez, and it might have worked if you'd been mobile. But once we lost you in that blast, we just couldn't move you and the colonel through that tunnel and cover our flank effectively. Fighting our way back out going forward was our only option, and it was looking pretty bleak until McCartney showed up. I think you ought to hire that guy."

Dawson smiled. "I probably couldn't afford him," he said. "Have you heard anything from Kelly?"

"No, but Kelly doesn't really have a secure channel to me," Winger replied. "I think he only knows how to reach you. I assume you are using the Gmail method?"

Dawson nodded. "Can you get my laptop for me?"

"Be right back," Winger said, and strode out through the doorway. A few minutes later Dawson had his laptop hooked up to a satellite communications device and was looking at the message from Kelly.

"Bi-shou," Dawson said aloud.

"Bi-shou, the Chinese assassin?" Winger asked. "She's mixed up in this?"

"Evidently Bi-shou sent some operators in to get Carolyn Menlo," Dawson replied, "but it sounds like Kelly got *them* instead."

"Man, if it was really Bi-shou, Kelly got lucky," Winger said. "I hear she has a near-perfect batting average."

"Apparently not anymore," Dawson said. "Which means that if she is still alive, then…."

"Right," Winger interjected, "if she's still alive, Kelly had better keep out of her way, because she is going to be *pissed*."

Dawson sighed. "Just what we need," he said.

Dawson responded to Kelly via Gmail. He communicated that the package had been recovered intact, but they had encountered some challenges that would delay their return by a few days. He went on to say: *Expect us back within a week. In the meantime, please inform the doctor that her item is being cleaned and packaged and should be prepared for shipment soon. I am informed that she should have the item she ordered within a couple of weeks, in good working order. As to the product from China you mentioned, I am passing along that information to company headquarters; they will want to look into the matter. Based on what you have related, however, I recommend you remain extremely vigilant. This carrier will not be pleased the package she was tracking has been lost.*

Then he used the Gmail account he had set up to communicate with Carolyn Menlo and simply sent: *MENLO5; Kelly has more.*

Finally, he went to the account where he left messages for Jennings. In it, he alerted Jennings cryptically that there had been an attempted abduction, but that Menlo and her son were safe. He also passed along the most critical information he had—the fact that the operators had been engaged by Bi-shou and had used two telephone numbers for contact. He provided the numbers Kelly had extracted from the operatives in Virginia. Then he closed the laptop and unplugged the sat-comm device.

"So," he said to Winger, "if I am ambulatory, do you think we can get under way back toward the States tomorrow?"

"Absolutely!" Winger replied enthusiastically. "I really need a beer, and Biggles is calling my name." Biggles was Winger's favorite bar at the Millennium Hotel in Dubai. A few years earlier, after a particularly arduous deployment in Afghanistan's Helmand Province, he and Dawson spent a big part of several days watching World Cup soccer on the big screen at Biggles. Dawson had enjoyed observing the broad array of people from all over the world cheering on their favorite teams while he relaxed and drank copious amounts of iced tea. Winger had also consumed copious quantities, but in his case of course, it wasn't iced tea. "I can call in our ride whenever you're ready to go," Winger said. "We have a chopper on call. Axis will pick us up just outside of town."

Later that evening, Dawson was able to walk to the eating area and sit down for a meal. Koofi joined them for dinner but then excused herself and went to handle a few more Women's Center matters. After dinner, he strolled around the grounds of the compound with Winger and tested his legs a bit. It was a comparatively cool evening with a light breeze, and the fresh air felt good. Eventually, dusk closed in and the men went back inside. "You all right for tonight then, Boss?" Winger asked. "I'm gonna turn in."

"Of course," Dawson said through a stifled yawn. "See you in the morning."

Dawson spent another hour checking and packing his gear. Then he extinguished the single light source in the room, a small lamp on the bedside table, shoved off his sandals, and fell back onto the pillows. He had been in bed about thirty minutes and was finally drifting off when he felt something soft and warm on his outstretched arm, then easing over onto his shoulder. In the near-total darkness, he could just make out the form of Koofi's head.

"Najia?" he said.

"Yes, Ben," she replied, and he realized that this was the first time she had ever called him by his first name. "I am here. I would like to speak with you now."

"Oh, of course," he said, and began to turn his body to face her.

But she pressed her hand against his chest, pushing him back toward the mattress, and said: "Just stay where you are and relax." She left her hand there, and eventually, as she spoke, lightly traced the tips of her fingers across his chest in soothing circles. "When you were here the last time," she said, "I told you that Commander Ahmadi has asked me to marry him. You asked me a question then. You said, 'Do you love him?' Do you remember that?"

"Yes, I remember," Dawson replied. "But you never answered me."

"I did not know what to say," Koofi replied. "Here in Afghanistan, as you know, things are very different than the way these things are in the United States. Women here do not often have the opportunity to choose, or to decide. We are simply given in marriage by our families. I am different, because my parents were from other countries, and because my family no longer lives. So I have a little choice in these matters. But the way things are here in this country, I am very blessed that Allah has caused Commander Ahmadi to want to make me his second wife, and to care for me. To receive such protection for myself and my women here, it can only be from Allah."

"I see," Dawson replied, believing that Koofi was concluding what she had to say, and was likely to leave him to rest.

"I believe you do understand that, Ben. You have spent much time here in this part of the world, and you understand many things that others do not. But when I kissed you tonight, I know you felt another answer from me as well."

"Yes, Najia," he admitted, "I did, and I was very surprised. But you know that I must…."

"Yes," Koofi interjected, "I do know that you must leave tomorrow. It is the right thing to do. You have others to protect, and another life you must lead on the other side of the world. Allah has woven our destinies together like this," she said, lacing her fingers in his, "but our destinies are not the same. I have decided that I will marry the commander because Allah would not have caused him to ask me to marry him if that was not his will. But we both know that none of that would have happened if Allah had not sent you to us, to me, first. And because you asked me if I love Commander Ahmadi, I want you to understand. If my decision was based only on the desire of my heart, my decision would be different, and I would beg you to take me back to America with you. I love you, Ben, in ways that I could never love anyone else, not even the commander. You alone, in all of my life, are the only man who ever asked me what *I* wanted."

"Najia, you don't need to…."

Again she stopped him by placing her fingers gently across his lips. "Ben, I know you have been very badly hurt by the events in your past, and that those things have something to do with your wife. I can tell this from things that you said before, and from some things your friends have said. I think you have hidden your feelings and your needs away and starved your heart for a very long time. I know you must leave tomorrow, but before you go, I will feed you tonight. I will feed the part of you that you have denied for so long and try to restore your heart so it can beat again. You have done so much for me, and for all of us. I promised myself when you were here many months ago that I would show you my gratitude one day. Now I want to do this for you. *Please.*" Dawson could find no words, and so he kissed her, tears slipping from his eyes, and Koofi fulfilled her promise.

CHAPTER 23

After Charles Jennings received Dawson's Gmail message, he reviewed the NSA's available information on Bi-shou. The assassin's record of known kills outside the United States was staggering. She was strongly suspected of many hits in the US as well, but none could be tied to her with sufficient evidence to make a case that would stick. Her reputation was well known throughout the intelligence community and the upper echelons of federal law enforcement organizations, so Jennings was not surprised to see her name surface. But this strongly confirmed the link between attempts to inhibit and steal the Salacia technology with the Chinese government and in particular the MSS. Jennings immediately pulled in his best team of analysts. He provided them with the information Kelly had obtained, and they set to work.

Two analysts started with the telephone numbers, one attacking each of the two numbers. Two more went to work on Bi-shou's known movements based on credit card records assigned under her name, and under the names of those who worked directly for her in her office. Another analyst reached out to operatives assigned within NSA and also from other agency branches to gather all of the information available on Bi-shou's known and suspected clients, especially within the Chinese government, and most especially within MSS.

There was a camera trained on the front entrance of the building containing Teng-hui's office twenty-four hours a day, seven days a week. The CIA had the camera and transmitter housed within a telephone transformer shell, and mounted on the telephone pole across the street. The video captured faces with good quality, and automobile license plates with near perfection. Analysts began to scour the footage in detail beginning thirty days prior, and identified at least two occasions where Bi-shou had visited the office building.

When he had the dates and times of Bi-shou's visits, Jennings scheduled a lunch with John Deering, a close friend, in the Taft Dining Room at the Washington University Club. When Jennings and his friend met there, it was always to trade favors, and usually those favors involved information. Deering was deputy director of the Central Intelligence Agency and had, for a number of years, led the counter-espionage organization within the agency. They had been friends since college, and both had benefited richly from the friendship, especially on a professional level, over the years.

The two men had a wonderful lunch and had settled back in their chairs with coffee to chat afterward. Jennings always enjoyed the sheer sumptuousness, not just of the food, but of the dining room itself. Adorned with a grand piano, rich tapestries, and silver candelabras, Jennings almost wished he needed favors more frequently.

"So, Charles," his friend asked, "is there something particular on your mind today?"

Jennings sighed and resigned himself to business. "Yes, John," he replied, "there is. It's Bi-shou. I need your help."

Deering took a sip of coffee from the delicate cup in his hand. "Shouldn't you be speaking with our friends at the Bureau? I presume you're referring to some kind of recent activities on US soil."

"Yes, and yes," Jennings replied. "But I don't have time for formalities right now. I realize the camera in place outside Teng-hui's building officially belongs to the FBI, but I also know who monitors the footage, and for the most part, that's your people. I know of two specific times Bi-shou entered that building within the last thirty days, and I need to know who she visited when she was there along with anything else I can learn about the content or duration of the meetings."

"I see," Deering replied, replacing the delicate cup on the equally delicate saucer in his other hand. "Well," he said, "I suppose that if it was something easy, we would not be here."

"No," Jennings was forced to admit. "We would not."

Deering didn't bother to ask Jennings just how he thought Deering could get such information. The CIA had at least one operative well placed inside that building. Jennings knew that, and Deering knew that Jennings knew. "What would those dates and times be, Charles?" Deering asked. Jennings withdrew a business card from his pocket with the dates and times listed in neat script on the back, and passed it to Deering. Deering glanced at it briefly, and placed it immediately in his pocket. "How urgently do you need this information?"

"Oh, you know how these things are. The sooner the better."

"Well then," he said, placing the coffee aside, "I suppose I had better get back to the office. I will send along whatever we come up with as soon as possible."

"Thank you, John," Jennings said, rising. "I appreciate it."

By the time Jennings returned to his office, there was already news waiting for him. Dan Winters, one of the department leads, had asked Jennings' administrative assistant to alert him as soon as he returned, so he was only moments behind Jennings when he arrived at his desk. Winters, an ambitious and talented thirty-something up-and-comer, was nearly giddy. "You're going to like this," he grinned as he crossed the room. "We ran the cell records of Bi-shou against the known times and locations you got from your source with no hits."

"And I like this because?" Jennings asked.

"Because," Winters replied, "we then checked similar circumstances against cell numbers listed under the names of Bi-shou's direct reports at the office she runs here in DC. When we checked the records of a cell number listed under Michael Guo, we got location and timing matches for not only the times when she visited the building where Teng-hui operates his little MSS storefront, but also several calls between that number—" he said, pushing a piece of paper across the desk where Jennings was now seated "—and this one. This one belongs to a man named Jing-ti."

"Ah," Jennings responded. "Teng-hui's chief of operations."

"Exactly," Winters replied. "Of course, we'll need a court order to open up the actual conversation and listen to its content. But frankly, given the timing here and the position fixes we've established...."

"Yes, I see where you're going with this," Jennings interjected. "And now that you have *this* node in the network, there will undoubtedly be other nodes and tendrils."

"Yes, Sir," Winters agreed, "I'm on it. By tomorrow morning, I expect to have a number of requests for court orders on your desk. In addition to the communications, I'd like to look into funds transfers."

"Yes, there is very likely to be a relationship that can be developed there as well, I realize," Jennings said. "All right. Let's go for broke here. Bank records and funds transfers—especially any which cross national borders. We'll look at real estate holdings as well. Pull together a list for the lot of them, and I'll take them over for signatures at one time. I am running a trapline of my own as well, but this is excellent work, Daniel. Please keep me apprised. I'd like to know where you are at—" he glanced at his watch, "—say around 1800 hours."

"Yes, Sir," Winters responded, and hurried out, reminding Jennings of a dog with a fresh bone.

After Winters left, Jennings sat quietly and thought about the current circumstances in light of recent developments. Something was bothering him, and he wasn't precisely certain what it was. He pulled out a blank sheet of lined paper and began to scratch out a set of timelines and activities.

Finally, he punched a button on his desk and asked his administrative assistant to come into his office.

"Yes, Sir?" Gloria Treadway asked as she approached his desk.

"I'd like you to reach either Max Kelly or Lily Gerard at Kelly & Gerard Enterprises, and determine whether I can have a personal chat with one of them this afternoon."

"Yes, Sir," she replied. "Is this a local company?"

"Yes, here in the DC area."

"I'll get right on it," she replied, and left the room.

About three minutes later there was a gentle knock on his door, and Treadway slipped back into the room. "Sir, there is a bit of a complication with your request to meet Mr. Kelly or Ms. Gerard. I did reach Ms. Gerard, but apparently they are in the midst of a rather delicate case, and Mr. Kelly cannot be reached until sometime this evening. Ms. Gerard is working from home this afternoon and is unable to leave there for some reason."

Jennings thought about this for a minute, and then said, "Very well. Please provide my driver with Ms. Gerard's home address, and tell him I'll be down in five minutes."

"Yes, Sir," she said, and wheeled for the door.

Because it was now mid-afternoon and traffic was relatively light, Jennings' car pulled up in the driveway of Gerard's condo just thirty-five minutes later. Jennings instructed his driver, who was also his bodyguard, to wait outside, which also meant to make himself as inconspicuous as possible. Jennings rang the condo's doorbell twice before Lily Gerard answered.

Gerard had watched as the blacked-out government-issue VIP sedan pulled up in her driveway, and although they had never met, she knew exactly who the man was emerging from the car.

She quickly considered ordering Menlo and her son to the bedroom, but then thought better of it. It would have rattled them again, and as nearly as Gerard could tell, there was no need for that. So she merely warned them that she had a visitor, but that they should just continue what they were doing. In this case, that meant finishing another brick oven pizza they'd ordered to Andy's great delight. *For heaven's sake,* Gerard thought, *doesn't she ever let this kid have pizza?*

She opened the door on the second ring.

"Ms. Gerard," Jennings said, "my name is Charles Jennings, and I'm a deputy director at the National Security Agency and a very close colleague of Ben Dawson."

"Yes," Gerard responded as impassively as she could, "I recognize you."

"May I come in?" Jennings asked. "I'd like to speak with you for a few minutes if I may."

"Of course," Gerard said, backing away to allow him to step inside and then closing and dead-bolting the door behind him. "Please have a seat in the living room, and I'll be right with you. May I offer you something to drink?"

Jennings smiled. "No thank you," he replied, "but that's very kind. I don't intend to take more than a few minutes of your time." He walked across the hall and took a seat on the living room sofa.

"OK. I'll be right back," Gerard said, and disappeared a few steps down the hall. He could hear muted conversation from what he believed was probably the kitchen, and then Gerard returned.

Sitting down across from him in a small rocking chair, she asked: "How can I help you, Mr. Jennings?"

Jennings cleared his throat and launched. "Well, first of all, I know that you and Mr. Kelly are working on a case for Ben Dawson related to Dr. Menlo of the Brystol Foundation. I was forwarded some information from Ben this morning about events that transpired a few days ago, and something about the timeline and events is bothering me. I was wondering if either of you could help me with it," he said.

"Well, Max is in the field, but I'll certainly help you if I can," Gerard said. "What is it you need to know?"

"As I understand the sequence of events, Ben has engaged your firm to perform personal protection services for Dr. Menlo and her son Andy, and he engaged you before he left for the Middle East. Is that correct?"

"Yes, that's correct," Gerard responded, wondering what exactly Jennings was getting at.

"And so I presume you have had the Menlos under surveillance since that time?" Jennings asked.

"Continuously," Gerard replied.

Jennings continued: "Ms. Gerard, at any time during the last several days, did you notice anyone watching the movements of the Menlos?" Gerard thought about this. The only person they had seen observing Menlo was Fengche, and that was before Dawson left Dulles Airport.

"Not since Ben left the country, Sir," Gerard said, "and believe me, if there was a tail, we'd have known."

Jennings smiled reservedly. "Yes, Ms. Gerard, your reputation, and of course Max's, are well known to us at the agency. I have no doubt about the quality of your work." With that, Gerard relaxed a bit.

"So here is my conundrum," Jennings said. "How did the enemy know that Dr. Menlo had been issued a warn order and was leaving for her sister's home in Atlanta? The fact that they were prepared for her during the drive means they knew almost as soon as she knew herself that she was going. Do you see what I mean?" Gerard thought about that. "Yes, I do," she said slowly, a frown clouding her face, "and it's an interesting point. I wonder whether she made a call from the road. I know Ben would have instructed her *not* to, but I think we should ask."

"I agree," Jennings replied. "Can you reach her now?"

"Yes," Gerard smiled, "she and Andy are eating pizza in my kitchen. Would you care to meet them?"

Jennings was already standing. "I would very much, thank you," he said. He followed her through the hallway and into the kitchen, where Menlo and her son were still chewing on their margarita pizza.

"Carolyn, Andy," Gerard said by way of introduction, "surreal as it seems, this is Deputy Director Jennings of the National Security Agency. Deputy Director, this is Dr. Carolyn Menlo and her son Andrew."

Menlo hastily wiped her fingers on a napkin, and stood to extend her hand.

"Dr. Menlo," Jennings said, shaking her hand firmly, "it is a great pleasure to meet you. I know recent circumstances have been very difficult for you, and we are doing everything we can to sort things out. I understand your husband is now recuperating in one of the best medical facilities in the world, and we hope to have him back here to you very soon."

"Thank you, Sir. That is my understanding as well. We, I mean Andy and I, are *extremely* grateful to Ben for all he's done, and especially grateful to Lily and Max as well. If it hadn't been for them, I don't know what would have happened to us."

"Yes, I understand what you mean," Jennings said, "but Ben clearly placed you in capable hands." He glanced at Gerard. "By the way, I would appreciate it if all of you would call me Charles, and if you would allow me, I'd like to call you by your first names as well. I think it would just be easier. Now," he said, waving them all to a seat at the table and taking one himself, "I'd appreciate it if you could answer a question for me."

"Of course," Menlo responded. Andrew stared at Jennings, but kept eating his pizza.

"I'm trying to determine how the people who attempted to abduct you from the highway knew about your route and that you were under way. Could you tell me, please, who knew where you were going and when they knew it?"

Menlo thought about the question. "*No one* knew," she said. "I received the notice from Ben when I woke up, and had Andy in the car about a half hour later. Ben had told us to pack a Go Bag, and I threw it in the car, woke Andy, and left. We didn't stop to tell anyone we were leaving." Jennings' brow furrowed. It didn't make any sense.

Suddenly, a light came on in Andrew's eyes. He stopped chewing and sat bolt upright in his chair. "What about Gillian and Kristi's mom?" he said excitedly. "They knew, 'cause we called them from the car!"

Menlo covered her mouth for a moment. Andy was absolutely right. "Of course," Menlo said, returning her gaze to Jennings. "Joan. We had an appointment with her and her kids, Gillian and Kristi, and I had to call her so she wouldn't be waiting for us at the park. I told her my sister had some problems, and I had to drive down there at the last minute. But Joan wouldn't have—"

"Carolyn," Jennings interrupted her, "the call was probably intercepted. But we have to find out. What is your friend Joan's last name, and how do you know her?"

"Her name is Joan Wu," Menlo said, noticing a momentary flicker in Jennings' eyes when he heard Joan's surname, "but she works for me, and I have known her for years. She has a Secret clearance, and she would never do anything to jeopardize Andy or me."

"I'm sure you're right," Jennings responded, although his tone was less than convincing. "As I said, the call was probably monitored. Do you have the mobile phone that you used to make that call with you now?"

"Yes," Menlo said. "It's in the bedroom."

"I'd like to borrow it if I may, and have it checked for bugs. Would you mind? I can have it back to you in the morning."

"Of course not," she said. "Andy, would you please get my cell phone from the bedroom for Charles? I have it plugged into the charger." Menlo smiled to see that Andy, entrusted with such a grown-up task, actually pushed his chair back and strode in an orderly fashion from the room rather than engage in his normal shove-off-and-run routine. She met Gerard's eyes and saw that she had noticed it, too. She was smiling.

"Carolyn, are you *absolutely certain* that you made no other calls, and no one else called you right up to the moment of the attempted abduction?" Jennings asked.

"Yes, absolutely," Menlo replied. "Ben had given me very clear instructions, and I violated them only that one time. It looks like that one infraction nearly got us kidnapped and got a couple of the bad guys killed." Jennings was hearing about that for the first time, and shot a glance at Gerard. She carefully didn't meet his gaze, which spoke volumes to the veteran intelligence officer. He decided, quite deliberately, that he didn't hear that remark.

"Don't be too hard on yourself, Carolyn," he said, standing to leave. "This cloak-and-dagger work isn't what you are trained for, and your professional contributions, if I may say so, will greatly eclipse all of ours combined. I think you can be forgiven the occasional infraction. That's why Mr. Kelly and Lily are here."

"Yes," Gerard said in a tone of self-rebuke, "and I should have asked that question immediately when we got on the road. That was an oversight on my part."

"You saved our lives, Lily," Menlo told her. "I'd say that was a pretty good day."

Andy returned to the room, handing the phone and the charger to Jennings. All three adults noticed that he had neatly wound the charger cord around the charger and presented both the phone and the charger assembly to Jennings. "I thought you might need the charger, so I brought it, too," he said to Jennings.

"Yes, I see," Jennings replied. "And a very neat job you've done here, too. Good thinking, Andy. I'm sure your mom and dad are very proud of you, and I have a feeling that you and I will be seeing each other again one day. We have need of young men like you." With that, he placed the items in the pocket of his suit jacket, excused himself, and walked with Gerard to her front door. "I'll have someone return the phone tomorrow morning," he said quietly to

Gerard. "Do you want them brought here?"

"Yes, I'm keeping them with me until I see the whites of Ben Dawson's eyes," Gerard replied. "We'll be right here."

"Do you require any backup, or other assistance?" Jennings asked.

"Not that I can think of," Gerard replied. "But I'll call you if something comes to mind."

"Please do," Jennings said, pressing a business card into her hand. This is my mobile number. Use it day or night."

"Thank you," Gerard responded, "I will."

CHAPTER 24

Jennings returned to his office about an hour later, having dropped Menlo's cell phone off with the tech support people in another part of the building. He told them he needed the device returned to him by eight a.m. the following day. The 1800—six o'clock in the evening—status update with Daniel Winters went even better than Jennings expected. By that time, Winters reported, they had confirmed that Bi-shou was in fact using her subordinate's cell phone and had been able to pinpoint her location at critical times over the last three weeks, and especially over the last week. They were now working on identifying the owners of all of the other numbers who had called that number, or to whom that device had placed calls.

"Remarkably," Winters told him, "these people don't change SIM"—Subscriber Identity Module—"cards very often. Bi-shou hasn't changed this one for a month. We have a pretty complete call history spanning the last thirty days."

"She probably simply changes phones," Jennings mused, "alternating between the phones of other subordinates. It reminds me of the way Ben Dawson exchanges rental vehicles." As it happened, Jennings was right. Bi-shou exchanged phones with one of her staff on the first day of each new month of the Chinese calendar.

"So what do we know so far, Daniel?" Jennings asked.

"We have calls and likely physical meetings between Bi-shou and Teng-hui,

Bi-shou and Jing-ti, and Bi-shou and both Teng-hui and Jing-ti," Winters replied. "We are a little murky here, but we believe that Teng-hui has used Bi-shou on at least two earlier occasions, and probably more. They have been seen together on eight occasions under various circumstances, and each time they are involved in earnest conversations. However, we have no information about the content of those conversations. They have been very careful. We believe," and at this point he placed a printed list of times and dates on Jennings' desk and pointed out one line of text, "that this visit by Bi-shou to Teng-hui's building was probably the occasion when Teng-hui introduced Bi-shou to Jing-ti. He may well have engaged Bi-shou and placed her under contract with Jing-ti as her handler for this assignment. You'll notice all of these subsequent calls, as well as the meetings listed here between Bi-shou and Jing-ti, follow that initial meeting that we believe was the introductory one. As you can see, the volume of communication traffic continued to escalate between then and the abduction attempt a few days ago."

"Yes, I see," Jennings replied. "I may be able to confirm or refute that in a day or so, but we need to move on this quickly. What else has come up?"

"Well," Winters responded, "once we had the number that Bi-shou has been using to communicate with Teng-hui, we discovered an interesting pattern between the Teng-hui number, which, by the way, appears to be a burner. We saw a frequent communication pattern between that number and another number which corresponded in proximity to the Pentagon. It never originated inside the Pentagon, of course, because—"

"Because cell signals are blocked in the Pentagon," Jennings interrupted.

"Exactly, Sir," Winters continued, "but as you know, most Pentagon employees who want to use their cells just walk outside to the courtyard to make a call. That's exactly what has been happening with this number. So we went back and looked at the badge swipes for Pentagon employees going out to that courtyard and returning at times that bracket these specific calls. One name comes up every time."

"Daniel, that is excellent work!" Jennings exclaimed, with uncharacteristic enthusiasm. "Just excellent. And that name is…?"

Winters' eyes flicked around the room as if someone else might be hiding. He lowered his voice and said, "Ralph Simons, Sir."

Jennings just stared at Winters for a moment, unblinking. *Ralph Simons?* Simons, a career US government official, held the purse strings for most covert activities related to the Department of Defense. As such, he knew who was spending how much and on which programs. He had the trust of the most senior levels of the military, including the Joint Chiefs of Staff. This wasn't looking good at all. When he emerged from his momentary reverie, Jennings said: "I want court orders as soon as you can get them to me. We need to know the content of those conversations. Anything else?"

"Probably, Sir," Winters replied, "but I honestly don't know what yet. We are continuing to dig, and depending on what's contained in those conversations...."

"Quite right," Jennings interjected. "Obviously, this has just become the most important and urgent project in the agency. Treat it that way, especially as regards resource allocation and urgency. Take whatever you need, and send anyone who objects to me."

"Yes, Sir," Winters replied, and charged from the room.

When Winters was gone, Jennings dialed the personal cell number of Cal Ingram, director of the Federal Bureau of Investigation. He had done this only twice since assuming his position at NSA. Ingram picked up on the third ring.

"Hello, Charles," Ingram said. "It's been a while."

"Yes, it has," Jennings replied, "and like the last time, I wish it were under more pleasant circumstances. Would it be possible for you to meet with me this evening? I believe this will take less than thirty minutes."

Ingram agreed to meet at the wine bar at the Four Seasons Hotel. It took Jennings about an hour to get there, and when he arrived, Ingram had already secured a corner table out of the main traffic pattern. Jennings filled him in on what had transpired thus far, carefully omitting certain facts to avoid unnecessary scrutiny around the activities of Kelly and Gerard as well as his conversation with John Deering at CIA. After bringing him up to speed, Ingram agreed to quietly begin looking into the Simons end of things, and the two agreed to meet again each evening thereafter. "I'd like to bring John Deering in, as well," Jennings said. "Some of this is clearly tied to external players, and I think leaving CIA out of the loop would be problematic."

Ingram considered this and then, much to Jennings' relief, agreed. "I think you're right, Charles. CIA will need to come into this at some point, although the bulk of it sounds like the Bureau's jurisdiction to me."

"I understand, Cal," Jennings replied, "and I appreciate it. I'll talk with you tomorrow then. Shall we say the same time and place?"

"That will work for me," Ingram replied.

Over the course of the next few days, the investigations at NSA, CIA, and the FBI built a very tight case against Simons. Work by the NSA identified communications between the burner phone used by Simons and several other numbers used by Teng-hui, as well as another operative who Winters believed to be a Russian agent. That one was likely to take a while to unravel. There was some disagreement between Ingram and Deering about how to deal with that problem. Ingram wanted to wait until they were able to identify the agent, determine what he had, and roll up as much of his network as possible. Deering wanted to wait only until they had enough damning information to squeeze Simons, and draw the rest of the information out of him that way.

Winters tasked one of the NSA systems to identify any correlations between Simons' communications dates and the dates of funds transfers into and out of his accounts, and came up dry. So then he began to look at the federal accounts over which Simons showed up in the very short list of people who had authorization to disburse funds. Eventually, the analysis of those correlations flagged a recurring distribution pattern that always resulted in what Winters referred to as a "weak echo with extraordinary fidelity." When one account under Simons' control disbursed a million dollars, a $100,000 deposit was received into another ostensibly unrelated account within thirty days. That account, by virtue of the "echo," had grown to more than $100 million. Because it was tied to a budget number that was allocated to clandestine operations, it was subject to almost no scrutiny whatsoever by normal oversight committees at the congressional level, and it appeared that Simons had managed to assign himself as the only authorized disbursing agent for that account. From there, the funds were moved on a quarterly basis to a bank in Latvia, where they were being withdrawn monthly.

From there the trail went cold. The funds could have been converted to cash or bearer bonds or some other form of liquid asset. However, the name on the Latvian account was Sergei Machetsky, who was well known to US intelligence agencies. Not even Winters could get to Latvian mobile phone records. However, he did have the international country code for Latvia, and so he began another series correlation analyses aimed at the timing of these monetary transfers and telephone calls between Latvia and Simons as well as Teng-hui, Jing-ti, and other known and suspected MSS agents in the DC area. Several hits appeared that tied Teng-hui, Machetsky, and Simons together.

From that point in the network, Winters was able to see another pattern that he thought was quite interesting. It appeared that Machetsky was also embezzling money somehow from the Russian government. *Well*, he thought to himself, *I believe I'll follow this up as soon as we complete the warrants we need for the Simons case. That will likely provide the boss with some serious bargaining chips.* In the meantime, Winters had already identified the source of the original account from which the funds were disbursed. It was designated Afghan Counter Insurgency Operations (COIN). It made Winters wonder how much of the disbursed money was ever really distributed where it was supposed to be distributed. While the vast majority of the US servicemen and women handling the funds were trustworthy and accounted for every dime they handled, funds were clearly being skimmed off at the highest levels before it even got to the field. Beyond that, the actual funds distributions at the other end were frequently made through Afghan officials who were notoriously untrustworthy. These men were selected precisely because they knew and dealt with the Taliban and were, in many cases, Taliban sympathizers themselves. Many in Washington simply viewed such losses as "the cost of doing business in Afghanistan."

In the meantime, Jennings had discovered that there was no bug implanted in Carolyn Menlo's cell phone. It was not impossible that her call had been intercepted electronically, but a thorough examination of her residence and her vehicle showed no indication that eavesdropping devices were present there. Jennings asked Ingram for a deep background check on Joan Wu, but the FBI came up dry. So they brought her in for questioning. When she was interviewed, Wu said that she had informed only Dr. Brystol that she would be covering Menlo's appointments the following week, and that she had left that message on his answering machine. Wu had explained that Menlo was called to help a family member with an urgent matter, but expected to return in a few days. Since it was a Saturday, she merely left the message on Brystol's office answering machine. She flatly denied informing anyone else, and seemed to be genuinely concerned that Menlo had gone underground and that the FBI was involved. But, as Jennings knew, that didn't mean anything. Good operatives were good liars.

Dawson and Winger returned home from their trip three days into the official ongoing investigation. Deering and Ingram were still debating about how to handle the Simons matter, but Jennings remained generally quiet about that. He continued to grapple with the fact that someone somewhere—Joan Wu, or perhaps someone else—had nearly caused Dr. Menlo and her son to be lost and the Salacia technology compromised. He was convinced that the spy was embedded somewhere within the Brystol Foundation. Jennings met Dawson at the Rock Quarry Tavern following his evening chat with Deering and Ingram to bring him up to speed.

"Are you experiencing any lasting effects from the blast?" Jennings asked.

"No, the only damage was to my head, so as you can imagine it was nothing debilitating," Dawson replied.

"I see that your sense of humor has not been impaired, in any case," Jennings said. "Seriously, Ben, aren't you getting a bit long in the tooth for all of this globe-trotting kinetic activity?"

"In a word," Dawson replied without hesitation, "yes. If you will stop asking, I will stop going."

Jennings sighed. "Of course, I never *officially* ask you to do this sort of thing. All of my expense line items for you simply say 'intelligence gathering.' If it ever became public knowledge that you perform, well, more kinetic tasks, I would probably have to fire you."

"That's easy; I'm an independent contractor anyway," Dawson said. "Just don't renew my contract."

"Well, of course the problem with that is that you have become rather a *favorite* contractor over these last few years," Jennings said. "Beyond that, Dr. Brystol, and now Dr. Menlo, are both ardent admirers as well. So even if I were to discontinue using your services, the Foundation would merely build your fees into their future contracts, and I would end up funding you anyway."

"Well then," Dawson replied, "I guess the thing for us to do is keep rolling along until I become so 'long in the tooth,' as you say, that someone finally takes me out of commission permanently."

Jennings nodded sadly in agreement. "All too often, I'm afraid, that is precisely what happens. Which brings me to a side conversation. There is a point that I want to cover with you unofficially, just between you and me."

"Oh?" Dawson said, his virtual antenna rising.

"Yes," Jennings said, leaning forward a bit, "it has to do with the events several days ago when Dr. Menlo and her son were rescued by your subcontractors. I know Max, of course, from his time with the Agency, and I had the pleasure of meeting Ms. Gerard last week. Obviously a very capable, and, I might add, attractive woman."

"Yes," Dawson responded, "and a close personal friend. So is there a problem?"

Jennings said, "I hope not. One thing that came out in conversation was that at least some of the operatives working for Bi-shou were killed, presumably during the events that transpired that day. No bodies were ever found, and no report was ever made to authorities about the event at all. The operatives simply disappeared."

"I see," Dawson replied. He had intended to get around to that discussion with Kelly soon, but now it sounded as though it had just escalated to *very* soon.

"Ben, both of us know this is a very imperfect world," Jennings said. "Dealing with terrorists and enemies of the United States requires, at times, that the normal rules be set aside. National security is a concept much more easily understood in the classroom than in the field, in day-to-day operations. People like you and Max Kelly who understand that and agree to operate in that world must accept that your decisions—decisions that you make in light of the very best interests of the United States—sometimes pull you across the lines of legality and even morality. Many of us in Washington understand that, but not all of us do. The ability of men and women like you to maintain perspective is critical. You can't allow yourself to become convinced that you are a law unto yourself, that normal rules just don't apply to you. In your case, I have never doubted your moral compass or your judgment for an instant."

"Thank you, Charles," Dawson said. "That means a lot."

"However, I think you know that, from my perspective, Max Kelly is a different case," Jennings said.

Dawson did not respond, and Jennings continued. "As far as I'm concerned, I know nothing about the specific events that occurred around the attempted abduction of Dr. Menlo. In addition, the information which came to me containing the telephone numbers and name of Bi-shou originated from an anonymous source. Once we started looking at known operatives in this area of espionage, the coincidence of telephone conversations and GPS coordinates drew our attention to her likely involvement, which is how I obtained the warrants to open her telephone conversations and other correspondence and transmissions. Hence you are not connected, nor are Max Kelly or Lily Gerard. The fact is, of course, without the information that was passed to us from Max, I have no idea if or when we would ever have put this all together, and the results for the United States would almost certainly have been severe."

Again, Dawson did not respond so Jennings continued. "Ben, over the last few times I have been aware of Max Kelly's involvement with projects here on US soil, the methods used in those activities have appeared to me to be questionable. I *don't* question them for a number of reasons, including the fact that he is a former NSA operative and that he is a close personal friend of yours. But you should be aware that his actions are becoming a liability not only to himself, but to you. I have seen cases like this before. When people like Max move beyond the scope of moral conduct often enough, they can go very dark very quickly. My advice would normally be to sever ties in such cases. But you are anything but 'normal'; your sense of loyalty to Max is, I believe, what caused you to leave the agency in the first place."

"It was one factor," Dawson grudgingly admitted, swirling the iced tea in his glass with a swizzle stick.

"All right," Jennings conceded, "it was *one* factor. But please heed my advice and think about how to handle Max. Things are, in my view, going to spiral out of control eventually."

"The attempts of others to 'handle' Max are part of the reason Max became whatever he became," Dawson said, realizing he had just become defensive, even though Jennings had been exceedingly kind and even-handed in his comments. "But I do understand what you're saying, and you are not only justified in saying it, but you're saying it in my best interests. I appreciate that, Charles. I will think about it."

"Good," Charles continued, apparently relieved to have that behind him. "Now on to what I believe is the most relevant and urgent topic at hand. Clearly, there is at least one bad actor at the Foundation. We need to identify and remove that operative before Dr. Menlo can safely return to work there. Do you have any thoughts about how that can be done?"

"I do have one, but it's pretty embryonic at this point," Dawson replied.

"What lines are your thoughts taking?" Jennings asked.

"I think we may have to allow Dr. Menlo to return to work in order to flush out the bad actor," Dawson said.

"You would put one of the nation's most important scientists at risk in order to identify her potential assassin?" Jennings asked, a bit incredulously.

"At the moment, that's what I have in mind," Dawson replied. "I don't like it either, Charles, but thus far neither the agency's analysis of communications records nor the Bureau's interrogation of Joan Wu and other Foundation employees has yielded anything of value. Something has to be done soon."

"Keep working on it, Ben," Jennings said, as he checked his watch. "I have to wind this up for now. I'm picking Rita up from her bridge club in just a few minutes. I hope we can come up with some alternative, though, because this sounds awfully risky."

"You're right about that part," Dawson replied, shaking Jennings' hand as both men stood to leave. "I'll talk with you tomorrow."

CHAPTER 25

Jing-ti's assistant placed the tea service on her boss's conference table. The cups, teapot, and tray were all beautifully adorned with an intricate pattern of copper plates and enamel inlay. The tea was a special blend of jasmine and deep orange pekoe that Jing-ti had developed a particular fondness for over the years.

"Will there be anything further this evening?" she asked him deferentially.

"Is Bi-shou here yet?" he asked her.

"She should be here any minute now," the assistant responded.

"All right, as soon as you admit her to my office you may leave for the night," he said. "I will walk her out myself."

"Yes, Sir," she responded, and quietly closed his office door behind her. Bi-shou entered moments later, and the assistant showed her into Jing-ti's office. Then she diminutively closed the door and departed for the night.

The meeting between Jing-ti and Bi-shou was much less cordial than their earlier rendezvous at the coffee shop. Bi-shou was defensive about having to ramp up her operatives with almost no notice, but both of them knew that hadn't been the cause of her team's failure. The problem had been that there were other operators involved, and the worst aspect of all of this was that at the moment, because her operatives had completely disappeared, no one had any idea who those operatives belonged to. With Dr. Menlo absent from the Foundation, even Brystol didn't know with certainty when she would return and the MSS operative or operatives inside the Foundation didn't know, either. The situation was as professionally perilous as any Jing-ti had ever faced. He had envisioned a much more fruitful relationship with Bi-shou on several levels, and now he was scrambling just to survive.

"What we have to focus on now is recovery," Jing-ti said. "The only option left to me is a very dangerous path, and frankly, under these circumstances, I am uncertain about whether you are the right person for the assignment."

The humiliation of her recent failure was transformed by Jing-ti's remarks from embarrassment into anger. She could have killed the man sitting across from her in seconds in a hundred different ways. She had no need of minions like this, and his condescension was nearly insufferable. After all, he's the one who didn't have the full information on the risks of the project. He should have known—or anticipated—other operatives would be involved.

Bi-shou said, "I accept full responsibility for our failure. We had no idea that another team was involved. I do not believe you knew either—" She was satisfied when she saw Jing-ti stiffen as that remark struck home, "—but I should have been prepared anyway, and I was not. I will understand if you wish to choose another contractor, but I do not believe that you will find one who is more capable."

Jing-ti thought about this. Bi-shou was almost certainly right, and then there was the fact that his boss, Teng-hui, had directed him to use her services. As long as she remained the point of failure, Teng-hui shared the blame. If he selected an outside contractor of his own and there was a failure, he was certain that it would be the last straw.

"Very well, then," he said, "let us discuss the way ahead. The only way I can see to move this project forward and obtain the technology we need is to enact a plan that requires two phases. Phase one is the abduction of Menlo's three key technology leads, Wu, McCallister, and Hoffman. With the technology we are seeking so far along in development, we are confident that all of the critical breakthroughs have been made, and now the project comes down to implementation. Therefore, the project leadership is less important. If we have the three pieces, we can do the integration ourselves. The second phase of the project is the assassination of Dr. Menlo. With the three technical leaders and the program leader all out of commission, there is a real chance that the program will stall, or at least slow substantially, enabling our team in China to surpass them. Now let us discuss the details, and then you must convince me that you can complete such an ambitious undertaking."

Over the next two hours, Jing-ti revealed more of the reason for the mission than he had planned to, but he felt that it would expedite matters and help Bi-shou to understand the gravity of potential failure. They went over every detail, nearly scrapping the endeavor at one point, then reconsidering and starting almost entirely from the beginning. They were hampered somewhat by the lack of available information about Menlo's subordinates. It wasn't that they were more difficult to examine, quite the opposite, actually. The problem was that for many months the MSS had been focused almost exclusively on Menlo. Doing a thorough enough job of reconnaissance on three individuals to pull off simultaneous abductions takes time, and the clock was ticking. Nevertheless, by nine that evening the details were in place, and Bi-shou was once again the principle actor engaged to make it all happen.

At six the next morning, Jing-ti's assistant opened up the office as usual. She turned on the lights and unlocked the inner door to Jing-ti's office. She picked up a few scattered papers and used napkins from around the tea service, and brought the tray with the teapot and discarded items back out to her own desk. Then she relocked Jing-ti's door. Checking to ensure there was still no one approaching from the elevators down the hall, the assistant reached under the base of the ornate teapot and carefully detached a flat bayonet-mounted disk that was completely inconspicuous to anything less than a detailed examination. She placed it in her pocket, and walked to the elevator with the tray. She took the elevator to the first floor, and walked briskly to the back of the building where Food Services was located.

She placed the tray on one of the racks for dirty dishes and, as expected, she was greeted by the manager of Food Services just coming in for the day. The Food Services area served the entire building, and over the years, Jing-ti's assistant had become friendly with the rather severe woman. It was a morning ritual with them to step outside the service door in the back of the building to begin each morning with a cigarette and a cup of coffee, and today was no exception.

On this particular day, however, as the two women finished their forbidden ritual and were walking back up the three concrete steps to the service doorway, the assistant dropped her empty cup, sending shards of porcelain in a four-foot radius around her. Uttering mild expletives and looking apologetic, she began to pick up the shards. Her companion admonished her slightly, and told her that she would retrieve the broom and dustpan. As she disappeared through the doorway, the assistant slipped the disk from her pocket and pressed its magnetic surface to the underside of the metal junction box affixed to the exterior wall near the door. An hour later, the entire conversation between

Jing-ti and Bi-shou had been uploaded, translated, and delivered into the hands of John Deering at CIA headquarters. By midafternoon it was also in the hands of Cal Ingram at FBI and Charles Jennings at NSA.

* * * *

Around noon, Dawson found a sullen Max Kelly doing squat thrusts at Shock 'n Aw's Gym. "Hi, Boss," was all he got out of him.

"Hi, Max," Dawson replied. "How long until you're finished up here? I'd like to talk with you when you have time." Whenever Dawson visited Max before, he had always just stopped what he was doing. Today was different. Max continued his squatting and thrusting and grunted through the process. "Should finish up here in about thirty minutes."

"OK, I'll do some time on the treadmill downstairs; just come and get me when you're done," Dawson said.

"Got it," Max replied, without meeting Dawson's gaze.

Dawson went to his locker and retrieved an old pair of sweat pants, a T-shirt, and running shoes and hit the treadmill.

Almost an hour had gone by when Kelly finally showed up. "Boss, is this important?" Kelly asked him. "I gotta check on Boxer across town." Dawson powered down the treadmill and slid down to the floor.

"Anything I can help with?" Dawson asked. "I'd be happy to ride shotgun."

"No, nothing like that," Kelly replied. "I just need to relieve him so he can get something to eat and take a break."

"Oh, OK. Well, it's not urgent," Dawson said, "but I really do need to talk to you sometime this week."

"No sweat," Kelly replied. "Today's just busy. I can catch up with you in the next couple of days."

But he still wasn't making eye contact. It was very unlike the Max Kelly Dawson knew so well, and, after what had happened with the Menlo job and given his conversation with Jennings, he was concerned that Kelly was going into one of his dark places. He'd never seen Kelly "go dark," and Lily Gerard had never come out and described what it was like, but she'd come close. Now, Dawson was getting worried. He stepped in closer, right at the edge of Kelly's personal space, and dropped his voice. "Max, is everything OK? You seem pretty distracted."

Kelly stepped back, making just flickering eye contact while saying, "Geez, Ben, I said I'll talk to you later. It's just been a hellacious week, that's all. Cut me a little slack." With that, Dawson wheeled and headed for the showers. He hadn't seen this side of Kelly in a long time, and he wanted nothing to do with it. Kelly made no attempt to call him back.

CHAPTER 26

The specific information provided by the eavesdropping device from the teapot was sufficiently detailed that the FBI was already working on warrants for operatives who did not have diplomatic immunity and extradition orders for those who did by the time Jennings met with Dawson that evening. Jennings pulled up the transcript of the conversation on his iPad and waited while Dawson read it. "Amazing," was all Dawson could say. He was already going through implications and possible courses of action in his mind.

"No one is going to move on this until we have identified the operative at the Foundation who is feeding critical information to the MSS," Jennings said, "and distasteful as it sounds, your concept of using Carolyn Menlo as bait to draw them out is the best idea any of us has. Have you given any thought to how we could go about it?"

"As I said before, Charles, I don't like it, either," Dawson said, "but it's all I can come up with. Now, as to how, we could do one of two basic things. Our first option would be to wait until Bi-shou enacts her scheme, and try to thwart her on four different fields of battle. We certainly have her outgunned here on our home turf, and right now we know what she knows, which offers us tremendous leverage. The problem is that we don't know who she will send and how or when they'll move to take out Dr. Menlo, because she doesn't know herself. She doesn't know when Carolyn will surface. In addition, the variables around the three simultaneous abductions are extensive, and an awful lot can go wrong. The second option, and the one I prefer, is to go on the offensive. I think we can draw out the bad actor at the Foundation by basically announcing Menlo's return soon, and crafting a story around it. Here's what I have in mind."

Over the next hour, Dawson laid out his thoughts. The two men talked over a couple of the details, but essentially Dawson got approval on the entire plan. Then, when he had parted company with Jennings for the evening, he called Kelly and asked him to meet him at Gerard's condo. Kelly didn't sound happy, but said he would be there.

When Dawson arrived, he found Kelly and Gerard sitting at the kitchen table, Kelly downing a beer and Gerard with a glass containing what looked like an Arnold Palmer. Carolyn Menlo was in the living room working on her laptop, and Andy was tucked into bed. Dawson excused himself for the lateness of his visit, and asked Menlo to join them in the kitchen. "First of all, Carolyn, you have heard, I trust, that your husband is due back in DC in three to five days?"

"Yes," Menlo beamed, "thank you. You cannot *imagine* the weight that has lifted from my shoulders. Now I can finally focus again on my work, but of course the downside of that is that I'm not actually back to *doing* my work."

"I understand, and that's what we are here to talk about," Dawson replied.

Dawson spent the next thirty minutes carefully reviewing the events of the last few days. He left out the classified details, of course, describing specific information gathering techniques, personnel, and other details of the plan for going forward. "The only way to identify who at the Foundation is leaking this information is to put you back in the mix, Carolyn," Dawson said. "This puts you at risk again, but we just don't see another way. The leak could be anyone from your own staff members up through Dr. Brystol himself, and we have to smoke the person out. The concept is this: Charles Jennings, who I understand you met a few days ago—" Menlo nodded and smiled "—is going to contact Dr. Brystol tomorrow, and tell him that you will be returning to work the day after tomorrow, Wednesday, but will take a few days before resuming your normal duties in order for you to complete a special project."

Menlo's eyebrows arched in a question, but feeling certain that he was about to answer that question, she remained silent.

Dawson continued. "When Dr. Brystol asks Jennings what the project is, he will be told that for reasons of national security you will be putting the finishing touches on a complete description of the Salacia system. Your deliverable from this activity will include a detailed explanation of the various technologies involved, so that even if something should happen to you and your department heads, the project would move forward unabated. Jennings will make it clear that by *the end of this week*, the Foundation will no longer be dependent on you and your staff for the scaling-up and deployment of Salacia."

"But there is no way that could be done in three days," Menlo objected.

"Yes, I suspected as much," Dawson said, "so Jennings is also going to tell Brystol that you have been working on this for the NSA since you left so abruptly several days ago. You just need a few days at the Foundation to finish it up before you can resume your normal duties."

"And this would cause the MSS to believe they are about to lose their opportunity to get the technology and set back the US development effort. Correct?" asked Gerard.

"Exactly," Dawson replied. "When MSS hears this news, we believe they will conclude that it's now or never. They must stop this at any cost, or lose their window of opportunity. They will mobilize very quickly, and we'll be ready for them."

"What's that going to involve?" Kelly asked. He still seemed glum to Dawson, and he noticed that Gerard and he were sitting at arm's length. Dawson wondered if he had walked into the middle of some kind of tiff. *That could be a problem,* he thought, *but we're all professionals here, so we're just going to have to work through it.*

"I'd like to pair Lily up with Carolyn posing as her assistant, ostensibly assigned as a loaner through NSA, to help her with data gathering and documentation," Dawson said. "Lily will need to be armed, of course, but not overtly. The idea is to be a covert personal bodyguard, and nobody does that better."

Gerard couldn't help smiling a bit at the compliment. "Why, thank you, Mr. Dawson," she said. Kelly looked as though he was going to gag, and Dawson moved on.

"Max, if you're available I would like you to manage physical site security," Dawson said. "I'd like your ideas about this, but I'm thinking we may need to ask Carolyn's department heads—Hoffman, Wu, and McCallister—to physically operate at a central location with Carolyn through the end of the week. It would make all of our lives easier that way."

"Since it's just for a few days, we could all work out of the lab area," Menlo said. "That would put us all in one building, and we'd all be on the same floor."

"What do you think, Max?" Dawson asked.

"Well, I can make the time available," he said, "but I'll want to get out there and do recon. I need to know the lay of the land and will need to bring Meriwether and Boxer with me to cover the various access points and sightlines, especially since we have four people we are now covering. That's a lot of moving parts."

"That sounds right to me," Dawson said. "I'll walk you and Lily around tomorrow if you can both get away, so you'll understand what you're getting into."

"I can do it, but I can't speak for Lily," Kelly said. Gerard frowned openly at Kelly. Without addressing either of them by addressing *both* of them, Dawson asked, "Can Meriwether or one of your other operators do PSD for Carolyn and Andy tomorrow while you two come out to the Foundation for initial recon?"

Kelly continued to stare at Dawson, while Gerard looked at Kelly. Gerard said, "Of course, we're not going to leave Carolyn uncovered tomorrow. We'll have someone in place here while we're gone."

Holy cow, I'm too old for this kind of nonsense, Dawson thought. "Great," he said. "I'll meet you out there at ten a.m. tomorrow then." *I hope you two work out your own problems before then.*

"Carolyn, we'll want you and your three subordinates to look as though you are doing systems integration activity or something like that, creating the perception among observers that the four of you are collaborating on the documentation of the entire program. Can you and your team manage that?" Dawson asked.

"Sadly," she replied, "we ought to be very good at that by now. It seems like we're doing dog-and-pony shows for Pentagon brass all the time. We have to keep the funding flowing, you know, even if it slows our actual progress, which it sometimes does."

"Excellent," Dawson said. "Hopefully, in a few days this will be behind us so that you'll be able to focus more on your work and less on security. For the longer term, I have an idea that may help to alleviate that problem as well, but let's focus on the near term for now."

"Are you planning to be *her* personal security detail after this weekend?" Kelly asked. The way he asked it contained an unkind and unsavory edge that Dawson had never heard from Kelly before, and he didn't like what he was hearing.

"No," Dawson replied soberly, wiping the fraction of a sneer off of Kelly's face. Gerard was actually turning red. Menlo just looked confused.

"Are there any other questions?" An uncomfortable silence ensued, and after several seconds, Dawson ended it by announcing, "OK, then, I'll let you get back to your evening." He stood to leave. "Lily, thanks again for letting us use your condo for a safe house these last several days."

"That was my decision," Gerard responded. "It was convenient for me, and I like the company. Besides, it's not every day I get paid to have house guests."

"Well, I'll let myself out then," Dawson said. "Good night, everyone." Gerard and Kelly stayed at the kitchen table to work out their scheduling details for the next day, and Menlo walked with Dawson to the front door.

"You know, Ben," Menlo said to him as he was about to reach for the front door, "I'm kind of a movie fan."

"Oh?" he replied, not understanding where that came from.

"Yes, I've loved movies— especially the old ones from the fifties and sixties—since I was a kid. Anyway, I always used to think the ones where someone gets rescued from certain death and they end up saying something corny like 'I just don't know how to thank you enough' were pretty sappy. But now I find myself trying to say the same kind of thing to you. I truly cannot *imagine* where I would be right now, whether Tom or I would even be *alive*, not to mention what would have happened to Andy." At this point her voice broke and she covered her mouth with her hands, crying hard but as quietly as she could.

Dawson took her by the shoulders and pressed her gently into the rocking chair, seating himself on the hassock in front of her. Quietly he said, "Look, Carolyn, you've been through a living hell these last few months, and I honestly don't know how you've done it. But you held together your family, your own sanity, and the foremost R&D effort on the planet. Believe me, *you're* the hero here. I don't know another person who could do what you have done—and are still doing. I have more than respect for you. I *admire* you, and that's not something I say very often." She started to calm down a bit.

"One more thing," Dawson continued. "You need to understand that we're not out of the woods yet. Crazy as it seems, the most dangerous part of all of this is just about to start, and we are triggering it on purpose to get it behind you. Those two rascals out in the kitchen are among a very small circle of people that I'd entrust the lives of my children to, if I had children. They would step into the line of fire for you, as long as you are their responsibility. They've already saved your life once. But that doesn't mean there is no risk here. It just means we're doing our best to manage it. You need to be alert, focused, and have your head in the game over the rest of this week in order for everything to work out. If one of us tells you to do something, don't think—just do it. OK?"

She snuffled one last time and nodded fiercely. "OK," she said, "I understand. But I also understand other things, Ben. *You* also saved my husband's life and not because you were paid to, but because I *asked* you to. And it was *you* who put me into the care of Lily and Max, even before I knew about it. So in that sense, *you* saved my life as well. I don't devalue what they did, but I also know better than to think you weren't responsible for it."

"You know, Carolyn," Dawson said grinning as he stood up again to leave. "We'd better get you back to work so that you have more important things to think about."

In the kitchen, the conversation was much less pleasant. "I know you've gone through rough patches before, Max, but you're turning into a different man than the one I met, loved, and started a company with," Gerard said. "I don't know what's eating at you, but the tiny dark streak that was in you a few years ago seems to have resurfaced. Those snide remarks you made to Ben about me, and even about him, were *totally* uncalled for. And you're surprised I've been pulling away from you? We both have things in our past that we're not proud of, Max. Everyone does. And whatever your demons are, they're eating at you. Everyone has noticed it lately, and the way you've been behaving the last few days, since that day on the highway, well, it's like you're putting every baser instinct you have on display deliberately. I haven't asked you what happened after I drove away with Carolyn. Do I need to? Do we need to talk about it? What is it you aren't telling me?"

"You have no idea," Kelly groused.

"So *tell* me!" Gerard said. She reached out to put her hand on his arm, but he pulled away.

Kelly took a long, deep breath and said, "When I was deployed in Iraq the first time, back in 2005, my unit searched out and destroyed cell after cell of Al Qaeda, Al Qaeda sympathizers, and just plain thugs who wanted nothing more in life than to kill Americans. I can't begin to describe what I saw, and what we came to live with as just an ongoing day-to-day reality over there."

Gerard waited. She knew all this. There had to be something more.

He continued, "One night we crashed into some hovel up in Tikrit looking for two missing GIs, and found them still surrounded by local Al Qaeda sympathizers, not even the hard cases. They had the GIs strapped to shipping crates, seated and facing each other. First they brought in local girls from the village and started doing things to them with knives and other assorted tools in front of the GIs, asking the GIs for information, but mostly just taunting them because they knew it would tear them up that they couldn't help those little girls. Then they went to work on the GIs themselves. When we got to the right alleyway, we had no trouble finding the place. We just followed the screams. We crashed in to find that they were using a cordless electric drill on one GI while the other was being questioned. If the GI didn't tell them what they wanted to know, or they didn't believe the answer, another hole went into his buddy while he looked on. Eventually they made it up to the unfortunate buddy's head with the drill. It would probably surprise you, Lily, how long it can take a man to die when things like that are done properly." Gerard's eyes were watery and she had a lump in her throat, but she said nothing.

Again, Kelly continued. "Then, late in 2006, I was working up in Fallujah. The Al Qaeda boys up in that neck of the woods had been having some trouble recruiting from the local villages; it seems the local sheiks didn't want any more of their sons turned into murdering marauders by those SOBs. So the Al Qaeda leader up there decides to send a message to the community. His men come around at night and kidnap some of the local children. The next morning, several boxes are found on the front steps of the local city center. Each box contained the head of one child. Oh, and then there are the Taliban. These are the guys who have convinced a big part of the population of Afghanistan that no girls should be educated, that women are property to be bought and sold, and that it's just as good an idea to target civilians— women, children, it doesn't matter—as it is to target enemy military forces. They are, even now as we sit here, stoning women to death who try to tell their fathers that they don't want to marry whoever the father has arranged for them to marry in trade for two goats and a used motorcycle. They're killing teachers who dare to help girls learn to read and write, and murdering little girls because they are walking to school in the morning." Kelly stopped and took a breath, but he was on a rant, breathing hard, staring off somewhere over Gerard's shoulder.

"And then a few years went by, and I came back home, where life seems normal again. I tried to put that stuff all behind me, but as I think back on it, I realize that finding and killing those people is probably the most honorable thing I ever did in my life. Now I run into those same terrorist SOBs *right here*. Right here at home, trying to pull the same crap *right here*. And I find myself standing there, holding my M4 and they're right in front of me. I know what would happen if I called the cops, and I know I can take care of things there and then. So I do. I stop these animals from wreaking havoc on innocent Americans here at home. But I know that's making me a criminal, no different from them in the eyes of the law."

Gerard was staring at him wide-eyed now, tears running down her face, but unable to speak. "So when I run into people like that, Lily, I do what I was trained to do; *I kill them.* I get whatever information I can and then I kill them. And do you know why? *Because some people just need to be killed.* But it changes you inside when you do that for a while. I've seen it in other guys. They're good men, but something hardens inside them and they come to understand that someone has to do what needs to be done. Guys like me and Ron, we understand that it's got to be done, that most people can't do it, and so we do it."

Gerard said, "Max, have you been—" But she was cut off by Kelly.

"Lily, you don't want to know, so don't ask me. I know you think Ben is a great guy, and the fact is he really *is* a great guy. I love him like a brother. But when it comes to doing the things I'm talking about, Ben doesn't have it in him. You don't either, and I get that. I'm glad you don't. What that means, though, is that people like me have to make up the difference. We have to meet these snakes where they live and kill them. Period. So when I see you and Carolyn and everybody else fawning all over Ben like he's something special, when other guys like me are doing what's *necessary*—what guys like Ben don't have it in them to do—then yes, it pisses me off. I start feeling inferior and guilty and really, *really* pissed off. And when I'm in this frame of mind, you don't like me very much, Lily. I guess I don't like me much, either. But I am who I am, and I'm going to do what needs to be done. You'll just have to figure out whether you can live with that."

Leaving her there at the kitchen table alone, Kelly got up and walked out of the condo.

CHAPTER 27

Jennings placed the call to Brystol at eight o'clock the following morning. The call was cordial, but there were a number of dynamics at work. Brystol was not pleased that the NSA seemed to have a better handle on where his prized employee was than he had, nor that—for a short time, at least—that agency appeared to be directing her work. However, in light of what Jennings related to him about recent events, coupled with the very high degree of dependency that the Brystol Foundation had on government contracts for their funding, he decided that discretion was the better part of valor, and agreed to the arrangement Jennings had suggested.

This also meant that Brystol would have Menlo back physically on site again, which he knew would have a restabilizing effect on her team. Finally, he believed the story Jennings related about building a more secure envelope around the Salacia technology, which should improve the security of the Brystol Foundation's intellectual property at the same time it bolstered this aspect of national security. All in all, he decided it was best to cooperate fully.

Within the next eight working hours, Menlo and her team would literally move into the laboratory facility. There were already sleeping quarters on site with showers and a small living area, so they wouldn't be too indisposed. Menlo decided Andy could accompany Joan Wu's children to their aunt's home in the Richmond area for the next few days. Dawson was OK with that, as long as he could post someone outside the aunt's home to make sure they remained secure. Dawson made a phone call and got Romero signed up for that duty. In turn, he indicated he could enlist whatever assistance he needed to cover the house 24/7. None of Menlo's direct subordinates, Wu, McCallister, and Hoffman, objected much after Brystol recounted what had happened to Menlo, and explained that the objective was to make all of them non-targets for future abduction attempts. Keeping themselves and their families safe was pretty high on their priority lists.

The building that Menlo and her staff were working in and would be residing in was three stories tall not including the basement, but the second story, which contained the labs and the short-term living quarters, was a "high-bay" facility that accommodated large equipment, and so the laboratories included twenty-foot ceilings. The building was designed to support two overhead cranes in the lab area, and the facility was comprised of heavy-duty components from the foundation to the structural members, floor load capacity, and door openings. The building was also designed around stringent safety measures to resist lab accidents and equipment failures.

In addition, the building itself, already within a gated campus, was designed with current technology security equipment ranging from surveillance cameras to badge readers, cypher locks, and biometric readers at critical points of egress and ingress. The security cameras were monitored in another building, but there was an armed security guard on duty in the lobby of all ten of the primary buildings on campus, including the one containing Menlo's lab. It was, by all normal standards, a very secure facility.

Dawson met Kelly and Gerard at the Foundation and got them signed up for regular passes with the same level of access he had. He noticed they had arrived in separate vehicles, and things between them didn't appear to have improved over night. They walked the perimeter of the building, outside first, then inside the ground floor. Next they examined the basement level, and Dawson showed them the underground tunnel connecting the buildings. It was pristine, lit with recessed fluorescent light fixtures, floor drains, and enough width for golf carts to pass one another. Golf carts were quite a popular means of conveyance on the campus grounds.

The long tunnels were enclosed by metal fire-resistant doors and badge scanners at each end. A badge was required for entry at each end, but no badge was required to exit the tunnels. The basement contained a backup power plant for the building, should grid power be lost, so that critical lab work was never interrupted by the errant lightning strike or a wayward vehicle strike on some power transformer somewhere in the neighborhood. There were also several fenced-off storage areas with walls made of chain link fencing that ran from floor to ceiling, as well as the custodial offices and equipment rooms that supported the building. Some of the storage areas contained vats of substances such as liquid nitrogen, argon gas, and so on.

Toward the back of the basement area, near the opening to the tunnel, was a room simply marked: *AUTHORIZED PERSONNEL ONLY. Alarm will sound when this door is opened.* Some employee who saw himself, or herself, as a comedian had attached a paper sign with transparent tape under the official sign, which warned: *Trespassers will be shot. Survivors will be shot again!*

Dawson badged in, keyed in the cypher lock, and pressed his index finger against the glass of the biometric reader. Inside the small room was a floor-to-ceiling, wall-to-wall walk-in vault. "This vault," Dawson explained to Kelly and Gerard, "is the on-site storage of an extremely rare crystalline material we recovered from the Middle East a few months ago. This material is required to enable the Salacia technology, and it doesn't take much; a chunk the size of a shoebox would enable enough Salacia-equipped vessels to cover an entire navy. If we really are attacked here at the Foundation, this is likely to be the secondary target."

"Who has the credentials to get in here?" Kelly asked.

"Only two people," Dawson replied. "Dr. Brystol and Dr. Menlo. The physical protection mechanisms are a biometric reader, fingerprint based, and an eight-digit numeric code."

Since they were looking at the tunnel anyway, Dawson took the opportunity to walk Kelly and Gerard over to the next building in the chain, and led them inside the lobby to the security office where all of the security cameras were monitored. There he was able to introduce them to Jerry King, the retired Richmond, Virginia, police chief who ran the security department at the Brystol Foundation. King was a likeable man, but direct. He seldom engaged in small talk, and when it came to security at the Foundation, he was all business.

Dawson introduced him to Kelly and Gerard, and told him in broad strokes that Kelly would be looking after the facility's security at the opposite end of the hall for a few days while Gerard would be providing additional personal security services for Carolyn Menlo and her immediate staff during that time. He explained that a government agency was concerned about their safety through the balance of the week, owing to some very sensitive information that was being put together in the lab. King seemed to be good with that, and asked Kelly if there was anything they needed.

"There *are* a couple of things I could use," Kelly replied. "The architectural plans for the Salacia building would be a big help, for one."

"I'll have them to you in an hour," King responded. "What's the other thing?"

"What do you maintain for an armory here?" Kelly asked.

"Each of the people on my team carries a nine-millimeter automatic, and we have a cabinet here in the security room with ten M16s," said King. "They are all capable of single shots and three-round bursts. That's about it. I have no vests or helmets here. We don't exactly have to repel boarders at this facility," he chuckled.

"How about the sentries at the gates?" Kelly asked.

"Pretty much the same," King said. "They are both armed with nines, and they each have Remington twelve-gage pump actions in a locked cabinet below the desk in the guard shack."

"Do they have vests?" Kelly asked.

"Nope," King replied, "we've never needed 'em."

"I understand," Kelly said, "but that's likely to change."

Suddenly King began to get a grip on the gravity of the situation. He looked at Dawson, who also wasn't smiling, and then back at Kelly. "Damn," he said.

"So," Kelly continued, "Mr. King, this is what I need you to do. I'd like you to get vests on the people in the guard shacks and on the floor security man in Dr. Menlo's building starting with second shift tonight. Call each of the guards in and alert them of who I am, and tell them that I'll be coming around on regular spot checks throughout the shifts—not because I'm a stickler, but because I'd like them *and* Dr. Menlo—to stay alive. You're going to need two sentries at each of the gates, and two driving the fence line in those golf carts you have all over the place here. If you don't have enough people to cover that, just let me know and I'll supplement your staff with people from local agencies I work with all the time. They all have clearances."

"All right," King said hesitantly, "are you guys really expecting an attack?"

"We don't know with any certainty," Dawson said, "but it seems likely."

"One more thing," Kelly said to King, "Tell the sentries starting on second shift tonight that the shotgun comes out of the cabinet. It needs to be loaded, safety on, and in the hands of the second sentry at each guard shack *at all times*. OK?"

"Yes, I have it," King replied, but he clearly wasn't happy about it.

Dawson continued his tour with Kelly and Gerard back at the laboratory building. They began on the second floor, which was the area of primary interest. Gerard was surprised at the comfort of the living quarters, but as Dawson pointed out, lab technicians and staff members often needed to remain on site for multiple shifts, sometimes even for days, monitoring particularly complex and lengthy procedures and experiments. Each living unit, and there were ten of them all situated on one long hallway, had in-suite bathrooms. Every two living units shared a small kitchen, living room, and entertainment center in common. All of them were professionally decorated, and serviced by the custodial staff daily. Kelly muttered something under his breath about "your tax dollars at work."

Next they toured the office areas on the third floor, which were pretty standard fare. The nicest offices were around the perimeter facing the windows, with large office cubicles occupying the central area of the floor. "Looks like there's a stairwell in each corner," observed Kelly, "and passenger elevator banks on the north and south walls."

"Right," Dawson replied.

"And downstairs there is also a west wall freight elevator that only moves between the shipping and receiving docks, the second floor labs, and the basement," Gerard contributed.

"What else is relevant that we haven't seen?" Dawson was thinking, but he asked it aloud.

"The roof," Kelly and Gerard both spoke simultaneously.

Gerard and Dawson smiled at this, but Kelly's face remained impassive. "So where's the access?" he asked.

"It's back in the stairwell in the northeast corner," Dawson said. "Not much up there; air conditioning compressors is about it, I think."

"Flat roof, right?" Kelly asked.

"Right," Dawson said.

"No skylights?"

"None."

"Looking at the rest of the construction," Kelly said, "I'm guessing it's not plywood or something like that which would be easy to cut through?"

"Right; it's not flimsy," Dawson replied. "Coming through the roof would not be among my top three choices for penetration of the perimeter."

"Now that's interesting," Kelly said. "So what would your first three choices be?"

"I think my third choice would be right through the front door. One guard, glass entryway, level with the ground. Drive an armored vehicle through it, or even a dump truck, full of operators, and follow it with a bus to close out responders. There are disadvantages galore though; a lot of circus to draw attention even on the way in, and a lot of moving parts to coordinate."

"Agreed," said Kelly. "There's also the front gate to contend with, although at the moment that's a pretty soft point in the campus perimeter. What would your second choice be?"

Gerard just watched them and smiled. *They just love thinking through this kind of thing.*

"My second choice would be the tunnel," Dawson said.

"The tunnel was interesting to me, too," Kelly said. "There were no security cameras, motion detectors, or suppression systems there. Seems like a soft spot to me."

"And it has a couple of other advantages, too. You come from the other building, where you could disable the security monitors and deal with the normal security escalation path before ever coming to this building. You also come into this building right next to the room with the secondary target, the vault in the basement."

"Of course," Kelly said, "you also have to get up to the second floor to hit your primary target, but there are two elevator banks and four stairwells; a lone armed security man in the lobby isn't going to be much of a deterrent. I think that's the way I'd come in."

"Hmm," Dawson said.

"Oh, that's right," Kelly interjected, "you have another way in mind. So what is it? You said you wouldn't try to cut or detonate your way through the roof...."

"Yes, that's true. I wouldn't be coming in that way, either," Dawson said. "In fact, I'm not sure I'd come in *at all*, at least for the abductions. The tunnel seems like a reasonable approach for the vault, especially if they had time to cut through the wall from the tunnel, I guess, but for the abduction I'd make the *targets* come outside to *me*."

Kelly stood there and thought about that for a minute. Then a smile finally stole across his grizzled face. "Very interesting!" he said, and he couldn't help it; the smile spread into an ear-to-ear grin. "Makes perfect sense. That's *exactly* what they're gonna do, if they do it at all," he said.

Then Dawson turned to Gerard, and said, "Lily, I think this is going to make things interesting for you."

While Dawson, Kelly, and Gerard were doing their tour of the Foundation facility, Jennings' team at NSA was obtaining court orders for wire taps on the telecommunications of Brystol and everyone on his immediate staff as well as Menlo's entire project team. They received authorization to monitor telephone, email, and text messages retroactive for thirty days. Historical communications were relegated to the least experienced analysts, with current message traffic monitored by the most experienced members of the team.

All communications were then transcribed by advanced speech recognition software for further review by automated systems. Those systems were looking for code words and other phraseology and wording combinations that would indicate the possibility of hidden messages.

Between noon and four that afternoon, all three of Menlo's immediate subordinates appeared on site, and moved into their quarters. Menlo showed up at five, and spent the first hour getting caught up on both personal and professional activity since she last saw each of her staff members. Then she introduced Kelly and Gerard. Kelly, in turn, introduced Meriwether and Boxer. That team, along with Dawson, also moved into the living quarters in their building. With the introductions complete, Kelly and his team excused themselves and set about briefing the Foundation's security team and establishing their own routines. They installed some equipment of their own, including additional stores of weapons and ammunition, their own webcams to supplement the security cameras already in place, and communications gear that operated on different frequencies to connect them with each other as well as Dawson and Gerard.

Dawson and Gerard drew Menlo and her three subordinates off to one corner of the lab and talked about how they could remain reasonably productive while presenting the appearance that they were collecting and collating designs, formulae, processes, and specifications of the Salacia technology. At that point, Hoffman, McCallister, and Wu went to work, and Dawson and Gerard walked with Menlo back to her quarters.

Once there, Dawson and Gerard briefed Menlo on what they called the Exit Protocol and the Deep Dive Protocol. Essentially, they covered what they believed the most likely scenarios were, and how Menlo should respond in each of those cases. It had been decided that, with the exception of things like bio-breaks, Gerard would be with Menlo at all times, 24/7. Dawson would cover for her when Gerard had to be away for any period of time.

The first day and night went off without a hitch. On the second day, NSA analysts began to notice some interesting message traffic. It was buried in text messages between one of Brystol's staff and what appeared to be family members, and the messages each seemed fairly innocuous when considered independently. The messages said things like, "Your eight shirts will be ready for pickup at the cleaners in the morning," and "We need to have furniture out of the way for the carpet cleaners by noon tomorrow."

When the messages were flagged by the speech analysis software, analysts began to pull the staff member's other message traffic, reaching backward in time and looking for message traffic correlated in time with specific events such as Menlo's telephone call alerting Wu that she was leaving for her sister's home in Atlanta. While the process was lightning fast compared to the speed such analytical work entailed even a few years earlier, in the end it still required talented and experienced analysts to piece the various elements together. By noon on the second day, the analysts at NSA headquarters in Maryland had a suspect, and a greater than fifty percent confidence level that they had the right person. Then they started to pull badging information and security camera footage to look at what the suspect had been doing during windows immediately preceding and following critical events.

Around seven that evening, Dawson wandered through the cafeteria and grabbed a salad and a bowl of minestrone soup. When he turned the corner to find a seat in the dining area, he saw Kelly perched at one of the high-tops and working his way through what looked like a BBQ sandwich, so he pulled up a chair. "How's the physical security looking?" he asked.

"Much better," Kelly said, "though I have to tell you, Ben, this place is an incredibly soft target when you consider what they do here. I'm surprised the government allows it. It's not that they are lax, exactly; Jerry King's a straight shooter and they follow their procedures well. It's just that they aren't designed to be resistant to any serious assault. If this technology is as important as it seems to be, I would have thought they'd have beefed up physical security. Especially after 9-11, this just seems eerily soft."

"I understand," Dawson replied. "I have spoken with Dr. Brystol about it before, but he keeps saying that he wants the place to feel more like a Microsoft or Google campus than a nuclear reactor site or a federal prison. It seems to me that he just has no appreciation for what could happen."

"A lot of folks are like that until they get hit," Kelly said. "Looks like this may be another case like that."

"Agreed," said Dawson. "It's a problem. Jerry has tried talking sense into Brystol, too."

The two men ate in silence for a moment, and then Dawson said: "I'm glad to see you're in a better frame of mind this afternoon."

Kelly shrugged and kept eating. Then, a minute later, he said, "It helps to have something to think about, and getting ready to engage always keeps me focused."

"Yeah," Dawson agreed, "it will do that." He sighed, and continued. "Well, we all go through ups and downs. But this last week or two, you've seemed to be on the down side more than usual. That's why I asked you the other day if everything was OK."

Kelly stopped eating and shoved his tray away from him a few inches. "This sounds like something maybe Lily has been saying?"

"Nope," Dawson replied, "Lily hasn't said a word. Just a couple of things *you've* said, grumbling under your breath, mostly."

"Well, it's like this, Ben," Kelly said. "You and I came from different places. I know you have spent a lot of time in bad places, and more time outside the wire than a lot of the GIs who get posted to bases like Bagram and Kandahar. And we've been in enough firefights together that I know you're solid. But I'm a soldier, and beyond that, I came out of Spec Ops. I have seen and done things you've *never* seen or done, and I've done those things *a lot*. It changes the way you look at the world, and the way you look at life, I guess."

He looked down at his hands. "So sometimes," he continued, "when I think about the absolute *nonsense* of what we have to do—the hoops we have to go through—just so that some bureaucrat will let me do my job, it makes me crazy. Honest to God, Ben, do you know that before I left NSA they had me putting together slide decks to brief the brass before they'd let me do a covert op?"

Dawson nodded. "Sure, Max. I remember. And you're right; it's nuts. You were right to leave when you did, and I followed you out the door. I remember Stan McChrystal's guys even developed a term for it: 'Death by PowerPoint.' Making warriors do that stuff is just crazy. But you don't have to do those things anymore."

"Yeah, well that's part of it, anyway," Kelly replied. "I look at all this stuff," he waved his arm to take in the room—"I don't know; scientists and bureaucrats and politicians, and all this technology they sit on, and the way we all kind of say 'How high?' when they say 'Jump.' It doesn't make a bit of sense. We are literally *killing* ourselves and each other out here, and I don't think most of them give a tinker's damn. I guess I'm losing respect for the lot of them, and sometimes I wonder why we keep doing what we do."

"Well, in some ways at least, I think you're absolutely right, Max," Dawson said, scraping the last of the soup out of the small cardboard bowl. "Most of the politicians in DC have never seen combat, very few have ever seen what goes on in places like Darfur or Afghanistan, and most Americans these days think they know all they need to know from what they read in the press, or, even worse, what some pompous ass taught them in their undergraduate world history class. It would probably surprise most people how few of them, politicians or professors, have ever lived anywhere other than the good old USA for any significant period of time. Yet they talk on TV and teach our young people as though they have some clue what they are talking about, having sat under the tutelage of some other ass that's just as ill-informed as they are."

"Absolutely," Kelly said.

"And for what it's worth, my friend," Dawson continued, "I fully realize that the places I've been, the things I've done, and the things I've witnessed are a mere *shadow* of what you have done for this country. I can't even imagine what you carry around in that thick head of yours, not to mention your heart."

"I hear a 'but' coming," Kelly said through a tiny smile.

"Yeah," Dawson said, "*but* you can't let it change who you are. I have seen you carry wounded men across killing fields without hesitation. I went in *behind* you in Kandahar, when you knew damned well that we were outnumbered, what, six or seven to one? I know things about you that not even Lily knows, and more importantly, I know that I don't know it all. I doubt *anyone* does."

Kelly just looked at him and said, "Are you *sure* Lily hasn't been talking to you?"

"Listen, Max," Dawson continued, "you know that the American military, like any other group of human beings, is a bell-shaped curve as a population, with most people in the middle. Average intelligence, average height, and so on. The smaller populations on either end of that curve are the smartest and dumbest, the most courageous and most cowardly, the tallest and the shortest, and so on. But as a population, there is no group of men and women anywhere in the world, and never has been, that I have more respect for. They get paid subsistence wages in most cases, leave their lives of relative comfort here at home, and go over there where they're exposed to almost every imaginable physical, mental, and psychological challenge."

Kelly nodded in agreement, and waited for Dawson to continue.

"Nineteen and twenty-year-old kids were over there standing on the wall and living in abject fear just waiting for some terrorist or criminal or wannabe to shoot them or blow them up. I'll *never* forget that first ride I took with kids like that, going through Baghdad back in '06, just waiting to get my legs blown off. You know how it was; there were no MRAPs, in those days, just flat-bottomed Humvees. While we all dreamed about Mine Resistant Armored Personnel vehicles, IEDs were *everywhere*. I could hear them going off, shaking the ground, at least every forty-five minutes. It was awful. Even on base back at Camp Victory, Al Qaeda was rocketing us from surrounding houses all the time. Then there was Afghanistan. Those soldiers we worked with up in Wardak Province, and the Marines down in Helmand just outside of Marjah, even the ones who made it home in one piece physically will never be the same. And I know you Special Ops guys had it even worse. But I'm begging you man, don't let it ruin you. You are without a doubt the most courageous guy I have ever known. Probably Billy Winger is the only man I know that could hold a candle to you. If you need some kind of help...."

"I don't need help, Ben, and it wouldn't do any good anyway," Kelly said. "The things I have done can't be undone, and that's the only thing that would change anything. I appreciate what you're saying. I really do. But we all change, and I'm no exception. I just am where I am, and there's really nothing that anybody can do about it—including me."

CHAPTER 28

The next morning Margaret appeared for work around seven a.m., her usual time. She got Brystol's coffee started, checked the office's voicemails, and booted up both her computer and Brystol's. Then she grabbed a denim tote bag she'd brought in with her and walked down the hallway to the elevator. She took the elevator to the lab floor and did a walking tour of the office area, depositing eight small, cheerful-looking artificial potted plants about ten inches tall on various desks and conference tables. Finally, as was her custom, she picked up the interoffice mail from the outgoing mailbox at the end of the lab and took it back up to the main office with her. Between seven-thirty and eight a.m., the rest of the lab technicians and staff reported to work and got started.

Dr. Menlo, Gerard, and Menlo's lab assistant appeared in the lab about eight fifteen and held an all-hands, stand-up meeting for about ten minutes. Menlo took some notes on the previous day's progress, shifted a couple of work assignments, and dismissed everyone to get back to work. About ten, a call came in for Gerard on her cell. It was one of the analysts working the desk at Kelly & Gerard Enterprises. She listened for a minute, and said, "Got it. We'll take a look. Thanks." Then she placed a call to Dawson, who was still in his quarters, briefing the most recent member to join the team. "Ben, bring your laptop and come out to the lab, will you? Ann says we need to look at something she thought was odd on the webcam footage from this morning." Dawson was in the lab in about three minutes, and set his laptop up on one of the conference tables.

They began to watch. "Did she give you a time marker?" Dawson asked.

"She said it was around 0715," Gerard replied, "and that it might be nothing at all. It just looked odd to her. Something about plants. She said we'd know it when we saw it."

At about that same time, Margaret was on the elevator again. But this trip didn't stop at the ground floor. She rode the elevator to the basement. She looked around the area, and not seeing anyone, walked immediately to the custodial offices. There she found that, as she expected, Jack Coleman was on duty. He was readying the floor-polishing equipment, and looked up in surprise to see Margaret. A gentle, balding, somewhat stooped Norwegian man well into his sixties, Coleman was one of the best liked and longest tenured employees of the Brystol Foundation. "Why Margaret, it's not often we see you down in this area," he said with a smile. "What are you doing on this fine morning?"

"I've brought you something, Jack," she replied, reaching into her denim tote.

Coleman looked puzzled and started to walk toward her. "Something for me?" he asked incredulously.

"Oh, my yes," Margaret said, withdrawing a nine-millimeter Beretta with a silencer attached to its barrel from her bag. Before he could even form a cogent thought about what he was seeing, Margaret whipped the pistol up into position and spat two rounds in a tight grouping through Coleman's forehead. The man folded up like a rag doll, crumpling in a pool of blood just where he had stood. Margaret replaced the pistol in her bag and then stepped over and tugged loose his big belt-mounted key ring. Then she exited the tiny custodial office, locking the door behind her, and jammed three flat toothpicks into the lock, breaking them off at the surface to prevent anyone from using another key to enter the room.

She crossed the basement and unlocked another door with one of Coleman's keys. This door led to the power room, where both the grid-based power from the city and the power from the backup generators fed through the main switch-and-breaker bank. That device routed power to the various equipment, lighting, HVAC, and telecommunications throughout the building. On the top of a console-size breaker box with conduits running out of three sides, she placed a small block of C4 explosive with a digital timer-based detonator. She pressed a button and the digital readout flickered to life, counting down from thirty minutes. Finally, she turned and left the power room, repeating the process she had used to disable the door at the custodial office, and returning unobserved to the elevators.

Margaret had been waiting for this day for years. She realized that she might not survive it, but who could really tell? In the meantime, she focused on all of the times she had been considered old and frail and foolish by so many in recent years. Most recently, there was the terrible indignity that she had suffered when that pig Biwu had literally slapped her so hard it drove her from her chair and onto the floor. She spent no energy considering whether her rage should really be directed at the MSS rather than people like Coleman who had done her no harm. They were just collateral damage, and all of these intellectuals who comprised the upper classes in the West needed to suffer. This was her small contribution, and she was happy to be even a small part in such a staggering blow to America.

CHAPTER 29

Bi-shou was taking no chances this time; she had decided that she would lead this mission personally. *If this mission fails, I may as well be dead anyway,* she thought. *My career will be over.* The team was comprised of twelve operators and Bi-shou. They were transported in two vehicles; one was a standard Ford Econoline van and the other was a video uplink truck, both emblazoned with the local news station's emblem on the sides. They were quite realistic because they were perfectly authentic; they had been stolen less than two hours earlier. Bi-shou had also prepared authentic-looking forged badges and identification papers for herself and both drivers. They were about five miles away from the Foundation when a call came into the guard shack at the front gate from Brystol's office. It was Margaret, Brystol's secretary. Brad Schreiber, who normally worked third shift, was on duty. With the doubled guard routine, a lot of the security people were working double shifts, and Schreiber was one of them.

"Yes, Ma'am?" Schreiber said, seeing Margaret's name and extension come up on the phone screen.

"Who is speaking?" Margaret asked.

"This is Sergeant Brad Schreiber," he said, unconsciously stiffening his posture.

"Very well, Sergeant," Margaret continued, "we have a news crew coming into the campus this morning to do an interview with Dr. Brystol. They are on their way and should arrive within twenty minutes. Dr. Brystol will begin his interview at the research building, and so the news team will be coming through your gate. Do you understand?"

Schreiber was frantically leafing through the paperwork on his clipboard and on the desk. He replied, "Well, not exactly, Ma'am. We are at a very high level of alert here, and I am not seeing anything about a news crew on my log of expected visitors."

"*Sergeant* Schreiber, I am calling you on behalf of Dr. *Brystol*. This is the *Brystol* Foundation. Dr. *Brystol* is preparing for the interview. Would you like me to interrupt him and explain that Sergeant Schreiber says he cannot do an interview today, even though the news crew is undoubtedly already en route? Should we just turn them around and send them back to the station, Sergeant, because you don't have them written down on a *piece of paper* somewhere?"

"No, Ma'am, I just—" Schreiber began to respond, but she cut him off.

"Do I need to come out there and write it down on your paperwork for you, Sergeant? Is *that* what you need in order to do your job?" she demanded imperiously.

"No, Ma'am," he replied, now completely undone. He grabbed a pen from the desk, saying: "I'll do that. Just give me their names, please?"

"You know, Sergeant," she replied icily, "that is precisely what I was calling you to do. But now that I understand just how utterly incompetent you are, here's what I'm going to do instead: I'm just going to tell you this. When a news crew shows up in vehicles that clearly say 'Channel 2 News' in letters three feet high on them, you just *open the gate and let them through.* Do you think you can handle *that*, Sergeant Schreiber?"

"Yes, Ma'am," he replied, "but—" It was too late; she had already hung up. Schreiber was perspiring heavily at this point, even though it was a cool morning.

His counterpart, who was even newer in his position than Schreiber, just shrugged and said: "Man, that was uncalled for."

"You can say that again," Schreiber responded.

Brystol, of course, was oblivious to all of this. He was in his office, door closed and classical music playing softly from the stereo behind him, going over budget and expenditure numbers for the coming quarter-end financial close.

In the meantime, Dawson, Menlo, and Gerard were scanning the webcam footage and had just come to the point where Margaret was walking through. "Oh, that's Margaret," Menlo said. "She always comes through in the morning to pick up and drop off inter-office mail. Nothing suspicious about that." Dawson and Gerard were about to agree with her when something caught Menlo's eye, and she turned back to look again. "Wait a minute," she said. Menlo watched the image another several seconds, and then began to glance around the work stations. "What are those?" she asked herself aloud. They all saw it then; Margaret had been depositing the small artificial potted plants at various points around the work station area of the lab. "That's odd." Menlo mused aloud. "I wonder...." Then she looked up and began searching the work area for one of the plants.

All three of them started looking around, and Gerard found the first one. "I've got one over here," she called out. Menlo and Dawson converged on her position at a desk near the back of the work area. Dawson pulled a Leatherman tool out of his pocket and slowly pried up the top of the faux turf at the top of the pot. He tipped the plant just enough to allow fluorescent light from the bench-mounted magnifier to spill into the pot beneath the surface as he held it in place with the blade of his Leatherman.

"Smoke bomb," Dawson said. "Looks like it's on a remote detonator, probably RF-based." He gently extracted the blade and replaced the surface. "Lily, alert Max immediately about what we found and who put it here. Then try to figure out how to minimize the impact. I'm going to Brystol's office to look for Margaret."

In Brystol's outer office, Margaret was already preparing for the arrival of Bi-shou's team. Since Brystol's office door opened outward, blocking him inside required only that she remove the heavy, plastic wedge-shaped doorstopper that she kept in her desk drawer and place it quietly under the door from the inner office. She took her phone off the hook and placed the line on hold, making it impossible for it to ring and also making it look to Brystol as though she was on the line, should he glance at the telephone in his office. Then she grabbed her bag, turned off the lights in the outer office, and locked the outer door. She strode quickly to the end of the hall and turned left, going a few office doors down and walking into an empty conference room to watch through the window for Bi-shou.

Precisely twenty-five minutes after Margaret started the digital timer on the detonator in the power room, Bi-shou's team arrived at the gate. Margaret watched with satisfaction as they were all waved through. No one tried to check the cargo areas of the van or the truck. As soon as they cleared the gate, she reached into her bag and withdrew the remote detonator.

Dawson found the office dark and the door locked when he arrived at

Brystol's office, and knew that he was too late to stop whatever Margaret had set in motion. He began to marvel at how the MSS had gotten someone so close to Brystol for so long, and it drew him back to one memory in particular of sitting in Brystol's office while he complained under his breath that Margaret was always cleaning his office up, and it took him forever to find all of his papers again. The woman had been privy to everything—schedules, expenditures, Dawson's work assignments, the office communications—*the answering machine! That's how they knew Menlo was on the road. After Menlo called Wu as she headed for Atlanta, Wu left a message for Brystol on his office answering machine.* At that moment, the lights flickered and an alarm began to emanate from the Salacia research building, and he knew he had to get back over there fast. About five seconds later, his earbud crackled and he heard Gerard say: "The floor show has started, Ben; better get back over this way."

* * * *

Nearly twenty kilometers away, Billy Winger was performing his morning exercise regimen when he heard Gerard's statement. He shut down the treadmill. He took a moment to towel off, and pulled on cargo pants and a long-sleeved shirt. After grabbing a Go Bag lying near the garage door, he started his 1985 Ford pickup. Then he pulled out onto the street and turned the old pickup truck toward the Leesburg Executive Airport.

* * * *

Margaret's timing had been perfect. The news vehicles had barely cleared the gate when the C4 in the power room detonated. She watched the office lights in the windows of the building extinguish, and as they did, she triggered the radio frequency switch, detonating the smoke grenades she had deposited in their little artificial plant version of Trojan horses, and smiled. It was all in motion now, and neither Ben Dawson nor anyone else could stop it. Within twenty-four hours the Salacia Project and the people who built it would all be in the hands of the MSS, and China would, at last, be on a level playing field with the rest of the world.

Dawson was rounding the corner in one of the stairwells heading down when he saw the news vehicles backing into position near the building. "Max, it looks like the bad guys are in Channel 2 trucks," he said. "A white van is backing into the loading dock area now, and a truck is right behind it."

"Roger that," came Kelly's reply, "I'm on it. I guess if there was any doubt about who's who in the zoo, it's gone now."

"I think so," Dawson replied. "Have you got our ground team moving?"

"They're in the pipe now; should be in position in sixty secs."

"Roger that," Dawson said, "Lily, give us a sitrep."

At that moment, the back end of the two news vehicles opened and Bi-shou's twelve tier-one operators emerged. All of them were dressed in navy blue windbreakers with POLICE emblazoned on their backs in bright yellow block letters. They wouldn't fool anyone who checked their credentials, of course, because they had no credentials, not even fake IDs. But no one was going to be looking for IDs while they were engaged, so Bi-shou was fine with that. All of them were armed with AK-47 assault rifles.

Inside the lab, as soon as Dawson had bolted for the door to try to track down Margaret, Gerard told Menlo. "Let's find all of these we can. We'll turn waste baskets upside down over each of them. Should contain a lot of the smoke until it can be released deliberately—in fact it will probably seep out rather than billowing." As it turned out, they found and contained over half of them before the remote trigger was engaged.

Fortunately, the grenades were potassium chlorate-based devices rather than the white phosphorus units, so there was no real explosion, just a great deal of smoke and heat. The heavy metal waste containers positioned at each work station, overturned on the hard concrete-and-tile floors, made an effective suppression mechanism in those cases where they were applied. As a result, when the devices were triggered, there was far less smoke than Bi-shou had expected; the resulting events caused alarm, but didn't result in the panic that she had tried to engender among the lab technicians and staff. Instead, when the smoke billowed out of the remaining containers, setting off the fire alarms and suppression systems, the lab personnel all moved in an orderly fashion toward the nearest exits.

Gerard responded, "Initiating Exit Protocol."

"Roger that," Dawson replied, and repeated, "Initiating Exit Protocol. Everyone copy?" Everyone on the team responded, including one last voice at the end that the rest of the team hadn't heard yet that day. "Roger that," came Winger's voice. ETA ten mikes."

Bi-shou's operators split into two teams. The first team of three, carrying a large equipment bag, shoved their way through the crowd of exiting workers near the receiving docks and moved immediately toward the closest stairwell, descending toward the basement. The second team, including Bi-shou and the other nine operators, split up into pairs and spread out to cover the four exits that Menlo and her staff were expected to use. They moved to positions just inside the doors, carefully reviewing the faces of everyone who passed them on their way out of the exits. Each operative had the four faces they were watching for memorized, beyond which almost everyone was wearing a lab coat and a name badge, so identification was pretty straight forward.

The team descending into the basement moved immediately to the vault room. They made short work of the pedestrian door using a small C4 charge at the lock, and the technician of the group began to work the various locking mechanisms of the vault. Since Margaret had already provided a fingerprint lifted from one of Brystol's drinking glasses, the biometric part was easy to defeat. However, Margaret had tried repeatedly to identify Brystol's eight-digit numeric code without success. So in order to gain entry, the technician would have to pull the cover off the cypher lock, find the appropriate locations to which he could attach leads, and start a computational decryption device that basically ran through every possible eight-digit numeric code. The device would then recapture the biometric pattern that he had pressed against the screen with a latex facade, and trigger the combination of those two until it finally presented the correct pairing.

Just as the technician was about to pull the cover off of the cypher lock, the door opened from the tunnel adjacent to the vault room, and Ron Meriwether poked his head through the opening. Boxer was immediately behind him. Meriwether just glimpsed the operators posted outside the vault room as the closest one wheeled to fire at him. He jerked his head back inside the door frame less than a second before thirty-nine-millimeter rounds began tearing up the surrounding wall and severely denting the metal frame. "Hold on, Ronny. I'm almost there," Kelly said as he opened the door from his stairwell and rolled into the room. Kelly came up on the other side of a pallet load of copy paper. A couple of seconds later, bullets began thudding into the boxes of paper, but Kelly was reasonably well protected for the moment.

He shifted around and pulled out his smart phone. Thumbing the keyboard, he brought up a grainy image from the webcam he secreted behind the ductwork leading to an exhaust vent near the ceiling in the area of the vault room. He couldn't make out the entire area, but he could see both of the operators outside the vault room. Kelly keyed his mike and said: "Ron, there are two operators I can see. When you open the door, they will be at nine and eleven o'clock. You'll know when to come in, 'cause I'm about to make some noise."

"Roger that, Boss," Meriwether replied. "All set here."

With that, Kelly looked one more time at the position of the two operators, jammed his phone back in his pocket, and then rolled out to one side. From a prone position behind a metal pillar, he began firing on the two operators. Both had pretty decent cover in their positions from the standpoint of Kelly's sightline, but they were flanked by Meriwether when he came out of the doorway.

Meriwether had been one of the best in his training class at the shooting-while-running maneuver, and he put those skills to work. One of the operators was hit twice, right arm and rib cage, which took him out. The other one jumped backwards behind the open metal door of the vault room and continued to fire on Kelly from there. He had no sightline to Meriwether, but of course the opposite was also true.

The technician had been trained to focus on the matter at hand and allow the other two operators to handle any outside interference. But while he was inside the small vault room he was waiting for the cypher lock combination to be identified by his machine. This left him free for a minute or two while it ran through the possible combinations. So he picked up his rifle and moved to a position where he could see Meriwether when he stuck his head around the corner. Since Meriwether wasn't expecting movement from inside the vault room, the technician got his first quick look unassailed. Both he and Meriwether knew that wouldn't happen a second time.

Meriwether keyed his mic and said, "Boxer, can you hear me?"

"Yeah, Boss, I hear you," came Boxer's reply. "What do you want me to do?"

"First check your 6," he said. "Anything back there?"

"Nope. No one coming from down the tunnel as far as I can see," Boxer said.

"Good," Meriwether said. "Now when I count three, I want you to rear back and kick the crash bar on that door coming into this room just as hard as you can. Don't come into the room or you'll get shot up. Just kick the door open as hard as you can for a distraction and stay back out of the line of fire. Press your back up against the wall. You got that?"

"Got it."

"Good thinking, Ron," Kelly whispered into the radio. "Give me a second to get ready over on my end. OK, I'm all set whenever you are."

"All right, Boxer, here we go … one … two … *three!*" Meriwether stood and sighted in on the edge of the door at head level just as the metal fire door was crashing open. As he expected, the operator behind the door started to peek out behind his weapon, and that was all Meriwether and Kelly needed. He was caught in the cross-fire, and no one knew whose shot actually killed him. They were all head shots, and there wasn't much left.

This left the technician, who realized he was in trouble. He had alerted Bi-shou that they were losing a firefight on the lower level, and Bi-shou dispatched the operator she was paired with to assist. He found the stairwell that Kelly had used and headed down as quickly as he could. He could hear the firing reaching a crescendo as he eased open the door at the bottom of the stairs just a crack, peering carefully and quietly inside.

At this point, less than ten minutes had elapsed from the time the alarms had sounded. Even so, the security center in the headquarters building was now swarming with security personnel. Jerry King was barking out questions and orders faster than the console operator could comply. He knew there was a fire of some kind in the lab, but he didn't know that anything else was really wrong. As nearly as he could tell, the power was out over there, and it looked to him as though people were exiting the building in an orderly fashion.

Then King noticed the Channel 2 News van just protruding from that corner of the building where the receiving docks were located, and said: "Who authorized the news people to be on site today? I didn't hear anything about it. Surely they aren't already here about the fire—and even if they are, who let them through the gate?" He snatched up the keys to the security golf cart and turned to head outside. Dawson's report about the news trucks was coming in on King's radio as he was preparing to leave the building.

Just as he was about to go through the door, Margaret entered. She didn't even speak to King; she just spat three rounds into his chest from her pistol, and before he hit the floor she was already reorienting her Beretta to shoot the console operator. He died slumped back in his chair with his eyes and mouth open, trying to understand what was happening. Then Margaret moved toward the tunnel entrance.

On the main floor, Bi-shou had figured out that Menlo and her staff were not exiting through the doors as expected. The crowd of Foundation employees was dwindling, and she was going to have to do this the hard way. There was less smoke than expected, and the twenty-foot high-bay ceilings permitted what smoke remained to rise much higher than it would in a normal room. As a result, Bi-shou was getting a clearer and clearer view of what were fewer and fewer people in the lab area.

After a bit, Bi-shou saw what must have been the group, flanked by

Dawson, going into the stairwell and headed up stairs. She signaled her operators to follow her, and ran for the stairway. As she was on the run, she called out to one pair of operators: "Take another stairway and get around them in case we need a cross-fire." She realized, after they had disappeared, that she needed either Menlo or the three subordinates alive. But she would have to cross that bridge when she had them all in her sights. *Just keep moving, Dawson,* she thought, *you're so predictable; how did you ever live this long?*

She hit the third floor followed by five of her operators, just a few seconds ahead of the remaining two operators who burst through the opposite stairwell fire door. It took less than a minute to determine that Dawson and the others were not there, and since this was the top floor of the building, that left only one place to go. Bi-shou smiled; this was better than she could have expected. "The roof," she called out. "This way!" They all raced for the stairwell that contained the exit to the roof.

In the basement, Kelly was unaware of the operator that had slipped in behind him. He and Meriwether were both moving slowly in a crouch toward the vault room, rifles up and in position to fire. Then several things happened at once. The operator/technician in the vault room slid out from the doorway on his side in a prone position, requiring Meriwether and Kelly to use a precious split-second to reposition their weapons and compensate for a moving target at floor level. They exchanged fire with the prone figure, and at the same time, Bi-shou's newly arrived operative stood and fired on Kelly. The operator on the floor was severely wounded, with only a few shallow breaths remaining in his lifetime, but Kelly had been hit, too. An unimpeded three-shot burst hit Max Kelly at the base of his neck, just above the top of his vest, before Meriwether could instinctively pivot and return fire. Meriwether's burst was low, and hit the man in the groin. The operator fell heavily forward, and Meriwether followed up with a shot to the back of his head. Then he called for Boxer to come on in, while checking on Kelly. "Max?" he said, kneeling over his longtime friend. "Where are you hit?" But it was too late. Max Kelly was already dead. *Funny thing,* Meriwether thought, *the big man's face looked as though he was finally at peace.*

Boxer joined Meriwether on the floor beside Kelly and said, "I'm sorry, Ron. I'm really sorry." As the last syllable of that sentence left Boxer's mouth, his face was suddenly covered with a look of wild surprise, then the light left his eyes and he fell forward, face down. Only peripherally, Meriwether made out the movement to his far left and realized the coughing sound he heard was a silenced pistol round. He rolled to his right, but already felt a searing pain in his left shoulder before he heard the cough of Margaret's Beretta again. She had slipped quietly through the tunnel and come in behind Boxer. *I told him to watch his 6,* Meriwether thought, *and he didn't, and now he's dead.*

Meriwether managed to come up from his roll, though still in terrible pain, holding onto his M4. He had to fire it with only his right hand, since his left arm and hand were now basically useless. Fortunately, the pipe-stocked weapon is relatively light at seven and one-half pounds, even with a full magazine. A former Delta Force member, Meriwether was strong, even at his age, and accustomed to working through great pain. Margaret, though clearly no ordinary sixty-something, was not limber enough to effectively throw her body around in order to survive a firefight. One-handed, Meriwether traced the bottom edge of her heart with a three-round burst.

Upstairs, Gerard and Dawson escorted Menlo and her three subordinates onto the roof. They moved them to a far corner, and settled them into a seated position behind one of two large air-handling units there. The air-handling units, each of which was about five feet high and twelve feet square, were the only structures that afforded cover, visual or physical, on the otherwise flat roof. As soon as he saw they were all safely there, watched over by Gerard, Dawson started back to replace the hatch to the roof. Recognizing that this was likely to be their exit strategy, Kelly had equipped the hatch with a special locking brace made of iron bars that could be closed from the outside, preventing access from below. As he rounded the corner to run back to the opening, though, Dawson realized that he'd made a big mistake in not securing the hatch immediately when he reached the surface.

Bi-shou was already on the roof, and one of her operators was pulling himself up behind her. She spotted Dawson over the air-handling unit, and didn't hesitate. She pulled a Mac-10 machine pistol that was slung from her shoulder around and opened up. She missed Dawson with the first spray, but really did a number on the massive air-handling unit. Then she pulled the strap off to get more freedom of movement and slowly began to sidestep so that she could peek around the big metal air handler, with the Mac-10 poised to unleash the next burst. Dawson had two problems—getting that hatch secured and keeping the people on the roof from becoming some combination of corpses and hostages. He realized too, however, that there was only one entrance to the roof. If he could maintain a line of fire over that open hatch, he could keep any other operators from coming through it alive.

Gerard ran up behind him, crouching. Dawson said, "You stay with Menlo and company. I'm going to try to make it to that second air handler.

They will have to come through that hatch and they have no cover, so they will have to rush us."

Gerard, who, unbelievably it seemed to Dawson, was pulling her hair back into a ponytail, nodded in the affirmative. Then she grabbed her pistol and got ready to spring into position, replacing Dawson as he ran the fourteen feet to the second air handler. Again, the Mac-10 started to track Dawson down with rounds splintering the rooftop and sending debris into the air, but this time Gerard spun out from behind the air handler at Dawson's previous position, let her breath out slowly, and squeezed off two rounds at Bi-shou.

Dawson slid the last few feet behind the air handler as though stealing second base. He recovered visual perspective just in time to see Bi-shou looking very surprised and grimacing in pain. Gerard had hit her center mass with two rounds. She was wearing a vest, it seemed, because there was no blood. But the sheer force had knocked her over backwards and sent her Mac-10 flying over the edge of the roof. This distracted the operator immediately behind her, but not for long. He immediately realized that he was in the open and any distraction would likely ruin his entire day.

Coming to the same conclusion Dawson had reached a minute or two earlier, Bi-shou's operator ran toward the first air handler, firing in Dawson's general direction as he ran. Anticipating the assailant's move, Gerard had run from her previous position, around Menlo and her team, to the other end of the air handler and worked her way around the far end. As she heard the gun fire, Gerard spun out from the other end of the air handler and fired again. No more of this center mass crap, she thought, and she steadied herself and took the shot. The assailant's head exploded. Then she spun to her right in time to see another operator's head come cautiously up through the hatch. She fired again, grazing the back of the man's head. She heard him scream as he fell back down the ladder, undoubtedly tumbling over other operators that were in position following him up.

Bi-shou had some rib damage and the wind was knocked out of her, but she had recovered her senses enough to pull a nine-millimeter automatic from her vest. It did her no good; Dawson was already there, and yanked it out of her hand. Gerard approached the hatch quietly from behind and quickly swung the top over on its hinges, throwing the crossbar into position. In response, a few bullets made their way through the metal cover, but hit nothing and careened off into the sky. Then more gunfire broke out below, and Dawson assumed that Kelly and Meriwether had caught up.

He would have been surprised to know that it was the Foundation's own security team. Although they were technically inferior in skill, sheer numbers and the fact that the remaining operators who could still resist were so depleted gave the advantage to the security team. One more operator died in the battle, and the last three operators who were fully functional finally surrendered just as they heard a helicopter overhead.

Dawson looked up to see Bi-shou's MD902 NOTAR helicopter descending and flaring off to a hover just a few feet from the rooftop. At the controls was a grinning Billy Winger. "Anybody need a lift?" Winger's voice came through Dawson's earbud. Gerard already had Menlo and her team up and running toward the helicopter door. While they were on the run, Dawson zip-tied Bi-shou's wrists and ankles and moved her to the chopper with a fireman's carry. He threw her in like a sack of potatoes, and admonished Gerard to be careful with her. Gerard was the last one aboard. Dawson remained behind on the roof, and signaled Winger to spin up and take off. In seconds, Winger was lifting away into the sky and saying through Dawson's earbud, "You know, Boss, if we're gonna keep stealing these choppers, one of us really ought to get a pilot's license."

At that point, Dawson finally realized that the gunfire had settled down below. After a minute or so, he keyed his mike and said: "Max, Ron, somebody give me a sitrep please?" Only silence answered, and Dawson knew that something down below had gone very wrong.

CHAPTER 30

Dawson threw the cover off of the hatch and looked cautiously down the steel-frame ladder that led up from the third-story stairwell. Even with the power still out, there was enough sunlight and emergency light spilling through the stairwell to see that matters had been settled there. Dawson could see that there was still a little movement just out of his visual range, so he shouted down: "This is Ben Dawson. Who is below?"

A voice responded almost immediately. "Mr. Dawson, this is Captain Mitch Genio of the Foundation security department. Is everything secure up there?" Dawson remembered Genio, who was, to the best of his recollection, a member of Jerry King's staff.

"Yes, Captain; It's all secure up top. I'm coming down."

"Yes, Sir," Genio responded, "we're all secure here, too. It's all clear now."

Dawson thought, *I hope this isn't an ambush,* grabbed the rails of the ladder, and descended as rapidly as he could, slowing himself just a little at every third step. When he touched the floor, he could see Genio and two other Foundation security staff. He saw more as he moved out of the stairwell. "The FBI is on their way, and they said they would call in the Virginia State Police," Genio said.

"Where's your boss?" Dawson asked.

"He was killed, Sir," Genio responded, his voice cracking.

"I'm sorry, Mitch," Dawson replied. "I truly am. Jerry was a good man. Do you know what has happened with my folks?"

"No, Sir," Genio replied. "Haven't seen or heard from—" He was interrupted by a crackling voice on his radio, and pulled it off his belt.

"Mitch, we need a medic down here in the basement ASAP," came the voice on the radio. "Dawson's team is down here, and they're shot up pretty bad. A couple are already dead, along with a bunch of bad guys and Dr. Brystol's secretary. We also found Dr. Brystol. He's OK, but he was trapped in his office all this time, and he's pretty pissed."

Genio began moving even as he acknowledged the transmission and began barking out orders to the other officers. They had some bodies of their own there outside the stairwell, and a couple of the operatives had surrendered. They were on the floor, facedown with handcuffs and zip-ties restraining them. In the ten seconds it took Genio to make sure his officers were going to remain in place and turned for the stairs himself, Dawson was long gone.

When Dawson arrived in the basement, the situation washed over him like a wave. All the adrenaline from the firefight on the roof and the sheer stress of recent days seemed to converge on him. It was as though his field of vision progressively narrowed to the face of his friend Max Kelly, and all he could think about was how he was going to tell Gerard. He knelt there for what seemed an eternity, replaying that conversation he and Kelly had in the cafeteria. "The things I have done can't be undone, and that's the only thing that would change anything," Kelly had said. *Maybe you were right*, Dawson thought, *and if you were, I guess this keeps you from fighting your demons anymore. But my God, how I am going to miss you, my friend. You have left a gigantic chasm on this earth. There are certainly more virtuous men than you, or me for that matter, but I know none who are more honorable than you.*

Finally, he heard Meriwether groaning not four meters away. Meriwether was still alive! Dawson could hardly believe it. At that moment, he realized they had lost Boxer as well. He remembered how close these three had been, and in some ways was almost relieved that Boxer had gone with Kelly. Dawson thought, *I don't know how Boxer would have gotten along without Max.*

Dawson moved over to Meriwether and saw that a Foundation security officer was applying a compress to Meriwether's shoulder wound. "Thanks," he said, replacing the officer who had been kneeling to assist Meriwether. "I'll take over until the medics arrive." Between the shock and blood loss, Meriwether was floating in and out of consciousness. "Ron, can you hear me?" Dawson asked him.

Meriwether's eyes fluttered a bit, and he tried to move his lips, but it just seemed too much for him. "It's all right," Dawson said. "Don't try to talk but try to stay with me; stay awake if you can. I'm really sorry about what happened here, Ron. I should have called in more operators."

At that moment, there was the shuffling sound of people descending the stairway at the far side of the room, and a man in a lab coat ran over followed closely by two others in similar attire. It was the Foundation's on-campus medical doctor, Oscar Silverman, and two members of his staff. The doctor began working on Meriwether, while his two assistants prepared a stretcher. They got Meriwether onto the stretcher, transported him quickly but carefully to the freight elevator, and started up with Dawson alongside. There was nothing more he could do for Boxer or Kelly, he knew, and his remaining responsibility lay with Meriwether. Once Meriwether was stable, Dawson would have to find some way to break all of this to Gerard, and he wasn't sure he had the strength.

"He's lost a lot of blood, and I'm pretty sure his scapula has been shattered up here at the top. Must have penetrated the top of the shoulder and come down between the ceramic plates in his vest," the doctor said to Dawson. "I think he'll recover. We have our ambulance outside the loading dock, and we'll have him at the trauma center in a few minutes. We have room for you, if you want to come along."

Dawson nodded and followed as they got the stretcher onto the portable gurney and moved it to the ambulance. Within three minutes, they were out the gate and headed down the road.

* * * *

Winger set Bi-shou's helicopter down, as planned, in an empty field outside Leesburg. Waiting at the edge of the field were three SUVs, one of which contained two NSA operatives and Charles Jennings. The other was an extended capacity up-armored vehicle containing only a driver. Winger shut down the helicopter's rotor and unloaded his last passenger, Bi-shou, almost as unceremoniously as Dawson had deposited her in the bird about thirty minutes before.

Jennings walked quickly over to speak with Menlo and Gerard, inquiring to assure that they were both unscathed, and then met and checked each of Menlo's staff. He thanked each of them for their courage and told them he would be meeting with them all later to thank them properly, but noted that he really must see to their other guest, Bi-shou, right away.

Bi-shou was lifted to her feet by two of the NSA operatives as Jennings walked over to speak with Winger and shake his hand. Then he turned to the assassin. "Bi-shou," he smiled, "I am Charles Jennings, and I work for the United States government." She glowered fiercely at him, but said nothing. "You have been the subject of much conversation recently," Jennings continued, "and I will be speaking with you more when we reach the detention center. But there is something I'd like you to know before we begin our journey, and that is this: You are a very fortunate woman. This is true for many reasons, among which is the fact that you have been captured by men and women of great gallantry. Others who could as easily have been your captors today would have dealt with you in a much different manner."

Bi-shou looked sullen, but unconvinced. Jennings continued: "The other reason you are extremely fortunate is that I was successful in lobbying for you to be treated as a US citizen, although I'm sure that your dual citizenship with China will be wielded skillfully by attorneys in the days ahead. Other US government agencies argued strongly that you should be treated as an enemy combatant and interrogated more aggressively. My dear, you would not have cared for that. But you will be afforded complete security as long as you cooperate in our discovery of the network who hired you. The moment that cooperation ceases, we will avail you of more *typical* security measures. Not long thereafter, I'm sure, operatives of the MSS will undoubtedly find some way to dispatch you in order to mitigate the risk of greater damage. So I advise you to tell us everything you know as quickly as you can, so that you no longer remain a significant liability. We shall give you time to think that over, of course, but I recommend that you do so expeditiously. Your proverbial clock is ticking."

Straightening her posture, Bi-shou finally looked Jennings squarely in the eye. She said, "Mr. Jennings, I do not fear the MSS; I have defeated them before. I know who *you* are, Mr. Jennings. I know where you live. I know all about your wife, Rita, and about her weekly bridge games. I know about your children, including your pregnant stepdaughter, almost six months along now, I believe, and I know about your grandchildren. I can tell you where all of them live, and for those grandchildren old enough to be in school, I can tell you which grammar schools they attend, even the ones in Denver. If you release me before midnight tonight, I give you my word that all of them will remain untouched by me and by my associates. Whether you release me or not, however, will not alter the very special plans I have for you and Mr. Dawson. I believe you are familiar with my reputation, Mr. Jennings. I would advise you to consider carefully what you choose to do next."

With that, Jennings signaled the NSA operatives, who escorted her to the rear seat of the SUV in which they arrived.

* * * *

About thirty kilometers away, Jing-ti paced around his office like a caged animal. It was past time for him to have received a report from Bi-Shou. But when information began to trickle in from local television stations about a fire and undetermined police activity at the Brystol Foundation, he knew his worst fears were being realized. Bi-shou had failed again, and it was likely they now had nothing—not Menlo, not Menlo's key staff, not Menlo's husband, and most importantly, not Salacia.

At that moment, there was a discreet knock at his door, and his assistant quietly entered. She bowed slightly, and said, "Teng-hui requests that you attend him in his office, please."

"Yes, all right," Jing-ti replied. The assistant repeated the slight bow and exited as quietly as when she arrived, closing the door silently behind her. Jing-ti stood there, unmoving for a full two minutes, his mind racing through options and scenarios. Finally, realizing that he really had no options left, he walked through the door and down the hall toward the office suite of his boss.

When Jing-ti arrived in Teng-hui's office, he found two very serious-looking men whom he had not met before. They were both large men, dressed in dark suits and wearing ominous expressions. Teng-hui said, "Jing-ti, these gentlemen are from MSS headquarters in Beijing. This is Bing Lee, and Huang Tang. They arrived yesterday to review your operation at the Brystol Foundation, and your progress toward obtaining the Salacia technology."

Yes, Jing-ti thought, *suddenly it's my progress and my operation, no longer our progress and our operation. Teng-hui is attempting to use the famous tactic of "plausible deniability" employed by American presidents like Nixon and Obama, both of whom had been elected by these gullible Americans to a second term of office in spite of their behavior. But the Chinese government is not as blind as these Americans,* he thought. *Teng-hui surely cannot survive if I fall now.*

When Jing-ti turned and bowed respectfully to them in greeting, they did not return the gesture. "Good afternoon," Jing-ti said to them anyway. The larger of the two men said, "Please tell us, Jing-ti, whether this is correct: You have spent more than three million US dollars in your recent attempts to obtain Salacia, and as of this morning, you are no closer than you were a month ago. Biwu is dead; Bi-shou is captured or dead, and more than a dozen Chinese operatives have been killed in the last few weeks related to this endeavor. Fengche has been recovered, but he is injured and our relations with the Iranians are severely damaged. You do not have the technology, you do not have the inventor, and you do not have the critical material required to enable Salacia. Is that correct?"

"Yes, that is correct," Jing-ti replied. *No point in denying it now,* he thought. *As the Americans would say, Teng-hui has thrown me "under the truck." No wait, that's not right; Teng-hui has thrown me "under the bus." Yes, that's it, "under the bus."*

"As to the cost and the reasons for my actions, and the sequence of events over these last few weeks, I have all of those records here," he replied, holding out his hand and offering up a flash drive. "You may download that information through any device with a USB port." *Now we shall see who is embarrassed,* he thought. *They will find that this has been my responsibility for only a few weeks, that the entire debacle around Biwu and Fengche belongs to Teng-hui, and Teng-hui is also the one who brought in Bi-shou.*

Teng-hui interjected, "That information may be tainted or untrue. I must review it before it goes anywhere else!" He wasn't fast enough, though. The smaller of the two MSS operatives had already pocketed the flash drive. He ignored Teng-hui, and said: "You will come with us, Jing-ti. You will have an opportunity to explain your actions in Beijing."

"May I close things down here first?" Jing-ti asked. He already knew the answer.

"Teng-hui will take over any open matters remaining here," the larger of the men replied. "We will go to your apartment and you may pack some clothing. However, leave everything else, including your car keys here on the table."

"I understand," Jing-ti replied and did as he was told.

"I will also need the passwords to your computer files," Teng-hui said, placing a single sheet of paper on the conference table with a pen, and then returning to his own desk.

Jing-ti smiled to himself. *It's too late for that, Teng-hui,* he mused. *It's all gone. Everything pertinent was copied to the flash drive, or put into an electronic folder in the cloud, and even that is encrypted. My hard drive is being wiped as we stand here, and you will find nothing until Beijing asks you about it. When that happens, there will be nothing left here for you to defend yourself with. But* he dutifully wrote the passwords for Teng-hui as requested, and placed the pen on the table beside the paper.

When they had left, Teng-hui walked rapidly to Jing-ti's office and discovered, to his great dismay, what Jing-ti had done. With the drive wiped, even the passwords were useless. His hope of plausible deniability was crumbling around him.

* * * *

Across town, technicians at the FBI were using photographs provided by Winters at the NSA to run facial recognition routines on the security video from Fairfax Metro Hospital, and discovered Fengche in the footage of the lobby. The images of Fengche in the corridor outside Biwu's room the day he was assassinated were lost in the subsequent fire, so it was impossible to place him actually in that room, but the lobby time stamps, along with reports from Jennings that had been forwarded by Dawson, made the sequence of events and Fengche's involvement pretty clear.

Fengche, by that time, had been moved to the Chinese Embassy in Tehran. He was recovering well. The MSS had already informed him that he would be flown directly to Beijing from Tehran as soon as he was well enough to travel, and before he could be debriefed or coached by Teng-hui.

Late that evening, Dawson rang the doorbell of a sprawling, secluded two-story home in the hills outside of Richmond. The home was a safe house owned by the FBI, and it had been loaned to Jennings by Cal Ingram for purposes of housing Menlo and her team while things settled down around the Salacia project. Menlo, McCallister, Hoffman, and Wu had been sequestered there until their safety could be assured. He was pleased to find that when the door opened, he was greeted by a somewhat wan but smiling lieutenant colonel in a US Army uniform. "Colonel Menlo," Dawson said, "it's good to see you again."

"Hello, Sir," Menlo replied. The colonel had begun to straighten himself to salute, but realized that Dawson was actually a civilian, and instead, offered his hand. "It's great to see you again, too. I have been looking for an opportunity to thank—"

"Now don't start that, Colonel," Dawson cut him off. "We all did our jobs, and you more than anyone showed us how it's done well. We're all very proud of you, Tom, especially your wife and son."

Menlo nodded sheepishly and said, "Will you come in, Sir?" Dawson stepped inside, and Menlo closed the door behind him. "Just about everybody has gone to bed for the night here, but I can find some coffee."

Dawson replied, "Thanks, Tom, but no. And please call me Ben. I am here to see Lily Gerard."

"Oh, of course," Menlo said. "If you'll have a seat in the living room, I'll track her down for you." He turned and disappeared down the hall and up a staircase. Dawson found the living room pretty much directly ahead of him, and took a seat as suggested. About three minutes went by, and Dawson could hear the sound of a grandfather clock chiming somewhere on the second floor.

When Gerard padded into the room, she was wrapped in a terry cloth bathrobe over a plain V-neck T-shirt and sweat pants. Although it appeared that she had taken a moment to run a brush through her hair, she had clearly been sleeping when Dawson arrived at the house.

Dawson stood and said, "Oh. Lily, if I had realized you would be sleeping, I would have waited until morning for this. I should have called you to check, but I didn't...."

"What is it?" Gerard asked. "Has something happened to Max? I haven't heard from him since we jumped on the chopper."

Dawson took a deep breath, deciding that telling her outright was the best course of action now. "Lily, Max and Boxer were both killed during the firefight at the Foundation. Ron was hit, too, but it looks like he is going to be OK." He let her process that for a moment. She fell heavily into a seated position on the end of the sofa.

The look on her face told Dawson that she had almost expected this. "I thought something like this must have happened," she said, covering her eyes with her hand as she rested her elbow on the arm of the sofa. She seemed to be refusing to look at Dawson, as though this would somehow keep reality from flooding in. He could see tears leaking through her fingers, and then her shoulders began to shake.

Dawson rummaged around the adjacent rooms and found a box of tissues. He returned to the living room and sat them on the end table next to Gerard. While she was blowing her nose and wiping her eyes, he sat down beside her. "I'm really sorry, Lily," Dawson said softly. "I just don't know what to say."

"What happened?" Gerard asked, looking up at him through teary eyes.

"He was hit from behind. A three-round burst from an AK. He never saw it coming, Lily. I honestly don't think he felt a thing. His face looked, I don't know, peaceful, I guess. Meriwether got the guy who did it. But then Meriwether and Boxer were both shot by Margaret. Boxer was killed instantly, but Meriwether will make it."

"Margaret?" Gerard asked.

"Meriwether got her," Dawson replied. *There's almost no one left to hate for this,* he thought.

"I feel so guilty," she said in barely audible tones. "Max wasn't himself lately. It'd happened before, and … I tried to talk to him. But he just built up that wall around him."

"I know," Dawson replied, "I talked to him about it, too. I asked him to let me get him some help, but he said 'no.' Said he was just who he was, and there was no going back. In some ways…."

"I know," Gerard said. "In some ways, this may be exactly what he wanted. He was going to end up in jail or dead before long, wasn't he?"

Dawson just looked at her, exhaled, and nodded. "I think so, Lily. I really do," he replied.

"What a day this has been," she said. "What is that phrase: 'It was the best of times, it was the worst of times'? Today the Menlos were reunited, and today we lost Max and Boxer forever."

Gerard reached over and took Dawson's hand in hers. Then she simply lay back against the sofa and closed her eyes. Dawson did the same, and she laid her head on his shoulder, and her breathing slowed.

Eventually, they were asleep.

* * * *

Two weeks later, Dawson was called to a meeting in Brystol's office at the Foundation. When he arrived, he saw that a number of things were changing there. The simple wrought iron fence that surrounded the campus was being replaced with a higher and more substantial one, adorned with outward-facing spikes. Dawson also recognized the elements of an electric charge distribution mechanism going into place as a part of the remodel of the gates at the Foundation's entrances. Both the north and the south gates were being equipped with inground pylons that could be raised and lowered from within the guard houses.

The guard houses themselves were being modified as well, with surveillance monitors that utilized cameras extending along the perimeter fence on all sides. The new structures were almost three times as large, with a two-guard compliment now the standard at each gate, and a small armory in each that included M16s capable of fully automatic fire selection and fitted with forty-millimeter grenade launchers. Bullet-proof vests were no longer optional, and the sentries themselves were employees of the Axis private security firm.

When Dawson pulled up to the main building, he could see that there were three of the all-too-familiar black government sedans parked in the VIP area nearest to the building's front lobby. As he entered, he could see evidence that the interior security equipment was also being upgraded. *This place will never be the same*, he thought.

Margaret's successor met him at the front door, and escorted him up the elevator and to Brystol's conference room. She introduced herself as Diane Maretti, and appeared to be the model of efficiency. She looked to Dawson to be in her late thirties, about five feet eight inches tall, athletic, and perhaps of Italian descent. Ascending in the elevator, Dawson asked her: "Which branch of the service were you in, Ms. Maretti?"

She stared straight ahead, but smiled just a little. "Captain in the United States Marine Corps, Sir," she replied. "I'm still a reservist."

"I'm curious, Ms. Maretti," Dawson said.

"Yes, Sir?" she replied.

"Do you carry a weapon?" he asked.

As the door was about to open, she said: "I *am* a weapon, Sir."

Ah, Dawson thought, *we're going to get along just fine. I can't wait for you to meet Lily.*

As he approached, he could see that Brystol was locked in an intense conversation with Cal Ingram, and standing to one side were two other men, John Deering and Charles Jennings. When he entered the room, all conversation stopped and the four men all moved to greet Dawson warmly. There were a number of questions from Brystol, Deering, and Ingram, which Jennings patiently endured while he poured drinks at the side bar. He returned with a scotch and water for himself, and Dawson's "usual." Dawson accepted the iced tea gratefully, and was a little amused to find that the deputy director had even remembered the Splenda. Jennings was starting pretty early with liquor, Dawson observed, but given what they had just experienced, the man certainly deserved a break from regimen.

The group never did bother taking seats at the conference table. This was more by way of an after-action report than an actual meeting; there was no formal agenda. Essentially, it boiled down to personal assurances by the FBI and the CIA that the actions taken by Dawson and his team were classified and were viewed to be actions necessary to protect US national security. There was a brief discussion about whether any future events such as this one should involve official Bureau employees when they occurred on US soil, but Ingram was gentle about that, and even then he produced rather embarrassed glances from his two colleagues.

In response, Dawson said to the group: "I accept full responsibility for the lives we lost during the attack here. I should have had more operators in place. I simply underestimated the force that would be deployed. We would never have been able to bring in official law enforcement people en mass such as Bureau people, because whoever the mole was at the Foundation would have warned off Bi-shou. The other side would simply have waited us out until they had a better shot. But I might have been able to slip more operators in without the spy—Margaret, as it turned out—seeing the added manpower."

"The upshot of our meeting with you today is this, Ben," Ingram eventually said. "Under the circumstances, we believe you did the right thing. We aren't here to issue recriminations. However, going forward, we would like to hear from you from time to time. Now, I know you work for Charles and Kenneth here, and I'm not asking you to tell us things that they don't already know. But it would be to everyone's advantage if, oh, you know, once a month or so...."

At this point, Jennings cleared his throat. "Or even just, oh, quarterly, let's say," Ingram glanced at Jennings, and seeing no objection, continued, "you could just drop by my office and have a chat about what you're working on. We all work pretty closely on things like this, and it would help us all to stay on the same page. Isn't that right, Charles?"

"Of course," Jennings replied through a smile, "and I'd be pleased to accompany Ben whenever he does that."

"I'll be happy to do that, Sir," Dawson said. "Charles, may I rely on your office to set those meetings up?"

"Absolutely," Jennings replied, smiling like a Cheshire cat.

Whew, Dawson thought, *parried that one*. If there was one thing Ben really didn't want, it was two more bosses from two more government agencies as overseers.

EPILOGUE

Three months had passed since the battle at the Brystol Foundation. The summer had been a beautiful one across the eastern half of the United States. September had painted the hillsides in brilliant autumn colors, and retained enough warmth to keep the voices of children echoing from parks and football fields. The air seemed fresh and clean to Dawson as he stood there listening to the rustle of the leaves.

He had been there at the grave of Max Kelly in Arlington National Cemetery for about forty minutes when he could tell that someone was approaching from behind. He waited until the footsteps drew closer and said, "Hello, Lily."

She slipped up on his right and laced her arm through his. "I didn't mean to disturb your reverie," she said. "I didn't know you were here. Just came by to say hello to Max."

"Me, too," Dawson replied.

"How did you know it was me?" she asked.

"Sand & Sable," he replied. "You were upwind, and I like that fragrance a lot."

That made her smile, and she squeezed his arm. They both stood there for a while longer. After ten minutes or so, Lily spoke again. "When are you coming back, Ben?"

"Oh, I'm ready to go. I've been here long enough, I think."

"That's not what I meant," she said, leaning her head on his shoulder. "I mean when are you coming back to work, to your friends, and, selfishly, I guess, when are you coming back to me?"

"I could any time I suppose," he said as they turned to walk back toward the road. "Hearings are over on the Hill, and everybody seems satisfied. Jing-ti has been sent back to China, and it looks like his boss Teng-hui may be close behind. Bi-shou is out of the hospital and in prison, but will undoubtedly fall victim to an untimely 'accident' at some point. She's just too great a liability to the MSS now. Ralph Simons will spend the rest of his natural life behind bars. Fengche is still in the wind, of course, and no one knows when he'll show up again. As long as he's still out there somewhere, he's going to worry me, I suppose. The trial run of Salacia on the Vicksburg was a big success. The Navy is equipping its other ships just as fast as they can. Carolyn Menlo has her husband back...."

"Oh, and I've been meaning to congratulate you on that," Gerard interrupted, still walking with her arm tightly laced through his.

"Really?" Dawson asked.

"Oh, not on getting him back; everybody knew you'd pull that off."

Dawson's eyes widened as he said, "Everyone except *me*, maybe."

"But the thing I wanted to congratulate you on was getting the Army to detail Colonel Menlo to you, so you could assign him to bodyguard his own wife. That was some pretty fancy string-pulling for a guy who loathes bureaucracy."

"Oh, that," Dawson replied with a smile. "Well, sometimes I can get the old boys club to see things my way. Not often *enough*, but sometimes. As Carolyn moves into the next phase, converting Salacia technology to a configuration that supports underwater vessels, she's going to need longer-term security than I can provide. It seemed like a good arrangement."

"I think you're understating that," Gerard agreed. "I think it's *perfect*. Now that you don't have to think about Carolyn Menlo any more, perhaps you have time to think about *other* things."

Dawson smiled down at her. "Subtle," he said, and chuckled. "Very subtle."

"Have you given any thought to my proposal?" Gerard asked him.

"Yes, but I think I have to turn you down, Lily. I'm just not willing to leave the Foundation right now. Brystol has several new technologies coming down the pipe right behind Salacia, and some of them are quite interesting to me. One of them, code named Angelia, is developing some challenges not unlike the things we encountered with Salacia. I'm guessing I'll have my hands full, and I'll need your special kind of help."

"So, let me see if I understand this," she said, allowing her mouth to pucker. You want me to just go on running my business now that half of the team is dead, just like nothing happened, and keep following you around, cavorting all over the country while you cavort all over the world doing God knows what with heaven knows who, and…."

"Calm down," Dawson interrupted, "and stop putting words in my mouth. That's not what I said. I think you ought to hire Winger and Romero if you need more help. I already ran it by them, and they like the idea."

"You *what*?" She spat back at him, planting her feet and stiffening.

"Look, Lily, you're going to need help, and these guys are both top shelf. You *know* that."

"Yes, I *know* that," she admitted, "but don't you think I should interview and hire *my own* people?"

"Well, if you had time, of course," Dawson replied, "but we've got a lot to do, and, like I mentioned, things are heating up on Angelia."

"Ben Dawson, you are *incorrigible!*" She retorted. "Why do you assume that every time you get yourself into a mess, all you have to do is come by the gym and I'll be just waiting for—"

He kissed her then, hard and for a long time, and in a few seconds, she was working pretty hard at it, too. When they came up for air, he said, "Listen Lily, I *want* you to be my partner. I don't know exactly what that means, but I don't think it's a good idea to become *business* partners right now. I think this works best if you're the leader of a contract house and I can bring you in that way. It keeps a degree of separation that I believe, rightly or wrongly, makes you safer. Losing Max was hard enough, but if something happened to you—"

She kissed *him* this time, and he never got to finish that sentence. Both of them decided that they had time to work out the details later, and would go forward on what Dawson called "an agreement in principle." In the meantime, they had more important things to do.

THE ANGELIA PROJECT

If you liked *The Salacia Project*, you'll love *The Angelia Project!* Ben Dawson and his team are back, rescuing another world-changing technology from international thieves and assassins. As a bonus, here is the first chapter from this next installment in the Brystol Foundation series. Enjoy!

CHAPTER 1

It was a beautiful spring evening in the bustling Athens neighborhood of Ilisia. The campus of the National and Kapodistrian University of Athens was uncharacteristically crowded, as visiting faculty members from a wide array of international partner universities were arriving for a presentation on Thermoelectrically Powered Computing Paradigms. Representatives from Carnegie Mellon University in the United States, Aalborg University in Denmark, the French National Institute for Research in Computer Science and Control in France, the University of Southampton in the UK, the Technische Universitaet Berlin in Germany, Instytut Chemii Bioorganicznej Pan W Poznaniu in Poland, and many others were there. Other participants included Greek government officials and several representatives of leading research and development corporations such as RTI International, Tellurex, and Sigma-Aldrich.

Among the VIPs attending the presentation that evening was Dr. Kenneth

Brystol, a physicist and entrepreneur of some renown and CEO of the Brystol Foundation. Brystol was always scanning the landscape of scientific research to identify potentially world-changing technologies, and he had demonstrated an uncanny knack for finding them. The Brystol Foundation, headquartered in the Washington, DC vicinity of Virginia, maintained an ongoing portfolio of about ten such technologies at all times. Many of them were obtained by convincing the US government that they were vital to national security and that the Brystol Foundation was uniquely qualified to complete the development of the technologies and turn them into strategic advantages for the United States. Brystol had traveled to Athens for this event to see a presentation by one of the Athenian researchers, Eleftheria Karounos, who was working in a very specific area of computer-based telecommunications.

Eleftheria Karounos was a PhD candidate at the National and Kapodistri-an University of Athens, researching signal processing for encrypted commu-nications. While the university had no particular interest in this specific field, the program funding was quite attractive, and like all Greek institutions in recent years, the university was in no position to shirk sources of revenue. The relative abundance of funding had sprung from the advent of cyber warfare, especially since the trouble in America following September 11, 2001.

Karounos was a dark-haired and bespectacled woman of twenty-eight, not unattractive, and was most often described by friends and family as cute, but rather dowdy. She had very little social life; she loved her research, and the interchanges with colleagues satisfied her social interests. At five feet ten inches tall, her body was more angles than curves. Karounos maintained a slightly stooped posture that did nothing to cause any significant interest in potential suitors. As long as funding continued to flow to her work, she was satisfied with her life. And at that moment, it seemed to her as though funding was likely to continue.

The Chinese, the Russians, and even the North Koreans had developed substantial capabilities in cyber warfare, and the United States had found itself on the defensive. After Chinese MSS operatives managed to introduce a computer virus into one of the defense networks at the Pentagon, the US Department of Defense began to issue laptops to its employees that had all USB ports and print capabilities disabled, and banned the use of flash drives in the Pentagon. The situation was ludicrous. But the upshot of the debacle was that rivers of revenue opened up from the coffers of the US government and several of her allies, that branched out into many streams of research and development into all types of anti-hacking hardware, software, and skills. As the Americans' capabilities in this field matured, it also occurred to the CIA and the Israeli Mossad that their newly developed tools could be an effective offensive weapon. Working together, the two organizations used cyber warfare to set the Iranian nuclear development program back by more than five years.

Karounos had no interest in cyber warfare or even in cryptography for that matter. But she did love research and was fascinated by the possibilities of changing the medium of telecommunications. During her doctoral studies, she came across an obscure article written by an information technologist at Boeing titled, "The Quantum Universe: An Information Systems Perspective," and it started her down a mental path that changed her perspective forever. It postulated that the fabric of the universe at its most fundamental level is information and that information adequately and correctly configured comprises mass. The relationships between mass, energy, and information became her mental laboratory, and it led her to devise breakthroughs in the construction of materials that were themselves not only containers of information, but actually *comprised* of information. When some of her work became known to the scientific community at large, the telephone of the dean of the Informatica Department at the University of Athens began to ring. That was about thirty days prior, and as a result, many of the intellectual and scientific leaders of related industries were assembling in Athens to listen to a presentation by Karounos and her research partner, Tom Iliopoulos.

Iliopoulos had a burgeoning reputation in the field of thermoelectric materials science. Essentially, he was on the forefront of developing materials that converted thermal energy—heat—into electrical energy. Karounos and Iliopoulos had met only six months earlier as part of a Friends of Athens event. A few months hence, they decided to partner in order to work on a research project related to self-sustaining computers. Their project involved using a very small amount of solar energy to power laptop computers. After the initial kickstart from solar energy, the computers then generated sufficient internal heat from their own processes via the thermoelectric materials inside the computer structure itself to make additional external electricity requirements practically nil. It wasn't quite a perpetual energy machine, but it was closer than anyone had ever come.

And yet this area of research was really only of passing interest to Iliopoulos. His real interest was in the work of his fellow researcher, and his purpose was to learn everything possible from her just as quickly as he could. Iliopoulos' name was an alias. Born Steven Rosen, Iliopoulos was recruited by the Mossad while he was a student of one of Israel's Haredi secondary schools. He demonstrated a facility for languages early in life, and his mother was Greek. The result was a complexion and natural affinity for the Greek language that made him an excellent choice for his assignment in Athens. He had always been an excellent student and very adept in the sciences.

He was dispatched to Athens University following the completion of his studies at the Weizmann Institute of Science in Rehovot, Israel, to continue in his studies and, more importantly, to get close to Eleftheria Karounos. When Iliopoulos had obtained everything he needed, or when he had obtained everything she could provide, he had known that he might be ordered to kill her. That time was now at hand, and he was relieved he had not received a kill order. Evidently Tel Aviv had decided against terminating her life at this point; they rarely vacillated about such things. A different course had now been plotted, and the plan was about to unfold. He would disappear with the critical information, and no one would ever come looking for him after tonight.

The presentation that evening was titled, "An Analysis of Thermoelectric Opportunities in Polymers and Composite Materials." While it wasn't on a par with a major cinematic release, the presentation had generated a real buzz in the scientific community. Of course, attendance was also boosted as a result of the venue. Athens was a spectacular tourist destination, and most attendees would undoubtedly take advantage of the trip to visit the Parthenon and many of the other local landmarks. Between the commercial attractions and the cuisine, few destinations were more attractive to academics and professional researchers who were typically locked up in classrooms and laboratories every day.

The presentation was, as is often the case in similar situations, designed to provide only information that would be discovered by others over the next six to twelve months. So, while groundbreaking, it would provide only a marginal boost to those seeking to accelerate their own R&D efforts. Still, it would serve to enhance the image of the university, further establish Karounos and Iliopoulos in the eyes of the scientific community, and provide further assurance to their financial sponsors their money was well invested. The real value of the ongoing collaboration between Karounos and Iliopoulos was in a technological offshoot the two of them simply referred to as "our side project" when speaking privately, and never referred to at all when speaking to anyone else. Iliopoulos had nudged Karounos gently into this project over the last few months, mining the information and mental models that she had constructed carefully, bit by bit. He now had a working approach to the problem he was sent there to solve, and he was convinced that he had plumbed the depths of Karounos' intellectual capabilities to assist him. It was time to move on.

The presentation was held in the University's OIKONOMIDOU Auditorium, housed in the Nomiki Building. The Nomiki Building and the Palamas Building, containing the computer lab used by Karounos and Iliopoulos, were directly across from one another, with the central courtyard of the campus separating the two structures. Mature, graceful cypress and non-fruit-bearing olive trees surrounded the campus, and the courtyard was adorned with fountains and statues consistent with many such university campuses across the industrialized world.

Karounos and Iliopoulos were listed on the agenda as "discussants." The session chair was Professor Jürgen Bleckhaus from the Technische Universitaet Berlin. Bleckhaus was much better known in international circles as a speaker on various scientific matters than as a real contributor to serious science. He was frequently seen on BBC and Das Erste as the guest expert on various science-related matters that surfaced in the daily news. Bleckhaus was a portly man in his fifties, five feet seven inches tall, and weighing about two hundred and sixty-five pounds. His international travel had provided him with a wide array of opportunities to sample cuisines from around the world, and Bleckhaus was not one to pass by an opportunity of almost any kind.

Karounos had told Iliopoulos that she would be rehearsing her part of the presentation in her apartment, and established a meeting time for them just outside the Nomiki Building twenty minutes before the session was called to order by Professor Bleckhaus. They had decided it would be best to arrive in the room together.

Ninety minutes before the session was to begin, Iliopoulos was standing outside the rear entrance of the Palamas Building holding a small duffle bag when a catering van approached, then backed up close to the steps. Iliopoulos signaled the driver with a brief "stop" motion to stay in the van. He continued to smoke a cigarette, scanning the vista around him as it was disappearing into the deepening twilight. The only people he could see were a couple of young lovers strolling away from him hand-in-hand as he exhaled his last drag and flicked away the remaining butt. He beckoned the driver to come ahead then, and the man behind the wheel killed the engine and opened the squeaky, old door. Without a word, he strode to the back of the van and opened the door. Iliopoulos and the driver each took one end of what appeared to be a large catering cart and lifted it gently out of the van and onto the ground. The driver disengaged the braking mechanism on the wheels of the cart, and both men wheeled it up the ramp to the door of the building.

They took the freight elevator to the third floor and then pushed the cart down the hallway to the lab. While riding in the elevator, both men donned clear disposable plastic gloves. Most of the labs and offices in the building were dark and empty at this point, with only an occasional sound of someone locking up and their retreating footsteps echoing down the hallways. Retrieving his key from his pocket, Iliopoulos quickly opened the outer door to the lab. Then the two men pushed the cart through the doorway, and Iliopoulos closed it behind them. In the small reception area between the outer and inner doors, Iliopoulos dropped his duffle bag on the floor. He punched in his five-digit code on the mechanical keypad at the inner door and opened it. He and the driver pushed the cart into the lab, and the driver lit a very dim electric lantern he had carried inside his white apron, setting it on the floor.

Iliopoulos set to work unplugging and gathering up computer CPUs and disk drives. At the same time, the driver unlatched the side of the catering cart and dragged a large, black plastic body bag from inside. The corpse inside the bag was selected to mimic the body of Iliopoulos in every important detail. The local Mossad technicians had even redone the dental work to match any records on file related to Iliopoulos, and there weren't a lot of those since Rosen's alias had only existed for a few years. The body had no identification papers on it, and Iliopoulos tossed his wallet to the driver who placed it into the rear pocket of the corpse's slacks. The corpse was dressed in Iliopoulos' jacket, which fitted a bit tightly over a shoulder holster containing a MP-433 semi-automatic pistol. The corpse was positioned as though it had fallen backwards from a standing position facing the northernmost wall of the lab. In that wall was a medium-size fireproof wall safe where backup disk drives were kept to prevent the loss of important research records. When he had placed the CPUs and disk drives from the lab in the catering cart, Iliopoulos stepped over the body positioned in front of the wall safe and opened it. He removed the external hard drives from the safe and placed those in the cart as well, then left the safe wide open.

Then the final component of the catering cart, a canister about the size of a typical office paper recycling bin, was removed. This was a larger explosive device, already fitted with an RF receiver. When detonated, the device was designed to ignite all of the flammable materials across the lab, even as it blew out the windows and the inner door. If all went as planned, it would appear that some terrible accident engulfed the lab just as Iliopoulos was retrieving something from the fireproof safe. The great tragedy would be that Iliopoulos and the ostensibly protected backups of critical research materials were all destroyed by one enormous fire. If anyone sifted through the debris looking for salvageable computer drives, they would never find them. And in the unlikely event that anyone realized several CPUs were missing from the wreckage, that discovery would come only after many weeks, and since he was supposed to be dead anyway, any suspicion cast in Iliopoulos' direction wouldn't matter much.

Iliopoulos and the driver then retraced their path to the catering van, reloaded the cart, and fixed the braking mechanisms. The driver took both sets of the clear plastic gloves with him.

The entire process took about thirty minutes from the arrival of the van to its departure. Iliopoulos walked casually across the campus to his small dormitory room where he changed for the presentation. By six-thirty p.m. he was back in front of the steps to the Nomiki Building, ten minutes early for his rendezvous with Karounos. She was only five minutes later than he was, which barely gave him time to finish a cigarette. Karounos was dressed in a burgundy gown with her hair fashionably piled atop her head, making her large horn-rimmed eyeglasses and fluorescent-light pallor the only remaining semblances of academia about her appearance. Her neck was longer than Iliopoulos had noticed before, and a flickering memory of an American film star from the 1960s movies was illuminated in his mind. Her last name had been Hepburn—was it Katharine? No, that wasn't right. Audrey. It was Audrey Hepburn. Again, Iliopoulos was grateful that he hadn't been ordered to kill her.

"El, you look ravishing," he said to her, and watched her blush as he took her arm and escorted her up the steps.

"I feel ridiculous," she confided by way of response but gratefully leaned on his arm. Clearly, walking in heels was not something with which she had much experience. The gown was slit to a point just above the knee, which made things easier, but the marble steps were still a challenge. "At least it will be over soon."

Yes, Iliopoulos thought, *it will all be over soon. And then you will never see me again.*

ABOUT
THE AUTHOR

Bill Duncan worked in Iraq in 2006–2007 and in Afghanistan in 2010–2011, as a Special Assistant to the Deputy Undersecretary of Defense for Business & Stability Operations. At the completion of his work in Iraq, Duncan was honored by Deputy Secretary of Defense Gordon England at a ceremony in the Pentagon's Hall of Heroes. At the conclusion of his work in Afghanistan, Duncan was awarded three medals from the Office of the Secretary of Defense and the US Joint Chiefs of Staff. Details may be viewed at: www.billduncanscareer.com

Before and after his work in the Middle East, Duncan has been a member of executive management teams at major manufacturing companies such as John Deere, McDonnell Douglas, Boeing, JDS Uniphase, and Emerson. He is the author of several business books and dozens of business-related articles. He has earned a bachelor of arts degree and a master's of business administration/technology management, as well as multiple professional certifications. Duncan currently lives and works in St. Louis, Missouri.

More information, photographs, and background about the experiences that inspired *The Salacia Project* can be viewed at: www.bill-duncan.com. Additional copies can be purchased there as well.